We are US...

Sarah Ann Walker

We are US...

Also by Author Sarah Ann Walker

I am HER...

THIS is me...

My Dear Stranger

LOST

Choices...

Copyright © 2015 1127 Sarah Ann Walker
Cover Design: James Freeburg
All rights reserved.
ISBN-13: 978-09917231-57

This book is a work of fiction. Any reference to real people, or real locales are used fictitiously. Other names, characters, places, and incidents are the product of the author's imagination, and any resemblance to actual events or locales or persons, living or dead, is entirely coincidental.

Sarah Ann Walker

We are US...

Sarah Ann Walker

Sarah Ann Walker

DEDICATION

To Jakkob

I truly have no words to describe my love for you.
I try and try, but nothing ever seems like enough.
You are just everything in every moment between us.
Xo
Mommy

To Mr. Z Zinfandel
What can I say?
I made you and I love you.
You are the most patient man on the planet,
And as Suzanne said, you are *everything* to me.

We are US...

Sarah Ann Walker

ACKNOWLEDGMENTS

James, thank you for another *amazing* book cover. I love it.
To my parents, thank you for reading my books and for always telling me you love them, whether they are too dark or not.
Brennah, thank you for giving me my handsome nephew Zakkary, and my 2 beautiful nieces Piper-Ireland and Teaghan.
Paola, thank you for being my longest, dearest friend.
Silvana, thank you for making me laugh, and for totally getting me (still).
Sam, thank you for being my BBE- Best Brit Ever.
Amy, thank you for pimping me endlessly and selflessly. I look forward to these newest pics.
Olivia, Thank you for being my BIE- Best Italian Ever.
Brenda, thank you for still holding my hand *way* too often.

Randi Newman, thank you for your amazing support with this book, and for your constant, beautiful friendship. You are my most special stalker turned dear friend ever, and I love you and Mike to pieces.
Enjoy your couch. ☺

Darcy Villalobos, thank you for your support with this book. When I was Suzanne-like neurotic and crazy, you never lost patience with me, and I truly appreciate it.

A special thanks to Darcy, Diana, Amy, Julianne, and the Twisted Sisters.
Thank you Deniro, Samantha, Eli, Megan, Michelle, MTO Diane, Jen, Katica, Glenda, Diane, Mark, Suzy, Carla, Alanna, Coach & Christine, Tracy, Samantha, Suzanne, Elizabeth, Carole, Christy, Lustful Literature, Triple M Books, and Mommy's Naughty Playground
to name a few…
And finally to Michelle New- you are forever my Teaser Queen.

I want to thank all the readers and bloggers who supported me these last 3 years. I wish I could name you all.

xo
Sarah

Sarah Ann Walker

Sarah Ann Walker

SHAKESPEARE SONNET 116

LET ME NOT TO THE MARRIAGE OF TRUE MINDS
ADMIT IMPEDIMENTS. LOVE IS NOT LOVE
WHICH ALTERS WHEN IT ALTERATION FINDS,
OR BENDS WITH THE REMOVER TO REMOVE:
O NO; IT IS AN EVER-FIXED MARK,
THAT LOOKS ON TEMPESTS, AND IS NEVER SHAKEN;
IT IS THE STAR TO EVERY WANDERING BARK,
WHOSE WORTH'S UNKNOWN, ALTHOUGH HIS HEIGHT BE TAKEN.
LOVE'S NOT TIME'S FOOL, THOUGH ROSY LIPS AND CHEEKS
WITHIN HIS BENDING SICKLE'S COMPASS COME;
LOVE ALTERS NOT WITH HIS BRIEF HOURS AND WEEKS,
BUT BEARS IT OUT EVEN TO THE EDGE OF DOOM.
IF THIS BE ERROR AND UPON ME PROVED,
I NEVER WRIT, NOR NO MAN EVER LOVED.

Sarah Ann Walker

Sarah Ann Walker

Shakespeare Sonnet 116

Introduction

Inhale

Exhale

Breathe

Live

Love

Author's Bio

Sarah Ann Walker

INTRODUCTION

"Suzanne... I have to go. I'm so sorry, love, but I'm leaving."
Huh. His words I understand- even his facial expressions are known by me. His face screams love, sadness, and a stubborn finality I have come to know intimately. I know that look, just not as it suddenly applies to me. I know what he said, but I have no concept of what he's saying.
"What? Um..." Giggle. Shit.
"I'll be at the Marriot. I already have a suite. The number is beside the bed. Call me for anything."
"But-"
"**Anything,** Suzanne. I will always help you if or when you need it."
"Um..." Holy shit. Can I speak? Can I say one friggin' word here? Just one word that doesn't sound like a grunt of some kind. "But..." Yup. That was a word.
"I love you, Suzanne. But I'm gone."

Ummmm...
Giggle.
NO!

Waking on a quick burst, Z reaches for me and places me on his chest while I struggle to breathe. Rubbing my back, Z kisses my head over and over again while I come back to us in our own room in our beautiful life together.
"I have you, Suzanne. I'm right here, love," he whispers against my hair as I exhale. I know he is. He's always right here with me.

Z would never leave me. He promised.

We are US...

Sarah Ann Walker

INHALE

We are US...

Sarah Ann Walker

CHAPTER 1

"Good morning," I whisper against Z's chest. "You've gotta go to work this fine, fine Saturday. And I have to go to the wedding studio," I groan.
"I don't want to get up yet," Z moans pulling the covers back up over our bodies. "It's Saturday."
"Me either. But I hear Mr. Zinfandel is a real prick to work for so you better get going," I tease.
"A real prick?" Z huffs. "I doubt he's ever been called a prick, Suzanne. Maybe a little demanding, but fair. Or maybe a little intense but accommodating. But a prick? I don't think so."
"Fine. Maybe I just added the prick part," I giggle into his side as he pinches my ass. "Get up, Mr. Zinfandel. There are too many women who need to swoon over you today, so you better get going," I growl.
"You're very cute when you get jealous. Adorable, really. No one ever swoons over me. And who says the word swoon, by the way?"
"*I* do. And yes they do. They all *swoon* over you and it's really annoying. I mean you're clearly married," I grumble. "But they don't seem to care."
"I *am* married- very happily married, I might add. But I don't need to add it because everyone knows I'm happily married and not the least bit interested in anyone else but my jealous, beautiful, neurotic little wife."
"They might know it, but they still flirt." Pulling me closer to look at his face, Z smiles at me in his super sexy way, and I want to hit him. "I hope to hell you don't smile at them like that!"
"Like what? Like *this*?" He says smiling brighter than before until I growl again and hide my face in his neck. "Suzanne, no one flirts with me."
"Every single woman who meets you, talks to you, or simply drives past you on the street flirts with you. What about that woman Deirdre? Did you see her wipe the drool from her chin last night when you were speaking?" I ask as Z bursts out laughing.
"Drool?"
"Yes, drool. God, Z, she was glaring at me all night but staring, smiling, and *swooning* over you at the same time. Right in front of me!"

We are US...

"No, I didn't notice. Which is kind of the point, isn't it? I don't give a shit who's looking at me, as long as *you're* looking at me." Oh. Damn, he's good.

"Okay, I feel better after that comment. Good one, Z."

"Thank you, Suzanne," he teases again pulling me closer to him.

"Can I dress you today?" I ask as he pauses suspiciously.

Looking at my eyes when I raise my head, Z grins, "What will I be wearing if I agree?"

"Um, those old holey sweat pants with the paint on them and that sweat stained uglyass pink t-shirt you won't throw out."

"Salmon," he says with the grin I love.

"Whatever. It's pink and hideous. So I'd appreciate it if you wore that today instead of one of your sexy suits."

"Though I'm meeting with a California buyer this morning and my clothing might look a little inappropriate as we settle in?"

"Yes, please. Have you seen you in a suit?"

"I have. Have *you* seen me in a suit?"

"I have."

"And do you like the way I look in a suit?"

"Yes. I *love* the way you look in a suit."

"Then I'm wearing a suit, so maybe my beautiful, stunning, amazing wife will swoon at me today," he says again kissing the top of my head.

"Okay." I snuggle into his side. "But don't let anyone else flirt with you, okay?"

"I don't even notice anyone else. You are *all* I notice, Suzanne." Again with the perfect comment. God, I love this man.

Smiling, I climb up his chest and kiss his lips even with our nasty morning breath. "Go to work, Mr. Zinfandel. There are women to ignore, and lots of wine to sell."

"And the Rinaldi's to avoid," he fake shudders.

"Thank god this wedding is only a week away. Wish me luck," I beg pulling away from Z to get dressed.

"Good luck. Call me if they get too crazy for you," he grins knowing full well I'm still the craziest of us all- but just barely.

"I love you, Z," I say simply as he nods with his sexy as hell smile which is all for me, apparently.

ααααα

Sarah Ann Walker

Walking into the wedding boutique, or *hell* as I like to call it, I'm immediately assaulted by Korn. Who the hell would've thought Kayla actually loved the band Korn, or that her mother would allow her to play them LOUDLY at her wedding preparations? I didn't know, and I still can't believe Kayla won this round against her mother. But here I am. Standing in the doorway to HELL with Korn blasting in my head.

"Suzanne! You're late and my mother is going to kill you!" Kayla yells over the music while pulling me further into the store.

"Well, as your fiancé once said, 'I'm only 5 minutes late which is actually 25 minutes early by Manhattan's standard of time.'"

"My finance is an idiot," she laughs looping her arm through mine.

"Suzanne!" Turning, I'm immediately afraid of Mrs. Rinaldi's tone. Coming at me like a friggin' bulldozer, she doesn't even smile. "Go try on your dress."

"Mom! Say hi to Suzanne."

Shaking her head like we're speaking a different language, Mrs. Rinaldi quickly clues in. "What? Oh. Hello, Suzanne. Now please go try on your dress. And make Kayla turn this ear shit *OFF!* I'm going to hit somebody soon out of sheer frustration!"

"Not gonna happen," Kayla pushes.

Turning into Kayla's side I beg, "Um... just a little lower? Please?" I'll support Kayla against her mom and sisters anytime but I've got to be honest, this 'ear shit' is making me a little mental myself. "It's bothering me a little," I whisper as Kayla stops moving to look hard at my face. Yup. She gets it. I can see recognition dawn on her face immediately.

"Jesus *CHRIST!* First the rosettes, now Korn? I really hate you, Suzanne," she pouts.

"Sorry," I breathe as Kayla storms off for presumably the sound system.

Leaning into me Kayla's mom whispers, "You are completely forgiven for the rosettes now."

"You're welcome," I laugh walking away for the change room with my name tag on the door.

Once inside, I again pause to look at the black monstrosity I have to wear. Originally, I was given the 'you're going to love the dress- and you'll totally be able to wear it again, it's so awesome' speech, which I quickly turned into the 'I love it!' response hiding my gag and an 'as if I'll ever be caught dead in this dress again' pout with a smile.

We are US...

Like all bridesmaid dresses, circa **1992**, you just hope people looking at you remember you had no say over the dress, and for whatever reason the bride who actually likes you wants to make you the most hideous creature imaginable on her special day, whether consciously or not. And sadly, Kayla is no different. She unconsciously hates me and wants me to be hideous so she is the gorgeous one on her wedding day. There is NO other explanation for the atrocious gown she wants me to wear.

Once dressed, which was really hard because of the weird crisscross back straps that turn into a giant friggin' bow on my already large enough ass, I walk out to Kayla, her sisters Paola and Laura, and Mrs. Rinaldi beaming. Smiling, I hold the dress nausea in check and do a little twirl for everyone. At least I got the dress in black, which was a major battle won, thank god.

"I still don't understand why *she* gets to wear black and we have to be in that gross purple color," Paola whines for the thousandth time. And here we go.

Yup. The yelling match gets heated once again. These 3 sisters are amazing, and truly, I think Mrs. Rinaldi is the craziest of them all. For 2 months now they have had this same fight every single time we all meet up for dress fittings. Out of desperation, I even offered to change dress color to the dreaded purple to help Kayla against the other 3, but thankfully, she refused. Without selling me out as *formerly* totally mental to her mom and sisters, she insisted I had to have the black dress to stand out as her maid of honor. But the battle continues anyway.

Walking to a big slouchy chair, I plop my fat ass in it, crush the giant bow, and reach for the bottle of wine sitting chilled in the ice bucket. Not even pouring into a glass, I take a gulp right from the bottle as I watch The Rinaldi Show, as Mack calls it.

Drinking, I watch as loudly they continue. Point. Counterpoint. Oh *no*... It looks like Kayla might actually lose, and I'm scared to death. Kayla losing isn't good for anybody.

And then I'm spotted. Shit.

"Oh my *god*, Suzanne. Could you be any tackier?" Laura suddenly yells as they all turn to look at me.

But before I can answer, Kayla jumps in yelling right in Laura's face, "Yes, she can!" Which I think was supposed to help, but came out backhanded at best.

Turning dramatically, Kayla practically rips the wine bottle from my hand as she chugs half the bottle in one breath. Jesus Christ!

"Pass it over," I try, but Kayla just shakes her head no as she plops down in the chair beside me.

"Honestly. Do you hate your dress?" She begs sadly.

"Not at all," I lie. A white lie. The good kind of lie. A little white lie only to ease her mind. So it's not really the bad kind of lie.

"Thank god. I've had that dress in my mind since I was a little girl." *No shit,* I almost giggle. "And it's always been my favorite. I'm so glad you like it," she smiles, and I just can't hurt her feelings. Taking her hand I squeeze until she smiles at me and hands over the bottle of wine.

"I have to go soon. Z and I are going to that party at Manchester's tonight for the Save the whales, or Save the environment, or the Save... something foundation. I can't even remember what this one is for, but I think Z knows. I hope he does," I grin.

"He's too funny with all his donating. Half the time he doesn't know shit about it. I've asked him myself why he does it and he just shrugged at me and said, 'I have it to give'," Kayla laughs.

"I know. I mean there are actual causes he really cares about, but then some he just does because an employee asked, or a friend of a friend asked. I don't know. But sometimes it's a bit much for me going out in public all the time," I confess.

"You're doing so well, Suzanne. Nobody would even know you're crazy," she smirks.

"Ha! Thanks," I grin taking the bottle back for another gulp of wine. "Um, are your sisters coming out or are they too pissed to let us see their purple nightmares?"

"They'll come out, if for nothing else than to bitch about their ugly dresses again," Kayla shakes her head.

"They're not ugly. And once they get their tans on Friday, they'll look awesome," I smile because she needs it. And so what if I told another tiny lie. It's for the greater good, *Kayla's* greater good.

"I can't wait for Kayla to get here," I admit thinking of how much fun it'll be to have the Rinaldi's take on my Chicago Kayla.

Though they've met a few times, Chicago Kayla was on her best behavior each time, letting a few comments go and a few looks go unpunished. But the few intentional remarks about Kayla's friends getting whatever *they* wanted almost had her engage.

We are US...

Apparently, after the rosette incident which thankfully Chicago Kayla was here for, the Rinaldi sisters were about to trash me but Chicago Kayla gave a death glare that shut them right up as I struggled with getting my shit together.

"Thank god, the seamstress has another store in Chicago. Could you even imagine my mother if she thought Kayla wasn't getting fitted until 2 days before the wedding?" Kayla shudders as we continue swatching her sisters come out twisting and turning to complain about their dresses to their mom.

Passing the wine bottle back, I know I've probably chugged a whole glass which is more than enough plus it's really time for me to go. I'm getting my hair styled in the afternoon before Z comes home to change for the benefit.

"I really have to go. But I'll see you tomorrow for brunch, k?"

"Oh, go ahead," Kayla huffs. "Leave me with this crazy. Honest to god," she whines as her accent thickens. "I don't want to be here either, but I'll see you tomorrow," she leans over and kisses my cheek as I rise for the change room.

Undressing quickly, I can still hear the group of them going at it, and I'm exhausted by them. Honestly, if I had the nerve I'd tell Kayla's sisters to shut the hell up, but I don't. They scare the shit out of me, and with the way they gang up on someone, they'd slaughter me in a heartbeat.

Passing by them, I yell across the boutique, "Bye, Mrs. Rinaldi. I'll see you tomorrow." Smiling at Kayla I remind her, "Only one week to go," as she nods walking away to engage her crazy sisters and mom.

Okay, so they aren't technically crazy like I've been, but they are seriously deranged, and bitchy, and just LOUD. I don't think I've ever heard them have a conversation that wasn't raised even when it was friendly.

Christ, the first 5 times I met them all I was sitting away from them breathing my way through a near panic attack at all the yelling until Kayla's mom smiled and hugged a yelling Laura and Kayla like they were just having fun.

It was a trip for sure realizing people can actually just yell and talk loudly, or even scream over each other to get their point across without it being about abuse, or hatred, and even anger. It was definitely a learning experience for me about families I never had from my own family growing up.

Not that my mother yelled. She didn't have to. My mother's cold tone of hatred, disapproval, and abuse was scary enough without yelling at me, too.

My mother could say she hated me and was going to punish me for absolutely anything at any given moment with just a look. She didn't need to even speak before I was cowering in a corner or hiding in the smelly hidden closet to avoid her.

When my mother did raise her voice though, only an octave higher than her usually calm, reserved tone, I knew I was going to suffer badly.

And I always did.

ϘϘϘϘϘ

Entering the hair salon, I don't remember hailing the cab, the drive, or even walking into the building. Looking for Dee, I exhale thoughts of my mother and smile at her in the corner.

"Hey, Suzanne. The usual?" She asks walking me to our corner chair as I nod. I love my sexy up do's, and Dee knows how to keep all the wispy front bangs and sides of my hair down so I can hide my face in public. She also knows I need to sit in the corner chair away from everyone else while she works my hair so no one can see me clearly. When she lifts my hair away from my face to comb and tease, I need the privacy of the corner so I don't fear anyone but Dee seeing my ugly scarred face.

"So, what's going on tonight?" She grins as I smile back through the mirror once I'm seated.

"I honestly don't know or remember. I think Z told me, but I've been distracted with Kayla's wedding crap and can't remember anymore. It doesn't really matter though. I have all the black dresses I need, and my hair will look fabulous," I smile at my favorite hairdresser.

"You would look fabulous anyway, Suzanne. Even without my hair magic," she laughs.

"Uh huh. Just work your magic, sister, so half the battle is over for me."

Nodding, Dee starts sectioning my hair, clipping it in place at the back first because she knows I hate having my face exposed for longer than necessary.

"How have you been? I saw that newspaper article on Wednesday," she whispers and I freeze instantly. Nearly panicking, I breathe hard until she quickly jumps in. "It's nothing, Suzanne. No one here knows, and I would never tell anyone. I was just curious, that's all," she tries to soothe immediately but it's too late.

Shaking, I try to fight the panic, but it gets me anyway. No. No. *No*... I'm so much better now. I'm almost *all* better now. Shit, this doesn't happen to me anymore.

Reaching for my own throat, I try to fight the hard swallows and the growing tightness as I stare panicked at Dee through the mirror.

"I'm so sorry. Just breathe, Suzanne. Let me get your medication," she whispers while reaching right into my purse as she turns her body to hide me from the rest of the salon. "Here..." she extends my pill bottle but my hands are shaking too badly to open it, so she takes it back from me again to open and pour a pill on my hand. "Can you walk?" She asks already pulling at my arms to lift me.

Standing, I'm barely breathing and my legs are shaking so badly Dee wraps her arm around my waist as we move into a little room at the back where woman get waxes. Once inside, Dee quickly closes the door as I slump into the nearest chair.

Hanging my head while deep breathing, Dee hands me an opened bottle of water so I can take my pill.

Swallowing between gasps for breath, I see Dee lean in my peripheral against the wall while we wait for the pill to take effect. With my hands on my knees and my head hung, I breathe in and out as slowly as I can while the panic slowly recedes.

This medication, found for me by Mack and Dr. Phillips through trial and error, actually works the quickest to numb me the fastest from the panic. I don't need it much at all anymore, but I always carry it with me in case of an emergency, which this just became. Right here in my favorite goddamn hair salon.

"Let me get my stuff, and we'll finish your hair in here. Okay?" Dee asks kindly and I can okay nod. I don't trust my voice yet, and I really don't trust my emotions if I start speaking.

Waiting in the silence once Dee leaves, I'm shocked by the suddenness of my panic. I haven't freaked like that in a while, even when I actually read the newspaper article she mentioned.

I know Z hid it from me because I couldn't find the paper Wednesday morning, but he obviously didn't think I would just go online to read the news. I'm sure in his ever-protective mode, he even walked the paper all the way down our building to recycling so there was no chance of me finding it in the hallway recycling room if I looked.

I remember sitting with my coffee Wednesday morning looking online for the paper, and there I was again. A front page picture, amazingly, a good picture of me smiling with Z. With my face covered by my hair, they talked about my horrendous past, the charges, the trials, and the outcome of pitiful Suzanne Beaumont-Anderson-Zinfandel, the wife of New York's famous bachelor extraordinaire who was so taken with his little wife he married her immediately.

Surprisingly, the article was somewhat complimentary about me and my charities and good works, and how I am the love of Z's life. But it was learning about one of the men making release early because somehow his sentencing conviction was lessened that prompted the article, and my past to rise up again to the collective surface of New York.

It also prompted me to feel pissed at Z for hiding it when *clearly* everyone else knew what was going on around me. Christ, my friends, the DA, everyone would have known, but Z chose to keep me in the dark. I assume to protect me, but it still infuriated me. I mean, come *on*. As if I don't deserve to know what's happening with my own life and past.

Anyway, the anger is what made the panic stay away Wednesday morning, and by the time I saw Z that night I wasn't in the mood to confront him, so I let it go. Until today apparently.

Today, the upset and panic decided to hit in a hair salon with my favorite hairdresser looking at me with pity again which I hate.

"Did you call anyone?" I ask immediately upon Dee's return to our room feeling much calmer and breathing almost completely normally.

"No. Would you like me to?"

"God, no. Please don't tell Kayla or Z. Kayla's a psycho right now with her wedding, and Z is Z," I grin lifting my head finally to Dee's understanding nod.

"I won't tell anyone, Suzanne. It's none of my business anyway, and I shouldn't have brought it up. I was stupidly bringing it up only to mention how great your hair looked," she smirks as I laugh a little. Dee did do my hair the night that picture was taken.

We are US...

"It's okay. I'm fine now," I exhale again straightening in my chair. "Can you hurry with my hair though because I have to be home in just over an hour which doesn't give you much time to work with."

"45 minutes then? No problem. I'm a professional," she grins spinning my chair back toward the only mirror in the room. "I'm so sorry, Suzanne," she whispers before taking my hair again. Squeezing her hand on my shoulder I let her know everything is okay between us.

Dee is amazing. She's actually Kayla's cousin's wife, and she knows enough about me to be supportive and sensitive, but she doesn't usually let it fill her eyes with pity when she sees me. Usually, she jokes and teases, and moans about 'sexy Z' like we're friends, without looking like she's worried I'll have a freak out at any second, which I usually don't. Actually, this is only the second time out of the many visits to Dee that I've lost my shit.

The first one was bad though, and it required Dee to call Kayla who promptly called Z to come get me because I couldn't recover or function enough to even make it to a cab for home. It was also the day Z explained a little about me to Dee with the strictest of confidence and gave her his phone numbers in case I ever needed him again.

After that day though, Dee acted like I was normal anyway when I returned and I've actually *been* normal at the salon ever since.

Smiling through the mirror while Dee pins the last few strands in place, my hair looks beautiful. She always seems to get my natural high and low lights on the surface of the up-do so the contrast looks amazing.

"You did it again, Dee. I love it," I beam to her return smile.

"You're too easy. I love working with your straight hair. It takes all the work out of blow-drying and straightening it first," she grins before I take one final look at my scarred face side all covered in cute little floppy layers looking like they artfully fell from the rest of my hair.

"I'll see you next Saturday morning. And I get YOU. I don't care how great the others are I have to have you for the wedding, okay?"

Walking out the little room back through the main salon together, Dee agrees. "I've already been told by your bitchy friend from Chicago that I was doing your hair or I'd be 'whacked, New York style' I believe she said, so I made sure you were my first of the morning," she laughs as I do. I can't believe Kayla said anything to her, but then I totally believe it, too.

After paying Dee and leaving the salon I feel emotionally exhausted. The panic attack was quick, no more than 10 minutes from onset until I could speak coherently, but it was enough to make me tired as I flag a cab for home.

And once inside, honestly, I can barely walk I'm so drained. It's only slightly after 2 and Z said he'd be home by 4, so there's plenty of time to relax before I start dressing for our night out.

ΩΩΩΩΩ

"Suzanne... It's time to wake up. Are you okay, love?" I hear Z whisper against my forehead as I smile.

"I'm good. What time is it?"

"5:00. I didn't want to wake you. You looked so peaceful," he whispers again.

"I did?" 5! *Shit!* We're supposed to be there by 6 aren't we?" I yell scrambling to stand up from the couch in the living room as Z leans away from me so we don't collide.

"So we'll be fashionably late. Who cares?" He smiles and I want to smack him.

I don't do late, and fashionably late is even worse. "If we aren't with the rest of the people arriving there's too much opportunity for pictures, Z. You know that. Why the hell did you let me sleep?!" I yell running for our bedroom to change.

I shouldn't have fallen asleep! Shit, now there'll be picture of us for sure. God dammit, I hate when they take our pictures at these things.

"Suzanne, stop for a second," Z says standing in our bedroom doorway as I grab a random black dress and run for the washroom.

"I don't have time!" I yell scrambling to pull out all my makeup while leaning my dress against the chair back beside the vanity. Oh my god, this is a disaster. I can't be late to these things. We were late once, and unknowingly we became the focus of too many pictures for way too many local papers and magazines. Friggin' New York! There's like 50 different articles on any given night about all the events that take place.

"Suzanne, stop. What's going on?" Z asks again from the bathroom doorway this time.

We are US...

  Glaring at him, I rip my clothes off and start trying to pull my dress overhead without screwing up my hair. I feel so pissed at him suddenly, and I know I'm being irrational but I can't help it. My fear is making me bitchy.
  "Nothing. Forget it. Nice suit, Z," I practically snarl at him because *he's* perfectly dressed and ready to go. The asshole!
  Walking toward me, Z leans against the counter and crosses his arms over his chest with his talk to me face. But I'm not doing it right now.
  Fixing my dress, and turning for the mirror, I notice my hair slightly messed up from sleeping, but not too bad. I think I can fix it myself with a few more bobby pins. I think I can, but Dee is magic, and I'm not, and with my shaking hands and growing anxiety, I'll probably look really bad.
  Stopping everything, I just close my eyes and place my hands flat on the counter as I breathe slowly. I don't want to do this again today. I can't do this twice in one day. And I know Z's waiting for me to speak, but I can't yet. I have to let this stress and anxiety pass first.
  Okay. Be rational. So we arrive late. I don't have to look up, and I don't have to acknowledge the cameras. If I asked Z to ignore them with me, he would. If I asked Z to just hold my hand and run inside the building with me, he would. This late doesn't mean I'll end up in the paper again tomorrow morning before the big wedding brunch. It doesn't have to mean an article, or an exposé, or a spread in a local magazine. It could mean nothing at all except simply arriving late. Then all this anxiety is for nothing. Okay. Deep breath.

  Keeping my eyes closed, I whisper in our silence, "I know about the article in the Times Wednesday morning. I know what happened, and I know you hid it from me. I'm mad that you still think I can't handle anything, and I'm mad that you think I'm too stupid to know what's going on around me. It's embarrassing and frustrating. And I'm mad at you."
  "It wasn't like that."
  Shaking my head, Z stops speaking immediately to wait for me to finish. "When everyone around me knows things about me that I don't know, or that you *think* I don't know I feel embarrassed and belittled, and actually I feel like I did growing up. It makes me feel like everyone has secrets about me and are talking about me behind my back. And not only is it scary for me feeling like I used to, but it hurts me, too. It makes me feel like a child who has no control over her life, like I didn't in my past. And

it makes me question why I've worked so hard to get better and to move forward, especially when I'm just going to be talked about and lied to like I *am* that little girl again. It makes me feel like you don't trust me, and it makes me feel unsettled."

Okay. Whew. I know I'm crying a little, but they're those annoying frustrated tears falling down my cheeks, not sad ones.

"I'm so sorry, Suzanne," Z whispers in his sad voice, and finally my sad real tears fall. "I fucked up, love, but not intentionally. I actually just had a moment Wednesday morning."

Opening my eyes, Z hasn't moved, but his upset face says everything to me suddenly. "A moment?"

"Yes. We had gone out for date night Tuesday, and you were so happy and just adorable with all your laughter. And then when we came home we were together and you seemed so happy still, I felt happy because I did that for you."

"You always do that for me," I whisper.

"I know I try to. But Tuesday night everything was just effortless and fun and sexy, and when I woke up for work, you grumbled you loved me, and when I kissed you, you barely moved but your smile was amazing. And you forgot to cover your face from me, and I felt so big and strong and loved and *trusted* by you in that moment when you forgot to hide your face that I couldn't stop my own smile, especially when I slid my hand down your back to your ass and you moaned like a content little kitten," he smiles as I grin back.

"Z, you are always big and strong and loved and trusted by me."

"I know. But you have to work to feel that way most of the time. Wednesday morning though, half asleep and completely satiated by me through the night you didn't have to think about it. I saw you just *feel* it. And that made me feel so happy and loved I never wanted you to ever have that scared look again you get in your eyes that destroys me when I see it. The look I've watched come into your eyes thousands of times over the past couple years. The look that breaks my heart when you struggle with your past, and struggle to accept our present."

"What happened with the newspaper, Z?" I need to understand this so I don't feel angry anymore.

Exhaling, Z reaches out his hand slowly and takes my own into his when I don't object. Intertwining our fingers he looks so intense, I brace myself for the bad.

We are US...

"After I showered and dressed I leaned down to kiss the beautiful pale skin on your back and you moaned again with a smile. Do you remember?" He asks as I nod. "Well, I left you and grabbed the newspaper from the hallway, walked to the kitchen for coffee, and just as I sat down there it was. Our picture folded on the front, and your name plastered across the front page again. So I had a moment as I said. I couldn't even swallow the mouthful of coffee in my mouth. I just grabbed the paper and took the elevator all the way down to the utilities room, reading it as I went to throw it away when I was done," Z exhales again looking at me with his beautiful dark eyes, almost like he hopes I'll understand, which I actually do.

I know Z is always protective, but we've talked about him hiding stuff from me out of his attempt to protect me, and he's promised he wouldn't do it anymore.

"What else did you do?" I ask without anger.

"Um, I called everyone. Mack, Chicago Kayla, Glenn Rose, our lawyers, Dr. Phillips, and even the security company we use sometimes, because I had a moment, Suzanne. I just couldn't have you lose the look I saw, and I didn't want you to be afraid. So I panicked. Ah, after the quick calls I entered the condo again prepared to explain why I was back with a lie about forgetting some papaerwork if you were awake, but you weren't around."

Smiling, I know where I was. "I was still in bed. I slept way too late Wednesday morning because someone loved me thoroughly through the night and I was exhausted," I smile so Z knows I'm not mad at him anymore.

"Yes... I checked on you one more time before I left, and leaning against the doorway I saw you still sleeping as I had left you and I justified everything I had just done. I wanted you to sleep like that, and I wanted you to feel happy, even in your sleep. So I left for work feeling good about what I did."

"But you-"

"Were sneaky. And manipulative, and too overprotective, I know. I did everything wrong Wednesday morning, but it was for the right reasons I think. I did it to keep you feeling happy for just a little while longer. That's all it was. I don't think you're weak, and I do trust you to deal with everything going on around you. I just didn't want you to have to deal with it Wednesday morning. I figured we'd have time to deal with it later. But then you didn't bring it up, and I was happy to let it go," he exhales again, almost pleading with me to understand.

"Okay. I understand. But you can't do that ever again. No matter what you think I'll do, or what my reaction will be. You can't hide anything from me, Z. You know that. We either do this together, or we don't at all. *You* promised me that, remember?"

Nodding, he says firmly, "I do."

"Okay. I don't want to talk about that pig Sheran tonight, or what happened, or what this means for me. But tomorrow after the wedding brunch you have to promise to tell me everyone you know. Okay?"

"Absolutely. Can I just say one more thing?"

"Of course," I agree bracing for more.

"Suzanne, you are the strongest person I have ever known. Please don't ever think I don't feel that or believe it. That isn't why I get all protective, or why I overreact from time to time regarding your safety. You need emotional security in your life, and I need to be the one who provides it. That's how we work, and I love how we work. I love that you can come to me with anything, and I love that I try to fix everything. You feel most secure when you're with me, right?" He asks as I nod yes. "Well, that security is what makes me happiest. When you need something, I need to be the one to provide it. Sometimes, I just go a little too far though, like on Wednesday morning. But it is *never* because I think you're weak, or because I don't trust you. It's only because I want to be the man who loves and protects you. I promise you, Suzanne." Pulling me into his arms, we have a collective exhale and cuddle up until the tension slowly slips away from our bodies.

"Z, I really don't want to go tonight," I whisper against his chest.

"Good. Because I really don't want to either. Let's just have a Saturday night in together," he says against my head as I squeeze him a little tighter.

"Can you help me get the 412 bobby pins out of my hair?" I laugh pulling away.

"Certainly. But then I also get to strip you of this dress as well," he replies seriously, followed by an eyebrow wiggle.

"Yes, please..."

We are US...

CHAPTER 2

Watching Z enter our bedroom makes my heart speed up as usual. Looking at his face looking at me makes me smile. Looking at his return smile makes me hungry for him.

"Hi, Love. How was your day?"

"Good. I thought about you all day. It was weird. Oh! Ha. Not like that. I *always* think of you, just more today," I say grinning like an idiot.

Smiling back at my stupidity, Z walks toward me, leans down and gives me a quick kiss hello. "Why more..." kiss "... today?"

"I don't know. The wedding, I guess. Kayla is so cute right now. Well, as cute as a 6 foot bridezilla can be. Anyway, she was brutal today, barking and demanding at her mom and even at me a few times, but then she suddenly stopped, plopped down in the chair beside me, took my hand and whispered, 'God, I love him, Suzanne.' And when I nodded her eyes filled with tears until mine did as well and then she yelled at me to stop crying like a wuss. It was just so cute I hugged her tight and told her Mack felt the same about her. But with only 3 days to go, it seems like she isn't enjoying anything about this wedding which is kind of sad."

"And that made you think of me?" He asks smirking.

"No. After she had another freak out 5 minutes later because she couldn't choose between the 2 shades of purple table clothes, I thought of how grateful I was that we didn't have a wedding like theirs."

"I would have that kind of wedding in a second. I would do all of that for you," he smiles sitting beside me on our bed.

Shaking my head no, I'm glad we didn't. "No, thank you. Ours was perfect. Spontaneous. 2 witnesses. No fuss and no drama. Our wedding was perfect for us," I say wrapping my arms around Z's side.

"Can I be honest?" Z asks turning me in his arms as we lean against the headboard together.

"Of course. Unless it's mean- then lie to me," I grin.

"When am I ever *mean* to you?" Z asks kissing the back of my head.

"There was that time last Wednesday when I made the Swiss steak that you hated."

Barking a laugh, Z squeezes me tighter while muffling his laughter in my hair. Trying to turn to him, he holds me tightly where I am until just the sound of his laughter against me makes me start laughing a little.

"I wasn't being mean, love. Actually, I was being very, *very* kind to both of us," he says still laughing.

He really was doing us a kindness by pulling away our plates of *horrible* leather meat mixed with the worst tasting chunky, watery, reddish sauce imaginable.

I remember that afternoon and I'm not sure what happened. I either misread the ingredients, or didn't follow the directions, or maybe just added my own take to the recipe. But whatever happened, it *was* truly, undeniably atrocious.

"That was a weird day, I know," I laugh once more thinking about his initial face, followed by the hard gulp, finished with a stunned expression as he picked up our plates and walked quickly to the kitchen to dump them.

At first I was shocked and pissed off, but I too was still trying to chew and swallow the inedible food in my mouth. So I got over his dinner rebuff pretty damn quick once I swallowed and we made grilled cheese sandwiches instead.

"How are you feeling?" Z asks quietly against my hair as all his laughter fades.

"I'm fine, Z. I promise I'm good."

"You've been grinding your teeth badly and lashing out a little at night."

"Oh, well I always do."

"Actually, you haven't in quite a while. Is there something going on besides Sheran? Something else you're struggling with? Suzanne, you can tell me anything. You know that. I will always-"

"I'm perfectly fine, Z," I say turning in his arms.

I know he worries about me, but I'm sure I'm fine right now. Kissing Z, I try to stop him from worrying, but he's not really into it I can tell. His hands haven't gone for my face to pull me close, and his body hasn't moved against me as it usually does when I'm this close to him.

"Please stop looking for problems that aren't there, Z," I huff against his lips.

Pulling away from my face Z looks intensely at my eyes. "*Really,*

Suzanne?" Z replies with a bit of tone.

Trying hard to ease the situation, I climb Z's legs to straddle him and kiss him desperately as I breathe into his mouth. I don't want tension, and I don't want to argue. Not that we argue much; we're actually pretty great with each other. But I can feel this tension is the kind that'll lead to distance between us, and I don't want any distance.

"Suzanne?"

"I'm sorry. It's just you think something's going on with me and there isn't. But the more I say there isn't it sounds like I'm protesting too much, which makes you think there IS something going on. But there really isn't right now. I would tell you if there was, I promise."

Looking at my eyes closely like he always does when I speak to him, Z seems to accept the truth in front of him. I do tell Z almost everything, and I would tell him if something was wrong, but I know there isn't this time.

"You're right. I'm sorry."

"Don't be sorry. I love that you worry about me, but I would tell you. Don't I always tell you?" And smiling, I think of Kayla and her red rosettes, and how unknowingly I had smashed them all to shit with a mallet in her kitchen. "Remember the rosettes?" I grin.

Nodding, Z smiles again. "I remember. I've never heard Kayla sounding so shrill before yelling at Mack and I to get the hell to her apartment to get your crazy ass out of there."

Laughing, I remember coming back to myself with the mallet as Chicago Kayla reached for me while Mrs. Rinaldi stared silently for once while I got my shit together.

God, they really did look like drops of blood all over her kitchen counter. And before I knew it I was crying and smashing the hell out of them, moaning and struggling until there was nothing left but red powdery sugar all over Kayla's counter until Chicago Kayla yanked the mallet from my shaking hand.

Smiling at the weird memory, I'm glad those moments are few and far between. I'm also glad I rarely have panic attacks, and rarely freak out anymore. Since Z and I have been together I've grown very strong, sane, and happy.

Looking in his dark brown eyes as he watches me I can't help the smile from spreading across my face.

"I love you," I whisper before kissing him again.

We are US...

Straddling his lap with his arms wrapped around my waist I kneel up and kiss him harder.

I love, love, *love* kissing Z. I always have. When Z kisses me there is nothing in the world but us. I have no past when we kiss, and my future looks amazing.

Slowly moving on Z's growing erection, I deepen our kiss as his hands travel up my back. Pushing harder into his chest, I can't get enough of his kiss. As usual, Z is deep, and dark, and delicious against me. He is everything in every moment between us.

"Take what you need, love," he groans against my mouth as I smile. I love those little expressions of his, and I love that I can take or give with Z always. He loves me and gives or takes as we each need, whenever we need each other.

Pulling away, I lift my black silk nightie overhead and wait for the heat to come into his eyes, which it always does. And there it is instantly. His eyes always narrow slightly, highlighting how long his lashes are, and his breathing always gets deeper when we're together like this.

Pushing my body back a little from him with a kiss, he quickly unbuttons his dress shirt. Kissing me as he strains, he shoulders out of his shirt while my hands slide down his chest to his sexy as hell stomach. Nothing like my super white, slightly flabby, scarred stomach, Z's is ripped and dark, and so lickable, I never get enough of touching him.

Looking at the tattoo of me on his heart, my hand massages it and him. The beautiful strawberry blonde with the stunning blue eyes looking back at me never seizes to amaze me.

I am HER... And over time I actually felt and became her with Z. On his gorgeous chest, against his heart sits the stunning woman smiling back at me. THIS is me... with Z. And when we're together like this, we are US...

"I love when you look at me like that," Z whispers before palming my head for a deeper, harder kiss. It is the kind of kiss you use to center you. The kind of kiss that makes you feel alive and whole. It is the kind of kiss I have only ever known with Z.

Moving my hands to his pants, I quickly rip the button through and unzip him in my hands. When I tug at his pants and boxer briefs, Z bends his knees against me and lifts us to help me remove them as I sit up on my own knees. Kicking his legs out of his clothes, Z is suddenly naked under me as I settle back against his erection for another kiss.

Cupping my breasts in his hands, Z tugs and lightly pinches my nipples between his fingers as I push closer to his hands. Z knows what I like and he knows the balance between the pleasure I need and the pain I fear, and his touch is always perfect for me. *He* is perfect for me.

Lifting again, I take Z's erection in my hand for a few strokes until shifting I attempt penetration. Rocking back and forth, I try, but I'm a little too dry still and he's a little too big always.

"Let me help you," he moans against my mouth again as I moan in turn.

Lifting my hips right off of him, Z shimmies down the bed quickly until I'm holding the headboard positioned right over his mouth. Looking down my body, Z's eyes match mine and when he suddenly tongues me slowly I cry out against him.

With eyes that never leave mine, Z flattens his tongue against me and licks me slowly from back to front until he flicks my clit as I settle closer to his mouth.

Oh *god*... His eyes. It's always his eyes for me. Everything good and bad between us has always been in his eyes. When I almost died I remember his beautiful marble eyes crying for me. And when he held me after Thomas died, it was his eyes that centered me. When he married me it was his eyes smiling that pushed me to say 'I do'.

Why does tonight feel so different?

Z and I have sex all the time. We have hot sex, fun sex, and sexy sex. We make love frequently, and we even fuck from time to time which is amazing.

But tonight feels different and I don't know why. Tonight I really see him and my heart hurts. Tonight I really feel Z with such love I can't hold in the emotion.

"Please don't cry, love,' he whispers against my wet flesh as I smile down at him.

"They're definitely good tears," I whisper back wiping away the tears from my cheeks.

Lifting me and pulling me back down his chest, I'm laid flat against his chest as I try to impale myself on him. Stretching backward, my hand moves back to his erection as I rock against it and slowly take him in. Sitting up, Z leans forward to kiss me again as I start my slow sexy decent on him.

Pushing Z back flat I rise on my knees with my hands on his chest and I start to move. Slow and tentative at first while I adjust, then faster and harder as I start to feel. Leaning forward and away, my hips rock as his

We are US...

knees bend behind me. Thrusting into me as I lower, I moan and shake as my need builds.

When Z raises a hand to my mouth, I open for him. Sinking his thumb in my mouth I suck as hard as I can and feel a harder thrust inside me. Wetting his thumb he pulls away with a groan until he trails down my body, pinching my nipples as he ends his slow torture on my clit.

Circling and pressing down on my body, I'm instantly aroused higher. Gasping and quickening my movements, I need more of him. I need him inside me harder and I want him in me deeper.

"*Please...*" I cry out suddenly.

"Take me," he growls as I move harder.

No longer a sexy rhythm, my movements become crazed and aggressive. My body lifts and crashes down on Z as he grunts and lifts beneath me. I'm crying out and groaning and moving and breathing in shallow bursts as I feel myself burn inside forever. No matter how long, no matter how hard I take him in the burn continues, but nothing happens.

I can't get over, and I can't get there. I'm burning and struggling but my release is just out of reach.

"No. No. *No...*" I chant.

"Suzanne?" Shaking my head, I'm not doing this. Not this time. I am not losing this time. "Suzanne. Stop, love." No!

Frantically I bounce on his body as I try desperately to get there. When Z suddenly sits up I push his chest back down as hard as I can and shake my head no.

I'm fine. Everything is fine. There is nothing wrong, and I want to come with Z. *Shit*.

"Help me!" I scream desperately as Z attempts to rise again before I shake my head no. I don't want him to soothe me, or kiss me, or talk to me. I want him to get me off!

And then he does that thing to my body and I immediately go from frustrated to holy *shit* in a second. Rubbing my clit, and pushing and wetting me again with his wet fingers from his own mouth, I'm almost there. It's RIGHT there. I'm almost over...

"Ohhhhh.... Um?" Shaking my head I try to stay coherent. I'm with Z. Nothing is wrong. Everything is really, really NOT wrong. And I'm with Z.

"Suzanne, let go. Right now. Let go for me," Z begs and I do.

Looking at his dark eyes tight and hard waiting for me, I can finally feel

my body letting go.
　Screaming and grunting another hard orgasm, Z is all I know, and smell, and taste, and feel around me. Z is everything right here, right now with me. I am with Z and everything is okay.
　Collapsing on his chest, his arms immediately circle me to pull me tighter to him. Moaning the after effects of my orgasm, I writhe a little against him as I try to breathe fully.
　"I love you," I whisper against his damp chest as he pulls me in tighter.
　Breathing in slower, I try to stop my pounding chest while I acclimate to our room. Rolling off Z to his side, I feel myself pull from him and realize quite quickly he's still hard. Like rock hard. As I look at his erection lying on his stomach I also realize I have a complete lack of moisture between my legs from Z, and I'm stunned. We always come together. Always.
　Sitting up on my elbow, I don't even know what to say as Z lies silently beside me staring at my face. With his dark eyes waiting for something from me, I don't know what to say.
　"Why didn't you...?"
　"It's okay, Suzanne. I didn't feel the need, and tonight was about you," Z says calmly.
　Looking at Z, I'm struck with the memory of our very first time together. I remember the tacky hotel room outside of Chicago where it all began for us. The time when I didn't know anything about my past, and I didn't know anything about what was to happen to me. In that hotel room I remember I was a scared married woman fighting her attraction and want for a man way out of her league.
　Gulping the memory down, I whisper, "You didn't feel the need?" What the hell does that mean? And why doesn't Z want me anymore? He always wants me.
　Leaning into me, Z kisses my forehead and releases a breath against my head like he's thinking of what to say to me. Attempting to pull me over his body again, I fight him. I have NO idea what's happening here, but as the seconds tick by I want to cry in his arms until I understand why he doesn't want me anymore.
　"I see..." I mumble as my heart breaks. I knew this would happen eventually.
　Pulling away from Z, he holds my arm before I rise off the bed. "Don't go, Suzanne. We need to talk."
　"There's nothing to talk about. You didn't want me, and I'm fine."

"Suzanne. That's not what happened. I do want you."

"Whatever. It doesn't matter," I smile as I slip off the bed, pulling the throw blanket from the end to cover my nudity quickly.

"Stop, love," Z barks and I stop my retreat instantly. I hate that commanding voice he uses sometimes because it always works on me. The need to please, though relatively dormant in me now, still surfaces from time to time, especially when Z uses that voice on me.

Holding in my tears, turning to look at the most gorgeous man I've ever known, I wait for him.

"Talk to me, love. *Please*..." Z begs as he leans against the headboard. But I don't know what to say. Nothing is wrong, but I can tell he doesn't believe me, and I don't know how to convince him. "Suzanne, please?"

Shaking my head to clear it, I whisper all I can give him. "I'm not freaking out, and I don't think there's anything wrong. I promise," I say as honestly as I can.

I know I have to maintain eye contact with Z so he believes me, and though it's hard under the circumstances, I do it until he nods slowly.

"Why didn't you...?" I ask embarrassed.

"Because you weren't acting normal and I was worried about you," he responds still looking at my eyes.

"When do I ever act normal, Z?" I grin, and finally the mood changes in our bedroom.

Exhaling a smile, Z nods, "Point taken. However, you were more *ab*-normal than usual, so I was concerned," he grins.

"Well, I was fine. Just a little weirder than usual, but otherwise, I promise nothing is wrong." Blushing like we're new to this still, which we aren't at all, I ask, "Would you like to join me in the shower?" And before I even finish the words Z is standing, walking toward me in all his 6'3, ripped, darkly tanned glory as I walk backward from his body and erection toward our bathroom with a nervous smile.

Turning on the shower, Z tugs the blanket from my body and waits behind me rubbing my back as the water warms. When I turn back to him, he immediately lifts me in his arms and pushes the shower door wide open to carry us inside until I'm pressed flat against the shower wall by his strong body.

Kissing me hard, Z moves one hand between my legs and touches me making me moan from his touch and from my own sensitivity. Arching into his kiss, I'm desperate for him. Pulling him closer with my ankles against his ass, he positions himself and enters me slowly as I moan again in his arms.

"Hold on, Suzanne," he growls against my mouth as he moves. Lowering himself, almost bracing his thighs wider he suddenly takes me hard and deep as I cry out against the wall from the quick pleasure.

Pulling Z back to my mouth, I kiss the holy shit out of him as he takes me hard. Fucking me, he never breaks the connection of our mouths, he never pulls away, and he never lets me forget its Z I'm with this way.

Gasping in his embrace as he holds my ass tightly, I am fucked by my love, and it's so, so good. There are no demons or ghosts here. I'm not being hurt or tortured in our shower. I am simply being fucked by my beautiful husband and I love it.

"Z..." I whine as the pressure builds inside me again.

"Open. Your. Eyes," he grunts as his pace continues, punctuating each word with a thrust. "You know I need those gorgeous eyes of yours."

Quickly opening my eyes, I'm struck with the beauty of his own. With water in his eye lashes they look impossibly long, highlighting the dark brown of his eyes watching me.

"God, you're pretty," I grin as he laughs.

"Pretty? I prefer manly," he grins thrusting a little deeper than before as I gasp his point made quite well. Nuzzling my neck, Z whispers, "Are you ready, Suzanne?" as his hand slides around my front to touch me.

Gasping at his touch I moan 'always' before Z takes my lips hard once again. Kissing the hell out of me, Z pumps and thrusts into me making me wild in his arms gasping for breath until I pull away.

Waiting with my eyes open as Z likes, my head turns back and forth against the tile wall as my chest pumps against his. Pulling his shoulders closer, I need to get inside him. The intensity of us like this always makes me try to climb inside him as much as he's inside me. Pulling and kissing and moaning, his legs are pumping faster while he works my body with his hand quickly.

I'm almost there. I'm right there, I know it and he knows it. I think I have that hideous distorted face of the almost orgasm and my eyes constantly close until I open them for him.

I'm right *there*.

"Ah! Oh, *shit!*" I scream as the orgasm takes me over with him.

Practically pushing Z away as the shudders wrack my body, Z holds me up until I hear and feel his own climax all around and inside me.

We are US...

Collapsing against my body, I hold Z tighter to me and kiss the side of his face that's buried in my neck.

"I can't move," he groans breathing heavily.

"Me either. My hips are locked in place, and I don't think I can stand."

Pulling away from me with a grin, Z kisses my lips and whispers, "Well then, I guess I better do all the work."

Slowly unhooking my ankles from his back, my legs just touch the floor when I groan at my hip pain and numb legs. Holding onto Z, I laugh, "I think I'm getting too old for shower sex," before he looks at me with feigned disgust.

"Suzanne, you're not getting too old. You've just been well loved," he adds with a kiss, and I know I am always well-loved with Z. Nodding, I grab the handheld for a little clean up rinse before handing it to him as I step out.

"Suzanne?" Z asks again with so much emotion I feel it in my soul.

"There's nothing, Z. And I *will* tell you if there is. I promise."

Nodding, he smiles and accepts my words for what they are. I make promises to Z and I keep them, he knows that. I would never break a promise to Z by choice.

Crawling into bed with my wet hair and body I wait for Z as sleep bears down on me. I'm exhausted and refreshed and alive and whole. I am well loved.

Waking as Z climbs in and pulls me to his side and chest I mumble goodnight as he kisses my head.

Inhaling his scent I sleep away anything wrong inside me to sleep with everything right around me.

CHAPTER 3

Grabbing the keys to Z's truck, I'm almost out the door when the phone rings. Looking quickly like I always do because of the residual creepers who always seem to find our phone number, I see its Z. Again.

"How are you Mr. Zinfandel?" I grin into the phone. Z was extra cute to me this morning before he left for work.

"Are you sure you're okay to get Kayla by yourself?" Z asks with his intense, concerned voice.

"Of course. I know where the airport is Z," I barely hold in my huff. For the tenth time today Z has asked me this question, and the answer is always the same.

"I know you do, but-"

"Can I tell you something?" I suddenly interrupt him before he starts again.

"Of course," Z breathes deeply like he's bracing himself.

Breathing out my growing frustration, I just speak. Z wants me to always be open and honest with him, and I usually am, unless it's about the really bad stuff. Most times though I still feel guilty or something close to guilt when I say anything negative to him about him or us.

"Suzanne?" He waits not so patiently until I just spill.

Practically whispering, I say the truth of my mental health right now. "Um... *You're* making me feel crazy, Z, with all the watching, and questioning, and constant waiting for something to happen." When there is only silence as he listens, I go for it. "I'm perfectly fine right now. I take my meds every day, and I'm very happy. I don't feel upset, or confused, or anything negative, but you're making me a little frustrated and crazy with all the watching all the time."

"What else?" Z asks with a soft voice.

"Um, Dr. Phillips and I have talked about it and he thinks maybe you need to see someone away from me, or even with me, or whatever you want because you seem way too tense and worried all the time. And *your* tense is the only thing stressing me out right now, Z. I promise."

We are US...

  Whew. Okay. That's been sitting on my chest for weeks now and I could never work up the nerve to tell Z.

  Waiting for Z to respond, I feel my stomach turning tighter and tighter into knots. Not that Z is ever mean to me, or even hard to talk to, but I certainly don't want him to ever think I don't love or appreciate his constant concern and sweetness toward me, because I do. Sometimes it's just too much to handle all the time.
  "Thank you for talking to me," Z breathes into the phone and I exhale immediately all my tension. "I don't mean to watch or question you all the time, but I find I still get nervous with you. So when things like Sheran happen, I think I'm going to lose you to your past or something. I love you, Suzanne, and I don't want you to ever go back to your bad place, that's all."
  "I know you don't. And you're amazing to me, Z. Like I always tell you, you are an absolute gift to me. But you have to relax a little, too. We have a wonderful relationship, and we've figured out so much between us, but I sometimes feel like you haven't let go of the past as hard as I've tried to, and I worry about you."
  "It's hard for me remembering everything from before," Z admits, and I would do anything right now to just hug him to me tightly.
  "I know it is," I whisper his truth sadly. "That's why I think you need to see someone yourself. You've been such a huge part of everything that's happened to me for the last 3 1/2 years, and I think you may have your own issues over everything to deal with. Am I right?"
  Exhaling, Z whispers, "Yes..." and I want to cry for him.
  "Oh, Z... You can be upset and freaked out and nervous, or even just scared around me. You can even be sad if you're sad. You *can* be, and it doesn't mean I'll freak out, and it doesn't mean you are anything less than what I need in my life. Shit, I *want* you to be less strong all the time, so I can help you for a change."
  "But then-"
  "Come on, Z. Think about it. You're not infallible or emotionless. You're amazing, and delicious, and sexy as hell, and sweet, and kind, and a million other things, but you're not supposed to be my caregiver. You're supposed to be my husband, and we're supposed to share this life equally. Even the bad stuff. But you never share with me. You only ever wait for me to have a drama so you can be there for me to fix it.

But I want to be able to fix you too when you need it. I have to, otherwise I feel like this whole relationship we have is based solely on me and I don't want that. I want *all* of you. Remember, Z; the good, the bad, the ugly, and the beautiful? I've tried so hard to give you all of that, but I know you hold back from me. And it actually stresses me out a little."

Waiting for hours it seems, I start rocking in my heels as Z breathes into the phone. I'm going to be late to pick up Kayla, but Z and I need to have this talk whether the timing is right or not.

"I don't mean to stress you out," Z finally admits and again all I want to do is crawl up his chest and hug him.

"I know that, too. Obviously. But you need to chill a little."

"*Chill?*" When I suddenly hear his smile-voice, I exhale my nervous tension and grin.

"Yes, chill out. As in don't be all intense and strong all the time. Just chill."

"I can chill," he says sexily as I smile back at the door I'm waiting to exit.

"Okay, good. Let me see a chilled Zinfandel then," I laugh at the analogy. "This weekend. Through all this wedding nightmare we're about to endure, chill out and let loose a little. I seem to recall you used to be fun before we were married," I poke at him.

"I *was* fun. But I'm married now," he says poking back at me.

"Heaven forbid. What don't you try being fun *with* your wife? You might even like it."

"Okay. Fine. I'll be fun with my wife, though from what I understand that goes against the very concept of marriage," he teases again. "I'll give it a try though," he laughs and I know he's okay with our talk.

"Okay, good. I have to go though or I'll be late for Chicago Kayla."

"Drive safe. Call me when you have her, okay?"

"I will. I love you, Z. Will you think about what I said about therapy?"

"Yes," he exhales again before hanging up.

We are US...

I haven't seen Kayla in a month, though we've spoken almost every day, especially with crazy Kayla calling us way too frequently over the strangest, most asinine wedding crap neither Kayla or I could have ever dreamed existed for future brides.
  Cra-cra Kay, as Chicago Kayla calls New York Kayla is just mental over this wedding, and the effects of it are definitely showing. Chicago Kayla however always seems to calm her down with her blunt, don't give a shit answers to questions Cra Kay is totally stressed over.
  For me, Chicago Kayla is just my awesome, super sexy ex-coworker and friend who I love to death, no matter what shit we've gone through together in the past. And thankfully, my own crazy past has stayed in the past with Chicago Kayla since I left Chicago with Z.

  Waiting, I see Kayla descending the escalator with multiple carry-ons. Waving, she spots me immediately, and her smile makes me smile in return as I walk toward her.
  Dropping her bags she hugs me immediately. "You're lucky I look for solid chunks of black, otherwise I'd never find your short-ass among a crowd," she says pulling away as I burst out laughing immediately.
  "It's always a pleasure being insulted by you, Kayla," I grin.
  "You look awesome, Suzanne. I love your hair this way," she says pulling the piece of long hair that covers my face behind my ear before I immediately toss my head back and forth to let it fall back in place across my face. Old habits die hard as Mack says, and covering the damaged side of my face will never die I'm fairly sure.
  "Do I need to tell you to stop hiding your face?" She asks seriously.
  "No, you don't. And I'll never stop hiding that side of my face, so *you* need to drop it," I say just as seriously until she nods.
  Barking a quick laugh, she smiles and hugs me again. "You really are growing a set, Suzanne. Does Z like having a wife with some balls?"
  "Yup. He loves having a wife with balls, especially when she uses them against him. It's kind of a turn on, actually."
  "I can see that. Z's sexy as hell," she grins at my scowl. "Oh, come *on*. He's fucking edible. Anyway," she smirks again, "I could definitely imagine a little dual dominance role playing," she wiggles her eyebrows and after my immediate blush we both start laughing.
  "Can we please get your luggage? We redid your bedroom for you and I can't wait for you to see it."

"You did?" Kayla asks excited.
"Of course. After all your bitching about the boring colors last time you slept over, we made it *very* Chicago Kayla for you," I admit walking toward the luggage carousel. "Tell me that hot pink leopard print is your new luggage?" I grin knowing almost with certainty it has to be the 'awesome' luggage she told me she found on sale. Ugh.
"Of course," she laughs grabbing a trolley for her hideous luggage.

"So, how's Kayla?" Kayla asks as we settle into Z's SUV.
"Crazy. Seriously, she's almost previous Suzanne crazy," I grin while pulling out of the parking lot. "She isn't enjoying this wedding at all, and Mack is desperate for it to be over. I think Mack just wants to skip the whole thing at this point, but he knows Mrs. Rinaldi would chop them off, so he's being as supportive as he can. But honestly, this wedding is making them both so unhappy it's awful to watch. You'll see," I admit shaking my head again.
"They should've just continued living in sin," Kayla adds, and I have to agree.
I would've lived in sin with Z forever, but he wanted to get married. I didn't care either way about marriage having known what my previous marriage was like and was to become for me.
Thinking about that horrible wedding my mother threw and the endless bullshit fake friends, abusers, and even relatives who didn't know me or care about me at all for that matter feels like an entire lifetime ago. Another life, really.
Marcus was just so awful doing what he did, knowing what he knew about my abuse, sometimes I can't help but feel such betrayal from him it makes his death seem almost just or something. I can't explain it, but I don't feel bad about his death, more just about the way he did it. Or maybe it's a combination of both.
"Suzanne?"
"What? Oh!" Shit. "Sorry," I mumble picking up the speed. I didn't notice I had dropped down to a crawl on the throughway while I thought of Marcus again and our wedding.
"How have you-"
"Before you ask, I'm fine. Honestly. Z keeps waiting for some trigger but there aren't any. I've been really good with my own stuff, it's just Kayla I'm worried about. She's lost a lot of weight and she's so frazzled, I

We are US...

wish she had agreed to the wedding planner her mother wanted to use to take some of the stress off of her. Speaking of stressed out, I have to call Z," I smirk as I hit the phone icon on the steering wheel.

"Hi love. Everything okay?" When I see Kayla lift her hand to her chest I look over and she's swooning for Christ's sake. Mouthing, 'It's his voice that gets me', I shake my head at her. "Suzanne?"

"I'm here. But you can't speak anymore. You've got another *swooner* drooling over your voice."

"Really? *Hello...* Chicago Kayla. Are you *swooning* for me, darling?" He asks with his sexiest voice ever, and as I gasp, Kayla bursts out laughing.

"Holy *shit*, Z! You just made me wet!" She yells to my shock as I almost veer off the road to hit her until thankfully Z jumps back in.

"Wow. That was NOT my intention, Kayla. I see you are just as inappropriate as ever."

"Only with you, Z."

"Enough!" I scream as they both laugh. "Stop being a flirt Z, and ewwww Kayla. You're so disgusting!" I yell again to more laughter.

"I know, Suzanne. I'm just having a little fun at your expense," Kayla jumps in taking my hand for a squeeze. "Z's not even my type. He's way too manly and dominant for me. I like wimpy guys so *I* can dominate," she says as Z barks another quick laugh.

"Whatever. Gross. All I'm thinking about is the friggin seat now and the washable leather," I fake gag as she laughs at me. "We'll be home in 45 minutes Z and I'll make some dinner for us."

"Why don't we go out?" Z asks but I really don't want to.

"Um, I'm a little tired. And tomorrow is the pre-wedding dinner and rehearsal, then Saturday is the day from hell, so I thought we could just *chill*," I add with inflection to remind him.

"It's fine with me," Kayla pipes in. "But why don't we order in?"

"Sounds good. Z?"

"Sure. I should be finished up soon so I'll meet you two at home. Drive safe, love," Z adds as I roll my eyes.

"Yes, dear," I add quickly while ending the call before he can respond to my sarcasm.

After a few quiet minutes driving Kayla finally speaks to me. "I was only teasing, Suzanne. I promise," she says looking at me with concern.

"I know. I'm good, Kayla. No psychotic jealous freak out in sight," I smile though somewhat taken aback by her graphic teasing with Z.

"Suzanne, I'm sorry. I really was just being inappropriate," she continues like there's a problem between us. But there isn't with her. It's just every other goddamn woman who looks at Z I have a problem with.

"Honestly, I'm fine, Kayla. It's not you."

Turning against the door, Kayla gives me the Mack 'talk to me' face and I almost laugh. It's like he trained all my people how to give that look, knowing I can never fight it.

"Basically, I'm insecure. And neurotic. And-"

"Crazy," she adds helpfully as I laugh.

"Not that much anymore, but it's hard being with Z sometimes."

"Why?" She asks, and I can't help look over at her with an obnoxious 'Are you seriously asking me that?' face.

"You know why."

"No, I don't. Tell me," she pushes.

"Come on, you *know* why," I mumble embarrassed.

"I really don't. So tell me," she asks again looking honestly confused, which is bizarre considering the obvious physical differences between me and Z.

Eventually huffing a breath I spill. "Well, let's see. I have a lifetime of issues, and Z is Z. I have a scarred face, a lower belly flub I can't seem to get rid of, and I'm plain. But Z is still Z. Everyone looks at him and listens to his every word and just waits for whatever he says or does because he's Z. And I'm just Suzanne. The short, big-hipped wife with the facial scars and the very publicly known past from hell."

"So?" Kayla asks in almost a whisper.

"So, that's everything. Except for the women of course. Do you have any idea what it's like going out in public with him? *Everywhere* we go? Which incidentally is always, all the time, because he's really busy and he always wants me with him so I never get a break from all the looks," I huff again feeling totally insecure as I confess to Kayla.

"What looks?" She asks and I feel pissed off that she keeps playing stupid with me. Snapping my head to glare at her for a second she raises her eyebrow for me to answer.

"Fine. *THE* looks. First, the holy shit Z's hot look, followed by the check out the wife blatantly look, followed by the seriously? *That's* his wife look. Then I get the dreaded oh my god look at her face look. And if they aren't blatantly staring at my face while I duck my head and move my hair to cover my face they're almost scowling at me. And I know exactly what they're thinking as they look between me and Z- How the hell did *she* get him? I'm not stupid, Kayla. I'm well aware of the fact that Z is so far out of my league I should've run, but I didn't run. And now I have to spend a lifetime watching women watching us trying to figure out if we were childhood sweethearts, or better yet an arranged marriage or something. They're trying to find any kind of reason that makes some kind of sense to explain how I'm married to someone as amazing as Z. And it's exhausting," I finish lamely when I feel so insecure suddenly spewing it all in the front seat of Z's SUV I want to cry.

Shit. I didn't realize just how much this bothered me until I laid it out like that. Usually, I tease Z and he comforts me or says one of his perfect Z-isms until I calm down. But it really does bother me. Every single day, wherever we go, from the Benefits to the grocery store, I feel that intense insecurity and paranoia when I see everyone trying to figure out how the hell I trapped Z.

"I didn't trap him..." I mumble before realizing I spoke out loud.

"Are you high right now?" Kayla asks so seriously I burst out laughing.

"Um, no more than usual," I grin.

"Well, you are the most fucked up person I've ever met. Have you seen the way Z looks at you?"

"Yes. I know he loves me. It's the other people though. They're just so mean."

"Who *gives* a fuck?! Seriously, Suzanne. Stop feeling insecure for a second about all the things you think are wrong with you, physically and mentally and wear that shit. Own Z in public so they all know who his wife is. Sit up and be like, 'Fuck you Bitch- look what I got. While *you're* using a dildo at night to get off, *I'm* using his fine ass.'"

Turning to her, I'm stunned by Kayla's sudden anger. "It's not that easy."

"Actually, it *is* that easy. You're not hideous Suzanne, though you think you are. You're actually quite stunning, especially when you smile and your eyes light up like they do around us. But when you're around Z you both seem to glow, or some sentimental crap like that. It's awe-inspiring, especially watching Z- who incidentally loves you more than any man I've ever known loves his wife. So really, you need to cut the shit. Shine up those new balls of yours, and live in this awesome thing you have with Z. Because you are fucking fabulous, Suzanne. *Truly,*" Kayla finally winds

down by taking my hand for a squeeze.
  Breathing my way through Kayla's sudden outburst, I'm feeling a variety of emotions ranging from shock at her anger, love for her loyalty, and still the constant insecurity that has made me me weighing me down.
  After a few silent moments while I think about everything she said, Kayla finally whispers, "I'm sorry," in the quiet of the truck.
  This is so Kayla. Totally in my face bitchy which is meant out of love and support, followed by her reeling it back afterward when she calms down.
  "It's okay. It's just hard, Kayla. I'm not like you. I haven't had a lifetime of feeling fabulous, or being told I was fabulous. I was treated pretty badly my whole life, so even though I'm surrounded by love and support now, my past doesn't just go away in a few years. I don't just suddenly feel fabulous because you say I am." And that's the truth as I feel it. "Um, words aren't helping, I can only hope time makes me feel worthy of this wonderful life I suddenly find myself in."
  "You will, because you do deserve it. And if I have to yell at you until you finally get it, then I will," she says with a huge, devious Kayla smile.

ɋɋɋɋɋ

"Okay. I *love* it. I can't believe you 2 did all this in only a month," she says looking all around her room. Z and my city condo has 4 bedrooms remarkably, and Kayla claimed this one bedroom almost immediately. It certainly didn't hurt that 'her' bedroom had the only other bathroom besides Z and my master bedroom. But I think it was the view that got her.
  "It looks great, doesn't it?" I ask with pride.
  "It's fucking amazing. Thank you so much, Suzanne. I'm never leaving now. Chicago doesn't have anything like this, and I kind of miss you when I'm back home," she actually says quietly like she really means it. Kayla isn't particularly emotional so it feels great hearing she misses me.
  "You know you're always welcome here."
  "Uh huh," she says again distracted by the vivid black and white zebra prints and bright blue highlights all over her room and carpet.
  "Plus, you may find a reason to move to New York soon," I say knowing

that'll get her attention.
  Practically bouncing, Kayla looks so excited by my words. "And why would that be, Suzanne?" She questions almost threateningly.
  "Oh, I don't know... there's this guy named Marty I think you like. Oh, and Z told Mr. Petrie that you deserve to be promoted to Accounts Manager, preferably in a larger, busier location like New York for example," I say seriously biting my cheek to prevent my grin.
  Waiting, Kayla doesn't speak for second and then, "Fuck *OFF!* *Seriously?* He did that? He would *do* that?"
  "Yes!" I yell excited. "If you want it. Petri always listens to Z," I roll my eyes, "like everyone else does. Anyway, Z told him how great you were and how essential to the company, and basically said you needed to be transferred to the New York office because you were being wasted in Chicago. So Petri immediately agreed you were to be promoted to Accounts Manager regardless. And though the choice will be yours to move to New York or not, the promotion is a given, but the choice is still yours regarding where you want to take it. And yes, Z's going to kill me for telling you but I couldn't wait," I giggle at Kayla's silence.
  "I..." Ha! Her silence is awesome.
  "It'll be discussed with you officially when you return to Chicago and back to work on Wednesday," I grin again hoping and praying she chooses to move to New York. "Um, you can stay here till you find a place if you want. And to be honest Z already has a realtor looking for you in case you wanted the job transfer. Actually, he already found a cool apartment not far from here that will be available next month, and he already put down a deposit *just* to hold it so you could look at it before it was snatched up as soon as it went on the market," I grin. "It was a little presumptuous of us but when Z actually found an awesome apartment in Manhattan that was affordable we didn't want to let it go before you could decide what you wanted to do."
  Turning to me again, Kayla has such a shocked look on her face I can't stop the grin from spreading across my own. "You're too quiet, Kayla. You're kinda freaking me out here."
  Shaking her head, Kayla finally exhales and smiles back at me. "I'm stunned Suzanne, and happy, and excited, and holy *shit* do I ever want to take the job in New York," she says so excited, I too almost bounce with her.
  "You do?"

"Yeah... I do. Look, I love Chicago, but it's kind of been played out, ya know? After you and Kayla, and with everything that happened there I didn't feel the same about home. And I'm going to be honest, I've missed you and Kayla like crazy. I bonded with you two in a way that I've never bonded with any other women before, and I love my friendships with you both. I'm almost lonely without you guys around, and I really look forward to all my weekend shopping trips with you in New York. Even with all this wedding shit which I hate, I look forward to it because I get to come back and I love being around you." When I smile again, I know my eyes are shining with tears and she's gonna snap at me any second. "Oh, don't get all sappy for Fuck's sake! I'm just saying I like you and Kayla, okay?"

"Okay," I nod.

Walking closer to me, Kayla hugs me tightly. She's not a big hugger like my other Kayla is, but when she does it's hard, and engulfing, and almost sweet because they're so rare and special. Whispering in my ear, she admits, "I reeeeeally want to move here," as I nod against her shoulder. "Could Z be any more amazing?" She smiles pulling away from me.

"Nope. Z is everything, Kayla." When she nods back calmly, I know she knows it, too.

Z is everything to me, and he has made me everything I am, which is happy, and healing, and whole. Z makes every day beautiful for me. He makes every single day for me worth the nightmare I went through, because without the nightmare I wouldn't have found the dream I now live with Z.

"Look at this zit on my face AND I got my period this morning!" Kayla suddenly yells from the bedroom doorway. Spinning toward her, I almost laugh at her face but just catch myself. Wow. New York Kayla is a hot friggin' mess. There's no other way to describe her.

"Wow. You look like shit," Chicago Kayla says back and I can't hold in my shocked laughter.

"I *know!* Suzanne, I need that pasty white liquid foundation you use that covers everything. Please?" She nearly cries. "What was it? I don't have time to buy any, but I'll replace it I promise. I have to cover this thing- look at it! It practically has a pulse it's so big," Kayla yells again, and I know the crazy is coming. She's almost in tears, and I think Chicago Kayla is a little stunned by the changes to Kayla in just a month. I think she's lost at least 20 pounds and it *doesn't* look good on her.

Kayla is tall, and shapely, and her curves were to die for. Now she looks a little too skinny and her body looks almost awkward, or like disproportioned or something with her height.

"Cra... I need you to breathe slowly for me," Kayla says like Mack would and I start laughing at New York Kayla's face when she scowls at Kayla.

"Don't fucking start with the Cra-Cra Kay bullshit, Kayla. I'm losing my mind here! Who gets a fucking zit in the middle of their cheek 2 days before their huge wedding? *Me!* That's who. So of course I'm freaking out. My mother is going to point it out to everyone and make comments, and my sisters will love to torture me because they're bitches and where's that foundation, Suzanne!? I need it!" She snaps at me.

Shit, I know it's not going to work because I'm much more pale than Kayla but I'm not even going to try to be rational right now with her. Grabbing her hand we leave Kayla's bedroom for my own.

Walking into my bathroom, Kayla parks it on the long counter and waits for me to find it among the endless foundations and creams I've tried over the past 2 years to hide my red facial burns.

"I can't even have sex on my honeymoon," Kayla practically cries but before I can answer, Kayla does.

"Shower sex?" She asks leaning against the doorway watching us.

"For half the goddamn honeymoon? Fuck. We'll be waterlogged," Kayla says finally laughing a little.

Grinning at her, I try to calm her down. "You and Mack have a lifetime together for sex, and you'll probably be so exhausted when this is all over Sunday you won't even want to. Mack doesn't care about honeymoon sex Kayla, he cares about getting *you* back," I whisper as Chicago Kayla nods.

"I know. It's been just awful between us. And I'm so unhappy, I can't even get my Shrink to help me anymore," she grins until it fades away from her face slowly. "I'm scared I've ruined our relationship with all this wedding shit," she confesses as I pause in my cupboard of makeup.

Walking back to her, I take her hand as her eyes fill up, and smile my brightest smile for her. "You have ruined *nothing*. Mack loves you beyond anything this wedding has caused, and once it's over you two will be back to normal, I promise. He's just patiently waiting for it to be over, and then he's going to shrink you back sane. You know Mack, and there is nothing he wouldn't do for you, Kayla. Nothing," I whisper and I know I have her.

Nodding, Kayla exhales deeply and smiles sincerely for the first time in months. "You're good, Suzanne. Mack has taught you well," she grins.

"I know he has. Look, Kayla and I'll go buy you the proper shade of foundation tomorrow morning and bring it to you before the rehearsal, okay? My shade is the palest one they have, but it'll look like a dot of white on your beautiful, tanned skin. So let me grab a medium or slightly darker shade in the morning for you so you don't have to stress about it. Plus, that gives me and Kayla a reason to go shopping first thing in the morning," I smirk as Kayla nods from the doorway.

Exhaling, Kayla agrees. "Thank you," she smiles. "But I need it by noon before I see my mother. Is that okay?"

"Yup. We'll go out first thing and we'll have it at your place before noon. No worries about a little zit. We've got this. And you can use this foundation in the meantime to get you home so no one can see it pulsating on your face," I say so seriously both Kaylas pause for a second before they start laughing at the same time.

"Smartass! And nicely done," Chicago Kayla says entering the bathroom fully to take Cra Kay's hand. "We've got this. Is there anything else you need? Any last minute oh shits we can grab for you?"

"No. I'm good."

"We're ordering dinner and Z should be home any second. Do you want to stay for dinner?"

"Nah... I think I'll go home and snuggle up to Mack. It's our last night together living in sin before we're married and I really need to see him," she says hoping off the counter with the foundation. Dabbing a little amount on her cheek, she shakes her head at the horrible coverage but smiles anyway at us through the mirror before turning to leave.

"Thank you for everything," she says a little sadly until I hug her.

"3 days, Kayla. It's Thursday, and by Sunday *everything* will be over. Just 3 more days, okay?" I ask as she nods and walks away toward the hallway and my front door.

Opening the door to Z just walking in, Kayla almost jumps into his arms to hug him tightly all of a sudden. Watching, I instantly see Z's concern for her as he hugs her back with everything he has.

Kissing her head, Z whispers, "Just 3 more days, Kayla," as my own eyes fill up immediately hearing his soft voice. He and I are so similar now, I can't believe he just said my exact words to her from only seconds

We are US...

before as she exhales and hugs him tighter for a second.

"I can't wait to see you in a tux, Z," she smiles pulling away from him. "You're going to look so hot," she laughs as I roll my eyes again to Z looking at me over her head with a smile.

"Yes, I will," he grins letting her go.

"See you in the morning," Kayla says much happier when leaving us.

When the door closes Z walks to me for a Z hug, and I find myself exhaling in his chest as well. "How are *you*, love?" He whispers in my ear as I smile. Z's voice really does sound like the dark chocolate I always picture when he whispers to me.

"I'm good, and I'm glad your home. We have to still order though because Cra-Cra Kay interrupted us," I giggle when Z laughs and kisses my lips quickly.

"What are we having?"

"Chinese is good with me. Kayla?"

"Sounds good. Plus, Z and I need to have a little talk about awesome future promotions while we wait," Kayla says with excitement in her eyes and a huge smile plastered on her face as I groan.

Pinching my ass, Z whispers, "You're in so much trouble. I know where I'll find you later," with a fake scowl.

Smiling innocently I turn for our kitchen. "I'll be ordering the food while you two talk," I skip away before he can grab me again to take me to our room.

God, I love that voice, and I love that scowl. Usually, it means Z and I are having sex on our *special* couch in our bedroom. The couch we learned is absolutely perfect for sexy sex. The couch that is the right height and the right size for both of us. Whether I'm against the armrest, sitting, or lying down flat, it's a perfect fit for our bodies. It is our special sex couch and it always turns me on and gets me going.

If I'm sitting on it he knows I need him dark and delicious, and if he's lounging on it, I know he needs me to be ready for him. It is our special, secret sex couch and it has been very, *very* good to us, I giggle and blush.

CHAPTER 4

"Z, I need help," I giggle into the phone.

"What's *wrong?!*" He yells and I realize my mistake immediately. Shit, of course he'd think the worst. I just never thought about it. "Suzanne!" He yells again having a mini-fit.

"Shit! Sorry. I'm okay. But-"

"Is someone trying to hurt you?!" He yells again, and I can already hear the phone moving like he's running for the door.

"No! Stop, Z! Just listen to me. I. Am. Fine. No one is with us, but-"

"Where the hell is Kyle?" He yells again and I can't help my huff of frustration. I totally screwed this up.

"Ah, I think we kind of misplaced him."

"*Misplaced* a driver?" He asks like I'm mental. "What the hell does-"

"Z! Shut *UP* for a second!" I yell to get his attention and it works immediately. Actually, it works so well I almost forget what I'm trying to tell him.

"Where are you, Suzanne?" He speaks just above a whisper and I know he's trying so hard not to freak on me.

"Well, that's the thing... I'm not really sure. Kayla wanted to leave the one club, then Kayla found this other club, and then we met up with her cousin Tonia who is really sweet by the way. But then we ended up here I think, and now I'm not sure where we are."

Speaking as calmly as he can, Z asks the next question and I'm already giggling before answering. "Where are the Kaylas? Are they with you?"

"Um... Yes. Well, kind of. We're, well, *they're* still inside this dive club and I can't see a club name or a street sign, and they're really drunk, Z. Like fall down drunk, and I can't really carry them," I suddenly burst out laughing. "As if I could carry either of them, never mind both of them. They're like 12 feet tall combined!" I howl with my laughter.

"Are you drunk?" He asks so seriously, my giggles answer the question for me. "Okay, Suzanne. I have your location on my phone, so I'm on my way. Just stay right where you are. Actually, get your ass back inside the

club with the girls while you wait for me. Okay?"
"Yup. I love you, Z. Thank you for the awesome lovin' on our sex couch last night. You were very, *very* good, Mr. Zinfandel," I moan hoping for more of that sex tonight when we get home.
"I love you too, Suzanne," he says with his smile-voice making me giggle again when he hangs up.

Finding my way back to my girls, I can't believe Kayla is passed out on the filthy table while Chicago Kayla ignores her completely to talk to some hot young guy beside her.
"Holy shit! Is she drooling?" I ask as I sit my fat ass down. When Chicago Kayla looks over at her and rolls her eyes we both start laughing again.
Reaching in her purse Kayla pulls out her cell and starts taking pictures of drooling Kayla and though I think it's wrong I laugh as she does it anyway. Kayla is going to be a train wreck tomorrow at her wedding.
"We're in deep shit," I yell over the music.
"Ah, so you did call your daddy?" Kayla smirks turning back to the guy so she can't see my immediate reaction.
"He's not my daddy," I defend quickly while shaking my head to clear it. Z isn't like that. Z's never been like that to me. Oh no... *Please* not now.
"Whatever. You ran and called him, and now daddy is coming to spank us," she laughs with the guy she's flirting with. But I can't respond, and I don't really hear her anymore.
My whole body just became really hot, and my heart has started pounding. The jazz music is slowly receding, and everything is growing dark around the edges of my sight. Oh, *god*... I know what's coming.

Trying to breathe my way into the present, I know I'm in trouble. I didn't bring my pills like an asshole because I didn't think anything could hurt me tonight.
After the rehearsal and after dinner everyone was so happy, we all decided to split up for fun little individual bachelor/bachelorette parties. Spontaneously, we all split up and agreed to meet back up at my house at midnight before everyone went home. Chicago Kayla staying with us, and Kayla to her mother's house as tradition states she has to the night before her wedding.
But I never thought. And I never drink like this. And I didn't know.

"Z's **not** my daddy, Kayla," I moan trying to get her attention.
Moving closer to the guy, Kayla looks at me quickly and laughs like what I said is the funniest thing ever. But I don't care if she thinks I'm funny, I'm just trying to breathe right now. I'm trying to stay right here in this club in New York with my friends tonight.
This is not then.
But my everything has started shaking, and I remember Mr. Williams liked me calling him daddy, and though he's Z's daddy, Z's not *my* daddy. I know that. And I'm not little anymore.
Grabbing my phone again, I call Z before I'm completely incoherent. I know it's coming, and I hope he can help me before I freak out completely.
"We're only 20 minutes away," Z says calmly but I can only nod. "Suzanne? How are you doing?"
Gathering all my strength, I say the one word I can wheeze out of my quickly closing throat. "Trigger." And that's it.
The pressure in my chest is too great, and the memories are too close, and the feelings and memories are touching me all over my skin.
"*Trigger?!* Suzanne! I'm on my way, love. Mack's with me and we'll be right there. Just hold on. *Please?!*" He begs and I try really hard to hold on, but I just can't breathe. "What's happening, Suzanne?"
Gasping a breath, I tell him everything. "You're not- my- d-daddy..."
Standing quickly, I drop my phone on the table because I know I need air. Pushing past the guy Kayla's kissing, I stumble into the table beside us as she laughs when I walk run past them for the exit.
I don't think she knows. I really don't think she saw what happened. I'm almost positive Kayla would've helped me instead of making out with that stranger if she knew. But she doesn't know. And Kayla was passed out on the table drooling. So no one knows what's happening to me.

Tugging open the heavy wooden door, I just get a huge gulp of air when my stomach turns and I throw up on the sidewalk. Shaking, I try to stop the panic so hard, but it takes me anyway.
The feelings are all around me and inside me again and they're slowly strangling me from the inside out. They are spanking me, and laughing at me, and screaming at me, and grunting inside me.
Throwing up again, I land on my knees to crawl to the side of the building to the little alley in between buildings. Scrapping my knees on

pebbles and making my hand bleed on a piece of broken glass, I don't care. I don't want anyone to see me, and I can't have anyone know what's happening to me.

Maybe if I hide they can't get me this time. Maybe if I stay quiet in the alley they won't find me. Maybe if I stay little, they won't hurt me this time.

Leaning against the wall, I pull my legs up tight to protect my body as I breathe in and out as slowly as I can. Breathing, I feel the nightmare fear change to reality when the memories take me completely.

I know Mr. Sheran was there. He touched me all the time. He *always* touched me. He was very bad to me and I can't believe he convinced a judge that he didn't touch me that much. He must've said something, or lied, or told them something they wanted to hear. He did something to get out early, and I don't know what he did or said because he *did* touch me. Too often, and too badly.

Like Daddy Williams.

Throwing up again, I feel him all over me again. My little body is shaking and my arms have given out until just my cheek squeaks on the floor back and forth from my wet tears.

Grunting around me and pushing inside me, Daddy Williams spanked me and pulled my hair, and fucked me until I couldn't move anymore. He left me on the sauna floor gasping for breath, so hot and used my skin was burning. He was laughing at me until I crawled for the exit toward air and my freedom.

Reaching up, I remember the little click of the sauna door handle as I was blasted with cool air and my freedom. That time. But I was never really free, was I?

It was always the laughter and the pain that trapped me. So much pain all the time. If it wasn't the fucking, or the hitting, it was the awful words. Such mean words to say to a little girl. I never liked the words, but they always said them even when I begged them to stop.

"Suzanne?"

Oh, god. Here we go again.

Closing my eyes, I unfold my legs and turn over. Resting on my hands and knees, I lift my dress over my hips and pull my panties down quickly to my knees.

When I'm a good girl, they're usually good to me. When I don't fight them, they don't fight me. So I know to always be a good girl.

"Suzanne, it's me," he says, and I don't really care.

Mr. Sheran, or Daddy Williams, or Mr. Sheehan, or Simmons, or all the others. Or even my own mother. There are so many of them and they all do the same thing so it doesn't really matter who it is. All that matters is not fighting them. So I never fight them anymore.

When he places his hand on my back I freeze up tight but try to loosen the muscles of my dirty hole. If I clench in fear it hurts more and I bleed more. If I let the fear make me tight I always hurt so much more. So I have to try to not be afraid this time to make me looser and easier for them.

Wiggling my ass, I try so hard to make the muscles loose for him so I won't scream when he forces it inside me.

"Suzanne, it's Kyle. Z's on his way any minute, and I'm not going to hurt you. I promise," he says but Mr. Sheran always said that before he hurt me.

If there is such a thing as a nice monster, Mr. Sheran was probably it though. He didn't gag me, or hit me, or make me bleed too often. He was actually pretty nice to me. For a monster, I almost laugh. But thankfully I just catch the laugh in my throat and turn it into a little cough so he doesn't know I was laughing at him. Because laughing at him would be really bad for me right now.

Looking behind me, I don't know what's taking him so long. My muscles will only stay loose if I work at it and keep pushing out to accept him, and I'm getting tired as my arms shake holding me up. But he still isn't doing anything.

Kneeling beside me, his hand is still on my back, but he's not even looking at me. He's on the phone actually.

"...doesn't know me... I don't know... I'm just resting with her..." Oh yeah, sure. I'm resting? What an asshole!

I wonder if he's taking my picture. Spreading my legs further apart for him, I raise my ass so he can get a better shot of my little pussy, then maybe this'll be over quicker.

"There you go, sir. I'm all open for you if you want," I whisper so he won't get mad at me. But he still doesn't move, and he doesn't look at my body either.

God, I hate these mind games. I never guess right when they want me to, and I always get punished for not doing what they want me to do

We are US...

when I don't guess right.

"I'll do whatever you want. Please, sir. Just tell me what you want from me and I'll do it," I beg but he keeps talking quietly on the phone ignoring me completely.

"Suzanne! *Stop!*" Z suddenly yells in the street at the alley and I tense immediately. Oh *god*... He's going to see this and he'll never forgive me, and I can't do this to him.

"It's not my fault!" I scream desperately before flinching away from Sheran. "He did this! I don't want this anymore, but they make me and I'm not bad, but I can't stop them, Z. Please forgive me!?" I scream as the tears blind me to everything but the wavy street lights around him. Desperate for him to understand, I beg again, "Please forgive me, Z? This wasn't supposed to happen to me anymore."

I think I hoped Z would come save me. I think in the back of my mind I hoped he would somehow come get me this time. But he never did before, and I didn't think he really would this time. I just hoped he would.

"Suzanne, I came for you. And I'm not mad at you at all. This isn't your fault, I know that," Z says like he means it.

Crying out my relief, I let my arms slump to the ground as I feel my face scrap the filthy pavement. Rolling into a ball, I watch Z and Mack walk quickly towards me like they might help me this time.

Reaching out I cry *please* so Z will save me in time.

"I'm here, love," Z says bending down low in my face. And I know he is. I hoped he would and he came for me.

Bursting into loud tears and sobs, the relief is so sudden, I can help but reach for him to pull him to me until he collapses on the ground next to me.

Crying, I say everything in this moment. "You saved me this time. You didn't save me when I was little but you saved me this time. Thank you so much, Z. Thank you for stopping him from hurting me this time."

"Suzanne, no one was going to hurt you tonight, I promise. I wouldn't let them."

"Sheran was going to," I cry, trying to move away from him.

"Kyle wasn't going to hurt you, Suzanne. Do you remember Kyle? He's the driver we use. Remember Kyle and his wife Veronica?" Ummm... I think maybe, but...

"Kyle? I know Mr. Sheran was here because its Friday night, and he always visits me on Friday nights. I remember that now."

"Suzanne, you're in New York with me now. You're not in Chicago, and Mr. Sheran isn't here. There is no one here but your safe people- Me, Mack, Kayla, Kayla, and even Kyle. You're not at the country club, Suzanne. And NO ONE is going to hurt you tonight," Z says fiercely against my face and hair as he pulls me closer to him.

My safe people? "I think I know that. I think I do, but Mr. Sheran is going to come back now that he's free. They always come back for me, Z," I whisper as I start shaking again.

I knew this would happen. I knew he'd come back. Ever since I read the article in the paper I've known.

"Sheran isn't in New York, Suzanne. He's still in Chicago. Trust me."

"But he'll still come back, I think."

Squeezing me a little tighter, Z says, "He will NEVER come back to you."

Exhaling deeply, I feel everything loosen up inside me. Z is here. And my safe people are here. And I know Z won't let anyone take me. Z will protect me and keep me safe. I *know* that, I just forgot.

"I'm sorry," I whisper as Z kisses my forehead again. "I know you're not my daddy," I say and jolt.

Waking fully to my surroundings, I finally understand what's happening and what actually happened. Oh my *god*...

"Kayla said you were my daddy. No," I shake my head to clear it more. "She said I was calling my daddy and he was going to come and spank me. But I knew you weren't my daddy, Z. I knew that. But then I felt Mr. Williams all around me and inside me again and I couldn't breathe and I didn't want him to touch me, and I didn't want that bad daddy to come get me, and-"

"Suzanne-"

"Oh, god... You're NOT my daddy, but *your* daddy fucked me."

Turning my head quickly I throw up between me and Z on the pavement again as the shakes start working their way through my hands and chest.

Moaning, I almost collapse in my own vomit, but Z pulls me tighter to him, and instead leans in my vomit himself to keep me out of it.

"I'm so sorry, Suzanne. I am NOT him. Ever. I'm not my father, and I would never hurt you like he did. I'm so sorry for what he did to you. But I would never hurt you like that, Suzanne. *Ever*," he says choking up with tears I can actually hear. His voice is all broken and fading in and out as he struggles to be strong again.

Hearing Z's upset actually clears my mind a bit more, and I know I have to help him.

"I know you wouldn't hurt me like that. I just got confused about the daddy, but I know you're not like that. I'm so sorry, Z. I'm sorry I'm so dirty all the time."

"You're not dirty, love. You're beautiful and clean."

Shaking my head, I know he's lying to me. "I'm sorry I'm so gross, and I'm sorry I'm fucked up, and I'm so, so sorry I'm dirty and ugly. You deserve-"

"*You*, Suzanne," he says with such emotion I almost believe him for a second. But I know the truth.

"I will *never* deserve you," I whisper back staring in his eyes as he tears up again for me.

"I don't care about anything but you, Suzanne. Nothing. Don't say sorry, and don't cry, love. Please. Can I take you home now? Please? I need to hold you and care for you, and I need to bring you back to me," Z begs and as I burst into tears I nod yes against his shoulder.

"I need to go home. I'm safe there," I whisper and know it's true suddenly.

We have security in our building, and security in our condo. And only 6 safe people can come up with their keys. No one else can come up, not even for food delivery. We have to go down to get it, so I'm always safe in our home. Even Kyle can't-

Flinching, I realize what just happened and I'm so embarrassed I can't even look at him. Burying my face back in Z's shoulder, I think I'm going to die.

"Kyle saw me, Z. He saw my body, and he knows about the scars, and he saw my dirty hole," I cry desperately.

"Kyle didn't see anything, Suzanne. He didn't look, and he wouldn't hurt you. Kyle works for us, remember? Kyle and Veronica are good guys, remember?"

"I know but it's too late," I cry humiliated. "Please get me out of here, Z. *Please*?" I beg and he moves immediately.

Standing up, Z rips off his suit jacket and covers my waist. Lifting me, I try to help, but my legs feel tight until looking quickly, I realize my panties are still around my knees. Oh my god!

Reaching for his jacket, I cover my knees better and hide my face in his chest as he walks. I don't know who's around, and I don't care. I don't want to be here all dirty like this anymore.

　Whispering against my hair Z asks, "What do you need, love? Mack is here if you need to talk, and we've already called Dr. Phillips for you. Tell me what you need?"

　"Nothing. No one. I want to go home. I don't want to talk about this at all yet. Would you please just take me home so I can have a shower to get all this dirty off me?" I moan in his arms as we step up to his SUV.

　"Do you want to lie down in the back, or sit with me up front?"

　"I need to lie down, but would you hold my hand?" I ask choking up again as Z pulls me in closer and kisses my head. Whispering 'of course I will' against my hair, he unlocks the doors and helps me climb into the backseat.

　"Suzanne, I'm *so* sorry," Kayla cries stepping up to us but Z stops her from coming close to me with his body blocking her.

　In a deadly calm voice Z says, "NOT now," as I watch Kayla step back one foot and nod okay before Z shuts me in the cool, dark of his huge SUV.

　When I hear the trunk lifted I sit up quick but Z says simply, 'It's only me, Suzanne,' until nodding I lay back down.

　When Z opens the door again, he lays a blanket all over me, kisses my hair, and walks back away. Sliding into the front seat, Z immediately turns us around slowly, and before I can even think his huge hand moves toward me to grab.

　Crying, I know his shoulder is at an awkward angle, and I know it must be hard to drive that way. I know he's uncomfortable for me, but he does it anyway.

　"I'm really sorry, Z."

　"Suzanne, don't worry about anything."

　Cutting him off, I need to finish this for us. "I was doing so well, and I don't know what happened. Well, I know what words triggered this, but I don't know why they hit so suddenly. I was fine and then not fine at all so quickly there wasn't time to breathe. And I forgot my meds, and I remember being told I couldn't drink on my medication because it makes the effects unpredictable, but I don't think I've ever tested it before. I don't think I ever did because I never get drunk, and I guess one glass of wine once in a while is okay, but shots and other drinks and stuff aren't okay. And I'm really sorry, and this isn't Kayla's fault, okay?"

　When the silence continues, Z squeezes my hand from time to time to

We are US...

let me know he's still with me, and I always squeeze back to let him know I'm still with him.

Trying to understand exactly what happened, I know one thing to be absolutely true- this was coming. I didn't know what would do it, and I wasn't sure when it would happen. But I'm sure I felt the panic slowly coming for me. This was absolutely coming. I just can't believe how far I went with it so deeply and I'm stunned I went so dark so quickly.

"This isn't Kayla's fault, Z. Please don't be mad at her. She didn't mean to hurt me, and she didn't know what was happening because I left the bar when I freaked out. It's my fault for drinking and for forgetting my meds."

"It's going to be okay, Suzanne," Z whispers in the darkness and I almost believe him.

ϘϘϘϘϘ

Reaching for my pills I take 2 with shaking hands and a nauseous stomach. Tonight was so bad. I was so filthy and bad, and I honestly can't believe I lost it that badly. I didn't know where I was, and I didn't know who I was with. And that hasn't happened to me in a few years.

"I need to shower, Z. The dirty is all over me and it's still inside me," I whisper cry when we enter our bathroom together.

"Suzanne, there is *no* dirty inside you. None at all. You are clean inside, I promise," he says gently, but I know he's wrong. I'm filthy inside otherwise I wouldn't have done what I did in that alley.

Looking at myself in the mirror when Z starts the shower, I'm shocked and embarrassed, and really, just completely disgusted with myself once again.

Naturally, my mascara is smeared all over my face from crying, and all my foundation has been wiped off showing the red and pink scars clearly. I have a dark red scrape on my other cheek which makes me suddenly laugh in the dark silence of our bathroom because my cheeks match now and I'll never be able to cover both sides without just flipping my hair upside down to cover my whole face.

Sarah Ann Walker

Removing my beautiful pendant Z gave me on our one year anniversary, I see the vomit in my hair, down my neck and even wiped down the side of my dress. Giggling, I find this whole scene so goddamn nostalgic I feel like I need to take a picture to remind myself of just how bad I can get. Not that I ever forget, but sometimes I like to delude myself into believing I'm not as mental as others make me out to be.

"Can I be alone?" I ask in our silence.

I'm not sure Z heard me over the running water, but when he walks to me I assume he did. Placing his hands on my shoulders looking at me through the mirror, his eyes seem to be begging me for something, but I don't know what he wants. He looks so sad suddenly my heart hurts simply looking at him. Watching him staring at me like he still loves me, I just don't understand him.

"What is it?"

"I just want to help you, Suzanne. I *need* to help you, and I know you're going to need to take one of your moments, and I know that's perfectly okay, but sometimes I wish your moments didn't always exclude me," Z says hugging me tightly from behind.

Looking at his face, I feel my tears start again and I wish I knew what this man saw in me because I honestly don't understand him. Everyone else wanted something from me, so they took everything from me. But Z- Z takes nothing. And I don't understand him.

"Let me help you, please?" He begs and I can only nod as we hold each other captive with our eyes.

After forever, Z finally asks me to turn to him and I do. Raising his hands slowly behind me he unzips the back of my dress and lowers it off my shoulders. Never acknowledging my body, Z continues with my bra and eventually with my panties which somehow were raised back up my body from my knees.

"You're okay, Suzanne. And it's just us here," he whispers kissing my forehead like he knew the embarrassment was almost taking me to the darkness again which it was.

I remember my panties around me knees, and I remember my ass in the air, and I remember-

"Look at *me*," he says firmly, and my eyes immediately rise to his. Nodding, he kisses my head again and walks us to the shower.

When I step inside the door, Z quickly removes his clothes as I lean back and let the soothing warm water run through my hair and down my body. Moving when Z enters I can't look at him down there right now. It's too much, and it'll get all twisted in my head if I see his huge- oh! Z's under the water in his boxer briefs like he knew what I needed again.

"You're so good to me, Z" I whisper cry as he smiles slightly.

"I try to be. I want to be with you."

Exhaling, I tell him the truth. "You are with me. You are exactly what I need. And I'm so sorry it's always so hard with me."

"It's not hard," he grins when I give him a skeptical look. "It's not *hard,* Suzanne. It's challenging, and sad sometimes, and even a little scary at times. But when everything is good, and when you feel happy, it's all worth it to me. Everything about you, the good, the bad, the ugly, and the beautiful is worth every single day I have with you," he says so sweetly, I burst into tears again and lean into his chest as he hugs me.

After forever in silence, Z finally pulls away from me to clean my body. Washing my scraped cheek gently with a cloth, he kisses my nose when my eyes close from the sting, until he moves to my knees to clean the scrapes there as well. When he rises and turns my hand over, he pours some antibacterial soap and soothes me with soft sounds when I pull away from the sting.

Once my hair is washed I step out of the shower to give Z time to clean himself. Brushing my nasty teeth I watch his body move in the shower through the frosted glass and I can't stop thinking about everything tonight, everything between us, and everything that Z is.

But I still come up with no explanations to anything.

Sliding into bed once I'm dressed, Z follows me immediately dressed in black plaid lounge pants and a t-shirt. Usually Z sleeps naked which I love, but I'm actually glad he's dressed tonight. I don't think I could handle seeing a penis tonight, even Z's.

Smiling at me, Z settles in on his side so we're facing each other. "I wish I knew what you were thinking right now," he whispers.

"Um, it's mostly good now. Where's Kayla?" I ask concerned because I know Z's probably pissed at her.

"I really don't give a shit where she is, Suzanne. But to answer your question, she's at Mack's," he says with way too much anger.

"Z, you can't be mad at her."

"Actually, I can," he argues.

"Actually, you *can't*. Because she didn't do anything wrong. She made a normally funny comment to a not normal person. Anyone else would have reacted normally, but I didn't and that's not her fault. You know her, Z. She would *never* intentionally hurt me," I beg.

"But she did," he says flipping to his back.

Exhaling, I don't want to argue, but I can't have this animosity continue tomorrow. "She really didn't, Z. I hurt me by being careless with my medication and with all the drinking. I did this to myself, she just innocently used a trigger word which she didn't know was a trigger or you know as well as I do she never would've said it."

"I understand, Suzanne. But I'm freaked out by tonight and I need to be mad at her right now."

"Okay," I grin. "But just tonight when she's not here, okay? Then tomorrow you have to let it go. Deal?"

Turning to look at me, Z breathes nearly silently, "I don't think we should go to the wedding tomorrow. Kayla and Mack will understand."

Sitting up quickly, I'm not agreeing this time. "We have to go. And I feel much better and I won't drink. I'll make sure my meds are close, and really we *have to* go. We're the maid of honor and best man and we love them and even if they say they will, I know deep down they'll never forgive me for ruining their wedding. And I won't forgive myself either, Z. I won't."

"Suzanne, they'll understand," he pushes staring up at me.

"We have to go, Z," I whisper reaching over to squeeze his hand. "I know what happened, and I know what caused it. I'll call Dr. Phillips in the morning before we go, and I'm fine now. I promise I'm fine. I'm just really tired and we have to get up in 5 hours. But I'm okay, Z."

I know I sound a little desperate which kind of counters the 'I'm fine' argument, but I can't screw up tomorrow. I *won't* screw up tomorrow.

Mack and Kayla love me. And I love them. And I will never hurt them, ever. So I'll fake being well until I actually *do* feel well. And I'm going to their wedding with or without Z. Period.

Snuggling into Z's side as he wraps an arm around me, I whisper my plans. "We are going to their wedding. And I'm going to stand in that huge church with the ugliest dress known to man, staring at my gorgeous husband who tries not to laugh at me in my hideous dress. I'm standing up for Kayla as Maid of Honor because I love her like a sister. And Mack? Well, you know how I feel about him, and I know what he means

We are US...

to you. So we're going, Z. Okay?" I finish my little rant with absolute desperation and complete emotional exhaustion.
  "Okay..." Z breathes on an exhale.

CHAPTER 5

Pulling up to the hair salon after the makeup clinic in silence, I finally turn to Z before hopping out.

"Please stop, Z. I promise I'm okay. I know last night was really bad, and I know you're still freaked out by me and by everything that happened, but I *am* okay. I have an appointment with Dr. Phillips first thing Monday morning, and I feel much better after we spoke this morning. But you have to leave me alone now. It's too hard making myself feel okay when you're hovering around me like I'm not okay. Okay?" I ask with a grin at all my okays.

"Okay," he smiles before stepping out of the truck to open my door for me like he always does.

Once my door is open, he looks down at me so sweetly I kiss his lips quickly before struggling to get out. "I'm good, Z. But you're going to be late for your breakfast with the men. And no more driving me around. I was supposed to stay with the bridal party after our makeup, but now you've seen me in all my purple glory," I laugh thinking of my hideous makeup.

"You look lovely, Suzanne," he says against my lips before I shake my head and pull away.

Grinning at his blatant lie, I call him out. "I do not look lovely, I look awful. So you either need glasses or you *must* love me to even say such a ridiculous comment as that."

"I do love you *and* I'm getting glasses as soon as possible," he says like a smartass making me laugh against his chest.

"I'll see you in a couple hours, and I'm good. So stop stressing, and go have fun."

"You're getting quite bossy, Suzanne," he whispers. "And I think I like it."

"Good. Now go away," I fake glare until backing away with his hands raised in surrender he walks back around the truck to hop in.

We are US...

   Waving away Z and walking into the hair salon, I raise my hand to both Kaylas who are already standing away from the others near the door waiting for me. Smiling, I keep walking to the back room I hide in when I need it, motioning for them to follow. Waiting for them to enter behind me I close us in and purge before they can start on me.
   "Last night was awful. Or a clusterfuck, as you would say," I smile at Chicago Kayla. "But I'm not discussing it, I don't want to hear an apology, and we're moving on. This is Kayla's day, not the Suzanne Show, and I'm really good right now. I've taken lots of meds," I add with a smirk, "I've talked to my doctor this morning before we left, and I know exactly what happened and why it happened. And because I know what happened, nothing bad is going to happen today. I won't allow it. So I'm walking back out there to Dee, I'm getting my hair styled, and I'm going to put up with your bitchy sisters with Kayla's help of course," I say looking hard at Chicago Kayla for backup until she nods which prompts Kayla to laugh.
   "I really am okay now. And I don't want to discuss last night. It was my fault entirely, and I don't blame you Kayla and neither does Z *now*," I add with inflection. "We're just going to move on and have to best goddamn wedding New York has ever seen once you put on more makeup because no offense Kayla, but you still look horrible," I burst out laughing as Kayla does, thank god.
   "I'm dying," she moans. "I've already puked a few times, had to listen to my mother lecture me while puking in the toilet, taken 5 Tylenols, and Kayla here looks like this," she thumbs Chicago Kayla who really does look perfectly put together. The bitch.
   "Can I say one thing?" Kayla asks quietly and I shake my head no.
   "Last night was NOT your fault, I still love you, and we're absolutely fine. But that's it. It's over now, at least for today. Okay?" I ask them both until they nod. "Good. Well, let's get back in there before your sisters start trashing us."
   "I love you, Suzanne," Chicago Kayla suddenly whispers, and though I had put on my biggest big girl panties today, she just knocked the air from my lungs with that one.
   Tearing up, I smile and nod before opening the door to Dee waiting at my chair in the back ready for me with her own big smile.
   Inhaling deeply, I breathe, "Let's do this," as my Kaylas nod.

<u>ΩΩΩΩΩ</u>

"Holy shit, Suzanne! What the *fuck* is that?" Kayla yells as I panic and desperately shush her with my hands flapping in the dressing room lounge.

Trying to hold in my laughter, I whine, "It's a bow."

Looking at me like I'm mental, Kayla continues. "I know it's a goddamn bow. But it's wider than you are tall and its plastered on your ass. How the hell can you even sit?"

Mumbling, "Uncomfortably," we both start laughing. "Shhhhh... Kayla's only a few doors down and she loves this dress, so don't say anything to her. It's her wedding day and you're not allowed to hurt her feelings today," I glare as she nods still staring at my ass bow open mouthed. "Stop it," I laugh. "Like your Barney purple nightmare is any better?"

Grinning, "It's better than that thing. You could hide a family of 4 in your ass today," she says still laughing, and I can't stop my own.

"We're going to get in so much trouble if Kayla hears us. You have to stop with the ass comments because I'm dying here," I say with a sad twirl as I try to lift the huge ass-bow that I swear to god has steel planks in it to keep it stretched out sideways from my body. Christ, I thought it was bad before but now that it's been set to stay sideways it's horrendous.

"Z is going to-"

Interrupting us, Laura walks out already pouting. With her hair up, which apparently she hates, and with her makeup completed which she hates as well, she plops in the closest chair to us and grins at me like a bitch.

"Nice bow, Suzanne. I guess you regret being Maid of Honor now, don't you?" She smirks again, and I wish I could hit her. Being Kayla's older sister, Laura has clearly been pissed from the start that she wasn't chosen as Maid of Honor, but what could I do? I was asked, happily accepted, and I've had to deal with her shit ever since.

When Kayla steps forward I brace for it before Laura even knows what's coming. "She doesn't regret a thing. Why would she? Being chosen to be Kayla's Maid of Honor after only knowing her for a few years over her older bitchy sister of a lifetime is quite an honor. And it says a lot about how Kayla feels about *you*, doesn't it?" Oh. Ouch. Shit.

"Maybe she just felt sorry for her," Laura counters. Oh. Ouch again.

"Nah... Kayla clearly just loves us more because we're not bitches, I think," Kayla finishes with the last word just as Mrs. Rinaldi and Kayla walk toward us from their huge dressing room at the end.

Ignoring Laura completely, I take in Kayla and tear up immediately. Though a classically over the top, big puffy, white lacy dress, she looks gorgeous anyway- stunning, actually.

Smiling from ear to ear, Kayla quickly takes in me, Laura, and Kayla, but as I step forward she doesn't seem to notice any residual tension between us.

"You look beautiful, Kayla," I whisper as she hugs me. Obviously not a dress I would *ever* be caught dead in, but on Kayla her dress is the absolutely perfect, magazine-style, over the top wedding dress of most women's dreams.

"She does," Mrs. Rinaldi says from behind her.

"You look beautiful too, Mrs. Rinaldi," I add. "Your hair is amazing," I look at it closely because it really is. Wearing an up-do like the rest of us, Mrs. Rinaldi included purple and black dripping jewels throughout her hair. But not in a garish way, they're actually quite subtle but beautiful when you notice them.

"Thank you, honey," she says back and though I see Kayla flinch as her eyes dart to mine quickly, I only smile back. Nope. No freak out over 'honey'. Ha. I've got this. Smiling at Kayla, I let her know I'm good before she starts asking me questions in front of everyone.

"Wow. I love your dress now," Paola says walking toward us. "It looks way nicer on you since you've lost all your extra weight." Okay. A nice backhanded compliment, but thankfully, Kayla just rolls her eyes as she mumbles 'thanks'.

"When do we leave for the church?" Chicago Kayla jumps in with a little glare at Paola who shrugs at the look. Paola doesn't give a shit if she's nasty or not, but honestly, I thought Laura and Paola would play nice today on Kayla's wedding day at least.

"Um, we have about 15 minutes until the limo which will drop us off hopefully on time. We probably should have timed it with a little extra time for makeup touch ups, but so far you all look beautiful," Mrs. Rinaldi adds, and I relax a little.

That was another fight between them all. Kayla accidentally booked the dresses *after* the makeup, which was such a potential nightmare for Mrs. Rinaldi she screamed about it for days. Thankfully, we all seemed to have dressed ourselves without getting any makeup on our dresses or smudges on our faces though.

I know my makeup is okay, because I look at my face constantly to make sure all the thick foundation is in place to cover my scars. It's actually the bright purple eye shadow I'm wearing that is giving me the biggest worry. I know we had to match makeup, but still, bright purple on my eyes makes my face look even more pale. Actually, with my pale blue eyes, the purple color makes my eyes looks a little sickly, almost like I have a cold or something, at least according to Chicago Kayla who gently leaned over and rubbed a little of the purple out of the crease of my eyelids at the hair salon.

"Drink?" Kayla asks, and both Kayla and I groan.

"I don't think so. Kayla had more than enough last night," Mrs. Rinaldi snaps.

"Oh! That reminds me," Kayla says walking to her purse. Pulling out her phone I know what she's going to do, and I'm already giggling as Laura and Kayla step forward. "Here, Kay... Memories of your last single night for you," she laughs turning her phone around.

When Kayla gasps and Laura starts laughing, I can't help laughing too. These photos are priceless, and yes, the glare of Kayla's drool is clearly visible on the tabletop.

"Oh, *no*... What did you do?" Kayla glares and even Mrs. Rinaldi can't help laughing at the pictures as we all get closer to the phone being held up to us.

"Ah, let's see... I sent them to Mack of course," she says over Kayla's gasp. "I sent them to Heidi at the hospital so she'll let all your coworkers see them today. I sent them to Suzanne so we can print them off when you're on your honeymoon, and I sent them to your cousin Tonia because she was hysterical. That's it I think," Kayla adds with a triumphant smile, until finally Kayla bursts out laughing, too. "They were the perfect Bachelorette party pics, so I had to."

"You're such a bitch," Kayla laughs, and I know we're all okay. "But if you print those Suzanne, I'll kill you, understood?" She asks as I nod with a grin.

"Okay, enough shit, let's get all our stuff for the limo. Thank god, they have room for our bags, otherwise..." Mrs. Rinaldi let's hang in the air her disapproval again at Kayla booking the dresses in the boutique instead of at her mother's house, like tradition is supposed to do apparently.

ΩΩΩΩΩ

We are US...

After a long New York Saturday at noon drive to the church, followed by an unbearable attempt to get my ass-bow out of the limo, we 6 suddenly find ourselves the object of curious eyes and a few smiles in the street before we all head into the church. The wedding begins in only 20 minutes, which is to give us all time to freshen up, and 15 minutes for Kayla to try to pee with her dress on.
  "I have to pee now," Kayla says just as I imagined she would. She was chugging back water all morning to help her hangover dehydration and I was a little nervous she'd have to go during the ceremony.
  "Well, let's go Bridezilla," I giggle as she glares at me. "I believe helping the Bride pee is a Maid of Honor's job, so come on." Looking down the entrance hall to all the stragglers not seated yet, I see the washroom door and we make our way.
  "I'm not sure how to do this," she confesses and neither do I. Her dress is so big and floofy, and just huge.
  "I think I just need to get in there and lift this thing for you while you squat. Good?"
  "Uh huh," she groans like she's in pee pain. Crouching down in the large bathroom, thank god, I work my way up her dress until it takes me over completely.
  "Pull it away from my face!" I yell realizing its covering my face until I feel her hands flapping the material down so I can see and breathe. "Shit! Did I get any makeup on it?" I panic, but Kayla doesn't seem to care. Within seconds hidden behind the dress she starts going totally embarrassing me by the sound.
  "Sorry," she giggles making me laugh harder. "I *really* had to go." God, I'm thankful for all the dress material because eye contact right now would kill me. It's bad enough hearing her. "You would make a terrible nurse, Suzanne," she says as I nod silently behind all the dress.
  "I'm well aware. The fact that I can't even handle seeing a red rosette without mistaking it for blood and freaking the hell out is kind of a good sign I think."
  "Plus the fact that you're heavily medicated 50% of the time, and mental the other half doesn't really work in nursing. Typically, there's mayhem when the patients are more sane than the nurses. I'm just sayin'," she continues until she's finished going.
  "Okay, enough Suzanne crazy jokes. You're done peeing," I laugh knowing she was just trying to fill the air with humor.

"Can I say something slightly heavy but in a good way?" Kayla asks, again pushing her dress down a little so we can see each other.
"Of course you can. Always."
Waiting, Kayla says simply, "Thank you for everything." In a low moan filled with so much emotion her voice cracks, she smiles.
"You're welcome. Thank *you* for everything," I say just as quietly.
Grinning again as she flutters her eyelashes to keep any tears from falling, she finishes with, "We did pretty good, huh? Looks like we're both getting a happily ever after."
Though every single pessimistic, scared, nervous part of me wants to give her shit for jinxing us, well, jinxing *me* actually, I don't give into the fear. Smiling, I nod and flutter my own eye lashes to keep in my tears while she stands and I look away for a moment as she readjusts her dress to the floor.
"I guess we just have to work on Kayla."
"What the hell are you DOING in there?" Chicago yells banging on the door and we both laugh.
"Yup. With Marty," I say wiggling my eyebrows as Kayla agrees. "We're coming!" We both yell back as Kayla starts washing her hands.
Taking a big breath, Kayla says she loves me as she throws her shoulders back and opens the washroom door.
"Laura and your mom are fighting because she pulled some of her hair out and it doesn't look sexy like Suzanne's, it looks messy as shit. And now Laura's freaking out trying to fix it quickly, and your other psycho sister is gone to look for Dee in the church to help. And your mother was screaming at her for ruining your wedding with her selfishness, and wow- your sisters and mom are always a trip, Kayla. I see where you get the Cra from now," Kayla laughs as I giggle at the Cra Kay comment again.
"Listen. After this wedding when I'm normal again," Kayla smirks, "You don't get to call me Cra Kay ever again. Got it? The crazy title is reserved for Suzanne only. She's earned it."
Laughing, I add a thank you with a little bow as we start walking back to the sitting room to a flurry of activity and drama.
Dee is in the room already trying to bobby pin the loose hair and partial chunks that Laura pulled out in her attempt to pull solid hair pieces out, I think. Whatever. We didn't need this little delay or the drama.
Sitting next to Kayla her mom starts handing out tons of makeup, though surprisingly Kayla doesn't need anything. Kayla still looks perfect.

We are US...

"Ma... I'm good," Kayla shakes her head no, but Mrs. Rinaldi is already turning her face for more lipstick.

"You need more. People at the back won't be able to see how lovely you are without more."

"This isn't gymnastics or a dance recital. And I'll look like a freak all made up, so stop. Please," Kayla whines and finally Mrs. Rinaldi gives up with a huff to turn to Paola's face.

"3 minutes," Kayla's dad knocks on the door, and my stomach jumps. Jesus, it's not even my wedding and I'm nervous as hell suddenly.

Breathing deep, I smile at Kayla watching me through the mirror.

"I'm so happy for you. You and Mack are amazing together and I just couldn't love you both more if I tried," I whisper with Chicago Kayla nodding at her as well.

"Holy SHIT! I'm so nervous," Kayla giggles shaking, and before I can say anything Kayla actually hugs her from behind and whispers something to her. Smiling from ear to ear, Kayla nods and relaxes. Huh.

I'm sooo curious what she said, but they're allowed to have moments between them, too. I know that. I still get jealous sometimes though when they do. Call it residual insecurity, or potential insanity, or you know... just me. But I always get jealous that their relationship is stronger than mine because I can still be an immature idiot sometimes.

"Kayla! Let's *go*," Mr. Rinaldi barks making me jump again as Kayla grins with another deep breath. "Line up. Christ, Laura! Let's *go*."

Walking to the suite doors, I make sure to do my Maid of Honor duties, fluffing out and smoothing out Kaylas dress with her mom's help.

"I've got to go." Turning to Kayla, Mrs. Rinaldi smiles brightly and kisses Kayla right on the lips quickly, probably to prevent lipstick smearing, but when she smiles back at her I see the love between them instantly. "You look beautiful, Kayla. And your dad and I are so proud of you."

"Mom-"

"And Mack is just perfect. We know he's going to make you very, very happy, and we love him very much. You did good, Kay," she whispers as I watch in complete fascination.

Kayla looks so happy that her mom approves, and Mrs. Rinaldi looks so happy for her daughter. Again, this is a world I have no knowledge of, but it's amazing to see. A crazy mother and her loopy daughter who love each other is a comfort I find I enjoy watching from the sidelines.

"Mack's waiting for me, baby. I'll see you from the front row," Mrs.

Rinaldi says with such emotion in her voice, I can't help smile at the two of them. "Be good Laura or I'll beat the shit out of later," she threatens still looking at her middle daughter Kayla with affection as Kayla grins at the threat to her sister.

  Waiting, Laura, then Paola, then Kayla begin the slow walk down the aisle to way too many eyes watching.
  Turning to a fidgeting Kayla being held by her dad, I whisper sing, "You're getting married. Kaylas getting married," until she laughs and nods calming instantly.
  "Get going," she whispers back, so inhaling deeply I move slowly on an exhale.
  No one is here, and no one can see me. My giant ass-bow hides my real ass, and my black dress hides my lower belly flub. My hair is lovely, and the long side bangs and wisps falling hide my scars. My eyes are bright, and my pink lips are attractive. I don't look ugly or fat, and I can do this. No one is here anyway but Z.
  When I almost reach the front, I see Z smile at me and I find another huge exhale escape my lungs. He is stunning in his black tux, with purple tie, and handkerchief. He is a tall god staring at my eyes with a smile. He is willing me forward, and I'm walking toward the love of my life.
  Smiling, he doesn't acknowledge my ass-bow or my face or my belly flub, or anything else but me. He sees only me and as he nods his head slightly, I find myself entranced moving toward him.
  Z is always everything in every moment between us.
  Taking my hands, Z kisses my cheek and whispers in my ear, "Wrong side, love," with a cute little smile until I realize what I did.
  "Oh!" Looking at my Mack grinning down on me as well, I turn to him and just hug him.
  I don't care if it's weird, and I don't care if I should be on the other side. I need to give Mack a hug. Turning into him, he hugs me right back. A Mack hug. Hard and intense, and filled with so much emotion, I nearly choke up.
  "I love you, Mack. And I'm so happy for you both," I whisper in his chest as he says softly, 'I love you, too, Suzanne. Thank you for Kayla,' he grins pulling away from me as I nod.
  When Z nods his head toward the other side, I realize I'm still with the men and move quickly. Oops. I hope I don't get killed later, but I'm sure

We are US...

the bitchy sisters will point out my mistake as soon as they can.

   Noticing only one dirty look from Laura, I don't have time to panic before the music changes and everyone turns and stands to look at the back of the church for Kayla.

   Looking stunning in her huge white dress, her dark tanned skin and dark eyes are such a contrast to her dress, I don't think anyone could stop staring at her face if they tried. With a slight flush, and with her pink lips slightly parted she actually looks like a nervous virgin on her wedding day which really is too funny considering she and Mack have been having off the charts sex for a few years now. Smiling, I almost laugh at the thought of Kayla a virgin bride.

   Waiting for Mr. Rinaldi to shake hands with Mack and turn Kayla over to him, they smile at each other so beautifully, I find myself looking at my smiling Z. But when Kayla touches my arm, I jolt from my Z trance.

   Stepping forward, I know my ass is on full display, but I have duties to perform, so I get to them. Bending low to fan out Kaylas dress, I rise back up, take her bouquet and smile at my sister, for all intents and purposes.

   "Dearly beloved we are gathered here today..."

ΩΩΩΩΩ

   "I did it!" Kayla yells as soon as we've exited the main chapel for the exit hallway. "God, I didn't think I could pull this off, but I did it!" Kayla beams again with a smile as Mack leans forward to kiss her.

   "Have I told you how beautiful you look today?"

   "Um, no. You didn't say that earlier and I've been waiting," she grins as Mack kisses her again.

   "Sorry. Those annoying vows got in the way. Mrs. MacDonald, you look beautiful today. Well, all days, but today you look extremely beautiful."

   "Thank you, Mr. MacDonald," she grins as more and more guests walk out past us.

   "10 more minutes until we can relax in the limo with drinks," Chicago

Kayla adds and I'm so on board. I need to sit for a minute and I need to exhale all the residual tension and nervousness of a long day already, at only 2:30 in the afternoon with like 12 more hours to go.

When Z takes my hand, I lean into him and exhale. He is always so grounding for me, and just a comfort always.

"Nice ass, Suzanne," he whispers in my ear as I burst out laughing like he intended I think.

"Say another word about it Mr. Zinfandel and you'll never again get to see what's underneath this huge ass-bow. Are we clear?" I growl to him smiling and nodding.

"Very clear. Not another word, because I really want to see what's under that tent-sized bow later," he smirks as I hit his arm grinning. "Seriously, Suzanne. You look beautiful. I couldn't keep my eyes off you during the ceremony. I nearly forgot to give Mack the rings I was so distracted by you."

"Thank you. Now you may see what's under this tent-sized bow later."

"I plan on it," Z says in his sexy voice as I shiver, also like he intended I think.

"Are we ready?" Mrs. Rinaldi asks excited as we all prepare for the big dramatic exit on the church steps so everyone can pelt us with rice, and take our photos before we leave for the official photos.

Sarah Ann Walker

CHAPTER 6

Finally sitting at the head table, I hate being this far from Z in public. As the hundreds of people stare in our direction, I know sitting beside Kayla is a major disadvantage for me. Everyone who looks at her can see me just as clearly, and though I hate it I'm trying my best to pretend I'm not here. I'm pretending I'm at home around our dining room table with my people, calm and comfortable. I'm pretending really well, too.

"Everything looks really good, doesn't it?" Kayla asks at my side.

"It really does," I say lying again. Christ, everywhere I look I see purple something. From the table cloths, to the flowers on each table to the bridesmaids and even Mrs. Rinaldi, I'm drowning in a sea of purple. "Thank god purple isn't my trigger color," I mumble before realizing I said it out loud until Chicago Kayla barks a loud laugh on the other side of me.

"No shit," she smirks and thankfully Kayla laughs too before the glass tapping starts again as she rises to kiss Mack for the tenth time before dinner is even served.

Once dinner is over, Z finally stands to start the speeches. I've been dreading this, and Mack said I could opt out if I wanted, but I couldn't. This is important and I'm as prepared as I'll ever be. I'm Suzanne Zinfandel now, and though I usually stay away from ever standing out in public I'm going to stand at that goddamn mic and say what needs to be said about the people who mean the most to me in the world.

Laughing at a Z-ism, Chicago Kayla squeezes my hand under the table for support, and I wish I could take her up to the podium with me. With her beside me, I know no one would dare glare at me or question why I'm here or wonder what the hell Z sees in me. With Kayla standing beside me I almost feel like I deserve to be sitting among these amazing people who love me for whatever reason.

"Suzanne..." Kayla whispers and I jolt back to the present. I missed the end of Z's awesome speech which he only rehearsed in front of me once because he nailed it the first time. It was sweet, and funny, and just

We are US...

perfect for the lifelong friendship he's had with Mack. Z even managed to choke me up when he spoke about Kayla and how well suited they were for each other, and how shy of his own wonderful marriage, he couldn't think of 2 people who would love each other and support each other more in life than Kayla and Mack would.

It was beautiful and charming and funny, and so Z, I ended up happy-crying with him in our living room by the time he finished.

"*Suzanne...*" Chicago Kayla hisses to get my attention again as I stand too quickly and look like an idiot struggling to get out of my chair with my giant ass-bow.

Grabbing my speech, Mack squeezes my hand as I pass, and Z rises from his chair to kiss me gently on the lips for support as I pass him with a nervous smile.

Laying out my little card of notes, I know what I'm going to say. I even have a little poem, Shakespeare's Sonnet 116 as reference to marriage and love, and life as a couple. I wrote everything down so I wouldn't screw up or panic at the time. But now I don't want it.

Starting with the Shakespeare sonnet, I breathe my way through it verbatim and pause at the end. This is such a rehearsed speech, but suddenly I don't want a rehearsed speech. I need to just talk about them from my heart, I think.

"Um, I'm Suzanne, and Mack is my angel and my best friend. And Kayla is the most amazing sister and best friend I could've ever dreamed of having in my life. So, ah, they are my best friends, together and individually, and I love them both so much I can't really explain it. Mack saved me and loved me when I didn't know what love was, and Kayla held me and loved me when I didn't know what real friendship felt like." Don't choke up! *Shit.*

Taking a big breath, I continue. "I, ah, also get all the credit for getting them together," I smile quickly to a nodding Mack. "I wanted them to get together because I saw something so special in both of them. *I knew* they were special, so together they would be extra-special," I say like a dork. Ugh... I think I'm screwing this up. Shit.

"Anyway, Mack is always the calm to Kayla's *not* calm," I smirk as some people laugh. "And Kayla is the fun and light, to Mack's quiet reserve. Um, Mack spends his days with a lot of darkness, trying to help crazy people." Ooops. "Ah, what I mean is Mack has to deal with a lot of sadness and the dark stuff people go through to try to help them because he's a really good Psychiatrist. And Kayla spends her days helping people with her kindness and fun in a world of sickness because she's a really good nurse. So I think Kayla is perfect for Mack, because she can help him deal with all the stuff he has to hear and try to deal with by himself when he helps people with their own issues. And I think Mack is perfect for Kayla because of his constant understanding and knowledge of what she'll need in their marriage and life together. So, like I said, I think they are perfect for each other.

"And that's all I can say to you today. Mack and Kayla are my best friends, and I love them, and I know how much they love each other because I've seen it firsthand. Especially when Kayla tested their relationship when she became Bridezilla recently," I add to much laughter, thank god.

"Ah... Please raise your glasses to Mack and Kayla. The two most amazing, loving, supportive people I've ever known. I know they found each other for a reason, and I know they will love each other until death do them part, and even way after that, I believe."

Raising my own glass of water I mumble, 'To Mack and Kayla' as everyone else joins in. Watching everyone smile, I feel good. I think I pulled it off, and I doubt anyone will trash me for my speech later. I spoke from my heart and I know Kayla and Mack would want that from me.

Walking back behind all the groomsmen, Mack stands and hugs me so tightly, I almost choke up but hold it in.

"That was perfect, Suzanne. Thank you so much," he whispers against my hair as I feel Z's hand on my back.

"Enough! *God,* come here," Kayla laughs pulling me from Mack. Gently crying and sniffling, Kayla hugs me and whispers, "That *was* perfect, Suzanne. And you have a sister/best friend for life. Thank you for pushing me on Mack," she grins. "And thank you for always being the sweetest person in the room. I love you very much," she says pulling away as I smile like a loser before sitting down beside her.

"Good job, Suzanne," Chicago Kayla pipes up. "But watch how it's really done," she smirks standing up to walk to the podium gracefully.

Looking at Z past Mack and Kayla, he smiles at me so beautifully, my heart feels it, as usual. God, I love that man.

We are US...

"Hi everyone. I'm Chicago Kayla if you didn't know already, and I'm the better Kayla," she begins to laughter. "Kayla and I met through Suzanne, so I have to thank her as well for not only getting Mack and Kayla together, but for getting me and Kayla together as well. Through a serious of events I found a Kayla I actually liked, and we created a friendship I cherish. We..."

Zoning out, I think of everything we've all been through together. My past and my life, and their lives and futures. I think of my safe people and I thank god every single day for them. I know I have never taken even one moment for granted, and I have never wasted a single second with these people around me.

Together and individually, they have each taught me how to live, and they've taught me what love was. My Kaylas push me to continue moving past my pain, and Mack helps me when I make a mistake, or have a setback. Christ, even Marty has become a champion of mine whenever we see him with his ability to make me laugh with him always.

Looking at Z as Kayla continues to another chorus of laughter, I take in his profile and know nothing but him in this moment. Z is my own version of perfect.

With Z I know I will have a lifetime of love and support and a world filled with as much peace as he can give me. He pushes me when I should be pushed, and he holds me when I need to be held.

Turning to me, it's like he knew I needed to connect with him in this moment, which I did. Wiping my few tears I mouth the words, 'I love you,' as he nods and smiles his gorgeous smile for me. Standing casually, Z walks to me and bends down behind me without trying to interrupt Kayla's speech.

"What is it, love?" He asks in his dark chocolate voice.

"Nothing at all, I'm happy, Z. Totally and completely happy right now. And I love you very much. Um... And when I see Dr. Phillips on Monday I'm going to talk to him so I can figure out how to deal with, ah, so you and I can finally have that conversation you want," I whisper nervously.

Jolting, Z is visibly shocked and wordless until he breathes, "Really?"

"Really. *The* conversation, Z. But I don't want to talk about it anymore tonight, okay?"

"Understood," he says gravely though I still see the happiness in his crinkled eyes.

Kissing him quickly, I tell him to go back to his seat and with a slow smile and another kiss on my lips, he rises to walk back to his seat just as Kayla is finishing up. God, she's a wordy little bitch, isn't she? I giggle in my sudden nervousness with Z.

Holy *shit!* What the hell did I just do? Almost panicking, I grab for my water and chug it back like it's the wine I'm suddenly craving to take the edge off what I just decided.

"Thank you," Kayla laughs leaning around me to hug Chicago Kayla.

"I killed it, huh?" Kayla laughs and even Mack leans forward to agree. Shit, I wish I knew what the hell she said.

When Laura and Paola stand up together I almost cringe but hold it in hoping for the best, and thankfully they're done within minutes and it *was* their best. Gushing about Mack and Kayla, they played the proper part of the supportive younger and older sisters well, and I'm happy Chicago Kayla doesn't have to go after them later.

"Don't be good," I whisper in Kayla's ear as Marty walks toward her for the official bridal party dance. Waiting for Z to take my hand, I see even Z has a grin aimed at Marty and Kayla.

It's a not so secret secret that Mack, Kayla, Z and I all think Kayla and Marty would be an awesome couple, though both protest WAY too much how they would never work.

Personally, I think their relationship would be very spicy together. Filled with fights and hot sex all the time, which though not my thing is definitely Kayla's thing.

"May I, Mrs. Zinfandel? That huge ass-bow looks like it needs to dance," Z says like a smartass as I take his hand toward the dance floor.

"Giant ass-bow is what Kayla calls it too," I laugh as he pushes it around to rest his hands eventually higher on my back than normal.

Turning me into his chest Z bends low to ask how I'm doing. Even with my high 4' heels, Z still has at least 8 inches on me though somehow we always make it work.

"I'm really good," I smile just before he kisses me lightly. "I can't believe it's almost over. It seems like this wedding has been in the works for years now, and I'm almost sad it's over." When Z raises a questioning eyebrow, I quickly amend with a smirk. "Okay, I'm thankful as hell it's over. I think I'm just going to miss all the crazy Kayla time I've had with her."

We are US...

"She'll still be around. You two always see each other on weekends."

"I know. But it won't really be the same. We'll all go back to normal, which is still pretty good, don't get me wrong. But I kinda like the emergency phone calls and late night drop ins because they make me feel useful and almost special to her."

Leaning in low again as we slowly dance, Z says another perfect Z-ism as I melt in place. "You *are* special and useful, Suzanne. You make my life happy and filled with love. And you're so special we all love being around you, if for nothing else than to see your beautiful eyes light up when we're around. Don't underestimate your power over all of us. Just seeing you smile makes every one of us smile in return. That's your gift, Suzanne. Truly," Z finishes with a tight squeeze and a kiss on my forehead.

Breathing in Z's scent, I whisper 'thank you' against his chest as he nods against me. Honestly, this guy is too much but in good way. The best way actually.

When the song ends and the dance floor fills with the whole crowd Z asks if I need anything to drink. I'm sure he doesn't mean alcohol and he's just being a gentleman, but I tell him I'm fine anyway as he walks me back to my seat.

Sitting awkwardly in my chair, Z laughs once again at my giant ass-bow as I glare at him before he strolls off for the bar at the other end of the banquet hall.

Waving to a dancing Mrs. and Mr. Rinaldi, I turn just as Kayla drops in the chair beside me.

"Okay, so Marty is kind of hot," she says as an aside to me. "I still don't think he's my type, but I wouldn't mind screwing him once just to test him out."

"Test him out?" I ask surprised.

Grabbing her wine glass Kayla nods as she drinks back the last of it before reaching for another of the endless bottles on our table- a gift from one of Z's wineries.

"Yup. I like to test drive my men before leasing," she laughs at my stunned expression.

Humored by her weird car analogy, I have to ask, "Have you ever thought of just purchasing one 'sight unseen'?"

"Are you kidding me? Why the *hell* would I do that? If a man is terrible in bed there's only so much teaching I can do. If he's decent in bed, I have something to work with. But I sure as hell want to know what his stick shift looks like before taking him for a ride," she says as I burst out laughing.

"Jesus *Christ!* You really do sound like a man, Kayla," I laugh as she nods again.

Looking around us, I spot Z talking to a woman near the bar. A gorgeous woman actually. Even 75 feet away I can tell she's gorgeous. Huh. Well, this jealousy thing just hit me pretty quick.

"Watch this..." I mumble to Kayla, nodding toward the bar. "She'll start throwing her head back laughing and she'll touch his arm any sec-" and then she does it. Just as I predicted, or rather *know* from the endless women who flirt with Z, their moves are always the same. She's laughed loudly though I couldn't hear it, and she's already holding his forearm as he continues talking to her.

"He's just being friendly, Suzanne. Z is always-" but even Kayla stops talking when they're suddenly hugging. Um. Shit. Z never hugs women but my Kaylas. Actually, he told me he never touches women period. BUT me.

When she starts touching his hair talking to him again, I literally see red. Shaking in my seat, I feel the jealousy growing to nearly unmanageable.

"I've never seen Z flirt before. Like ever, Suzanne. Maybe he knows her really well or something. Z would never flirt," Kayla pauses watching the show. Holy *shit!*

"I'm going to kill him for this. Seriously," I growl as Kayla shuts up and nods beside me.

Watching Z pulled laughing back to the dance floor as he leaves his drink on the bar, gorgeous woman wraps herself around him as they begin slow dancing and talking very close to each other's mouths.

"Suzanne, listen to me closely, " Kayla says leaning into my side. "Every part of me sees this, and every part of me wants to go bitch slap him for you. However, this is Z. And Z is madly in love with you, *his* Suzanne, as he calls you. So though I understand why you might want to kill him as Gorgeous Giggles over there keeps him way too entertained, I honestly think there's another explanation. I also think you need to get over there to remind him you are his wife, remind Gorgeous Giggles he *has* a wife, and remind yourself that this shit doesn't fly. Got it?"

We are US...

"Got it. And I'm going to do it before she touches his chest one more goddamn time. And stop calling her *gorgeous*," I hiss as I stand awkwardly. "Christ! I wish I could get this giant ass-bow off before I approach them," I add as Kayla laughs.

"No such luck. Remember what I said. You need to put this bitch in her place, and then you need to put Z back on point when you get home."

"Oh, I'm gonna kill Z when we get home."

Walking away from Kayla I look back at her just once as she nods for me to engage. Like I need her permission? No way. I'm feeling totally pissed at the show Z's putting on publicly.

Z always tells me he doesn't notice the flirting, and he tells me he would never flirt back. He says he doesn't touch anyone ever, but as I walk closer I'm just stunned to see him hugging her closer, talking in her ear as she dances wrapped up in his arms. What the hell is this shit?

Pushing my way to him Z spots me immediately, and as he pulls away from Gorgeous Giggles slightly, I jump right in.

Finding my inner Chicago Kayla, I let them have it. "Hello, Z. Remember me? Your *wife*?" I sneer. And turning to Giggles I quickly continue. "Hi. I'm Z's wife Suzanne, and you are way too close to my husband right now."

"Suzanne-"

"Don't talk to me right now," I snap at Z. "Listen bitch," Ha! I said Bitch! "I get that he's hot and rich and sexy as hell. And I know when you're using your dildo tonight it'll be to thoughts of him, but *I* won't be."

"Suzanne!" Z yells pulling my arm.

"*I'll* be fucking him while you're sitting there alone fantasizing about him. Got it, Giggles? Now could you please go rub up on someone else? Because Z, my *husband* is clearly taken," I finish with just enough anger to make her nod.

Turning back to Z, Gorgeous Giggles actually has the nerve to laugh at me like I'm a joke to her. The BITCH! I'm so gonna rip her face off.

"Suzanne. *This* is my cousin Lucia who I haven't seen since my parents' funeral." What?! "Neither of us knew she knew the Rinaldi's, so this was a huge surprise for both of us." WHAT?! I can barely breath as Z continues in his scary pissed off voice.

"I used to visit Lucia and her family every single summer growing up in Italy but sadly we lost touch after my parents died." MOTHER *FUCKER!* "So though clearly you thought more was going on here, there wasn't.

We are just cousins reconnecting who haven't seen each other in years, who were very happy to share stories with each other about our *wonderful* spouses," Z finishes with nothing shy of disgust for me. Oh my **god.**

"And I won't be using a dildo tonight, little one," Little one? "I'll be using my husband over there," Gorgeous, or I guess *Lucia* says in her thick, sexy as hell Italian accent pointing to a man a few tables away who waves at us all.

Holy shit. What did I do? What the *fuck* do I do? Ummm...

"I'm sorry," I mumble shaking. "I didn't know, and you're gorgeous, and everyone flirts with Z, and I'm not gorgeous, and I hate it, and I panicked. I'm really very sorry," I cry desperately as I spin on my heels for anywhere but here.

Having my arm grabbed by Z as he says my name is too much right now. I don't want to cause another scene and I feel like a total piece of shit now.

"Suzanne! Stop doing this. You're embarrassing me," he says quietly but his anger is so clear the humiliation of this situation is suddenly strangling me.

"Please leave me alone," I croak just shy of full out sobbing. "I'm sorry," I try again but he won't let me go.

Turning me to him Z is speechless, which makes everything so much worse. "Just give me a minute. I need a *moment,* Z." And that's all it takes for him to release me instantly. Looking stunned and hurt by my word, he released me as quickly as I spoke.

'Taking a moment' is the equivalent of a safe word for us. If I tell Z I need a moment he backs off until I'm ready to talk. He knows the rule, and he always obeys it. I rarely need 'moments' anymore, but this one I need. *Badly.*

Sprinting for the bridal bathroom, I just close the door when the full crying begins. Shit! Sobbing in the only stall I can't believe how shitty I feel. I made an ass of myself to his cousin, yes. But the way I spoke isn't like me at all. I tried to channel my inner Kayla, but I don't have her in me. I'm not confrontational and I hate anger. I don't swear at people and I hate being sworn at. I don't like to be angry, and I sure as hell don't like it directed at me anymore.

We are US...

Planting my fat ass right on the toilet seat I let the tears take me for now. There's no way to fight them, and it's best if I just cry them out so I don't have another episode later.

God, I hate that I embarrassed Z. And I hate that he looked so hurt when I took my moment. I hate being like this and feeling like this. Shit, I keep screwing up lately, and I'm so scared he's going to leave me soon.

I mean really, how much shit can one man take before calling it quits? I think every other man on the planet would've left by now, so I'm just holding him by a thread at this point I think.

I have to stop this shit now though, because between last night's freak out and tonight's ridiculous performance, I know I'm going to push him too far soon.

God, I need to get my shit together for Z. And I will. I can do that and I will. For Z I can do anything.

"Suzanne?" Chicago Kayla calls out and I want to cry all over again.

Hiding in my stall, I try for just a little more privacy. "I just need a moment, Kayla. Please leave me alone for a minute," I beg but I can almost guarantee she won't follow the 'moment' rule.

"Ah, Suzanne? You've been in here for close to an hour." What? No friggin' *way*.

"I have? I swear it was like 2 minutes," I confess feeling confused. "I screwed up Kayla. Gorgeous Giggles was his long-lost goddamn cousin."

"I know. Z and Lucia explained everything so you can come out now. Z's been waiting for you in the hallway since you came in." Shit. How many ways can I say sorry to this man? "Z wants to see you, Suzanne, and I think you should let him. I explained that I may have egged you on a little," she says with a laugh.

"Ya think?" I huff thinking of Mack's license plate.

"Yeah... My bad. But as I explained, it did look pretty bad from where we were sitting, and even Lucia agreed she would have freaked out, too. She's very nice, and she finds this whole thing pretty funny actually. She even laughed about the dildo comment to me with a gag as she pointed at Z like he's repulsive. Which I guess as her cousin he would be to her," Kayla laughs. "Anyway, it's okay now. Z doesn't seem angry anymore, just maybe a little hurt that you don't trust him, I think," Kayla says softly which again makes everything seem worse.

Feeling like a total piece of shit is one thing. But hurting Z is entirely different. I've hurt him too often in too many ways to count over the years. And though it's never my attention, I always seem to do it anyway.

   Pulling in a big breath, I open the stall door and walk out to a sympathetic looking Kayla.

   "Does Mack and Kayla know what happened? Did I ruin their wedding?" I ask desperately. If I did, I'll never forgive myself.

   Shaking her head and reaching out to me, Kayla whispers, "Not at all. They're too busy to notice you missing, and we kept this on the down low. I saw you run away and Z told me everything immediately. So we've just been waiting for you to resurface while mingling casually."

   Exhaling my relief I turn toward the mirror. "Oh my god! I need my purse, Kayla. *Now!*" I scream in a panic as she jumps beside me.

   "No problem. Breathe sweetie," she says and I feel the sting of the name immediately. She forgot! She fucking forgot because she's trying to help me. "I'll go get it for you, okay?" She says kindly as I nod like I'm okay. But I'm not okay.

   I look like HER again, but worse. "I'll be right back. Just relax, Suzanne," she says again all calmly like I could possibly relax if she speaks calmly.

   Staring at the mirror after Kayla leaves I see I'm beyond gross. Just like last night and the good old days, I've managed to get makeup everywhere except where I need it. Somehow I wiped most of my scar foundation off completely, or smeared it in a way that it's essentially pointless now. All the red and pink scars are showing, and the texture is very distinct without the makeup globed into the creases of the scars.

   I can't believe I allowed this to happen again. I'm usually so good about never touching my face once the makeup is on so I don't mess anything up. Then again, I didn't realize I was crying in a goddamn bathroom suite for over an hour, so how could I possibly pay attention to my face?

   "Suzanne? I'm coming in," Z says firmly and I panic.

   Jumping at the door, I push against it hard and lock it. "Please don't, Z! I, ah, look pretty bad right now. But I'll be out soon," I say as the door knob jiggles.

   "I don't give a shit how you look I just want to be with you. Open the door, Suzanne," he tries still sounding calm. But that isn't going to last because Z hates when I lock him out of doors. "Suzanne, open the door, love. I need to see you now. I've been waiting for quite a while to talk to you." Shit. I can't yet. And he won't understand. And he's going to keep

We are US...

harassing me if I don't give in as usual. And I'm going to freak out worse.

"I'm just waiting for Kayla to bring my purse, okay? I'll be out in a minute, Z. I promise," I answer desperately.

Knocking again louder and harder, Z keeps pushing. "I have your purse, and Kayla is right here. I want you to open the door, love. It's just me."

Walking to the opposite wall from the door, I whisper, "I know it's you, but I don't want you to see me like this."

I know he can't hear me and that's good. When I say things like that Z is always sad or hurt. He hates that I think he cares about my ugly face, and it makes him sad that I don't trust his love enough to not care about my ugly face with him.

Z says he doesn't see anything past my eyes. He actually says that! He says such sweet things all the time to me but it's not enough. Well, what he says is enough, but how I feel never goes away no matter what he says to comfort me.

Banging on the door again as I think about all the good things he says, he isn't even hiding his frustration with me anymore. "Suzanne, this is only a knob lock which I can open within seconds with one of Kaylas bobby pins, so please just open the door for me. I need to see you, and I want to talk to you. *Now*, Suzanne," he growls.

Shit! He never leaves me alone. Storming for the door I slam my fist against it. "No! Leave me the *fuck* alone for once!" I suddenly scream in my fear, and even I'm shocked at my anger and language.

Covering my mouth quickly with my hand, I slam back against the opposite wall from the door and hide. I hide my face and I hide my fear. I have to hide Suzanne. This isn't supposed to be me anymore, and I don't know what's happening to me.

Crying my frustration I want to hit something so badly, I just need an outlet. I need to do something to get all this tension out of my body. I wish I could talk to Mack because he would know what to do to give me immediate relief from all this tension. Mack always knows what to do with me, but he's not here.

Mack is never here anymore. And Mack probably won't be here for me anymore because he's married now, and he works full time, and Kayla wants to have children right away because she thinks she's old in her mid-thirties, and I'm going to be all alone again.

Shit, the pressure just keeps building and I can't really stop the sounds of all the anger and fear from humming in my body and hands, and I just want to empty it all from my chest.

"Suzanne," Z suddenly whispers in front of me, and I'm done.

Diving for Z I scream everything he never listens to. "Don't look at my *FACE!*" I scream as I hit him. Slamming into him, I hit and punch and kick him until he listens. But he *never* listens. Z always does whatever he wants whenever he wants to me.

"You never listen to me! You said I wasn't invisible! *YOU* told me that! But I am. I'm invisible, and you always look at my face!" I scream again hitting him as hard as I can as he struggles against me.

When I'm suddenly pushed into the wall behind me by Z holding my arms at my sides, he snarls down low in my face. "Calm down, Suzanne. Now. Before you hurt yourself," he breathes like he gives a shit.

"Fuck. *You.* You don't give a shit if I get hurt! You never do. Stop looking at my *FACE!*" I scream again trying to turn away from his intense angry stare.

Struggling to breathe, I close my eyes and just wait. I don't think he'll rape me but I never know for sure what men want to do to me. And I've never fought them this hard before, so I'm not sure what they'll do this time. I was always pretty good but they hurt me anyway. But this time I was really bad, so I don't know what they'll do to me for punishment. And I don't want it, but I don't know how to stop them and it's going to hurt again.

Sobbing, I keep still against the wall with my face turned and my eyes closed. I don't know how he'll start, but I think my fight is gone now. I think I'm just ready for whatever he's going to do to me now. I think I can survive this. I mean I have before, and I will again, I think.

Exhaling my sadness I ask the question of my nightmares. "How do you want me?" I whisper as everything changes all around me.

Instantly, the air, the pressure, and the pain changes to calm acceptance. Everything I feel and thought was true of my new life disappears with my words as my past threatens to destroy me again.

"Suzanne, it's Z," he repeats further from me as I nod.

"I know."

"You know? And you still asked me that?" He says with shock clearly heard in his tone.

"Yes. I know it's you. Just do whatever you want-"

"Oh *fuck,* Suzanne. Please don't finish that sentence. *Please?*" He begs.

Crying, I don't know what to do or say or even feel anymore. I feel nothing but acceptance. This is going to happen whether I like it or not, and it's going to happen whether I want it or not. I have no choice but to accept this life of mine.

"Suzanne? I need you to open your eyes and look at me," he says so quietly I almost didn't hear him. But then I did.

If I open my eyes is it still Z? Ummm... I just can't be sure and I don't want to know for sure in case it isn't.

"I don't want to watch you hurt me," I whisper through my tears. I *never* want to see it. Z was a safe person. He was safe for me, but not anymore, I don't think. "You're not safe anymore. And I don't want to watch you hurt me," I moan.

"Suzanne! Wake up, love. *Look* at me. I'm Z. Open your fucking eyes. Right *now!*" He yells, and my eyes open instantly at his command. I never could disobey anyone. And I still can't.

Looking quickly at Z I see everything I forgot. He *is* Z. And he's crying for me I think, or maybe he's crying because of me. With beautiful dark eyes swimming in tears, he is still and silent as I try to *see* him clearly.

Oh my god... He is Z, and I'm losing it. He is Z and I made another mistake again.

Gasping awake my awareness of our situation I look quickly at the door and see I'm here in the private bathroom suite for the bridal party with Z. I'm not in my parents' house and I'm not on the country club floor. I am right where I'm supposed to be. With Z.

Feeling my stomach suddenly turn, I just reach for my stomach and the stall door as the filth spews from my mouth splattering against the stall and floor. Crying and moaning at once, my knees buckle as Z grabs for me when I hit the vomit-covered floor.

"I'm dying again, I think. Um, something's wrong, Z. There's something wrong with me," I sob in his arms on the floor.

"I know, love. I know there's something. But we'll fix it, okay?" He asks. "Okay, Suzanne?" He begs shaking me slightly as he wraps his arms around me tighter.

"I'm so sorry for this. For everything all the time."

"It's okay," he whispers against my hair.

"I didn't mean to be an embarrassment to you, and I didn't mean to fail you again," I cry because that's the truth. I work so hard at being good for Z so he'll love me.

"I'm not embarrassed and you've never failed me, Suzanne. Not once ever," he continues but he's lying to make me feel better. I know he is. How could he not be? Between last night and tonight, and his cousin, and the hitting. Oh *god!* I hit him again. I actually hit Z.

Crying harder, I barely hear him shushing me and I barely feel him holding me, my body is so numb. I've hit Z again. Only the third time since we've known each other, but 3 times too many. I've hit the one man who loves me beyond all reason and hope. The man who loves me way more than he should. The man who loves me even when he shouldn't.

"You shouldn't love me anymore, Z. I think you should leave me so you're free."

Pulling away from my body to look at my eyes, Z cuts me off immediately. "That is *never* going to happen, Suzanne. So cut the shit, love. We're going to figure this out," he pushes.

"There's nothing to figure out!" I scream in his face. "Christ! Nothing ever changes."

"Everything changes."

"*Nothing* changes, Z! Look at us. Look at *me!* Even after years with you, I'm exactly where I started. I'm sitting on a floor covered in vomit, scared and freaked out losing my mind again. I *never* change."

Growling in my face, Z yells back. "You *have* changed! Jesus Christ! Look at where we're at. Look at how far you've come. Look at how far our relationship has come together. Yes, this is an episode, or a something, but we'll figure it out. We always do," he yells again in my face. But I know he's wrong this time. I can feel it. This time there's no coming back for me.

"You have to make a change, Z, because I can't. I'm too weak to do it, and I love you too much to do it."

"Right back at you, Suzanne. I'm too weak and I love you too much to make a change. So we're not changing anything. We're moving forward together." God, he's so stubborn. He never listens to anything I have to say.

"Listen to me."

"I'm listening, but nothing is going to change."

"Because you never listen to me."

"I *always* listen to you," he argues back again, just adding to my sad frustration.

And I am frustrated. I think I see the whole picture now. I see how we

We are US...

coast along happy and then a thing hits and we go backward. We always do this. Or rather *I* always do this. No matter what happens though Z stays the same, and I never do. I can't keep up the good all the time, and we always slide back to the bad again. Yes, it's only been a few 'episodes' as Dr. Phillips calls them, but they've been there anyway. And it's always me and my shit that does it to us.

"I want to go home," I cry as he stands immediately. Not even acknowledging the vomit on and around us he stands and pulls me up with him. Leaning into me Z attempts to tuck me into his side, but I can't stand to be touched right now.

Pulling away I need my space if I'm going to keep thinking this clearly. If I give into Z loving me I'll go back to believing everything will be okay. I'll believe him because he tells me everything will be okay all the time.

But I know he's wrong this time because I finally see it clearly.

I'm crazy, and annoying, and so goddamn dramatic, it takes too much from people to love me. It is too time consuming, and too exhausting. I am annoying and screwed up, and just a total waste at this point.

I once believed I could be saved. I believed it and even wanted it for myself. I thought Mack was right about the good in me, and I believed my Kaylas friendships would help me. I even trusted Z when he told me we were meant to be together. I believed him when he said I was worth his love. But I know the truth now. And I don't believe anyone anymore.

I will always be this way. Annoying to some, and a burden to others. People think I don't know what they really think of me. People roll their eyes and bite their tongues. People shake their heads and want to smack me. I *know* that. But I can't help who I am or who I've become. I've tried so hard to get better for years now, but I always come back to this version of myself.

I am forever scarred and broken, no matter how lovely the bandage tries to look on the outside.

I will always be the screwed-up chick who was enslaved by her parents and abused by strangers. I am a horror movie. I am damaged beyond repair and I'm tired of trying to be fixed. I will never be fixed because it's simply too late for me.

"What are you thinking?" Z asks gently, and I tell him the truth. It's the least he deserves from me.

"I shouldn't have been saved," I whisper back as he flinches in front of me. But I don't care anymore what he feels. I know the truth, and I told him the truth now.

Walking away, right out of the bathroom suite, I pass Kayla and Lucia and her husband hiding my face as best as I can. With my hair wisps artfully falling around my face, I use them as the only shield I have to escape this wedding, and this scene, and this life I'm forever trapped in.

When Z touches my back, I shrug him off. When he begins speaking to me, I shake my head to stop. When he opens the front door to the banquet hall while ignoring other guests who call out his name, I'm grateful.

Hailing the first cab I see, I'm on autopilot. I'm not thinking, and I don't care about anything right now. I want to get this giant ass-bow off my body, and I want to shower away all the dirty.

Really, I just want to sleep with my new reality.

I shouldn't have been saved. I know that now, and everyone else should know it and accept it too.

It's time.

We are US...

CHAPTER 7

Entering our apartment, Z waits to see what I want to do. I know he is because he always takes his silent cues from me, which sucks.
A man like Z shouldn't have to worry or wait, or pussyfoot around because his wife is a goddamm psycho. He should walk however he wants wherever he wants because he is Z. Beautiful, delicious, accomplished, wealthy, sexy as hell Z.
But here he is pausing near the door to watch for my crazy before he can proceed once again.
"Will you help me get this dress off?" I ask quietly hearing my raspy voice for the first time since the banquet hall.
My voice is that desperate, sad sounding raspy voice of tears and anger and screams. It's the voice I hate. The voice phone sex operators would love to have actually, I suddenly giggle.
"Here?" He asks gently and I quickly understand his question. I'm still standing in the doorway of our condo.
"No. Sorry," I walk toward our bedroom.
Flipping on the bedroom light, I immediately walk to his side of the bed and turn on the lamp which gives off only a little soft light. Walking back to the door I turn off the overhead light as Z watches me from the door. I look mental I know, but I always hate walking in the dark, though I'm not comfortable standing in the bright light of our room either.
Huh. That's a fairly good analogy for my life as well. I hate walking in my darkness, but I'm not comfortable standing in the light of my life either. Wow, that was so Suzanne dramatic, I can only giggle again in the deafening silence around us.
"Let me help you," Z walks slowly toward me like he's nervous I'll freak out. And actually if he had walked to me quickly I probably would have freaked out any other night. But not tonight. Not when my mind is so clear and focused on everything around me. All my reactions, and all my behaviors are very clear to me. And also clear to Z apparently.
Turning, I feel Z unhook the little catch above the bow before he slowly loosens the zipper hidden under the giant ass-bow. Pulling my dress

We are US...

upward, I shimmy my arms up and out of the weird crisscross straps that are almost stuck in my skin because they held me so tightly all night.

God, I didn't even need a bra because the crisscross straps were so tight they actually pushed my breasts up and out almost like a bustier in the front, while providing lovely back fat gooshes in between straps. Overall, not a dress I would have ever picked for any woman bigger than a size 0.

"The straps left marks," Z says quietly as I feel his hand move down my skin gently.

"Of course they did. Did you see how tight they were on my back fat?"

Laughing, I remember turning in the mirror at the wedding boutique a month ago wondering how the hell I could lose back fat as quickly as possible before the wedding.

"I'm having a shower," I turn for the bathroom pulling off the little silk scarf I wore with my dress to hide my neck and shoulder burns as I feel Z's hand slide down my skin slowly before I walk away without looking back.

Flicking off my heels as I go with only my panties and thigh highs on, I wish this night was so different. I know the look I have now walking away from Z is one on his favorites. Thigh highs and heels. Like a total man, he loves it.

Whenever I've felt particularly naughty for Z I would pull out the thigh highs and heels knowing the look I would get. The dirty sexy Z look.

Totally unabashed, sexy as hell, and growly dirty, Z's eyes always lowered a little and his sexy smile would turn me on instantly. When I dressed like that, he knew I wanted the awesome couch sex we have, and I knew he wanted to give me our hot couch sex.

Tonight however, I'm filthy and post-vomit, and just nasty in my thigh highs and heels.

Stripping off my clothing, I turn for the sink to brush my teeth, which desperately need it. Turning the shower on I continue brushing my teeth without looking in the mirror. I know what I look like, and I don't want to see her right now.

After some mouthwash to aid the bad breath no amount of toothpaste could mask, I finally rip out as many bobby pins as possible, hastily brush out the ones I missed and enter the shower to wash away everything.

What a fucking mess.

When the water pressure changes slightly I know Z is showering in the other bathroom. He's probably taking his time hoping I finish first, so I'll crawl into bed first so he doesn't have to deal with me anymore tonight. And really, who could blame him?

I was Psycho Suzanne again. I embarrassed him, and I hit him. I was a mess again and *I* don't want to even deal with me, so I'm sure Z is dreading it as well. I hate the way I was so I can't even imagine what he's feeling towards me.

Scrubbing away all the makeup and repulsion from my face, I find I can't even cry anymore. I think my one hour crying jag in the bridal bathroom was enough. I think I got all the physical tears out, though admittedly, I still feel all the emotion trapped tightly in my chest.

The pressure and emotion is so powerful and strong it needs to somehow get out of my chest, but tears won't do it anymore. I don't know what will release the pressure though, which sucks for me.

All I can do is simply wait for this pressure to build until I either explode again, or I have to wait and hope it fades a little to more manageable for me. But either way, I'm waiting without knowing how to ease the pressure that is tightening my chest to nearly unbearable again.

Toweling off, I put on a nightgown from the little closet Z built in our bathroom so I always had post-shower clothes available for my spontaneous, 'Suzanne needs to wash away her past quickly' showers. Knowing I hate naked Z surprised me one day with the bathroom closet addition, even taking a little bit of room from the back of his own closet when I had been out all day with Kayla.

He planned it perfectly, and had the wall and closet guys show up as soon as I left, so when I returned 8 hours later after a shopping marathon with Kayla everything was finished. Z even stocked the closet full of both the silken black nighties he loves, and with the yoga pants and cami tops that I love.

Unbelievably, the closet door is even as waterproof as possible to prevent my clothes from getting steamy or damp, no matter how long my or *our* showers are together.

He thought of everything, as usual. And for just a closet, which I'm sure anyone could add to their bathroom, I was so overcome with the gesture behind it, I cried happily after the initial excitement of a clothes closet in our master bathroom.

I knew he knew what I needed. And I knew he paid attention every time I left the bathroom from one of my spontaneous I may freak out if I don't get clean showers, covered in a huge towel to cover my body shaking to run to my closet across our room so I could dress quickly to hide my naked from everyone, including myself.

Amazingly, Z always pays attention to the little stupid Suzanne things I can't help.

"Come here, love," he whispers from our bed.

With only the light from our alarm clock glowing turned toward the wall, he also knew I would need darkness tonight. I couldn't stand the thought of him seeing my face or my body tonight, because though clothed, the silken night dress shows off my ample chest, and because I'm going to sleep I couldn't put on my face foundation to hide the color or the scars on my face and neck.

I'm essentially naked though clothed, so I need the almost pitch darkness of our room to help me settle. And he knew.

"Can I say one thing before we sleep, Suzanne?" Z asks as I almost crawl in bed.

Pausing with my knee on the bed I exhale. "Of course you can," I whisper unable to see his eyes.

"You hurt me tonight."

"I know. I'm so sorry I embarrassed you."

"It wasn't that, though that was pretty gross for me and Lucia," Z almost smiles, I can hear. "You hurt me when you think the worst of me, and when you don't trust me," he says softly, and I can actually feel his emotion seeping from his skin.

"I do trust you. But some stuff I still can't talk to you about," I try, but he's already sitting up to argue with me.

"It's not that either. Have I ever given you a reason to not trust me with women? I know you think they flirt with me, and I know you're insecure about everything you think doesn't make you and I physically equal, but have *I* ever given you a reason to not trust me with other women?"

"No..." I breathe as our marital reality resurfaces once again. He has never given me a reason. It's always only me who does something wrong between us. "No, Z. You haven't. I'm just an insecure asshole," I admit before he laughs a little.

"Come here," he says reaching for me. Before I can even protest though I'm already lying awkwardly on his naked chest. "You're not an asshole, love. But you do try my patience with your insecurity. I will never cheat on you. I never *want* to. You're the only person I want in my life, Suzanne. And I really wish you would get that soon because it hurts me when you don't trust me or when you think I would ever do anything with anyone but you. There *is* no one but you for me," he says so softly against my hair I feel it straight through to my soul again.

"I'm very sorry," I moan because I am sorry I hurt him every time I'm too insecure to not trust him like I should.

"You're forgiven," he says squeezing me tighter to him with his smile-voice and I nearly weep in his arms.

"Can you talk about what happened tonight?" Z asks after a few minutes of silence between us.

"No." Whispering my reply I hope he lets it go, which he does when I feel him nod his chin against my hair again.

"Can I kiss you good night, Suzanne?"

"Yes, please," I barely say before I'm moved from his chest to my back with Z between my legs holding my face for an intense Z kiss.

And then he kisses me. Beautiful, intense and amazing. Z holds my face and kisses the holy shit out of me like he always does. From the little nips on my lips, to the gentle tongue movement in my mouth and on my lips, Z kisses me like he loves me.

Moving against me, his body may want me, but he doesn't react. He just kisses me because that's all I can usually handle after a night like this. But not tonight. Tonight I want him to make love to me to help release all the darkness and pressure from my chest.

"Please be with me. And before you ask, yes, I'm sure. I asked you. And I kind of need you tonight to make everything better inside me," I nearly beg in the silence between us when he stops kissing me.

Waiting for his reaction, I can't really see much in the darkness, though I do see his slow sexy smile before he kisses me again. A little harder and hungrier than before, I feel the difference in his kiss immediately.

Moving from my mouth, Z kisses my cheek which I hate, until he moves further to kiss my chest which I love. Lowering the spaghetti straps of my nightgown, Z clears my chest of material and as he takes a nipple into his mouth our moans are instantaneous. I love when he sucks me in deeply, and he loves when I move my body against his erection, which I suddenly can't control when he suckles me harder.

Grabbing his short hair I pull him closer to my chest as my left leg

We are US...

suddenly wraps around this back. Moving and moaning a little, I almost turn us when the quick pleasure consumes me.

"Touch me," he growls and I do immediately.

Sliding a hand down his back, I just reach his ass to pull him into me harder as he groans again against my chest. Grinding against him as he works my other nipple, I feel the burn build quickly.

When Z sits up suddenly on his arms, his knee slides between my legs and I find myself moving against it desperately. I need the pressure against my body, and I want to move against him as he watches.

"I need to see you," he whispers as I nod. I knew he would. He always watches my face and eyes when we're together and I'm usually okay with Z watching me.

Reaching for the alarm clock I flip it around quickly until there's just enough light to see his eyes clearly. Dark and delicious, and nearly closed he moves his knee between my thighs as I groan against him.

"Suzanne," he moans which makes my body react instantly. Grabbing at him, I pull down his lounge pants just past the huge erection waiting for me.

"Off!" I gasp as his knee moves harder against me before he pulls it away to strip himself.

Leaning back down to my mouth, Z begs, "Making love, sex, or fucking, Suzanne?" Pausing to absorb his dark voice, my body bows closer to him when I feel the sudden dampness I need escape me. "Which. One?" He asks with little thrusts against my body.

Pinching my nipple as he waits for my answer I gasp and cry out, "All of them. Everything!"

"*Everything...*" he smiles slowly as he moves away from my face again. Lifting me up, he rips my nightie from my body before stopping to stare at my face. "Everything?"

"God, yes," I moan before he kisses my lips hard again forcing me back into the pillows.

When Z works his way down my body, he pauses to kiss my huge belly scar like he always does. And though I hate the scar, I always accept the gesture behind it. I know that scar is important to Z, and I know he needs to kiss it so he feels like he won't ever forget his son.

Almost feeling the gesture myself tonight, I don't want to. Not right now, and not like this. I'll discuss the quick feeling I have for Thomas on Monday with Phillips. Right now though, I just want Z in our room with me. Actually, right now I just want Z.

"Stand up, Z," I say abruptly when he's almost where I want him to be on my body.

Raising his eyes to mine, he seems to understand, and though I sound a little weird with my demand, Z moves slowly off me and the bed anyway.

Watching him move, I see every muscle he owns and every bit of his flesh that I love. He is always darkly tanned, delicious, and sexy as hell. Even in the ugly pink golf shirts he loves he's so sexy to me.

Moving from our bed as Z waits silently, trying to breathe slowly I can see, I know he likes this. I also know I don't do it as much as he'd like, or as much as I should. He would never ask it of me though because he knows it's hard for me. Usually just the thought of this makes me think of when I was little and didn't have a choice, and couldn't fight-

"Suzanne?" He asks as I drop to my knees in front of him shaking my head to clear it.

Stoking up his thighs, I smile up at him so he knows I'm okay just before licking the tip of him as he gasps slightly. He loves my mouth on him, and I love him loving my mouth on him.

Grasping him in my hand I lean forward to take as much as I can as we stare at each other. Z always watches me and I love watching him watch me, too. There's something so intense and sexy about his body tensed up as I take him in my mouth. There's something almost special between us when he smiles down at me through gritted teeth when I start moving my mouth around him.

I never know exactly what to do, but I always seem to do it well. I mean I used to read my filthy novels before, and I watched a porn once at Chicago Kayla's, so I have the basic knowledge- lick, suck, move tongue around. But it's the complete knowledge of what will make Z absolutely out of control I don't know because he never loses control with me. Even like this, with his chest pumping and his fists clenching and unclenching at his sides, he is in control as he stares down at me without touching me because he knows I can't be touched when I'm like this.

Sucking harder we both groan at the same time. Me from causing his body to thrust a little harder in my mouth, and him from what I'm doing, I assume.

"*Enough.*" He growls and I can't help the smile on my face. I love that voice, and I love that intensity of his. "Lie down, Suzanne," he says dangerously when he pulls slowly out of my mouth with a moan.

We are US...

Moving backward toward the bed, my ass barely makes the mattress before he drops to his own knees and grabs my thighs over his shoulders as I gasp at the quick change in our bedroom.

"Oh! *God*..." I cry out when I feel his tongue enter me quickly. Ahhh... Not pausing for even a second, Z takes me hard. With his mouth, and his tongue and his fingers he is stretching me and burning me and eating me like a starved man.

Using his fingers in me the way that touches that spot inside, his tongue keeps lapping at me until his left arm pushes my stomach down flat to stop all my movement. Holding me down, my hips still buck as my hands reach and pull his head deeper into me.

"Please! Oh *god*..." I cry again when he impales me harder and faster. Flicking me with his tongue, I barely breathe until I hear his dark voice inside me.

"Look. At. Me," he demands and my eyes open instantly to his. Licking me from below to my clit slowly Z watches me watch him and its sexy as hell. I love when he does that. I love his eyes staring at mine when he licks me slowly.

I love when he "*Ah!*" Nearly turning us, my body jerks to the side as my ankle on his back pulls him in even closer when everything tenses inside me.

Locking down tight, his fingers are too big inside me and his tongue is too rough against me. But I need "more..." I groan on a hard exhale as I suddenly feel his more.

With his tongue deep inside me to catch my orgasm, Z pinches my clit until the white hot blast hits me as I scream and groan and flail on our bed. With my hands suddenly grasping the sheets, my head turns and I scream into the blanket next to my face while the convulsions keep going when Z continues.

"Stop! *Pleeeease*," I whine until he slowly rises to lean over my body. Keeping my thighs over his shoulders, Z advances on me until crunched up into a ball he kisses my lips, transferring my own release into my mouth which I kiss greedily.

Moving his body slightly, Z lines himself up watching me as he makes his slow entry. Lifting my ass right off the bed with our position, Z is inches from my mouth as he works himself inside me.

Too full, and nearly too tight for him, he always goes slow when he enters me. He works me slowly until I adjust and then he works me slowly until I beg.

Moving my left thigh around his waist, my right leg stays up high between us, and though I'm not quite as flexible as Z gives me credit for the position stretches me until all I feel is the fullness and the depth of him deep inside me.

"Look at me," he demands again and once more my eyes open instantly before he leans down for a kiss. "You are so beautiful, Suzanne," he whispers against my lips causing my slow smile and the tears that follow. He always gets me with his words, especially at times like this when I'm as free and as happy as I can be with him.

"Are you ready for some fucking, love?" He asks with his sexy grin, and I know what's coming- the hard, sexy fucking that is more than okay with Z. The fucking I never thought would be okay between 2 people who loved each other. The fucking that was always bad for me before, but is amazing for me now.

Nodding, I wait for his slow withdrawal before he enters me hard again on a gasp. Before I can even release my breath he's hammering into me and it feels so good, and I want it so bad, and I need this so much between us again. Moving against him, I find my hands ripping at his back to get him in deeper and harder and heavier in me.

Crying out and grunting with his own grunts of pleasure, my body feels everything all at once. Our emotional connection, our sexual connection, and the lifelong connection I have with Z builds. Everything fills me until I'm so full of emotion I need release again.

"I need..." but I don't know what I need exactly. I just need more I think.

"Some sex? Got it," Z grins pulling away from me quickly to turn us so I'm suddenly on top of him. Not even slipping from my body, Z flips us to continue his own movements inside me until I take over.

"Kiss me," he demands when I lean into him. Biting his lips first, he actually growls before thrusting up inside me so hard I cry out from the pleasure again. Huh. Lesson learned I almost laugh at his *I'm the man* sex grin.

When I plant my hands on his chest and grind against him, his neck suddenly pushes back into the pillow as his stomach tenses in a vision so hot, I know what sex fantasies are suddenly made of.

Grinding against him, lifting my hips and crashing down on him inside me, I realize Z is the ultimate sex fantasy. With his couple tattoos highlighting his abs and pecks and his delicious dark skin, he is the sexiest sex fantasy for any woman breathing. I know that, and I'm no more acutely aware of it as I am in moments like this between us.

It's no goddamn wonder women flirt with him. I did too, I suddenly giggle until he lowers his chin to look up at me.

"You are so sexy, Z. And I have you," I smile when he leans up on his forearms to kiss me.

"You do. Forever, Suzanne," he says using his feet on the mattress to push inside me when I stop moving because I'm thinking too much again.

Working against Z's thrust I counter thrust until I'm shaking and my body feels too heavy to continue, but still he moves.

I'm almost out of energy when I feel his hand slide from my hip to my body again. Oh! I know what this means and I know what he's going to do, and my exhaustion just disappeared with the appearance of his hand.

Smiling at my sudden harder movements on him again, Z touches me just enough to start the gasping. Moving between my legs, he rubs me just enough to work me back up. He moves his fingers around me until his other hand moves to pinch my nipple hard and the feeling is immediate. My pinched nipple just sent a spark straight to my clit and Z knows it even without the gasping sounds I make. With his sly smile, and his eyes watching me always, he knows I'm almost there.

Using his chest to keep me upright, I move and moan and writhe all over him. My rhythm is gone, and I know I'm moving like I'm desperate.

Grinding against his hand and fingers, my eyes close until I hear his little tongue click telling me to open them again as he pinches my body and stops my legs from working all together.

I'm gasping, and moaning, and just so ready to-

"Ah! *Ohhhh*... Um?" I cry out as I fall on his chest with my hard release to feel the low rumble of his laughter under my cheek.

"'Ah. Oh. Um?' You sound adorable when you're coming, Suzanne," he laughs again as I giggle against his chest.

"I sound like an idiot," I laugh until turning us again Z settles between my legs without breaking our connection once more.

"You don't sound like an idiot, love. You sound confused by your pleasure, which makes me feel like the best lover ever," he grins moving slowly inside me.

"You are the best lover. The *only* lover I've ever had," I whisper against his lips.

"The only lover you'll *ever* have," he says darkly as I nod yes.

Kissing me again, Z changes everything with his kiss. No longer are his kisses hard and sexy, and no longer are they desperate. Z suddenly kisses me like he loves me, and he kisses me likes he's loving me, which I realize he is.

"Making love," I whisper as he smiles before kissing me again moving slowly within me.

Forever it seems we move until I actually feel myself almost asleep. Strangely, I can actually feel myself falling asleep to his gentle movement, and though it's wrong, somehow I don't think Z would get mad at me or feel offended.

"Tired, love?" He asks as I nod again because talking seems like too much effort suddenly. "We really have to work on your stamina, Suzanne," he grins when I open my eyes to glare at him.

Z and his goddamn stamina. It's probably from all his gym visits and treadmill pounding that he has so much. Whatever. I prefer relaxing to working out any day.

"Suzanne?"

"I'm awake," I grin again just as I feel him move once more to finish inside me. Slowly, and without the noises or groans I made earlier, Z finishes us with sweetness and love and everything beautiful between us.

"I love you, Z," I whisper as he moves to my side lifting me on his chest like he always does.

"I love you too, Sleepy," he says kissing my head with his smile-voice.

And that's the last happiness I know before sleep- Z's love and his smile-voice.

Until I suddenly remember in agony it's that voice of Z's that creates false feelings like these that make me almost forget our actual sad reality together.

We are US...

CHAPTER 8

Waiting for Z to leave for the airport, I'm ready. I've done everything and put everything in order. I look the way I should and I've convinced everyone I'm on the mend.
For 3 goddamn days, I've had to deal with Z's constant hovering, and Kayla always watching me. I've spoken to Dr. Phillips every single day, even Sunday after the wedding, and I've played my part well. I know I have.
For having NO poker face I'm actually quite a good actress, which in another life could've made me famous for a good reason- not for the horrible reasons I'm known for by way too many people in this life.

Since I woke up Sunday morning after my horrendous night at the wedding, and my beautiful night with Z I've known what I had to do. I've never been more clear or so sure of anything in my life.
We even found out yesterday how Sheran was released early, which helped with all my fear and uncertainty.
First, he was released because he has testicular cancer that travelled to other parts of his body, which seemed way too fitting for a child rapist, if you ask me. And second, he gave some additional information he originally withheld from the D.A's office. Information I'm sure if Glenn Rose was still active D.A. wouldn't have been enough to secure Sheran's early release, no matter how good the information was. But the new D.A. doesn't really know me, nor did he feel the need to protect me like Glenn did when he was D.A. of Chicago.
According to Glenn, the new D.A. just wanted to make a name for himself by being involved in one of the largest, most famous cases in Chicago history. So he secured a deal with Sheran for his early release.
When Glenn called Z Monday morning he told him everything, which prompted Z to stay home from work to tell me everything. Which ultimately meant I was being babysat all day after the news.
But I didn't need a babysitter because I was fine. Nothing really surprises me anymore, and what I learned surprises me even less. At this

point there is very little that can still shock, surprise, or even upset me anymore. Though judging by Z and Kayla's reactions I'm assuming this newest information should have shocked me at least.

Instead of being hurt though, I laughed. But not in a trippy Suzanne's losing her shit sort of way, like Z assumed. I laughed in a 'wow, that's unbelievable, but totally believable' sort of way. And it didn't even hurt this time when I found out how much I was hated.

When I learned my mother paid the truck driver who hit me when I almost died a second time in New York, I simply laughed. Knowing he didn't succeed, I wasn't killed, and he received his money anyway from my mother 'to quietly go away' made me laugh even harder. Learning he also received an Insurance payout after the 'accidental' accident was too funny to me.

Knowing he failed to kill me as he was paid to do, and has been 'living large' as Glenn put it on my mother's money was hilarious. Knowing while I was in another coma fighting for my life but alive, he took a post-accident cruise with his wife while he recovered from his minor injuries was *beyond* funny to me. It was hysterical actually.

My mother must've been so pissed at the time that I survived.

Well, at least I was scarred and damaged for life which must be a small comfort to her. Between the chunk of my thigh missing, the burns on my neck and shoulder, and my hideous facial scars, my mother probably revels in laughing at pictures of me from prison. So really, even though her attempt to murder her only child failed she can still take some sick satisfaction from the damage caused by the attempt she made.

Remembering when Z told me, I almost cry. Now. He looked so sad, and so devastated for me, I wanted to comfort him badly. I wanted to tell him not to be sad for me, or to let this newest reality upset him at all. Because at this point in my life, everything just is.

After learning everything I learned years ago about Marcus, and my mother and her past, and even my grandfather's part in it all, I kind of just lost faith in everyone. I knew they were monsters, I just didn't know how truly evil they were until everything came to head. And since that time, when I was alone and pregnant and sad without Z in my life, something changed in me. I learned to *always* expect the worst of people so I couldn't be hurt ever again.

And really, it's worked out well for me, yesterday being the best example I can come up with. Whereas Z looked sad and devastated, and

Kayla walked away before she thought I could see her tears, I just laughed.

Finding out there was a warrant for the truck driver's arrest, and that the new D.A. in Chicago wanted to press additional charges against my mother didn't even phase me.

I could care less at this point. From what I've been told, my mother isn't getting out of prison until she's either very old, or dead, so additional charges and more jail time tacked on to her multiple sentences just seems a little redundant. But whatever, it's not my call to make.

Finally, I learned Z had hired someone 2 weeks before to always follow me wherever I went, just like in the beginning. When I thought I was driving alone to pick up Kayla at the airport, I was followed, and when I freaked out at the hair salon the Saturday before, I was followed to and from the wedding boutique and hair salon in the cabs I took. Surprisingly, I had NO idea though which was a little embarrassing.

However, when I said as much to Z he smirked and said that that was kind of the point of being watched by security. I wasn't supposed to see my watcher, so nodding I asked the obvious next question, *why?*

Straightforward, with very little emotion I could react to, Z admitted he wasn't sure why Sheran was released, and because I was in the newspaper article I was back in the forefront of everyone's minds again, so he thought it best to hire security again for my protection. He said he was nervous, and that was even before we knew about the killer truck driver, whose own injuries I had asked about and stressed over when I woke from my coma which pissed me off a little.

Anyway, after I was told I remember nodding, breathing, thanking Z for his concern about my safety, and for trusting and respecting me enough to tell me everything he had learned from Glenn. And then I remember walking to our bedroom for a much needed break from all the drama of the last 2 weeks.

When I woke from the little nap I took I was still numb though. I didn't feel sad about my mother's betrayal, again, nor did I feel upset by the newest developments in my life which once again I have no control over.

So I rose from my bed, greeted Kayla on the couch, smiled at a nervous looking Z, and asked if we could order in dinner, to which both agreed.

During dinner it was all over, as far as I was concerned. We didn't

We are US...

discuss the events taking place over dinner, and we three acted like we were all good. I ate and breathed and acted like I hadn't just learned about a failed attempt on my life By. My. Mother.

I even managed to sound well when I received a quick call from Kayla Monday telling me about her gorgeous hotel on the beach, and how happy she was to be on her honeymoon. I smiled and laughed and acted normal when I heard Mack growling in the background to get off the phone to her sexy giggles.

Anyway, since then Z is still treading lightly with me, and Kayla who has been way beyond sweet- nothing like her usual self- is finally leaving to return to Chicago. It is Tuesday night and I'm finally going to be alone. Because I'm fine.

Well, not fine by other people's standards but by my own I'm fine. I have known what I had to do since Saturday night, and I know that I'm ready to do it tonight.

Walking back in the living room with the last of Kayla's bags, I smile at her as she thanks me for having her over again. I convinced them both Z should drive her to the airport, instead of hiring the ridiculously expensive driving service, namely Kyle (who sadly I'll never be able to see or speak to again in my humiliation) or from hailing the cab she wanted to take. So they're ready to leave finally.

I convinced them everything was great, and I would see her soon, and to have a safe flight. I convinced Z I was fine at home and just wanted a little alone time while he drove to the airport, which though slightly suspicious looking was enough to get him to back off of all his hovering for at least an hour and a half to and from the airport.

Giving Kayla a final hug, I smile and giggle at her flirty Marty comments. Hugging Z I smile and squeeze him tight mentioning our secret sex couch in his ear so he thinks I'm happy. Waiting for them to descend the elevators, I smile and wave and just wait...

I'm almost free.

"I love you, Suzanne," Z says as the elevator door closes to my last smile and wave. But I feel nothing.

QQQQQ

Sarah Ann Walker

I am the world's best actress and I deserve an Academy Award, an Emmy, and maybe if I could actually sing a Tony award for my performance these last 3 days. Oh well. The first two at least.

Locking the door, I put the metal bar at the bottom which I know Z can't disengage from the outside. The metal bar was a gift to me for the rare nights Z travelled away from me, or for the times he was gone all day. It was a little metal bar, a gift from Z, to add a physical show of protection for me that all the hidden security alarms and cameras couldn't give me in our home.
The little metal bar gift that I'm now using against him was just one of the many gifts he gave me. The little metal bar that will prevent any interference I wouldn't be able to hear all the way in my bedroom if he came home too soon.

Walking back to our kitchen, I tidy up and wipe the counter clean. Passing the living room, I plump the couch pillows and refold the throw blanket neatly on the side of our huge couch as I run for the bedrooms.
Flipping off lights as I go, I throw open Kayla's door and smell her immediately. She has a lovely warm scent, mixed with old school Chanel that screams sexy and beautiful to me. She's also made her bed which is rare for her but appreciated with my time constraint.
Entering my bedroom, I walk to the little desk inside the glass atrium outside our room and sit for the last time to write. I have everyone else's finished because they were easy. Everyone else will understand. Everyone else won't really expect more from me but this, so I'm prepared.
Z, however, needed my special attention because he deserves it. I never want him to think he didn't mean to me what he meant, so I need to tell him now when I'm alone and the fear of being caught is absent.

I don't know which one will receive it, but I don't really care. Opening the first letter I read:

Mr. and Mrs. Beaumont,
I don't know why you hated me, but you've finally won.
You did this to me.
Suzanne

We are US...

Followed by another of little importance.

Grandfather,
I hear you're sick and dying. I hope you find peace in the end like I never could. You didn't do this to me, but your silence contributed to what happened to me.
And for me there has never been any peace in my life.
Suzanne

And now the harder ones. The ones that actually hurt when I do feel.

(Chicago) Kayla,
Thank you for being my fabulous friend. You really are, and I love that about you.
Thank you for helping when you could and for forgiving me when you shouldn't have.
I'm sorry if you hate me now.
Love,
Suzanne xo

Dear (New York) Kayla,
I'm so happy you found me.
You are the best friend and sister I always dreamed of having. Your friendship made me so happy I can't even explain it to you, other than your friendship was just so special for me I treasured it every day I knew you.
Please go love Mack forever. You both are amazing people and I know you'll be amazing together.
Help each other, always.
Love, Suzanne xo

And now for the heavy and the pain.

Sarah Ann Walker

Dear Mack,
I need you to go love Kayla forever. I want a happily ever after for someone I know, and I can't think of two more amazing people to experience it. Love Kayla forever, Mack.

I'm so sorry for this. Please believe me when I say you did NOTHING wrong, and you missed nothing. I was just that good of an actress. I've had to pretend my whole life, and I finally used it to my advantage. I'm sorry to put this last burden on you, but it IS the last one from me so I have to ask. Please take care of everyone for the next little while, but take care of yourself too. Please don't forget to care for yourself, Mack, like you sometimes do when other people's sad lives and craziness consumes you.

I have loved you from the moment we met, and I will always love you for believing in my life enough to want to save me. You didn't fail, Mack, I did. I was just too tired of the sad voices, and the nasty whispers, and the constant insecurity all the time. I finally woke up and realized I would always be screwed up to some degree, and I don't really want that for my life anymore. I actually want some peace now.

Mack, you are by far the greatest gift Z ever gave me, (besides himself) and I will love you forever.
You are 'my person' for eternity.
I love you,
Suzanne xo

Refolding the letters in my beautiful script, I feel okay with how I left things. It's not ideal certainly, but it is the absolute best I can do right now. And hopefully they'll eventually understand I did my best.

We are US...

   Walking to my bathroom, I grab what I need and place them on my bedside table before I begin my last letter. Z's was the only letter I couldn't write while he was in our home, because I knew he'd sense it.
   Also, having Z here felt too insulting, or tragic, or just sad or something. Knowing Z was around waiting for me to need him while I wrote him a goodbye letter felt like the biggest betrayal to the greatest man I have ever known, so I couldn't do it. Until now.

   Changing out of my yoga pants and cami, I wear my favorite black dress that Z bought me. It was a gift he had waiting on our bed as a surprise for an even better surprise night. He wouldn't tell me where we were going and though I barely held off begging it was so worth not knowing at the time.
   My dress was beautiful, and our night ended amazing. It was the very night Z asked me to marry him properly, and the night he convinced me to say yes.
   Finishing with my favorite ring from Z and a bracelet we both loved and bought in SoHo, I'm as ready as I'll ever be. I'm also so calm, I should be laughing at myself, but I feel no laughter right now. I feel no sadness, and I feel no fear anymore.
   I'm simply resigned to my fate.

CHAPTER 9

Entering the atrium dressed and ready, I sit for my final goodbye.

Dear Z,
I love you very, very much though I'm sure you don't believe me right now, but I really do. Hopefully one day you'll even believe me.
I won't say I'm doing this for you, because even though that's a small part of it, it's not the majority. Mostly, I'm doing this for me. When I say it's not you it's me, there are no truer words for us. This is all me this time. I've decided and I'm making the choice I didn't have when I was young. I'm making the choice to stop everything like I wish I could have done before. This is ALL me, Z.

I'm just so tired all the time now, and I don't want to be tired around you anymore. I don't want to be sad and confused and crazy any more around you. It's not fair to you, and it's not the life you should have to live. You are way too good to be trapped in this life with me.

Z, I want you to know I love you more than I've ever known love could be, and way more than I thought was even possible for me. Waking with you each day gave me a reason to fight for my future, and sleeping beside you each night gave me a reason to fight the nightmares of my past. Being with you has been the greatest joy of my life, because you have been the greatest gift I've ever known. You are my gift, Z, and I will hold you forever - just not here in this life any longer.

We are US...

So, again, it isn't you Z, it's all me. I'm too weak and too tired, and just too exhausted from pretending all the time. So I have to go now. I have to before I change you into someone else and eventually make you hate me, because I can't stand the thought of you ever hating me.

Z, I want you to find someone else to love. Someone who is easy and good, and who is actually worthy of you. I want you to love her and marry her, and even have those beautiful babies I couldn't give you. I want you to find love that is easy and makes sense. I want so much for you, and I want it because I love you. Walking on eggshells around a crazy wife who can't give you what you deserve isn't the life you're supposed to live. So please go find her and love her and be happy with her. Give someone who is worthy of you your good, bad, ugly, and beautiful, and make her give you the same in return.

Wiping away just one tear, I hold myself together with absolutely everything left of me to make this final goodbye right. Z deserves so much more than I'll ever be able to give him in this awful life of mine.

God, I love everything about you, Z. From your smiles and eyebrow wiggles, to your huge heart and your beautiful eyes. You are everything to me in every moment I've known you, always.
Please forgive me.
I love you.
Suzanne
xo

Finally crying my eyes out as I sign off, I feel my total despair so clearly, my heart and soul ache with it now that I feel again. I know Z will never forgive me for this. I can only hope he moves on and eventually forgets me. That's the best case scenario for both of us now.

ϘϘϘϘϘ

"What are you doing, Suzanne?" Z suddenly asks behind me as I scream.

Jumping, I nearly fall from the chair in my shock. "The security bar," I cry out.

"Yes," he glares at me. "I just learned if you slide a metal spatula through the side of the slightly opened door and wiggle it, the bar eventually falls to the side, which was a little too easy, I might add. Sorry for that breach in security, love. But I didn't know. I borrowed the spatula from Matthias down the hall by the way," Z says scarily calm. "Nice dress, Suzanne. Going somewhere?"

What the *hell* is happening here? He should have been nearing the airport by now with Kayla. He shouldn't be here. What do I do now?

Suddenly grabbing for my letters, Z actually pushes me out of the way as I dive for them. Shocking me motionless, Z holds the letters out to me and actually smiles sadly at me while I panic inside.

"Did you really think you fooled me, Suzanne? Do you think you fooled *anyone*?" What? "I *know* you, love. Or I did, I should say," Z says with a weird sounding huff. "But I guess I don't know you well enough to keep you alive and well, do I?"

Gasping, I scream, "Of course you do! I wasn't doing anything. I was going to surprise you when you got home from the airport. I wanted to maybe go out for dinner or to the movies or something. I was dressing up for you," I lie in my panic.

"Well, that's going to be difficult with Kayla waiting for Dr. Phillips and crew in the living room, and it's going to be difficult for us when I'm not here anymore," he spins away from me into our bedroom.

Grabbing the pills from my bedside table he actually throws them against the wall a few feet from me and just stops everything as the pill bottle crashes to the floor near me.

When Z stops moving entirely and stares at me I don't know what to do. He isn't even breathing, I don't think. Z is staring at me in the most silent stillness I've even known from him, and I'm scared to death.

"Never again, Suzanne."

"Never what? I wasn't doing anything wrong," I cry out walking into our room. I wasn't, because this isn't wrong.

"It doesn't matter anymore, Suzanne. Nothing between us matters anymore."

"What are you talking about, Z?" Shaking my head I almost walk toward him but his sudden glare freezes me in place.

We are US...

"I've agreed to a 72 hour psychiatric hold, and you'll be transported to Mercy as soon as Dr. Phillips arrives."

Staring back at Z with my mouth hanging open, I can't even laugh. I mean I want to, but I physically can't. I'm stuck again. There is just nothing but shock crushing me as he watches me watching him.

Finding my voice, I ask the obvious while I desperately try to understand what he just said to me. "Um, what do you mean? What did you do, Z?"

"Well, Suzanne," he says so deadpan, my heart aches hearing his voice. "I knew you weren't well, *everyone* knew that. But I really didn't know how unwell you were until last night. I saw you, love," he says so sadly a tear slides down my cheek as I stand frozen in place. "I watched you crying in the atrium from the door, but I didn't know what you were doing. I could tell it was bad though, so I left you alone in case you needed a moment. Once you were asleep however all bets were off. I tore through the books and drawers until I found all the letters, well, everyone's but mine apparently," he chokes out awkwardly.

"Because yours was special!" I yell accidentally. Holy *shit!* I just admitted everything in only 4 words.

Sneering at me, Z continues. "*Special?* Yes, I guess your suicide letter to your husband would be special, wouldn't it?"

"It wasn't-"

"*What*, Suzanne? A suicide letter? Then tell me what it was. Be honest with me for once in your goddamn life and just tell me what the fuck it was."

Exhaling, I can see he's mad, but I can't gauge how mad he is by his tone anymore. I can't tell if he's more hurt than mad, or just totally disgusted by me. I don't know what I should do because I can't gauge him at all anymore.

Sitting on the end of our bed I find the exhaustion so overwhelming I whisper, "I can't keep fighting anymore." And that's the truth of everything in this moment.

"What are you fighting?" He asks me nearly breathless. I know he's afraid I'll stop talking if he pushes too much. And I know whenever Z gets that soft voice he's trying to keep me talking. I know that. And honestly, right here like this with him I want to just talk for once.

Exhaling everything tight in my chest, I finally let go. Looking up at Z's beautiful eyes silently begging me to speak, I whisper my truth. "Life."

"Life?" Looking down at my hands, I nod. "How, Suzanne?"
"Um, life is hard, Z. Well, for me it is," I admit sadly. "I had to fight my whole childhood parents that hated me for some reason I'll never understand. Then I had to fight as a teenager bad men hurting and raping my body and even my mind at the clinic with Simmons, and then I had to fight as an adult my lie of a marriage. I had to fight my piece of shit husband and my parents still hating me even as an adult."

Pausing for a minute to collect my scattered thoughts I continue. "Um.... then everything happened, and I learned everything, and I had to fight to understand it all and I had to learn how to live after the tumor, and how to live with the horrific revelations and memories of my childhood. I had to fight the fear and the pain, and the constant barrage of darkness and horror that was my life. I had to fight after the accident, and I had to fight looking in the mirror every day because of the accident. I even had to fight what happened with Thomas," I cry gently grabbing my stomach to hold in the pain.

"And now I'm supposed to be all better, and an adult, and stable. But I still have to fight to just live all the time. Honestly, I don't think you know how hard it is for me every single day. Ah, it's not your fault, but it's hard to be with you sometimes," I whisper hoping I don't make him more angry with me.

"Tell me," Z breathes when I can't raise my eyes to him. I don't want to see his sad face or his angry eyes anymore.

"Um, you're so beautiful, Z. And I'll always be *just* Suzanne next to you. And that never goes away. So even though you're amazing and loving and wonderful and kind to me nothing ever changes inside me. I have your love, but the feelings inside me are still the same. Abused, hated, mocked, insecure, and just unworthy, I guess. I don't know how to explain it, but inside me is always sad darkness that I pretend doesn't exist so I can give you some moments of happiness so you'll stay with me. But they aren't real, or at least, they aren't as real as I pretended they were for you. Those happy moments were more like seconds of time when I felt *less* pain than I've known and lived with my whole life. So I didn't fake them for you, but they weren't exactly as real as I pretended they were because I just wanted to give you a little peace with me."

"You've been pretending with me?" He asks as a sad question rather than as an accusation as I nod. "Tell me."

We are US...

"Well, I know I'm annoying," I suddenly laugh on a quick burst and when I look up quickly at Z he's smiling a little until he nods me to continue. "I know people seeing me or hearing about me are thinking, 'Enough already. Get on with it. You got the guy and the life, and everything you ever wanted. So stop whining and freaking out, and move the hell on. Move forward with life already.' I *know* that. Just like I know I would be annoying to some people who are strong all the time, people who don't understand my weakness. But I'm not strong, Z."

"Suzanne, you *are* strong."

"No, I'm not, Z. I pretend I am, and sometimes actually believe I am, but I'm really not. I'm weak and tired and just exhausted from this life. But not with you. Please believe me when I say that because it's true. Life with you has been the greatest gift I've ever known, but it's not really enough to make all the other stuff go away, or like to balance it all out. But I really wish it was enough. Being with you *should* be enough because you are everything to me. But then all the pain and the fight and the exhaustion is still just always there, too. And I wish I was a better person, or a stronger person, or just a person who could get on with it, but I know I'm not," I almost cry, but just keep it in as I breathe deeply.

"How do you know that?" Z asks so quietly he makes me finally cry.

"Because even with you, I still have to try to not hurt myself all the time." Oh. And there it is.

Bursting out in a quick sob, I admit the truth finally. "They broke me, Z. And I've tried to get fixed so many times, but I was never fixed. I was taped up and glued shut but it wasn't real because I'm just broken," I cry as the pain lashes me from inside again.

"You're not broken, Suzanne, you're just-"

Shaking my head he stops speaking. "I am, Z. And that's what I don't think you, or Mack, or the Kaylas, or even Dr. Phillips understand. I actually *am* broken beyond repair. I will always be *HER*- that awful, insecure, loveless little girl who was hated and abused and so sad every day and every single night of her life she wished to die in her sleep, even at just 7 years old."

When our silence thickens, I continue so he finally understands. "I never told you that before, but it's true, Z. Even at 7 years old, before all the abuse that would damage me forever, even then as a very little girl I wanted to die so all the pain and abuse and *hate* from my mother would stop. I actually used to dream of dying in my sleep before I fell asleep. I used to pray for it and beg for it, and I even tried to figure out how to do it, but I was too young. I wanted to be the Cipher In The Snow," I whisper and look at Z. But when he looks confused by the movie of my childhood I continue.

"At 7 years old for god's sake, I wanted to die not even knowing what else was to come for me, or how much worse it could actually get. But then it did get worse, and I dealt with it however I could until I just didn't deal with anything at all. And now I'm expected to deal with everything so I can be happy. But there *is* no happy, Z. There is just nothing left. And I'm tired of fighting," I whisper.

"So you decided to kill yourself tonight?" He asks as I nod. Still staring at my hands, I can't look at his eyes anymore. Z's eyes always give me false hope and a temporary reason to try. "What happened that you finally decided?" He asks again when I still can't look up at him.

"Um, this weekend. Well, for a while now. But this weekend was the final straw for me. I was finally an embarrassment to you."

"You weren't an embarrassment," he lies quickly.

"Please don't lie to me, Z. I'm not lying to you anymore. I'm telling you everything so you can know why and move on."

"Move on?" He asks with a little tone in his voice, but I don't care anymore if he's mad at me. Maybe feeling angry will make him move on quicker. "Okay. So this weekend did what exactly?"

"Pushed me too far. My mother tried to kill me, and Sheran is free, and I can't handle all the fear and insecurity anymore."

"I told you Sheran would neved get to you."

"I know. And I believe you that he won't *physically* get to me. But it's the mental stuff I fear the most. He was a part of everything that broke me, and now he's free again to torture me with the fear of his return. But that isn't really the problem anymore, Z. It's the other stuff that bothers me the most."

When Z suddenly sits down beside me I flinch. I'm both surprised by the movement but mostly shocked he would be this close to me still.

"What stuff, Suzanne? Tell me..." he asks ignoring my flinch.

"Um, feeling worthless and unworthy. Feeling like a freak all the time. Feeling ugly and used and just insecure. You know, nobody understands why we're together, Z. *No* one. I've heard the comments, and I've seen the reactions from women especially, but even from some men as well because I'm so gross now. And I wish I wasn't as superficial as that, but I am, I guess. But it doesn't come from a superficial place, it comes from the nightmare I think. When they did those things to me, they always said I was pretty. They kissed my cheeks before or after and said I was a good, pretty girl. And they made me almost feel pretty too after what they did to me because I was so hurt and broken down. Or maybe I just needed to hold onto those little compliments because that's all there was for me then. If I wasn't being physically attacked, I was being hated by my parents. So those tiny little comments and compliments meant the world to me in my awful place of darkness. And now-"

"Your face is scarred," Z says gently as I nod.

"Yes. I don't even have a pretty face anymore like they said I did," I cry as he takes my hand and gently rubs my knuckles. "Um, I'm just all ugly now. Inside and out. And you're beautiful and people want you and you're just so amazing. But I can't stand the looks anymore. They make me feel exactly like I did back then, and still do I guess. I'm ugly, fat, worthless Suzanne born only to torture and abuse," I cry again as I feel him nod beside me.

"Have I ever tortured or abused you?"

"No."

"But it's still not enough?" He asks with the calm reserve I no longer fear. Z won't hurt me and he wants me to tell him the truth, so I do.

"Not really. And I'm sorry for that. *Truly* sorry. I wanted you to be enough, and you would be more than enough for anyone else. But for me, there's just too much to overcome."

"Okay, love. I understand, and I'm really sorry I wasn't enough, too," he says suddenly standing away from me. "Dr. Phillips will be here any minute if he isn't already, and Kayla wants to say goodbye to you. Will you at least come say goodbye?" He asks so calmly I start to feel real fear of him.

"Why? I can just stay here and wait, or you can just ignore all this and let me-"

"Suzanne. *Enough!*" Z yells suddenly making me jump on the bed again. "If you think for one fucking second I'm going to walk away and let you kill yourself in our goddamn bedroom you're crazier than I ever thought possible. You are doing nothing to yourself tonight, or ever for that matter. So cut the shit and get the fuck into the living room and wait for Phillips to try to help you. It's enough, Suzanne!" He yells one more time so loudly, I quickly cover my ears.

  Waiting for another explosion, or for the hitting, or for anything else he's going to do, the shaking starts so quickly, I have to start deep breathing to get control of myself again.
  "It's time, Suzanne. Let's go," Z says lifting me right off the bed by my arms as I give in. I'm not fighting him ever again, and the sooner this is over the sooner I can convince them all I'm fine until I'm free to be not fine again on my own.
  Nearly dragging me by my arm down the hall to the living room I just see Kayla's face for a second before I'm standing at the front door.
  "Where are we going?" I ask desperately.
  Turning me quickly, Z actually lifts me right off my feet by my arms to my shock and kisses my lips hard.
  Kissing me, he breathes deeply into my lungs but before I can reciprocate he places me back on my feet shaking and confused by his sudden passion for me. And then he turns away.

  "Suzanne... I have to go. I'm so sorry, love, but I'm leaving you."
  Huh. His words I understand. Even his facial expressions are known by me. His face still screams love, mixed with sadness, but his face also has the look of stubborn finality I have come to know intimately with Z. I know that look, but just not as it suddenly applies to me. I know what he said, but I have no concept of what he's actually saying to me.
  "What? Um..." Giggle. *Shit.*
  "I'll be at the Connaught. I already have a suite. I'll text you the number so you can call me for anything."
  "But-"
  "*Anything*, Suzanne. I will always help you if or when you need it, though we both know I'm not enough for you anymore," he finally says with tears in his eyes. Shocked, I dive for him but he actually hold his hands out to keep me away from him for the first time ever.
  "Um..." Holy shit. Can I speak? Can I say a friggin' word here? Just one word that doesn't sound like a grunt of some kind. "But." Yup. That was a word.
  "I love you, Suzanne. But I'm leaving you."
  Ummmm... Giggle.
  NO!

We are US...

Watching in shock as Z walks out our front door, I do nothing. I don't know if I'm breathing, or coherent, or even still mentally sound. I feel like I'm okay, but I know I'm not. There's no way I could be. Z is *everything* to me.

Waiting for him to renter, I try to be patient but I can't. Jumping for the door I rip it open only to hear the ding of the elevator already closed going down.

Still not believing he left I walk down our side of the hall and wait, but I'm not sure what I think'll happen. Maybe the old fashioned hands will slow their decent. Or maybe they'll just stop moving completely like they changed their mind. Maybe the little brass hands will change their mind and not leave me to slowly start climbing back to me.

I'm not sure, but it looks like they're moving slower. Maybe? Yes. I think they are definitely slowing down between floors 6 and 5.

Watching, I'm mesmerized. Watching, I'm hypnotized.

Watching, I'm stunned.

Did I know this was coming? Yes. Did I actually think this would happen? No. I really didn't think he would ever leave me.

Z promised me if I just loved him he would always stay. He promised no matter what happened, if I loved him he would never leave me. He promised. But I still love him and he's leaving me anyway.

Z said everything would always be us. He promised so many things, but he lied to me. Z left after he promised to stay.

Sitting in the hallway, I know I should be crying or something, but I'm just so, I don't know, I think stunned, or mad maybe. Yes, I'm mad at Z. No, I'm *furious* with him. He lied to me. Over and over again he lied every single time he promised he'd never leave me.

Every single, "Suzanne, I love you so much," or "Suzanne, there is only you," or even "I can't live without you in my life, Suzanne," was a lie. Z was a compulsive liar, and I believed him.

Just because I was going to leave him first, doesn't change the fact that he left me. He didn't know I was going to leave him, but he prepared to leave me anyway.

Okay. Done.

Z lied. And he left me just because I was going to leave him forever.

Sarah Ann Walker

EXHALE

We are US...

CHAPTER 10
Z

Well, that went well.

Holy *Fuck!*

What the hell just happened? I thought she would lie. I *hoped* she would lie. Never in my most insane nightmares did I actually think she would admit everything *and* say goodbye to me. Jesus fucking *Christ*. I actually thought I meant more to her than that.

Walking in the underground parking to my black Escalade, courtesy of Suzanne of course, I suddenly can't breathe when I realize what just happened in our condo.

Suzanne wanted to die *and* I left her. In one goddamn night.

Trying to breathe with my hand on my chest like that'll help, I start to panic a little. Fuck! Now I know what Suzanne feels like when she can't breathe. It's fucking scary, and weird, and just wrong. We're always supposed to be able to breathe.

Stopping to lean against a pillar in the garage, I really need to calm down. Slowly in and out like I always tell her, I start trying to breathe. Slowly, like I can control my lungs and my own body, I breathe. Slowly, like I always say to her... but it isn't working.

Almost laughing as I gasp a little for breath again, I want to howl at this sad irony now that I finally understand the panic she feels.

Fuck me. I can't breathe. And it sucks. And if I felt this as often as Suzanne does, I'd be fucked in the head too, I start laughing on another gasp.

Hunched over my own legs, I breathe as slowly as I can until the breaths come a little easier and the chest pain lessens slightly. Waiting, I find after a few minutes I'm functional enough to at least make it to my truck before collapsing in the garage where the cameras will see me.

It's bad enough they're probably watching me lean here like I'm going to puke or pass out, but if I actually do I'll never be able to face security again.

We are US...

Opening the door, I drag my numb body into the front seat, and the sight of my white knuckles clenched around the steering wheel look like claws but somehow clenching seems to help me breathe better. Maybe it's just the distraction, or maybe it's my intense need to strangle something distracting me so I can breathe. I don't know, but I'm slowly feeling better.

Waiting to leave my condo, I look around and realize I love my truck. It's a little *showy* as Suzanne said with a smirk, but it's also very functional and safe. I think I wanted the safety of a huge truck so no accident could ever hurt her again. Or maybe I wanted it so I could mow over anyone who tried to hurt her again.

Actually, I remember that from the dealership. I remember thinking I could run over anyone or anything trying to hurt her in this deluxe edition Escalade. I also remember how she thought it was way too much until I saw her look over at the solid black and chrome edition, and that was it. I had wanted silver before we arrived, but seeing her reaction to the black SUV sealed the deal for me.

Suzanne and all her goddamn black.

Eventually arriving at the Connaught, I don't remember driving the streets I've always known or passing the buildings that can still impress a homegrown New Yorker. I don't remember anything, and I really can't believe I'm here. I'm mean, yeah, there's really nowhere else for me to go tonight, but I honestly can't believe I'm actually here.

This wasn't supposed to happen to me. I wasn't supposed to be suddenly leaving my wife, or struggling, or living in a fucking hotel again. This isn't what I want, but it's what I'm left with suddenly.

Fuck! I wasn't supposed to lose her.

Entering the promenade, I hand over my keys to the valet and grab my wallet, phone and nothing else. There wasn't time to bring anything else, and really what the hell would I bring? Everything I've ever wanted is back in our condo. But everything I've ever wanted didn't want me back enough to live.

Fuck Suzanne, and her fucking shit!

Signing in and grabbing my room key card, I feel exhausted. I'm sure it's not the same kind of exhaustion that Suzanne struggles with, but I'm mentally wiped suddenly. I want to get in my room and chill. Christ, another thing she said to me. 'You have to *chill,* Z' with her little laugh that always made me smile.

God, I love her little laugh. Not her scary something's wrong giggle, but her actual laugh. Whenever Suzanne laughed I felt it inside me like it was my own. If one of the goddamn Kaylas made her laugh I always grinned as she lit up, even though it pissed me off, too, because I always wanted to be the one who made her laugh. I used to think it was my job to make her laugh, because Suzanne laughing is such a treat and an anomaly for all of us, we almost spend time trying to make her laugh, just to see her light up.

I'm pathetic, actually. Jesus Christ, there were days I stock piled funny moments at work so I could tell Suzanne at home, hoping to hear her laugh for me. And when I succeeded I could always count on her hugging me afterward, because that's what she does. After she laughs, she always leans into the person who made her laugh and she hugs them. It's such a little gesture, but it means the world to me. And really, to everyone else as well.

It's such a sweet Suzanne thing. Make her laugh, and she feels such happiness in that moment, she unconsciously needs to hug you to let you know she feels it and loves you for making her laugh. Or maybe she unconsciously needs to hug you because she actually found something to laugh about in her life. I don't know, but it's sad she still feels that way, almost surprised or confused that she laughed in spite of her life and past.

Okay... I'm becoming a chick.

Dropping my keys on the coffee table, I sink into the couch of my new hopefully temporary home and try to understand what happened. I don't know how I ended up here. And I don't understand what's happening anymore with her or us.

I thought she was better, or getting better, or just better enough that the darkness wouldn't take her away from me again.

But I was wrong.

I could even see it coming. I knew she was getting fucked up again. I could see it and feel it with her. I *knew* it was coming, so I tried to help

her however I could. I waited for her to need my help, and I watched to see the signs so I could get her help when I couldn't help her anymore.
 I talked to Phillips about it, and I talked to Mack a week before the wedding. I told the Kaylas I thought something was happening, and everyone knew to be on guard with her. They even knew to tell me if anything happened that looked like it might escalate. Everyone knew, but I'm still here anyway.
 I waited and watched and she even called me out on it. She accused me of making her worse with my watching, but she was wrong as usual. I didn't make her worse, she was getting worse. She just didn't know why, so she blamed my watching for it.
 I didn't cause this, or push it though. I was only watching what was already happening. I was trying to prevent it from getting worse by letting her know I was there for her if she needed me. I was watching and waiting and trying so hard to stop the darkness from taking her again, but I couldn't stop it.
 I didn't cause it though, her tragic past did, no matter what she thought or believed in her dark confusion. At least I know that to be true at this point.
 Slowly, I was seeing the changes in her. She was forgetting things, and messing things up. She was getting shaky all the time and I knew it was coming. I didn't know what was setting it off, but I tried to figure it out for her.
 I mean, I knew the newspaper article would hurt her. I knew that, so I tried to make it go away. In a mad panic I took the paper out of our condo hoping she wouldn't read the fucking news online that day, but she did anyway. And though she didn't say anything to me, I should've known she knew about it because of the Swiss Steak incident that very night.
 When I sat down for dinner that evening with her, her hands were shaking a little I noticed immediately. So I reached over the table to hold her hands without her knowing I knew they were shaking. I held her hands at the table and talked about my day until I tasted the meal, or whatever the hell it was she thought she cooked for us. And that's when I knew it was really starting. She was oblivious to what she served on our plates, and she honestly didn't know anything was wrong.
 Suzanne hates cooking, but when she does cook because she feels like it, it's always delicious. She cooks perfect meals when she cooks, and I

love them. So when I bit into the burgundy nightmare on our plates, I knew something was clearly happening again.
   I mean the food wasn't only inedible, it was just so wrong. From the weird watery sauce, to the partially raw steak, I knew she had been distracted or fucked up when she tried to cook for me. I knew something had messed her up enough that she didn't know what she was doing when she was cooking.
   Casually, I made it a little joke though. And after she relaxed, we did make grilled cheese sandwiches and laughed and held each other and watched tv and she seemed relatively okay afterward, for not being okay.
   But then the night terrors took over, and she was a crazy psycho in her sleep again. She started talking, and mumbling, and crying as she slept. She started hitting me to stop hurting her, or begging me to help her. She was so scary when she slept, I was exhausted from constantly waking her with hugs until she relaxed and fell back asleep peacefully on my chest like we both like.
   And every morning she was absolutely exhausted though pretending she wasn't. But I could see the bags under her eyes started, and she was dragging her ass all the time but trying to look happy for me. She didn't know she was acting out in her sleep again because she never remembers her nights, and I didn't tell her what she was doing at the time because I didn't want to freak her out if she didn't know.
   It was so bad that early last week, when my own sleepless exhaustion hit me hard, I found myself lying on the couch in my office, and before I knew it I had slept for over 5 hours. I was out cold, but no one knew I was sleeping because I had said I needed privacy and I shut my phones down. In my big office, I laid on the couch for just a minute I thought, and 5+ hours later I woke up feeling better than I had in a week.
   The sleepless nights were making me edgy, which of course made me edgier around Suzanne, who was also losing herself in her sleep, and in our reality. And yeah, basically, we were becoming a potential train wreck until I slept in my office and rejuvenated a little for her.

   Grabbing my phone, I can't wait. *Fuck!*
   "How was she?"
   "Good. She didn't fight or anything. When Phillips showed up only minutes after you left she was still just sitting in the hallway watching the elevators for you," Kayla says so sadly, I find my own heart ripped out of

my chest.

"She was by the elevators?" I choke trying to hold in the agony.

"Yes." When there's nothing else I suddenly want to scream. I didn't know what she would do after I left, but I didn't expect her to sit waiting for me in the hallway.

"Phillips helped her stand up in the hallway and before he even explained what was happening, Suzanne was nodding and handing over her purse for transport. She didn't speak, argue, or deny anything."

"Oh..." I feel like I was just kicked in the balls. When Suzanne doesn't even attempt to fight, it means she's just done with everything and everyone.

"Z, listen to me. You're weren't wrong, and you did everything right. I would've done the same thing for her, and once Mack and Kayla find out Mack will agree with you."

"I doubt Mack will agree."

"He *will*, Z. You had no choice. She was actually going to go through with it this time. I'm sure of it." When Kayla suddenly sounds angry, I understand her anger, but I hate it. She shouldn't be mad at Suzanne.

"Please don't be mad at her, Kayla. She doesn't mean to do this. She just doesn't see any other way out of the darkness. Or out of her past," I choke nearly crying.

"I'm not mad at her, Z. Well, I am. But not really. I just don't understand how she gets to this place so quickly and so badly. And it pisses me off that she can't ever keep her shit together."

"I know. Believe me, I feel pissed, too. But this isn't her fault. Suzanne can't help the way she thinks or feels, Kayla. It's just her and she doesn't want to feel or think the way she does, believe me. But she can't control it, so she chooses-"

"To fuck us all. And leave us because she's weak!"

"Kayla! It is NOT her fault, and she's NOT weak. She's fucked up again, and I won't have you trashing her for this. Understood?" I yell back.

I hate when Kayla gets all bitchy with Suzanne, even if it's to be supportive. Suzanne doesn't need bitchy, she needs understanding right now even if I *don't* understand her or what she wanted to do at all anymore.

"Sure, Z," Kayla says right back like she doesn't give a shit about my anger, which she probably doesn't. "I'm flying out in the morning. I need to get the hell out of here for this."

"Do you want me to take you to the airport?"
"Nah... I'll call you when I get back to Chicago, okay?"
"Thanks."
"You did *nothing* wrong, Z. And Suzanne will understand that eventually. There was simply no other way to make her wake up then to pretend you were actually leaving her this time. You probably scared her enough to make her fight hard this time. You did good, Z."
"Thank you. I, ah-"
"Z, get drunk. Cry your eyes out, feel hungover for the next 3 days, then decide what happens after her hold is lifted. You have 3 days to just be a pathetic, drunken idiot while Suzanne is assessed okay?" I can almost hear the grin in her voice.
"Okay. Thanks, Kayla. Have a safe flight."
"I will. I'll call you when I land. Let me know if anything happens or changes, okay?"
"I will."
"Good night, Z. You're the best, baby," she adds with a laugh as she hangs up.

Smiling, I wonder if I am the best. But as the sadness returns, I realize I'm not. I didn't save Suzanne as a child, and I couldn't save her as an adult. Being her husband didn't help, and loving her didn't help. And now I've locked her up. Something I promised never to do to her, I did.
In one night I did 2 of the three things she's only ever asked of me. Her 3 horrible requests; Don't ever lock me up. Don't ever leave me. And please don't ever rape me, Z.
In her broken, little voice, those were her only 3 requests ever of me, and I did 2 out of three tonight. The last one being so absurd, it was an absolute promise I would forever keep.
I remember the feeling I had when she begged me not to rape her. It was repulsion, and insult, and horror. But I swallowed down everything I wanted to say to her, and I made the promise to her.
Looking at her crying, begging eyes, I promised Suzanne I would never rape her. And I remember the exhale I received in return for my insane promise. She exhaled and again I was so offended I wanted to yell at her, but when she smiled I quickly realized it wouldn't matter to her if I was offended. She had to ask and she needed my promise.
As if I could rape or hurt my Suzanne. Just the thought of ever

physically hurting her makes me nearly violent. No one will ever hurt her physically again, least of all me.

But reasoning why I broke 2 of my 3 promises to her doesn't seem to change how badly I feel for doing it tonight. I broke my promises to her and I can only hope when she's rational again she understands *why* I did it. God, I need her to understand why I did everything I did to her tonight.

Walking to the minibar, I feel the sudden urge to be a drunken idiot. I know no one can see me lose control, and I have no meetings tomorrow, so I don't give a fuck how hungover I get. I need to drink this shit away. I need to numb myself a little from Suzanne and her desperation because she's making me desperate too.

Snapping the cap of the little bottle of Vodka, I grab the other 4 and settle in. Lining them up perfectly on the table, I gulp the first and realize quite quickly these 5 little bottles are going to do shit for my current mood.

What I need is to call Jon in shipping and have him send over a case of Z's finest, as Suzanne calls it, so I can get shitfaced tonight.

Waking 2 hours later, I'm still sober but feeling a little better. These last 2 weeks with Suzanne have been exhausting, not just physically, but mentally as well.

Knowing your wife was heading to her desperate scary place is beyond anything I think most people, especially a man could handle. But honestly, I thought I could.

I'm strong, and tough, and I'm Z. I'm a fixer and a doer, and I'm pretty amazing at controlling life and the people and events within it. But with Suzanne I always feel out of control. She makes me question every single decision I make, and she makes me fear everything I do. She makes me feel insecure in life, which truthfully, pisses me right off.

I mean, fuck *off* already. Get your shit together. Love the man who loves you. And get on with the life you have together.

But she never does. She tries, and I try, and we manage to get through for the most part. And then her shit resurfaces, and she changes back to fucked up Suzanne, and I can't stop it or control it. I can do *nothing*.

Fuck... I hate this shit all the time.

Storming into the bathroom I start the shower and try to exhale all my anger. I have to keep telling myself this isn't her fault, but yeah, I'm fucking pissed, too. Kayla's not the only one.

I want Suzanne to wake the fuck up and realize what she does have now so she stops all the shit all the time. I want her to pull her head out of her ass and get with the program- *my* program.

Suddenly laughing, I realize what an arrogant controlling dick I sound like. I remember when Suzanne once said to me, 'Dominant, much?' I laughed at the time before kissing the shit out of her. But she was right, and I knew it. I just didn't realize how right she was.

I am a dominant confident bastard, and the fact that I can't control her, or how she feels, or reacts, or even how she *lives* and views life pisses me off.

I'm patient and understanding, and really I just love her enough to deal with anything. But I'm pissed. I have never given her a reason to doubt me, or to fear me, but here we are again. Right back where we started.

I love a fucked up woman. And the fucked up woman can't see the love in front of her beyond the darkness suffocating her.

Because I'm not enough.

Stepping in the shower, there's nothing I can do right now, but wait. I have to wait for her, or for Phillips, or for Mack to tell me the next step. I have to wait, and the controlling bastard inside me hates the wait almost as much as the pain of knowing I'm not enough for Suzanne.

I'm not enough to keep her alive. And my love wasn't enough to make her live.

She didn't ask me for help, and she didn't want to hurt me. But that's been my life with Suzanne. One unintentional hurt after another.

Stepping back out of the shower as I look in the mirror I can see why I'm attractive to women. I'm also successful and wealthy which definitely helps. I know why I'm wanted by women, but I don't give a shit. I never have.

Christ, annoyingly, women still throw themselves at me, even though they know I'm married and I love with my wife. Woman want me for a good fuck, or to love them, and just even as a status symbol around town. But I'm not stupid. I know exactly what I am to the opposite sex. I've always known it, and I used to have fun with it.

I was a lover to many who loved very few. I was a man who knew

We are US...

exactly who he was and what he wanted, which was no one indefinitely, until Suzanne.

But I couldn't keep her from wanting to die, even with all my love and with my entire life given to her.

Because I am not enough.

CHAPTER 11
SUZANNE

Sitting back in his bland office again, I feel totally irritated and annoyed by everything all around me. For 3 goddamn days I've been medicated and talked to by Phillips and all the other staff endlessly. I've also done everything they ask me to do whether I want to or not so I'm compliant enough to get the hell out of here tonight.

"Suzanne, your husband left you, yes. But *you* were going to commit suicide."

"So?!" I yell angrily. I'm so tired of that excuse from him.

"So... You were going to leave him forever, and you told him he wasn't enough to keep you alive anymore, and you hurt him beyond anything he's ever experienced before I think. Therefore, he left you because *he* loved you too much to stay and watch while you attempted to kill yourself. Does that make sense?"

Huffing, I argue again, "Not really."

"Okay. Would you sit there and watch Z kill himself when he told you he loved you, but didn't love you enough to keep living with you?"

"Z would never do that," I answer again.

"Just imagine he did for a minute," Phillips pushes.

"But he would never do that, so I can't even imagine it. I was never enough for Z, and no one has ever loved me that much."

"You don't think Z did?"

"No," I whisper again now that the quick anger has faded.

"Okay. Just for argument's sake, pretend Z told you he loved you but he was going to kill himself anyway, even after you begged and pleaded and loved him and did everything you could for him. Would you stay and watch him die? Or would you leave him because the thought of Z's death was too painful to you?"

Staring at Phillips I think he truly underestimates my intelligence. Like most people he thinks I'm an idiot who will think whatever they want me to think. But I'm not, and I don't.

We are US...

"Of course I wouldn't stay and watch. But your hypothetical is so illogical and ridiculous, it would never happen. Z is amazing, and he would never do anything like that. So though you want me to imagine it, it's impossible *to* imagine. Z has too much going on around him, and too much going *for* him. He has too many friends and responsibilities and too big a life to ever feel like killing himself. So again, your ridiculous scenario is unimaginable. And a fairly useless comparison if you ask me." There! See, Suzanne isn't such an idiot.

"Suzanne, why are you mad at Z?"

"Because he left me."

"After you told him you wanted to leave him forever?"

"Yes," I huff for the fiftieth time. Jesus Christ, Dr. Phillips is such an idiot. I guess we're both surprising each other tonight.

"Suzanne? Why are you so mad at Z?"

Looking up at Phillips' face, I would love to smack him. His beady little eyes are waiting for me to answer the same goddamn question I've answered fifty *one* times now, and I'm done with this game tonight. My answer isn't going to change, no matter how many times he asks, or how many examples he gives. My answer will NOT change. Z is a liar, and he left me.

After all the promises and all the bullshit he fed me for the years we've known each other, he lied about his feelings for me, and he left me anyway. He also committed me which he promised never to do to me. The bastard.

"Are we done yet? I only have a few hours left of this forced confinement which is something else Z said he would never do. But here I am," I seethe at Phillips.

"We're done whenever you want to be done, Suzanne," he says in his annoyingly calm voice.

"Good. Then we're done. Thank you very much Dr. Phillips," I say politely as usual. Wow. You can take the Beaumont out of the Suzanne, but you can't smack the disgustingly polite out of her head.

When I stand to leave the room we're using, Dr. Phillips clears his throat which is another annoying way he either attempts to get my attention or tries to snap me out of my head.

Turning back with a fake smile plastered on my face, I ask sweetly, "Yes?"

"Suzanne, I'm not going to sign off on your hold being lifted this evening." *What?*

Smiling my best Suzanne smile I stay as calm as possible for this round of *are you FUCKING kidding me?* "And why is that, Dr. Phillips?" I ask sitting gently back in my chair with my hands folded in my lap and my back straight.

"Because you aren't ready," he says simply. Not even pretending, he just speaks which leaves me little to fight.

"Actually, I *am* ready."

"Suzanne, not 3 days ago you wrote suicide notes saying goodbye to everyone you love."

"And hate," I add with a poorly timed giggle.

"Yes, and *hate*. You haven't discussed anything about what you had planned, and what you were going to do. Or even what led up to your decision to kill yourself."

"Because I'm over it," I jump in quickly.

"Yes, of course. You said goodbye to the admitted love of your life, and you set up a situation to cause yourself if not death, immediate harm until you were found."

"But I didn't do it, so it doesn't count."

Shaking his head slightly, Phillips argues again like an asshole. "Actually, that's *all* that counts. You didn't do it because Z found you before you could hurt yourself. Not because you changed your mind and sought help."

"I was going to change my mind, and I was going to call you for help."

"But you didn't. Z did."

"I would have," I exhale slowly. This lying thing never gets any easier, even though I'm kind of a pro at it now.

"But again, *you* didn't. Someone else prevented your suicide. Your husband."

"Soon to be *ex*-husband," I growl.

"Really? So you're divorcing Z, then?"

"Yes," I admit then choke up.

Completely out of my control, like a physical reaction that wasn't even mine, my entire body just revolted against my words. I'm having an internal revolt. My organs, and heart, and even tear ducks revolted against the words divorce and Z in the same goddamn sentence.

But it is what it is.

Z left me and now we have to divorce. Period. I can't be married to a liar. And I won't be married to someone who doesn't want me. He left me and he committed me. He never loved me like he said he did every single time he lied to me and said he loved me.

"Why are you crying, Suzanne?" Phillips asks in his gross, slightly whiny voice, and after the initial repulsion at his voice I think of Mack.
My Mack wouldn't have asked such a stupid question. He would've explained why I was suddenly crying, what I could do to fix it, and what would help me. Mack would've helped me see another side to my feelings without belittling me or making me feel like my reactions were crazy and unjust. Mack would help me get out of this. But Mack's not here.
I know he's on his much deserved honeymoon, and I would never take that away from them. I even made everyone promise not to tell him what's going on while he and Kayla are away. But I need him badly right now because I know Mack would fix this for me.
Wiping away my tears without smearing my makeup- my *psychiatric approved* makeup, unlike even the tweezers that were taken from me in case I potentially *plucked* myself to death, I sit up straighter and look at Phillips as best as I can without the loathing I actually feel for him suddenly.
"I would like to be released this evening," I say simply.
Looking down at his papers than back to me he replies, "And I already told you I wouldn't sign off on your release tonight. I don't believe you're ready, and we haven't addressed any of the issues that prompted you to feel suicidal or to bring you here in the first place."
"Yes, we did. Z brought me to this place. Well, you *physically* brought me here, but with his permission." Wow, that one was hard. I almost scowled again at the thought of Z's betrayal.
"I mean emotionally, Suzanne. We haven't discussed *why* you felt suicidal or why you were going to kill yourself Tuesday evening."
"There's nothing to discuss," I huff for the hundredth time. "I was sad and now I'm fine. I'm all better now. I feel like I should, and I'm much better with all your help," I smile my bullshit compliment smile to flatter him. "If not for you these last few days, I wouldn't feel as strong as I do now and I wouldn't be ready to leave. But I'm much better, and I'm ready to leave now because of you," I smile again hoping to convince him with flattery.

"Okay, Suzanne. Unless you'd like to call Z to discuss lifting the temporary hold, we're through here. I'll set up another appointment tomorrow afternoon with you."

Looking at this weaselly piece of shit, I just barely hold in my rage. He thinks I'm so fucking stupid. Just like they did. Stupid, fat, little Suzanne, who always did as she was told, but it didn't matter. She was a useless fucking toy anyway. Actually, she was just a fucktoy, I suddenly laugh.

Oh my god, I never put that together before. I was a fucking toy, and a fucktoy. Laughing my ass off suddenly, I wish I was with anyone but this idiot so I could tell my stupid joke. Mack would get that one for sure.

Trying to fight off the laughter, I rise and turn for the door again. But this time I'm leaving. Screw him and his hold. I'll contact Glenn in Chicago, or the papers, or, or Mack. They can't do this to me, and I won't let them.

Stupid friggin' New York State and their forced 72 hour holds. Only half the States in the US even allow this but here I am. In the wrong goddamn state again.

"Suzanne, you could always call Z to lift the hold," Phillips says just as I'm opening the door.

Nearly ripping the door off its hinges to get out I scream, "Fuck him. And fuck *YOU!*" And the relief I feel is immediate.

Walking 5 doors down to my white, plain little room, or cell is more accurate, I close my own door before the orderly can physically check that I have nothing hidden on my body. Exhaling all my anger I find I'm barely breathing as the orderly throws open my door anyway before I can even sit on my bed.

Looking at his angry face, I feel the fear immediately. Shaking in an instant I know what this means for me. I know this room, and I know what gets done to me in psychiatric hospital rooms. I know it because I remember it all.

Oh *god*... Not this again.

"Please don't touch me," I beg shaking as he stares at me.

It's coming, I can feel it. The darkness and the fear and all the hands on me, and the disgusting slurping sounds and moans and all the ugliness I can't fight. It's coming for me as he approaches me slowly.

"DR. *PHILLIPS!!*" I scream as the man enters my room all the way to get me.

We are US...

No. No. *No!*

Fighting, I attack first. He's not doing this to me again. Simmons isn't touching me and fondling me, and fucking with me. He's not licking me until he gets off. And he's not fingering me hoping he makes *me* get off.

Never again.

Screaming bloody murder I fight with absolutely everything I have in me as the rage and fear consumes me. I will never again be easy, and they can't make me comply.

I am not little Suzanne anymore, and Z told me no one would ever hurt me again. Z promised me I was safe. Z said no one but him would ever touch me like this. But once again he lied to me.

Crying as I fight, the pain all over my body is so awful, my lungs huff and struggle for breath through the pain. My arm is killing me and my stomach feels like I've been kicked repeatedly. My face is sore, and my eyes are pouring pain tears, but I'm still fighting them. I'm going to fight this time until I just can't fight any more.

And then I just can't fight anymore.

Crying out my final frustration, I close my eyes and wait for them to start.

Staring at all the white, my face is pushed so hard into the tiles I can't even blink. They are touching me and fighting me, and they're going to fuck me again. They're doing whatever they want to me again because I can't fight them anymore. I am HER, and I will always be this woman to them. And that's why I want to give up living.

"I want to die," I moan through the side of my face as the darkness takes me completely. "Z? Help me..." I hear my own voice for the last time.

Beyond the screams and swearing, I begged him to save me again, but he never does. Z can't save me this time because he never could.

CHAPTER 12
Z

   Jerking off, I'm half asleep, but I know exactly what I'm doing. I can feel it. I can feel her holding me in her little hands as I semi-sleep.
   Picturing her sweet mouth on my cock as she holds my thighs tentatively is hot as fuck. I've always loved it when she went down on me- not that it happens often. Suzanne has to be feeling secure with me and in the right frame of mind to do it. But when she does go down on me, it's the sexiest fucking thing ever.
   I love looking down at her as she sucks me hard. Her eyes which always look up at me like she's nervous or unsure of herself and her abilities turn me the fuck on.
   Her gorgeous blue eyes that are so stunning to watch, watch my own reaction as she sucks me deep into her throat. And I love it. Knowing she has only ever trusted *me* enough to do this with by choice makes my head spin. Well, that and the fact that my mind is being sucked out of my dick makes my head spin.
   But when she looks up at me, I know she needs confirmation that she's doing okay. I know when her eyes are open looking at me, she's silently pleading with me to tell her she's good. So I smile down at her, and when she hears my little groans of pleasure, she always smiles around me. I can actually feel her smile around my cock and then she just let's go as she pleasures me like she actually wants to, as opposed to doing it because she thinks she has to for some reason I've never understood.
   I've never asked for a blow job or even hinted that I'd like one. I know it's hard for her, and I never want to make her uncomfortable or even scared with me. But when she drops to her knees without me asking, it's such a show of love and security from her, I could almost weep. Well, that and the fact that my half Italian side makes me an emotional pansy from time to time.
   Palming myself, I can feel her mouth around me. Not as soft, or as wet, but it doesn't matter. I need to get off, and I need to feel her loving me again.

We are US...

Moving my leg to the side imagining the vision of her eyes looking up at me, the couch gives me just enough room to... Oh, *fuck!*

Coming all over my own hand and chest, I wake fully just as the last shudders wrack my body. Coming on myself, I want to laugh at feeling like a goddamn teenager again, but I can't. Coming on myself is so pathetic, I'm embarrassed that I miss her so much I sleep imagine she's with me just so I can get off imagining her still with me.

Because honestly, even though it's only been 3 days without her, and almost a week without sex with her, I feel like I'm dying inside. My body is screaming to go get her, and my dick is aching with the need to feel her around me. Because being with Suzanne is all I ever want to know, and missing her is like a slow death for me.

God, I miss her.

Walking to the shower I know it's evening, but I haven't been sleeping all week and my couch at work isn't helping anymore. I'm exhausted and lonely, and just, yeah, I hate this fucking hotel. Everything here is the bland beige of our past until Suzanne warmed up a little to color in our lives. Color, except of course for the dreaded red.

Red, which ironically is the perfect color for her, is her worst nightmare. Red on a blue-eyed blonde is the perfect color, but not for my Suzanne. For her red is the unimaginable. Red is the nightmare awake, and the horror of her past. Red is death and pain and horror for her, and it breaks my heart.

To think a color could hold so much significance to a person as to break them is devastating. It's just about the saddest thing I've ever heard of, and watching it happen is something I never want to experience again.

Suzanne breaks my heart when she's broken.

Dressing, I grab my cell before calling for dinner because I'm waiting for Kayla to call about her promotion today. I knew it was happening today, so she had the weekend to think about the job and choices she was offered, and I hope her decision is the best one for all of us. New York.

Suzanne will love having Kayla always around, and truthfully, I'd love to see her more as well. Kayla is funny and crude, and just shy of being a guy around us, which is fun for everyone, though mostly for Suzanne.

Kayla makes her laugh even more than I do, and I like having that humor around. Plus, she fits in with our little group so well, even though I could kill her sometimes for upsetting Suzanne whether Suzanne needed the push or not. I like her more than dislike her though, but sometimes it's nearly equal like and dislike.

Like the night before the wedding? How fucking stupid, or I guess how drunk could Kayla be to say something so stupid to Suzanne? Bringing up not only spankings but a 'daddy' comment. What the fuck? Did she just meet Suzanne for fuck's sake?

I was so pissed at her for prompting that incident I almost told Kayla to fuck off forever. I wanted her to get the hell away from Suzanne and never look back. I wanted to tell her what an asshole she was, but thankfully, Suzanne explained the innocent comment under normal circumstances, and after I cooled down I could speak to Kayla coherently when she apologized.

And I knew she was sorry. Everyone knew it. Kayla would never hurt Suzanne intentionally, I know that. But for some reason Kayla always seems to be either a trigger herself, or she says something that triggers Suzanne, which is totally fucked up.

But Suzanne loves her, and I do, too. She's actually great when she's isn't the object of Suzanne having another breakdown.

When the phone finally rings, I smile. Kayla better pick New York, or I'll kill her. "Hello?"

"Z, it's Dr. Phillips. There's been an accident with Suzanne at the hospital and I need you to come down to sign some paperwork," he says like he's nervous or upset.

"Did she kill herself?" I gasp with no air left in my lungs at all.

"No! Absolutely not. But she was hurt before we could sedate her, Z."

Shaking my head while sitting on the couch I try to find enough air to speak. I try, but I don't have enough. There's simply not enough air in my lungs for words to form.

"Suzanne had just finished a session with me and when the orderly approached her for the mandatory pat down she had an acute attack. Actually, she attacked him as he entered her room and-"

Gasping, I find the breath to yell. "You let a man touch her?! Are you *fucking* stupid?"

"The orderly only touches her gently with a female present, with her door wide open in the hallway, so she doesn't feel threatened in any way. It's mandatory, Z. But we have accommodated all of Suzanne's issues with touch and with men in general. And so far, she has handled everything very well until tonight."

"What does he do to her?" I ask with a barely concealed growl.

Someone *touches* her? Not only does that piss me off because I'm a possessive dickhead, but its makes me enraged because I know she can't be touched by any man but me and Mack. Even Marty doesn't touch her still, though *she* might lean into him for a hug hello or goodbye if she's feeling secure around him. But *Suzanne* always chooses. We 4 people and sometimes Marty are the only people who can touch her because she can't handle hands on her.

"What is a mandatory pat down? And what the fuck happened to her?" I yell again already grabbing my keys walking toward the door of my suite.

"In case a patient steals something from the session room- a pen or even a paperclip is enough to hurt themselves with, we have to check them. The session doctor makes note of where the patient sat, and if there was any opportunity for the patient to even lean forward toward their desk. But before a patient can enter their room the orderly does a gentle pat down, trying not to touch anywhere inappropriate."

"*Trying?*" I yell as the elevator closes. If my phone cuts out suddenly I'm going to smash it, and anyone else who accidentally gets in my way.

"Yes, of course. They are watched closely, Z. And as I said there is a female present the whole time, plus it's in the hallway so it's in camera range, and they *try* to be as gentle as possible. Though it's a little invasive, the orderlies don't smile or speak, and they try to keep the emotion out of it so the patient feels like it's just a necessity, not a situation of any kind. And again, until tonight Suzanne was fine with it."

Reaching the promenade again, I can't even lower my voice I'm so pissed. "Then what the hell happened tonight?"

"Suzanne entered her room too quickly, and the orderly followed her inside to ask her to exit before she settled in."

"He went in her room with her?" I gasp jogging to the parking garage. Even without knowing what happened, I know exactly what happened. She freaked the fuck out on him.

"Yes, quickly without thinking *only* to ask her to step back out into the hall so he could pat her down, but it was too late. Suzanne-"

"Lost her fucking mind and attacked him. She probably screamed and fought him with everything she had in her to prevent him from attacking her in her room. Am I right?" I ask holding my truck door to keep standing upright.

"Yes," Phillip says so simply I want to cry for her.

Imagining the scene, I know exactly what she did. Suzanne tried so hard to protect herself, but eventually she failed. And then she became her young self again until she eventually gave up the fight and waited to be hurt again.

"Did she cry?" I whisper as my heart breaks all over again for her.

"Yes," Phillips whispers back sounding honestly upset. I'm glad to hear he actually feels bad for what happened to her or I'd kill him.

"You know what that motherfucker Simmons did to her in her room at the Psych Clinic. You *know* what he did to her over and over again and you still allowed a man to enter the room she's trapped in?"

"It was an accident, Z. All the staff know Suzanne's triggers and they all work around them. This was just a quick incident that had a tragic result."

"How tragic?" I moan turning onto 42nd street with my foot shaking on the gas pedal. "What happened to her? Is she sedated?"

"Yes, she's sedated right now. And once she wakes up I'll explain what happened and how the orderly made a mistake."

"What. Happened. To. Her?" I ask again. He's still evading and that shit isn't going to fly for much longer.

"Suzanne's right wrist was broken. And she was banged up and bruised before we could sedate her."

"Her wrist?" I say with murder in my voice I can actually hear.

"Look, Z. I was there. I saw the whole thing begin and I fought with her as well to try to get her under control before she hurt herself more. It was actually me who was holding her arm when she purposely twisted and threw herself to the ground, and that's when her wrist was broken. While I was holding her," Phillips says quieter.

If I gave a shit, I would almost think he felt bad about what happened based on his voice. But it doesn't matter to me what he feels. I'm going to sue the fucking hospital, and I'm going to ruin Phillips. He'll never again touch anyone else, and he'll never practice medicine again. He's a dead man walking as far as I'm concerned.

"Your medical career is over," I threaten calmly before ending the call.

We are US...

Is he fucking kidding me with this shit? I don't care how out of control Suzanne was, he broke her arm? She's fucking tiny. She might think she's fat, or has a huge ass, or whatever the hell else she's insecure about. But she's 5 foot nothing, weak, and incapable of fighting off anyone long enough to get hurt unless it was on purpose.

Phillips is a large man, plus there was a male orderly, and they couldn't restrain her without hurting her? Fuck, I can restrain her without hurting her. So clearly they didn't give a shit about her physical well-being. Maybe he even wanted to hurt her a little.

It's not easy to break someone's wrist, so I'm thinking maybe she frustrated him and he took the opportunity to work out a little payback on her body.

Breathing my way back to my SUV and the ride to the hospital I have to fight myself to stay calm. I have to fight to not kill him the second I enter the ward. And I know I'll have to fight not simply picking her up and taking her out of there when I see her.

This can't be happening. This wasn't supposed to turn out this way. Nothing was.

Walking to the ward, Phillips is waiting for me at the desk before I can even sign in. Before he has the chance to speak though I nail his mouth shut.

"Don't talk to me. Do NOT speak right now. Just show me Suzanne." That's it. That's all I have to say to make Phillips nod and start walking toward a room.

"Sir, I have to pat you down," a man says and before I can control myself he's flung against the wall.

"Are you the fucker who touched and broke my wife?"

"Z! Let him go. I will have you arrested in a second if you don't stop. *NOW!*" Phillips yells and seeing the asshole's face against the wall, I realize it couldn't possibly be the same guy. He was way too calm when he spoke to me and not scared of me at all.

Exhaling as I step off, I look at the guy moving slowly, and I squeak out an apology which he doesn't acknowledge. Not that I give a fuck, but I should at least try to make him understand.

"I'm sorry I shoved you, but I thought you were the bastard who hurt my wife tonight. If you'd like monetary compensation, call me tomorrow at work and I'll arrange it."

Smirking and rearranging his scrubs shirt, he actually says, "Oh, I will, sir. But I still have to pat you down before you enter a room." Like a fucking asshole, he even grins. I know he sees dollar signs, and I don't give a shit. I'll call my lawyer later to pay him off.

Opening my arms at my sides, I spread my legs widely, and smile back with a nod. "Go ahead and touch me, ya little bitch," I growl as Phillips jumps back in.

"Z, you aren't mad at Evan. So I think-"

"And I told you NOT to speak to me. I want to see my wife."

"Keys and wallet," the little bitch says and I hand them over.

"Go through the wallet if you'd like. There are a few hundreds in there to tie you over until tomorrow if you want them," I smile again as he laughs at me.

"Thanks," the little bitch says and I just stop myself, barely, from punching him in the face before Phillips opens the door to our left as I turn my head.

Suzanne...

Everything else fades away the moment I see her. Lying on her side, her arm is in a cast and she looks so lifeless I can't stand it. She's so much more pale than usual, and she isn't covering her face which seems wrong somehow. I know she always covers her face. Even in her sleep, she unconsciously manages to hide that part of her face in either the pillows, or with her hair. She always hides from everyone. She even hides from me still.

Walking toward her, I lean in and kiss her damaged cheek like she rarely allows me to do. She hates so much about herself, she never lets me have all of her. No matter how many times I've told her I don't care about anything but her, she has never given herself to me fully. And really, as I stand here looking at her I don't think she ever truly will.

Shit. I think I just had an epiphany.

No matter what I've done or said, Suzanne has still held back. And I think I finally realize no matter what I do or say she always will.

Suzanne will never give herself to me completely. And I'll always be waiting for her to love me back as much as I love her.

Wow. Wake up call.

Looking at Suzanne sedated and calm, I finally see her. Trapped in her own head, unable to love herself, she'll never be able to fully love me.

We are US...

Holy shit! I've *never* had her. We just went through the motions, living with each other, smiling and breathing, and laughing. We even loved each other. But it was never fully and it never will be, because it was never enough.

Suzanne isn't mine to love. She's not even her own to love.

"*Fuck...*" I whisper when reality finally shows me the truth I never thought was possible. "You will never love me like I want because you're incapable of trusting me with your own."

Falling into the chair beside her, I don't even know what I feel, besides utter devastation. Yes, that's about as close a word as I can find. I'm devastated and heart broken, and I feel such sadness baring down on me I can't move from this chair. And I don't know what to do with this reality now.

"I'm sorry, love. I thought my love was enough for both of us, but I know it isn't anymore. You were right all along," I moan our sad reality.

"Z. Suzanne begged for you before she was sedated. She screamed for you," Phillips says quietly beside me. But it's still not enough.

"That's only because she sees me as physically strong, and she thinks I could *physically* help her if she was attacked. It's because she wanted me to protect her body. It wasn't because she wanted *me*," I choke out the words I didn't understand before.

"Z, she does want you. She's just going through an acute episode right now brought on by stress and anxiety, and by the events in Chicago, and because she-"

"It doesn't matter why," I moan shaking my head as I finally understand everything between us. "The reality is she never believed I loved her enough for both of us so she never believed I'd stick around. She always believed I'd betray her, and I finally have."

"With good intention."

"The intention doesn't matter anymore," I admit shaking my head again.

"Z, the intention always matters- good or bad. It's what makes decisions so hard."

That I understand. I know what he means and I actually agree, but not with Suzanne. The intention doesn't matter in regards to Suzanne, just the end result matters.

"Dr. Phillips, I finally understand why she didn't cry over Thomas," I say not even fighting the tears falling down my cheeks. There is nothing in this room anymore but honesty, so my tears are irrelevant at this point.

"And why is that?" Phillips asks walking to lean against the wall in front of me with his arms crossed.

Raising my head I tell him what I've finally figured out. "Because she *didn't* love him. She doesn't love anyone truly, because no one ever loved her. She didn't learn about love until it was too late. And now Suzanne's version of love is equivalent to like, loving a stuffed toy or something. It's there, and you can play with it, but at the end of the night you put it back in its place until you feel like loving it again. That's Suzanne's love, I think."

"Are you trying to speak for her? Are you actually arrogant enough to know what she feels and thinks, Z? Because even for you, that's a little obnoxious," Phillips says seriously as I smile.

"Just call me a Shrink," I smirk sadly as he nods in deference.

"Touché. But you still don't know exactly what she's thinking or feeling, Z. No one does but Suzanne."

"And again, you're wrong. No one knows, *especially* Suzanne. She was right about everything the whole time. I just didn't want to see it or acknowledge it because I *am* arrogant. And because I love her."

Leaning away from the wall Phillips asks what I hoped he would so I could finally say it out loud. "What was she right about?"

Closing my eyes for a brief second, I expel my pain to admit the truth. "She IS broken beyond repair. She will never get over her past, and she will never fully live in the present. Suzanne is a shell of what she should've become, and only a little piece of the woman we see. She *is* broken, Phillips, and I should have understood it sooner to save us both from this heartache."

Standing, there is nothing more for me here. Suzanne knows I'm not enough, and now I know it, too. I could've handled her asking me for anything. I could've handled doing anything for her. But this I know I can't do.

I won't stay and watch someone I love, love nothing in return. It hurts too much, and it just delays the inevitable. Suzanne is broken, and I won't watch the final pieces of her die away before my eyes.

Leaning into her scarred cheek once again, I want to sob at the irony of her scars. She was also right every single time she argued she was damaged on the inside as well as the outside now. She was always right,

We are US...

I just didn't listen to her.

"I will always love you, sweetheart," I whisper the forbidden name against her cheek. "I hope you find your peace now, however you need it," I finally sob as I walk away from Suzanne, and us, and from everything I wanted with her.

If she dies tomorrow, I'll understand she needed the release, and if she dies in the future, I'll wait to be told she finally succeeded. But I won't wait to watch her fade to nothing anymore as she breaks my heart along with her.

Leaving the room and the hallway, and eventually the ward, and hospital itself, I move in a trance.

I have finally left the woman I love so she can end her suffering in peace. I won't stop her, and I won't make her fight anymore.

My poor, beautiful, sweet, sweet Suzanne shouldn't suffer anymore. I know that, and I finally accept it.

Sobbing against the wall outside as I hold my stomach contents in check, I realize I probably look like a man who just lost his wife to a tragic accident, or maybe to illness, or to something equally as sad. I notice people see me, but other than sympathetic eyes for the new widower they probably imagine, they do nothing but pass me. And that's it.

I am a widower, without the actual death yet.

I am a man who has suddenly learned the truth of his wife's illness and I have to just wait to know what her final death will be.

My Suzanne is broken. And I didn't love her enough to make it all better just like she always told me I couldn't.

"I finally hear you, love. And I understand now," I whisper to no one but her ghost in my soul.

CHAPTER 13
SUZANNE

"Suzanne? Can you hear me," Mack asks when I finally open my eyes. He came back for me. Oh *god*...

"You're here," I cry with such relief I can't stop from sobbing in my hands.

"Yes, I'm here. But why are *you* here?" Mack asks like he's confused or something.

What the hell does he mean by why am I here? He knows why I'm here, unless he doesn't. But he would know what happened because he knew to find me here, so he wouldn't know I was here without knowing *why* I was here. Right?

"Um, what do you mean?" I ask when the tears finally slow enough to talk to him.

"I mean exactly as I asked. Why are you here, Suzanne?"

"Ah, because I was put in a 72 hour hold that they won't lift. And it's been 6 days now, Mack," I cry desperately.

"Who won't lift?"

"Dr. Phillips."

"And who else?"

"Z," I whisper crying again. "Z betrayed me. He promised me. And he lied, Mack. He lied to me!" I yell as he nods like he understands.

"The same way you betrayed him?"

What? "No, I didn't. I was just... Um, it's not the same thing," I argue trying to make him understand.

"Correct me if I'm wrong, but YOU promised to never attempt suicide for Z, and for me actually if you recall our life-long contract," he says a little angrily, but not angrily enough to actually scare me. "And then Z had you committed which he promised never to do to you. Am I correct?"

"Yes," I nod not seeing where he's going with this, though I probably should.

"So you broke your promise first, Suzanne. Therefore Z's broken promise doesn't count." What?

"Yes, it does! He left me, too. Did you know that? Did you know Z also left me before he had me committed for a 72 hour psych hold? Did you!?" I yell at Mack because his calm is pissing me off.

"Again. After you broke *your* promise. So once again, his broken promise doesn't count. What else do you have? Are you going to blame me next for this because I was away on my honeymoon?" He asks much angrier.

"No, of course not."

Shrugging, Mack shakes his head like he could care less before asking, "Why didn't you call us? Or have someone else call us?"

"Because I didn't want to ruin your honeymoon. You and Kayla needed to reconnect after the wedding stuff, and I didn't want to burden you or make you angry with me," I fade out feeling a little insecure suddenly.

Leaning closer to me Mack asks, "Don't you think this ruined our honeymoon more?"

"Um, I don't know. I don't think so."

"Well let me tell you about my honeymoon. Kayla and I had a wonderful time, Suzanne. We were happy and relaxed and Kayla was even laughing again with all the stress of the wedding over. We drank and danced and just had fun like we used to. We actually reconnected again and everything was wonderful for us. And when our honeymoon was over we landed at LaGuardia ready to go back to our normal lives, still happy, cabbing it to our place. Then guess what happened?" Mack says beyond an angry I'm comfortable with as I stay quiet. "*Guess*, Suzanne?" He snaps at me.

"I don't know," I admit kind of scared.

"We entered our apartment, dropped our bags, exhaled from the flight, but before I could even use the bathroom Kayla was banging down the door crying about you because she listened to a goddamn message from Chicago Kayla telling us what you were going to do, or *wanted* to do. A message, Suzanne? *Really?*" He says so angrily I have no idea what to say. But he waits anyway with a glare until I cave under the pressure of his anger.

"Ah, I asked her not to tell you guys, or to leave you a message. I told everyone who asked if I wanted you that I didn't because I didn't want to upset you or ruin your honeymoon with this. Um, I made everyone promise me they wouldn't call you so you could enjoy your honeymoon."

"Did you?" Nodding, I whisper yes again trying to understand why he's so angry with me.

"Well, you managed to ruin our honeymoon anyway, Suzanne. So thank you for that. Instead of thinking about it with happiness, we're both scrambling to figure out what the hell happened while we were away. Kayla is bawling her eyes out, devastated and sad, and really fucking pissed actually- at you and at everyone else. And I'm just reeling from figuring out what the hell happened when I was away."

"I'm sorry," I blurt out quickly when he takes a breath to finally stop yelling at me.

Shaking his head again, Mack actually breathes deeply a few times like I do before he speaks. Leaning back in the chair a little further from me, he casually crosses his leg, ankle over knee and just waits while I struggle with what to say to him to make this better.

When he eventually lifts his eyes to me he still looks a little angry though his voice is much calmer.

"Suzanne. Why are you here?"

"Because I wouldn't talk to anyone after Friday night," I shrug lifting my arm for him to see my broken wrist.

"How did that happen to you?"

"Um, the orderly hurt me and Dr. Phillips broke my wrist," I whisper still afraid of Phillips but unable to get away from him. Whispering in case the room is tapped, I beg Mack, "Will you please get me out of here before he really *hurts* me Mack?"

"Suzanne, I need you to listen to me. Dr. Phillips isn't going to hurt you. He's a well-respected Psychiatrist-"

"Like Simmons was," I point out desperately.

"No, not like Simmons. Phillips is a colleague of mine and he would never hurt you the way you fear, or the way Simmons did. And that's the truth, Suzanne. I promise."

"But he did hurt me! Look at my arm!" I cry totally frustrated that Mack won't listen to me.

"I saw a little of the video feed, Suzanne. Once you were closer to the door the video picked up some of the struggle from the hallway, and I have to tell you Suzanne *you* hurt you this time."

"No, I didn't. Philips did!"

"When your wrist was broken, Phillips had you in a slight hold to keep your arms away from the closest nurse until you did some spin drop thing before you hit the floor. It's actually on the video feed, which was very lucky for Phillips and the investigation. I saw it, Suzanne. I also saw Phillips' shocked reaction when you suddenly threw yourself to the floor. There wasn't any time for him to release your arm before you threw yourself down, and he certainly didn't hurt you on purpose. You did that, Suzanne. I'm telling you what I saw."

"But they were going to attack me again," I whisper looking up at the light I know has the camera and sound recorder inside it.

Looking up himself, I think Mack understands what I see. "There is nothing in this room to record you. Nothing at all. It's against the law, and against hospital policy. I work here remember? My office is in the next ward so I guarantee you there is nothing in any of the rooms."

"Oh." Whew.

Jesus *Christ!* I didn't realize what a relief that would be until he said it. I was more afraid of giving them something to see and watch and maybe post online than I was of simply dealing with ignoring Phillips every time he and the other doctors tried to get me out of my room from the doorway.

"Suzanne, you attacked first. Blindly, crazily, and really fairly strongly. You attacked David when he was only 2 steps into your room. And yes, he shouldn't have been in your room- he's been suspended and he fully understand the protocol he broke when he entered. But it was just a poor judgment call on his part trying to do his job. You, however, kicked the shit out of him."

"I did?" I start giggling, though Mack doesn't laugh with me like I thought he would.

"Yes, you did. It was actually horrific and vicious, and it's so awful to watch that you were immediately upgraded from 'a danger to herself' to 'a danger to others'. And that's why the hold hasn't been lifted yet, Suzanne," Mack says so seriously my smile fades as quickly as the sadness returns.

After forever in my sad silence, Mack asks again, "Why are you here, Suzanne?" But I don't know what to say because I have very little left to give him. There's very little left inside me, and I'm so tired suddenly I want to be left alone.

When Mack waits patiently, I finally squeak out my answer to please him. "Because Dr. Phillips put a mandatory hold on me and he won't lift it," I say as he shakes his head no.

"Why are you here, Suzanne?" He asks again looking at my face like he's willing me to speak. But I already did.

"Um, because Dr. Phillips and Z agreed to a Psych hold," I try again.

"Suzanne... Stop playing dumb and answer the question. Tell me *why* you're here."

Oh. Huh. I wasn't *playing* dumb, I actually was. But I know what he wants now so I give it.

"I'm here because Z figured out I was going to kill myself Tuesday night, so he and Phillips put me away instead." There. It's out.

"You were going to kill yourself?" He asks as I nod. "Why, Suzanne? And be honest."

"I'm always honest with you," I snap as Mack smirks at me like I'm lying.

"No, you're not. You try to be, but you're not always. Often you say what you think you should say, or what you want me to hear. You even say what you think *I* want to hear. But you're rarely honest with me until I push you to be."

"That's not true! I never lie to you, Mack. I promise."

"Suzanne, evading a question, or only answering a question partially is still lying by omission. You know that. We've talked about that endlessly over the years. So don't start with this shit now." Before I can respond he asks again, "Why were you going to kill yourself Suzanne?"

"Um..."

There are so many reasons and so many things I want to say. I want to tell him everything, but he always just argues or tells me I'm wrong and tries to find another reason for my stuff. Mack always finds something that makes what I say, if not wrong, then just explained away differently and I don't want that this time. I need him to listen to me and I need him to accept what I'm going to say this time.

"Will you listen to me, Mack? Like, *really* listen?"

"Of course," he breathes quietly.

"No. I mean, will you hear what I have to say, and not try to change it into something else? Because that's what I need from you. I want to tell you but I want you to accept whatever I say as the truth this time without changing it in my head."

Nodding, Mack says exactly what I figured he would. "I'll listen to you, Suzanne. But I can't promise I won't tell you if I think you're wrong. That's the best I can do."

We are US...

"Okay," I nod because that's the best I'm going to get from Mack.
"Suzanne, why did you want to kill yourself?"
Inhaling deeply, I exhale with my words. "Because I'm screwed up, and I'm too sad to continue like this." Nodding, Mack prompts me to give more. "Ah, I feel bad with Z, and I don't want to feel bad anymore. Um, he deserves so much more than me. And I've embarrassed him finally, and he left me so-"
"Doesn't count," Mack interrupts. "He only left you after he found out about the suicide, so him leaving you doesn't count as a reason for your suicide. Try again, Suzanne," he says like an asshole.
"Okay, fine then. He was leaving me after he found out, but he still left me."
"Still doesn't count, Suzanne. So drop the Z left me part and tell me why you were going to kill yourself." Okay, Mack is just being annoying now.
"Fine!" I snap feeling pissed. "Because I was sad and tired, and I didn't want to feel like shit anymore. Nothing ever changes no matter how much time goes by." Breathing deeply all the pain inside me, Mack smiles at me and signals with his hand to give him more. "Jesus *Christ!* You're being really annoying right now."
"Don't care," he says with a shrug. "Continue, please."
"That's it, okay? Everything felt really bad, and I freaked out the night before your wedding, and a few days before your wedding, and then *at* your wedding. And everything was just so awful and I felt so shitty, and I was tired of feeling like shit, and looking like shit, and I hate the women who say mean things about me, and I hate Z for always looking and acting perfect all the time, and I just decided enough was enough."
"Because?" He interrupts again with a smile and I want to bash his face in. Z was right, dammit. I really do need to get into kick boxing or something to channel all this anger all the time.
"Because I was, okay?"
"Because you were what?"
"Depressed and-"
"**Bingo!**" Mack says with a triumphant smile as he claps his hands together.
Um... What the *hell* just happened? My whole room seemed to light up with Mack. It's like everything changed around me and now everything feels so different suddenly. I don't know what the hell just happened,

but I feel strange.

"You were *depressed*, Suzanne. That's it. Plain and simple. You felt depressed and you started freaking out. You were sad and depressed, Suzanne. And what happens when you get depressed?" He asks almost laughing at me.

"What? I don't know," I say totally confused by Mack's almost pleasure or something talking to me.

"Suzanne, when you get depressed your past haunts you and you struggle. When you get depressed nothing feels good anymore, and everything becomes darker for you. You don't feel anything good, and slowly your mind and feelings change everything that *is* good into something bad."

"I- *what*?"

Finally just laughing, Mack smiles as he reaches for my hand before I can even pull away from him. "For lack of a better explanation, when you get depressed, Suzanne, everything bad or *sad* in you becomes stronger and more amplified until you get totally fucked in the head," he says with a grin making me burst out laughing. He always cracks me up when he sounds totally unprofessional and undoctorly.

"You're depressed, Suzanne. And I think you forgot what this felt like because it's been a while for you. A good, *long* while. Your meds have been working and you and Z have figured out how to deal with all the triggers and the day to day life shit that could set you off. You've been really good for quite a while now, I'd say even happy. So I think when this depression hit you forgot what it felt like so you didn't know how to handle it. But it's a depression, Suzanne. That's all this is, and you can handle a depression. You have before and you will again," he finally squeezes my hand and smiles at the stunned expression I think I'm wearing.

"I- um..."

"Are depressed, Suzanne. Which is totally normal and even expected with you. You've had too much physical and mental trauma in your life to not experience depression for the rest of your life. And honestly, that's what this is. I promise," he says with a gentle Mack smile, and I almost believe him.

"But I really don't want to live like this. I'm tired of all the bad stuff, Mack. It just takes too much out of me, and it's not fair to Z to have to live with a woman like me. Someone who he has to walk on eggshells around or something in case I lose it. And I don't want to keep living like this all the time because-"

"You're depressed. Plain and simple, Suzanne."

Oh. Huh. Mack makes it sound so simple or something. "But it doesn't feel simple, Mack. It feels awful. *I* feel awful," I cry a little as he smiles at me.

"Of course it feels awful, Suzanne. Have you ever heard of anyone talking about an *awesome* depression?" He asks as he stands and I can't help but laugh again.

"Not really."

"That's right," he agrees sitting on the side of my bed. "Depression is awful and it sucks, and it's so intense you can't see past it without help and medication. But you know this. We've talked about this for years now. We've always acknowledged that you would have depressions, and we've agreed we'd work really hard at getting you out of them so you could live a happy, functional life as best as you can."

"I think I forgot," I whisper as he leans into my body.

"I know you did. But it's okay. You know now what's happening, right?" He asks before just lifting me right into his arms for a Mack hug. "Right, Suzanne?"

Squeezing Mack back as much as I can with one arm, I cry, 'yes' into his shoulder as he nods against my head.

He's right again. He's always right with me. Why don't I ever just ask him first what's going on so he can tell me and make everything more clear for me? Why do I always try to do this shit on my own so I get more messed up when I could just ask Mack? He always tells me the truth and he always helps me.

"Why didn't you come to me when things started feeling so badly?" He asks while not letting me go, which just makes me cry harder. "Tell me," he pushes.

"I didn't want to bother you, and I didn't know what was happening. And I was okay and then not okay so quickly, I didn't know what to do. But I tried to fix me, Mack."

"Without my or Dr. Phillips' help? Without talking to anyone?" Nodding against his shoulder I don't know what else to say. "When has that ever worked for you?" He asks seriously pulling away to look at my face.

"Um, it hasn't," I exhale as reality surfaces. I still feel like shit, but it helps knowing *why* I feel like shit this time. I'm depressed, which is just

about the best news ever, I giggle.
 "Feeling better?" He grins.
 "No. But I'm glad I at least know why I feel so badly. Does that make sense?"
 "Yes," he smiles rising from my bed to sit back in the chair beside me.
 Lying back down, I lean on my side so the pillow covers my ugly face and I wait for Mack to tell me what I do next.
 "What do you want to do now, Suzanne?" Oh, not what I had in mind. I have no idea what I do next.
 "Ah, I don't know," I admit.
 "Okay. How about we start with getting you ready to leave here. I know you hate the confinement, and I know you'll be much better at home when your healing. So why don't we work on getting you out of the depression first before we tackle all the reasons why you feel depressed. Sound good?" Not really. Crying out suddenly I realize what I've done and I don't know how to fix it.
 "What is it?" He asks quietly leaning forward again.
 "Z's gone, Mack. He left me!" I scream as the agony rips through me. "He left- me," I sob between breaths.
 "Suzanne. Look at me," Mack demands and I look immediately. "Listen to me for a minute. Okay?" He continues when I nod. "You need to work on *you* right now. And I know that's hard, and I know you want to crawl back into the darkness with Z gone, but you have to work on you right now. Once you're better you can work on the Z issue. But they aren't the same issue right now, and your mental health and life is the important issue right now."
 "But-"
 "Just think for a second. If you work on Z but you're still depressed the cycle will continue until you two break away from each other completely. Do you see what I'm saying? It's like this- you have to be *not* depressed to work on your relationship. Otherwise, it's just wasted effort that will fail as soon as the depression takes you over again. Right?"
 Nodding, I kind of see what he's saying, but I still want Z back. I didn't mean for Z to leave me, and I didn't mean to leave him.
 "Suzanne. Focus. You have to feel better to get Z back. Okay?"
 "Okay," I exhale because deep down I know he's right. I just don't like it. I want Z back with me now. But I *do* know Mack's right. If I'm not

We are US...

better, I can't make Z feel better about me. *Shit!*

"Wow. This sucks," I admit as the world's biggest understatement and even as he tries Mack can't hold in the laughter, which naturally makes me huff a laugh in return.

"Yes, it does. But it's going to get better, Suzanne. I promise," Mack smile-laughs squeezing my hand again.

"Will you help me?"

"Of course I will."

"No. Like *will* you help me? Like be my doctor again? Because I don't think Phillips is helping me much," I laugh a little at the obvious.

"No shit," Mack grins as we both laugh harder.

"Yes, I'll take you on again officially. But just like before Suzanne, no holds barred. I'm calling you out, and you are going to have to work really hard for me. Understood?" When Mack asks seriously I agree.

"Yes. Um, please help me, Mack? You're the only one who seems to get through to me, and I need you," I whisper again nervously.

"I got that. And we'll figure out how to do this again. Once again, Suzanne you drive me crazy, but I love you anyway," he says so sweetly, my smile is immediate.

"I love you too, Mack. So much. I'm really sorry for all this again."

Shrugging, "It was bound to happen, Suzanne. You're not the most stable person I've ever met," he says again so casually we both burst out laughing.

Thank god. A day without Mack's dorky humor would kill me, I think. Ooops. Laughing harder at my tragic analogy, I don't even need to share it. Mack knows the stupid things I think, so he can imagine for himself.

"Okay. I have to go calm my wife down," he smiles as I do. "That sounds kind of cool, huh?"

"Yes, it does. Very cool, actually. Could you please tell your gorgeous wife how very sorry I am that she came home to more Suzanne shit."

"Of course I will. Just relax now. We're going to fix you and then this situation you're in. But no more beating up the orderlies until I return, okay?"

Grinning, I just nod. "Thank you, Mack." God, I love him so much. Even when he goes no holds barred on me.

"You're welcome, Suzanne," he smiles heading for the door to leave me.

CHAPTER 14
Z

"Are you fucking retarded?!" Mack yells as I open the door shocked by his entry.

"Not that I'm aware of," I answer quickly to Mack's glare.

Mack rarely says anything inappropriate and he would never say something so politically incorrect unless he was hammered. *Maybe*. Laughing, I have to know. "Are you drunk, Mack? Because I can't think of any other reason you would say something so socially unacceptable in your life."

Turning back to me, Mack gets a little too close to me before yelling, "No, I'm not fucking drunk. But I need to be!" And as he storms away from me to the pathetic minibar, I want to laugh again. Mack hasn't been drunk since he was about 24.

"Over on the counter," I say pointing as Mack looks and exhales. There are 6 different high-end bottles of whatever the hell anyone could require to drown their sorrows.

Grabbing the scotch, Mack actually chugs without a glass until he stops to choke.

"That's gotta burn," I throw in for shits and giggles because I'm a bastard who's fairly annoyed with everything and everyone these days.

Turning back to me, I wait for whatever the hell he has to say. At this point, Mack would have to know what I did to Suzanne so I'm sure he wants to rip me a new one, but I just don't care anymore. I did what I did because I love her and I thought she needed it at the time.

"How was your honeymoon?"

Glaring at me again, Mack asks, "Really?" as I nod. "Fine! It was amazing," he says not sounding amazed at all.

Grabbing the bottle, Mack slumps into a chair at the table and just stares at me waiting for me to speak I think, but it's not going to happen. If he's pissed at what I did then he can bring it up. I'm tired of being the pussy around here. I've had enough.

I'm also *not* enough apparently.

We are US...

"Do you have any idea how hard it was to find you?"

"Not really. My cell-"

"Is shut off, you dickhead. And the hotel wouldn't call you for me or confirm a room number."

"I requested privacy."

"So I had to call your office which is closed, only to be transferred to the night service which I then had to convince to let me talk to *anyone* in your building, who it turns out was a shipping clerk named Jon."

"I know Jon," I answer deadpan. "He brought me the alcohol."

"Yes, I know. After much talking with Jon, nearly begging like an idiot, I finally convinced him I was Mack, your best friend. I then had to prove it was an emergency by explaining how you were my best man, until he found a goddamn picture of my wedding online and made me describe myself until he was sure I was the fucking groom in the picture and therefore *probably* your best friend before he would tell me where the fuck you were."

"Chicago Kayla knew which suite I was in I think. Oh, maybe not. I'm sure I told her the hotel, but maybe not the suite number."

"No, you didn't. She could only tell me the Connaught. Really, Z? The fucking *Connaught?*" He asks totally pissed at me.

"It seemed fitting suddenly," I breathe sitting down across from him in my exhaustion.

"Yeah, the hotel you used to bring women to is very fitting now. What the fuck, Z? Have you cheated on her?"

Growling, I want to punch him as I stand back up to approach him. Seriously. Just like Suzanne, I feel the quick anger well up until only punching someone will do. "Are you actually asking me that?"

"Well, why here? I know what you used this hotel for so don't bullshit me. I know this was the hotel you used when you wanted a little extracurricular fun, without the emotional trappings of having the women in your apartment. So why *here*?" Mack growls right back.

"I didn't know where else to go."

"Bullshit! Try again, Z."

"Fuck you, Mack! If you don't like the memories of this place, then get the fuck out! I seem to recall you using a suite once or twice, so don't suddenly play innocent with me!"

"That was a different time, and we were in a different place. And we weren't fucking *married!*"

"I'm *NOT* married anymore!" I yell standing over him until the sudden silence following my anger shocks me.
 I'm in a murderous rage or something. Fuck *me*... I don't think I've ever been this angry before in my life. I actually feel like I want to kill someone with my bare hands right now. And sadly, it may just be my best friend I kill if he doesn't shut the fuck up.
 "Sit down, Z. Now," he demands until I actually do as I'm told. Huh. I guess I *am* still the pussy here.

 Waiting forever in silence, I notice my hands shaking and I wish they'd stop. I also notice my heart is pounding and I can feel my pulse in my forearms and even behind my ears. I'm almost hyper aware of my body suddenly in a way that most people only notice after a hard workout. But I haven't worked out recently. I've done nothing for 6 days but simply function. The only time I switched anything up was to see Suzanne Friday night. And that was kind of the end of everything.
 So now I'm just waiting for Mack to yell at me, and I'm waiting for Suzanne to die.

 "What's going on, Z?" Mack asks gently and I feel such emotion suddenly, I barely hold in the sob I've been holding since Friday night to laugh instead.
 "Do you know what a pussy I am?"
 "Yes," Mack answers so deadpan, the quick laughter roars through my chest again in the room. I can't even hold it in anymore. I swear to god, it's either laugh my ass off or cry like I did when I said goodbye to Suzanne Friday night. And I have to choose laughter because crying feels so final to me.
 "Why are you laughing?"
 "Because I can't cry again. I feel like shit and I want to cry, and I can't because I'm a fucking man. But I actually want to cry like a little bitch again. You know what?"
 "What?"
 "I've cried 6 times as an adult. 6! That's it. I didn't cry when my parents died, not that they deserved it. Well, maybe my mother did if she didn't know what a fucking piece of shit he was. But I swear she had to have known. So whatever, I didn't even cry for my mother. But I've cried 6 times since I was a kid, and 6 times in the last 3 years, and 5 of

them were about or for Suzanne, and one was for my son, which is also kind of about Suzanne."

"Yes," he nods waiting for more.

"I'm a man, Mack! And I'm crying like a little bitch."

"So?"

"*So?* Ah, well, I feel like a pussy and I hate feeling like a pussy. I'm Z for fuck's sake."

"Yes, you are," he nods again. "What does that mean?"

"It means, I'm fucking Z!"

"Which means what exactly?" He pushes again, and I know what he wants and I know where this is headed and I know what he's trying to do. But I can't stop myself from playing his game anyway.

"It means I'm Z. So I don't have to put up with this shit, I don't have to feel this way, and I don't have to love a Psycho anymore who thinks I'm not enough. I could find anyone to love me. That's what it means!" I yell across the table. "Jesus *fucking* Christ. I'm so sick of feeling scared, and nervous, and fucking insecure around her. And I'm so sick of her fucking Suzanne *shit* all the time!"

"Bingo!" Mack claps stunning me silent after my outburst.

Leaning across the table, Mack hands me the scotch with a head tilt. "Drink up, Mr. Zinfandel. You're gonna need it," he grins and I actually exhale for the first time in 6 days, or for weeks I guess is more accurate.

"Am I?" I growl at his smile which only makes him laugh at me.

"Yup. I've just been to see your Psycho, so now it's your turn."

"For what?" I ask already chugging straight from the bottle.

"To delve deep," Mack laughs like that's the funniest thing ever.

"To *delve* deep?"

"Yup. That's a Suzanne expression, and when she says it we both know there's going to be tears and anger and eventually revelations and then maybe even some growth and healing. So we're delving deep tonight, Z."

"There's nothing to talk about," I say with just enough tone to make him not shut the fuck up, but actually laugh at me instead. The fucker.

"Man up, Z. It's time," he says waiting for me to get on board.

Trying to ignore Mack, I'm drawn back to him waiting for me, and as soon as I look back and we make eye contact he begins.

"Let's start with the biggest issue at the moment for both of you, but I think with your sense of honor probably mostly for you."

"Which is what?"

"You broke 2 out of 3 rules you promised Suzanne," he says without the anger I thought he would have on her behalf.

"Yes, but the 3rd one isn't a rule. It's an absurd statement she made once that was so insane and baseless and really fucking mental, I agreed only so she wouldn't be afraid of me, or afraid of something that would absolutely *never* happen to her in this lifetime."

"To not rape her," Mack says as I nod.

"I mean, really? Don't rape my wife? I wouldn't hurt *any* woman like that ever. But Suzanne? Just the thought makes me nauseous, and repulsed, and pretty fucking angry that she even asked me that. How the fuck could she ask *me* that?"

"Because she's scared of all men. Not because she's scared of you."

"I'm a man, Mack, so it's kind of the same thing," I say with a huff of frustration.

"No, it isn't. She asked me the same thing, and I agreed as well. Suzanne loves me and trusts me one hundred percent," Mack says without sounding like he's gloating, but it still pisses me off. "She even trusts me with her body." When I sit forward he quickly continues. "*Meaning*, I can touch her hand and hug her without any initial fear or panic, Z. You *know* that's what I mean." And I do, but it still annoys me that they're that close sometimes. "Suzanne *knows* inside her that I would never hurt her, touch her inappropriately, or even rape her. She knows that, but she still asked me to promise I never would. Just like she asked you."

"And that didn't piss you off?"

"No, it didn't, because it wasn't about me. I'm a man, so she had to ask. But it wasn't about me at all, it was just about my gender."

"You didn't feel like a monster when she asked you that?" I ask remembering exactly how insulted and repulsed I felt when she asked me.

"No, I didn't, Z. Because again, it wasn't about me. Just like it isn't about you."

"*Really?* Well, it felt like it was about me when she cried in my arms and begged me to promise I'd never rape her. That sure as hell felt like it was *all* about me at the time," I exhale thinking of that night. "I hated how awful she made me feel. Like she didn't trust me or think I would keep her safe."

"I know you took it that way, but why don't you flip it around. Do you think she asks random men to promise her that? Do you think she would ask Marty, or even Glenn Rose who she kind of trusts? Would she ask your driver, or your staff, or anyone else she sees regularly to not rape her? Would she ask Dr. Phillips, even though they spend a lot of time together in his closed office not to rape her? No, she wouldn't. She asked us because she is afraid of all men, but not of you and me. So she threw it out there for both of us to confirm our promises so she was free to trust us completely."

"That didn't feel like trust, Mack."

"But does it now? Think about what I just said. Can you see how she gave you an opportunity to make a promise to her so she could move on with you? Do you see how by asking you, she was actually telling you she trusted you *wouldn't* hurt her?"

Okay, I see his angle now, and it does make me feel a little better, but wow, "That's some fucked up logic right there. She doesn't ask monsters not to hurt her, but she asks those she trusts so she can trust them?"

"Do you have sex together?"

"Of course," I turn back toward his gaze.

"'Of course' shouldn't be such a flippant answer, Z," Mack actually says somewhat angrily. "Do you think there is any other man on the planet Suzanne could have sex with?"

"There better not be," I growl until he smiles and nods.

"There isn't, you idiot," Mack laughs. "She can't even have a goddamn pap smear without losing her mind. She can't be touched medically, and she can't have anyone look at her vagina. When she was pregnant and medical appointments were mandatory, she had panic attacks beforehand and she cried the whole time they occurred. Both Kaylas would have to arrange their schedules so they could be with her during pelvic exams, and even with them holding her hand and talking to her the whole time she freaked out anyway."

"I didn't know about that because she kept me out of that part of her life," I admit sadly thinking of everything I missed with Thomas again.

"Has she been to a doctor for a physical, or a pap since you've been together in New York?"

"I don't know."

"She hasn't because she can't. Even after Thomas when a gynecological appointment was necessary she almost lost her mind. She was just shy of totally sedated and Kayla stayed in the room and talked about me actually," Mack smirks, "to distract her. But Suzanne just barely got through it."

"When was that? I was around then after Thomas. Why didn't I know? I would've been there for her."

"She couldn't have you there, Z. She's too messed up about her body, and she didn't want you to know someone was touching her *there* as she sees her vagina. She still feels disgusting when she thinks of her body in any sexual context whatsoever. *Except* with you," Mack adds heavily. Exhaling, Mack looks so sad again thinking of my Suzanne I don't know what to say to him.

"So when you say 'of course' about sex I want to punch you in the face for being so blasé about it because I don't think you to truly understand what a gift that is between you. Suzanne doesn't have the ability to deal with anything sexual. Period. She rarely even talks about it. But with you she not only talks, but she actively participates. She wants to be with you sexually. She *likes* being with you sexually. Do you understand now?"

"Yes," I exhale as another goddamn reality smacks me upside the head.

"That is the biggest trust Suzanne can give you. Right there, Z. She has sex with you and she not only likes it, but she wants it with you because she believes you're safe for her because she loves and *trusts* you. And also because for whatever reason she finds you attractive," he says like a smartass as we both burst out laughing.

Smiling, I'll admit, "I like knowing she finds me attractive. I want to be attractive to her. And I've always loved the way she looks at me when we're together. Almost like I was her whole world or something."

"You are," Mack nods but the air changes a little around us again.

Shaking my head as we stare at each other, I admit where we're at now. "I really don't think I am. I'm pretty sure Suzanne's world is one of darkness, which I'll never be a part of. She doesn't want me to be a part of her world, Mack. She told me."

"How?"

"In our room before she was taken away and in her letter," I exhale as the pain returns.

"Can I see these suicide letters I've heard about? I assume you still have

We are US...

them. Would you let me read them?"

"Of course," I say and stop myself when I stand. 'Of course' seems too casual an expression suddenly for anything Suzanne.

Walking to the bedroom, I realize that expression can't be used with Suzanne anymore. I know that now. I think I took things with us for granted just a little. I assumed sex with me was okay for her because it was between us, and we've always had a strong sexual connection. I never really understood how intense that connection would be for her though. And it changes things for me.

Remembering the tentative movements, or the fear she'd suddenly get didn't necessarily irritate me, but I didn't quite understand how she could still feel nervous with me. I thought because I told her I didn't care about the scars or her past she should just accept my words and move on. I was patient, but inside I was always waiting for her to just get naked with me and have sex like she wanted to, without the initial love and emotional softness I always gave her first to get her in the right mood.

I think I thought she would one day just be sexually open or maybe *real* with me, but now I realize that'll probably never happen. If she can't even have a physical without losing her shit, I don't know that she'll ever be sexually free, and knowing that is better for me then naively believing she would one day come around.

In all honesty, I don't mind the loving and emotional softness first. I actually like it because Suzanne looks at me with those eyes of hers and with her little smile and I feel like the big man around her. I like it when I've soothed her nerves and made her hungry for me. I like pleasing her and being pleased by her.

So I have a lifetime of telling my wife she's beautiful and sexy and awesome for me. It's the truth, whether she ever actually believes me or not.

Taking the letters from my makeshift sock drawer, I immediately see the difference between them as my hands start to shake again.

4 of the letters are crisp and barely touched because there was little point and I didn't care enough to reread them. Mack's letter is a little more used and there is a smudge on his name that couldn't be helped.

But it's my letter that screams the loudest. It's bent, and crinkled, and covered in tear stains actually. Like a fucking pansy, I held the goddamn letter all night Friday as I drank and cried and said goodbye to her.

I said goodbye because I can't keep living like this, and I said goodbye because I don't think she *will* keep living like this.

I didn't know what else to do, so I read and drank and read some more until I eventually passed out to wake the next morning disgusted with myself and the letter.

And then I put it in the drawer and I haven't looked at it since.

Returning back to the living room, Mack hasn't moved from his chair. He's waiting and I think I actually want him to finally understand where she's at, and where we're at together. I need Mack to understand so he either helps her love, or helps me let her go. Maybe I need him for both of us at this point.

"Here," I pass over all but mine as I sit on the couch and chug another gulp of scotch. I doubt I can do this sober, and quite frankly I don't want to.

When Mack reads the letter addressed to 'Mr. and Mrs. Beaumont' he actually laughs which surprises me.

"Well, that was abrupt and horrible," he laughs again shaking his head, before reading her grandfather's next. I'm not sure how he'll read them, maybe in the same order of importance I thought they were, but it doesn't really matter. Mack will simply read them and understand where she's at.

"Have you read all these?"

"Yes. Just once."

"Even mine?" He asks with a smirk.

"Yeah. Sorry," I shrug. "I needed to know how serious she was, and saying goodbye to you seemed really important."

"I understand," he nods before starting Chicago Kayla's letter with a grin. "Kayla would love this fabulous comment," he smiles, and I don't understand his reaction.

Mack is too calm, almost enjoying the letters or something. Okay, maybe not *enjoying* them, but he's not freaking out or pissed off or acting like a guy reading about a woman who is saying goodbye to the people she loves for the last time.

We are US...

Opening his Kayla's letter, Mack smiles, which just confuses me more. "Kayla would be totally pissed at how short her letter is," Mack says with a little laugh. "Oh, but she'd love the best friends and sister comment."

"Mack, why are you acting like this?" I finally blurt out as the confusion of his callousness makes me angrier by the second. "I thought you loved her?" I nearly yell.

"Just let me finish, okay?" He asks so calmly my anger grows stronger. I don't fucking understand what's happening here.

Watching Mack read his own letter, he smiles sometimes, and shakes his head at others. He even smirks once like this is the best thing he's ever read, and I don't fucking get it.

"I did nothing wrong. There's the guilt she always feels and doesn't want anyone else to feel." Still reading, he pauses for a second. "A good actress?" Mack laughs but before I can speak he adds, "Yeah, *okay*. If actresses were terrible at acting, maybe."

Watching Mack read his letter, I find I'm stunned seeing his expressions and smiles as he reads. But when I finally see his smile fade I know he's at the end.

"Of course you want some peace, Suzanne," he whispers to no one and I feel the pain of her truth rip through my chest again.

"I'm her greatest gift, Z, besides you. And I'm still her person," Mack smiles at me still sitting here like a stunned jackass.

"I don't understand your reaction at all. You don't even seem to care, Mack," I can't help accuse.

"Oh, I care, Z. Very much. But we're not through yet. I would like you to read your letter to me."

"I can't," I whisper.

"Yes, you can. Honor Suzanne's final letter and read it to me." Shaking my head, I put the letter on the table between us and say no again. "Why can't you?"

"Because I can't. It's..."

"Too painful? Yes, I understand that. But I want to watch you read her letter to you."

"No."

"No?"

"I'm not doing it. I don't know what fucking game you're playing at, but I'm not doing this with you. This isn't about me anymore. It's about her."

"It's always about Suzanne. Isn't it, Z?"

"Yes," I say before I can stop myself. Shit. I know what that sounded like, but I didn't mean it like that. "What I mean is, these letters are about *her* saying goodbye."

"Yes, they are. But they're also about Suzanne as usual. It's always about Suzanne and her drama, right? Suzanne's crazy, and Suzanne's shit as usual. Everything about the 2 of you is about Suzanne's shit all the time, isn't it? Tell me, Z. I know it is, and you know it is, so why not just admit it. She's not here and she can't hear you and she'll never know what you said, so just say it. It's always about Suzanne and *her* shit, right? Just say it!"

"Fine! Fuck yeah. It's always her fucking shit between us and around us killing us always. Fucking *always!*" I yell before stopping quickly on a gasp.

"Very good. Now pick up her letter and read it to me, Z. *Now,*" Mack demands again. And for some reason I can't understand anymore, I pick up her stupid bullshit letter and read out loud.

Dear Z,
I love you very, very much though I'm sure you don't believe me right now. But I do. Hopefully one day, you'll even believe me.
I won't say I'm doing this for you, because even though that is a small part of it, it's not the majority. Mostly, I'm doing this for me. When they say it's not you it's me, there are no truer words for us. This is all me this time. I've decided and I am making the choice I didn't have when I was young. I'm making the choice to stop everything like I wish I could have done before. This is ALL me, Z.
I'm just so tired all the time now, and I don't want to be tired around you anymore. I don't want to be sad and confused and crazy any more around you. It's not fair to you, and it's not the life you should have to live. You are way too good to be trapped in this life with me.

We are US...

    Shaking my head, I realize how much I hate it when she says that. She acts like I'm some asshole who thinks or acts like he's better than her. She talks about me being trapped like she trapped me. Like I actually *could* be trapped. No one can trap me. I'm too strong for that.
    Looking at Mack, I say with nothing short of irritation in my voice, "There she goes again, taking the decision away from me to be with her like she forced it somehow. Or like I'm too weak to make the decision to be with her on my own because she trapped me into it."
    Nodding, Mack motions for me to continue.

Z, I want you to know I love you more than I've ever known love could be, and way more than I thought was even possible for me. Waking with you each day gave me a reason to fight for my future, and sleeping beside you each night gave me a reason to fight the nightmares of my past. Being with you has been the greatest joy of my life, because you have been the greatest gift I've ever known. You are my gift, Z, and I will hold you forever - just not here in this life any longer.

    Scoffing, I can't even hold it in. The greatest gift? Uh huh. That's why she threw me away like I didn't matter.

So, again, it isn't you Z, it's all me. I'm too weak and too tired, and just too exhausted from pretending all the time. So I have to go now. I have to before I change you into someone else and eventually make you hate me, because I can't stand the thought of you ever hating me.

    "What are you thinking, Z?" Mack asks quietly as I pause.
    "Um, I'm thinking she's so fucked sometimes. She doesn't pretend. Well, I guess she does but she doesn't actually *fool* anyone. Like I don't know when she's going off the rails? Like I can't see the changes in her when things are getting bad? Really? A fucking stranger could look at her and see the shaking and her eyes wide with fear, and everything changing from her breathing to her voice without knowing anything about her. She might pretend, but she doesn't fool anyone. And as for

hating her, yeah, I think I'm already there, Mack," I say on a long exhale as he nods.
 "Can you finish? I'm expecting something about finding someone better to love soon. Am I right?" Mack asks with another goddamn smirk that I return. He really does know her so well, I'm almost jealous of it, even though I know deep down it's a good thing between them, not a romantic one.
 "Yes, I can finish. And as usual, you're right about her," I shake my head before picking the letter back up from my thighs.

Z, I want you to find someone else to love. Someone who is easy and good, and who is actually worthy of you. I want you to love her and marry her, and even have those beautiful babies I couldn't give you. I want you to find love that is easy and makes sense. I want so much for you, and I want it because I love you. Walking on eggshells around a crazy wife who can't give you what you deserve isn't the life you're supposed to live. So please go find her and love her and be happy with her. Give someone who is worthy of you your good, bad, ugly, and beautiful, and make her give you the same in return.

 "Just find someone else," I whisper shaking my head again. "She's so fucked, Mack. As if I could just forget everything we've been through and move on easily with someone else. Fuck, if I wanted easy I would've been married before her. Easy wasn't a problem to find, true love was," I whisper as my throat tightens.
 "Yes," Mack agrees quietly before I finish the last paragraph.

God, I love everything about you, Z. From your smiles and eyebrow wiggles, to your huge heart and your beautiful eyes. You are everything to me in every moment I've known you, always.
Please forgive me.
I love you.
Suzanne
xo

We are US...

Exhale. Jesus *Christ!* This is such bullshit.

"She loves everything about me in every moment she's known me. But she doesn't love me enough to live."

"Yes," Mack agrees again calmly as I try to silence the anger and hurt inside me.

"What are you thinking, Z?" Mack asks after a few minutes of quiet between us.

"Nothing. Everything. I don't know anymore. I love her and I hate her, and I want to be with her and I want to let her go. I'm scared she's going to kill herself, but I want her to be able to die finally if it's what she really wants and needs to finally have some peace in her life," I admit sadly choking up a little.

Wow, is that true? Do I actually want her to succeed finally? No, I don't.

"Is that how you really feel?"

"No. I just want her to feel good for once. So I think I thought her suicide would finally free her from all the shit torturing her. I think I was ready to let her die."

"And now?"

"Now, I really don't want her to die," I exhale for the hundredth time this evening. "But I'm not strong enough to keep her alive," I moan.

"Holy shit, Z... you're so goddamn dramatic sometimes," Mack says mocking me. "Do you want her to live?"

"Yes," I nod feeling nothing but sadness at the loss of her.

Suddenly standing, Mack smiles and says, "Okay, good. That's something for me to work with."

"Um... *What*?" Fuck! I sound like Suzanne suddenly with my confusion.

"You're an arrogant asshole, and Suzanne is fucked up, Z," Mack laughs at presumably my stunned expression. "She's depressed, you idiot. I told you a thousand times this would happen, and I've told her 2 thousand times this would happen. You both knew it but didn't understand that it was happening. She doesn't want to die. Well, she did, but now she doesn't want to. She wants to get better and she wants to *feel* better."

"You don't think she would have killed herself Tuesday night?" I ask again just stunned by his carefree demeanor.

"Oh, I absolutely think she would have if you haven't realized what was happening Tuesday night and stopped her." Wow. Okay. I was just kicked in the balls again.

"But it would have been the biggest sadness and regret of all of our lives. She is very, very depressed, Z. It's soul consuming, and very real for her. It's her worst nightmare thinking and feeling only awful negative. She can't see anything good, and she doesn't *feel* anything good. But it's the depression, not her actual life. And I think I explained it and got through to her earlier, and she wants to get better, Z. She wants to live," he says so intensely, I find the change in my reality again so strange and overwhelming I can't help the release of all the pressure I've felt for the last 6 days.

Choking out a cough cry, I bury my face in my hands and try to get a grip. What the hell is happening here? I have no fucking idea anymore.

When Mack squeezes my shoulder from beside the couch, I almost lean into him, or shrug him off. I don't know which one I need because I'm so messed up.

"Christ, I feel like shit," I mumble.

"I know. Ironically, the more insecure and depressed she became, the more insecure you felt. And now depression has settled into you as well."

"I'm not depressed. I'm just mentally exhausted."

"Call it whatever you want, but it's essentially the same thing. And you need help, Z. Do you hear me?"

"Yes," I mumble again looking up at his smiling face.

"Okay. Get some sleep, figure out what you want with and without Suzanne, and I'll call you tomorrow morning. Got it?"

"Okay."

"And stop being such an arrogant dickhead, Z. You aren't the reason she lives or dies. You're just here to love her as best as you can, while you can. Her failure to be happy doesn't make you a failure as a man, or as her husband, or as anything else. Remember that when the insecurity sneaks up on you," Mack again smiles before walking to the door.

"Thank you," I stare hard at Mack as he nods.

"No problem. But I'm charging double time and a half with you two cuz you're both fucked!" He laughs as I do before walking out the door.

Being called an arrogant dickhead is so funny to me suddenly, like I didn't know that about myself already. Still. Twice in one night is a little much from Mack.

We are US...

Standing to go to bed, I don't even care that its 9:30. I'm just wasted from all this shit, but at least now I know Suzanne wants to live. And I want her to live. I just hope that's enough for Mack to work with.

CHAPTER 15
SUZANNE

"How are you this morning?" Mack asks walking right into my room- a room very similar to my first room in New York a few years ago. A room in his ward, and a room I'm dying to get out of.

"I'm fine. But I need to get out of here, Mack. Please?" I whine again.

Taking a chair to the little table of my past it seems, Mack smiles but shakes his head at me as he hands me a bagel. Shit.

"Fine? Come on, we've talked about that answer," he says just short of irritated with me again and I know why. I'm heard this lecture so many times, I know it verbatim at this point.

'Fine explains nothing. Fine is as uninspired as I'm good. Fine doesn't express feelings or emotions, or anything within us. Fine is a catch-all flippant answer that gets us nowhere.'

Waiting each other out, I know Mack's going to win because he always does. Mack has the patience of I don't know, I want to say a Saint but I think even Saints had limits.

Opening his coffee lid with a little snap, Mack takes a long gulp of the steaming liquid while relaxing and settling in. Oh crap. I think this is going to be *the* morning. Shit! And I already screwed it up with a 'fine'.

Smiling at me as he starts unwrapping his bagel Mack asks, "How are you this morning, Suzanne?" Ummm... "And if you say what you think I want to hear to get out of here, you won't. I know your lies, white and otherwise, and I know when you're simply trying to appease me. Therefore, I suggest you start with honesty this morning," he smirks to the totally offended face I'm sure I'm sporting.

"I don't lie, Mack."

"Yes, you do, Suzanne. Not bad lies, like the horrible kind that serve no purpose and have no merit. Not the kind people tell without a conscience, or just because they simply like to lie. But you know as well as I do you lie, or rather, you alter the truth to 1) make others happy, and 2) to make yourself look like you *feel* better to others. Both of which could be seen as somewhat harmless for a normal person, though not for you. Meaning, if you tell a white lie to not hurt someone's feelings most people think that doesn't count. But when *you* lie and say you feel good inside when you don't at all, you're not helping anyone. You're hurting not only yourself but those of us who *are* trying to help you. So, yes, Suzanne. You lie."

"Oh. I..." I've got nothing again. I hate when he does this to me.

"It's frustrating being called out on your shit, isn't it?" He grins. "It's probably as frustrating as when I'm trying to help you, but you lie to me instead of being honest with me so I can help you," Mack says again without anger as he squeezes my hand.

Exhaling, I feel like we've done this so many times over the years. Too many times actually, and it always comes back to the same thing. I get screwed up, Mack tries to help me, my life gets worse, Mack still tries to help me, then I lose it totally and Mack has to put me back together again.

Grasping for anything to talk about except all the obvious I'm avoiding, I beg, "I need some music in here."

"Not yet. You use music to soothe *and* to torture yourself," Mack says almost sadly. "I really don't think you're ready for music, Suzanne."

What?

"No, I don't. I just want to listen to some music because I'm bored and I'm going crazy here in all the silence," I actually whine again.

"Can I tell you something?" Mack asks like I would actually ever say no to him. Squeezing my hand again, Mack looks at me so sweetly, I want to just hug him. A huge almost crawl in his lap Mack hug. But instead I sit here anxiously waiting for whatever it is he has to say to me.

"Suzanne, you have a high audio perception and emotional reaction to audio stimuli. Therefore music, and sometimes even poetry draw you in to yourself deeper. I've watched it, and Z has spoken about it to me."

"He has?" I whisper trying to think of how I feel about music.

"Yes, he has. For example, there was a time when you and Z were driving to the airport for Chicago not too long ago and you were both talking and apparently everything was good and comfortable between you. Z describes the atmosphere in his truck as light and even flirty, but then some song began and before he could understand why you weren't answering a question of his he looked over and you had paled right out, shaking in your seat with your hands folded tightly in your lap, with tears streaming down your face. Z described trying to talk to you, and even trying to take your hands but you were almost catatonic as you sat there rigid and unaware of Z or even your surroundings. Z said he pulled over whispering your name but you were lost to him before he knew what had happened. And then you just snapped out of it, and Z says it was at that moment that he realized the DJ was talking and the song had ended, and you were back to normal totally unaware of what had just happened to you. Do you remember that day?"

"Yes," I moan. I remember Z explaining why I was crying and what had happened when I became aware of my surroundings again. I remember trying to understand what set me off and I remember being unable to explain anything to Z. He wasn't mad about it, but I know the fact that I couldn't explain what had happened frustrated him. "Z tried to figure it out when I couldn't."

"How?"

"He, ah, called the radio station while we sat on the side of the road to find out what the song was."

"What song was it?" Mack asks almost breathless himself.

"'I'm in here' by Sia," I suddenly cry. "It's such a good song, Mack, and it's like me, and I swear she wrote it for me, though that's impossible because she doesn't know me, or care about me, or like know anything about me. But that song is *me*, Mack. Totally," I cry again to Mack's silence.

Hearing Sia sing her song in my head I am me again. I'm lost and alone Suzanne, begging anyone to love her- anyone to *help* her. I am HER again and I hate it. I hate feeling this alone and not understanding why it's always this way, or why I feel this way, or just how I'm supposed to not feel this way all the time.

"I'm in here... Can anybody see me? Can anybody help?" Oh god...

"Suzanne...?" Mack calls to me gently to get me out of my head.

Suddenly back in my room with Mack I need to know. "Do you ever get tired of me?" I ask just above a whisper. I can't even look at him because I fear his answer so much. If he actually is sick of me I don't know what I'll do. There isn't anything I *can* do. "There is no one but Mack to help me," I moan out loud before catching myself.

"Suzanne...?" Mack whispers again before taking my hand as I lean my head on the table. Suddenly feeling everything horrible inside me, I can't even pretend I'm okay right now.

We are US...

"I'm very sad, Mack," I whisper cry.

Feeling Mack stroke my hair away from my face, I find myself still. I don't pull away because I don't have the energy, and really, what's the point? It's not like Mack hasn't seen my hideous face for years now, and he never seems to care.

Leaning into his hand, I actually feel comfort for the first time in forever. I feel the warmth of his hand, and I feel the depth of his caring for me.

"Tell me," he breathes quietly leaning into my side.

"Ummm... I feel like shit, Mack. Like everywhere and everything, and just all of me. My head is confused, and my heart hurts all the time, and even my body hurts. I can't explain it, but it's like there's a physical part to this that I've never had before. I find my arms and legs hurt, and even when I do try to sleep, all of me is sore or heavy or something which annoys me until I can't sleep. And I just feel terrible."

"And?"

"Ah, and I think I'm lonely," I cry wiping a tear that slides across the bridge of my nose. "I want to go home, but I don't want to go home to nothing. And I know there's nothing there anymore, and I don't want to feel that nothing in my home. But I hate this place, too. So I feel kind of trapped, even without the hold against me."

"What else, Suzanne?"

"I miss my life, but I also hate it. So I don't know what I want or what to do anymore," I admit as a sob breaks free from my chest.

Turning my face away from Mack, I still love the cool of the table against my cheek, maybe even more than I did before.

I know it's impossible, but I've explained to every doctor and plastic surgeon over the past few years that my cheek always feels hot, like I'm still being burned. Almost like phantom limb pain after an amputation, I swear my cheek feels hot inside and to the touch, though I never let anyone see what I mean by touching my face. Except for Z. Sometimes.

"Can you look at me?"

Turning back to Mack I realize I still love the cold on my skin. Just like in my parents' house, and in my house with Marcus. "I still love the feel of cold on my skin to cool the pain."

"Yes, but it's not the same pain as when you were abused, is it?"

"No. But I still like it."

"That's a memory of what you needed to aid you physically Suzanne, mixed up with the reality you don't have now. You aren't being abused, and your body and face aren't being hurt right now, but your mind likes to think the cool will ease some of the pain inside you. But it's not the same thing. The pain you have now is emotional, not physical. Though often it feels the same."

"It always feels the same."

"Do you still lie on the cool tiles in your home?"

"Yes. Whenever I feel all gross and Z isn't home, I lie down on the cold floor in his gym. Actually, that's the only time I enter the gym," I smirk a little laugh as Mack does.

Leaning his own face on the table mere inches from my face, Mack smiles at me. "It does actually feel good," he admits as I nod. "I didn't realize before how the cool feels on your skin. I might have to give it a try sometime."

"You don't have to, Mack. You're normal," I grin back. "Well, for a Shrink."

We must look so weird. Me crying on the table with my face pressed against it, and Mack's huge body pushing his chair back so he can lie his face on the table beside me. If anyone entered my room they'd think we were a murder-suicide, or just really strange or something. Not that Mack would care. He never cares how he shrinks people, as long as he's successful.

"You're a really good doctor, Mack," I breathe in the cool tabletop silence between us.

"Thank you, Suzanne. You're a really good test of my skills," he says so seriously I finally just laugh with him.

"I guess I'm not ready to leave yet, am I?"

"You tell me. Do you think you're ready to leave yet?"

"No..." I admit on a dramatic exhale.

God, I hate this. I hate my weakness, and I hate that it's never easy with me. I wish so much I was as strong as everyone else is. I wish I could just get up and get on with it. I wish I was like normal women. Actually, I just wish I was a little more normal. Just a little normal would help I think. Just enough normal so I could function without all this drama and upset all the time.

"I have to go. Our time is up, but I'll check in this afternoon, okay?"

"Okay," I agree finally raising my head from the table as Mack does.

"Do you want to ask me anything?"

We are US...

Shaking my head, I can't ask it. "No. If he's fine I'll feel horrible, and if he's not fine I'll feel worse."

"I understand. What are you doing this morning?" Mack asks finally standing with his untouched bagel, and his nearly full coffee.

Laughing, I burst out, "Knitting. 101," as he laughs with me.

"Well, you always did say you'd end up knitting in a padded cell, so..." he leaves the statement hanging in the air as he sweeps his hand out around us in my UNpadded cell. "Close enough?"

"Yup. It's official. I've become the old crazy knitting lady, with a broken wrist wrapping the wool around the tips of my fingers that can only wiggle."

"You're not old," he says deadpan until we both laugh again. Ha! I'm just the crazy knitting lady now. Wow, this sucks.

"I'll be back at 2. And I'd like you to think of the biggest issue hurting you emotionally right now. Be it your past or your current situation. I want you to really think about what you think is the most prevalent issue you're facing. The issue preventing you from getting out of your depression. Can you do that for me?"

"Yes, of course."

"Also, I have a request," he asks leaning against the door to leave me again for a few hours. A few long, lonely hours.

"Anything."

"Kayla would like to see you. She's been climbing the walls, and she really wants to see you. She even promises not to give you shit for all this," Mack smirks but I'm already shaking my head no.

"I'm not ready. But please tell her it's not her at all. I just don't know what to say or do with her, and I'm scared she's secretly, or maybe not so secretly angry with me. And I'm not ready to feel insecure with her yet because she's important to me." I breathe desperately hoping Mack understands.

"You're important too, Suzanne. But Kayla understands. She just misses you and wants to be here for you right now. But I'll let her know you're not ready yet."

"Thank you."

"But I would get ready soon. Kayla doesn't have much will power where rules are concerned," he laughs again at his major understatement.

Huh. If a rule is set, Kayla is exactly the person to question why, what's

the point, and how exactly she can work around the rule.
 "Mack, I feel scared of everything right now."
 "Of course you do. Everything is in a scary unknown place right now," Mack says seriously. And it helps that he acknowledges what I'm feeling. "See you at 2:00," he gives a final smile before shutting my door.

 Finally standing to throw my uneaten bagel out, I need to freshen up before my class.
 Reapplying my mascara and foundation, I'll admit I kind of like knitting though I'd stab myself in the chest with a knitting needle before ever actually admitting that to anyone else, I giggle.

We are US...

CHAPTER 16
Z

Parking at Mercy is a total pain in the ass. The lot closest to the main entrance is always full which means I have to park miles away from the doors to the individual wards. Not that I give a shit about walking miles, but it's annoying for me to always be late for everything when it's out of my control. Or maybe I'm just pissed again because *everything* is out of my control. Uh, yeah.

This last month has been so fucking annoying, I've become the prick Suzanne used to tease me about being. I can't stand talking to anyone, and I hate going into work. My office is just dark and depressing so I hate being there, but my hotel room is worse, so I need to get the fuck out of there every day which leaves my dark, depressing office as the only place I can go each day.

At this point, I swear if they had the balls, my office staff would either tell me to fuck off, or they'd tell me to take a vacation. Not that I've actually been a prick to anyone, I just haven't been myself. Or funny. Or happy. And I know my upset and frustration is showing to everyone who has the misfortune of being around me these days.

I haven't really done or said anything prick-like though, I've just been the anti-Z. Well, except for that annoying kid in graphics who I told to shut the hell up when he wouldn't stop singing some goddamn Miley Cyrus song. But come on, anyone would have told him to shut the hell up whether their life was falling apart or not.

Walking into the ugly grey, yellow interior of Mercy, I realize how much I resent this. I mean really, an appointment twice a week for a month now? I think Mack's taking this thing a little too far with me. I know he said he'd help Suzanne, but I didn't think he'd schedule appointments with me twice a week as well. I figured I'd talk to him and find out how she was doing and what was going on with her. But this? This is just stupid.

We are US...

Sitting in the even uglier waiting room of Mack's ward, I almost laugh at the interior. It's so depressing to look at, I don't know how anyone who needs to talk to a Psychiatrist could get better when all they see is this ugliness around them. Get a fucking plant, even a fake one, or some decent art on the walls, or something. Hey, I know! Switch out the grey plastic chairs for some color to liven the place up a little.

Scowling at the chairs, I just catch myself as a young woman looks at me and quickly turns her head away and down like I scared her, or like she's freaked about something. I don't know what's wrong with her, but I know that look all too well. That's the 'please don't be mad at me and hurt me' Suzanne look I dread.

Fuck! I can't stand myself anymore. I can only imagine what everyone else is feeling toward me.

"Z?" Mack smiles stepping into the waiting area.

Standing to follow, I just barely hold in my irritation and resentment toward Mack. I don't give a shit who knows I'm here, but does he actually have to announce my name like I'm some normal patient of his.

Sitting in front of his desk while he shuffles around paperwork and types something quickly on his computer, I feel pissed waiting again.

"I still don't understand why I have to come here. We could do this at my hotel. Or even at your place. Christ, we could go have a drink and talk."

Smirking at me, Mack stops everything to just stare at me for a minute before speaking. "Yeah, because most Psychiatrists sit in a bar with their patients and have a drink over their issues. That's what bartenders are for, Z. Not Shrinks."

"But I'm not your patient."

"Really? Do we have set appointments and talk to each other for an hour? Do you pay me?"

"Yeah, but that's a monetary courtesy for the time you're spending with Suzanne."

"Uh huh. A courtesy?" He scoffs. "News flash, Z. You ARE my patient, as is Suzanne. And that's why you're here, and why we talk in my office. We have to keep this as emotionally detached as possible. Well, I have to. I've known you for too long, and way too well to be professional with you outside of this room. It's hard enough for me not talking like your buddy, or not telling you when you're a fuckhead, instead of being doctorly with you while we figure all your shit out. Got it?"

"A *fuckhead*? Yeah, that's not all that professional or *doctorly*, Dr. MacDonald," I burst out laughing as Mack does.

"So what's been going on? How's work?" Mack asks leaning back in his chair as I get comfortable as well.

"It's shit. I hate being there, and I know the staff hates me being there right now."

"Why? You love your job."

"I do love it, but it's just not the same. Everything and every*one* irritates me now, and I'm having a hard time hiding it. I even cancelled going to a charity golf tournament the other day."

"Why?"

"I wasn't in the mood," I huff.

"Really? Well, what are you in the mood for?"

"Nothing. I don't know. Nothing, I guess. I just didn't feel like golfing, and I couldn't stop thinking about Suzanne that morning."

"Ahhhh... I see. Why Suzanne that morning in particular?"

"You know why."

"Because Suzanne thinks golf is stupid?" Mack laughs at my scowl. "Or because she associates golf with the horrific memories of the country club?"

Thinking about her eyes suddenly, I imagine telling her I'm golfing, and the sad look she'd get. "I don't know. Both I guess. It's just different now.

"You used to love golfing," he says as I nod.

"I did."

"But now you don't like golfing because Suzanne hates golf?"

"No. Yes," I shake my head. "No... more like because she hates it and associates it with the abuse she suffered I don't want to like golf anymore. I don't bring it up and I rarely play, and even when I do I don't tell her about it so she won't get upset." Oh, shit. That's kind of a lie.

"You hide it from Suzanne?" Mack presses.

"Yeah," I exhale. "But I didn't lie, I just didn't tell her." When Mack raises an eyebrow I quickly amend my statement. "Okay, I guess it's the same thing. But I only did it a few times and I felt so guilty *not* telling her about it, I didn't really enjoy playing until I just stopped. So, I don't play at all anymore."

We are US...

"Do you hide anything else from Suzanne?" Mack asks leaning across his desk closer to me.

"No." I answer way to angrily tipping Mack off immediately. He knows when I'm lying, and I couldn't have made that more obvious if I actually tried. Fuck me... here we go.

"What else do you hide from Suzanne?"

"Nothing."

"Z, talk to me. For this to work, you have to talk to me and trust me. Both you and Suzanne agreed I could share the basics- how you're doing, what you're doing, etc. But not our actual conversations or revelations. So I won't repeat anything said within these walls."

"There's nothing, Mack. Golf was the only thing I hid from Suzanne."

"And also your quick monthly day trips to Chicago to visit Thomas," Mack says barely above a whisper, but the result was the same as if he'd yelled it in my face. My balls just lodged in my throat with my breath.

"You know?"

"Yes."

"Who else knows?"

"All of us actually."

"*How?*" I croak. I always covered my ass with a meeting that 'couldn't be interrupted', or with a quick trip to the vineyards upstate. I always had a perfect excuse for Suzanne not being able to reach me during the flight.

"Thomas's grave flowers from his daddy. And Kayla Lefferts actually saw you once."

"What? *When?* Why was she there?" What the fuck?

"Well, she visits Thomas once in a while."

"*Why?*" What the actual fuck? "Why would she?" I ask sounding sad and confused. I can actually hear my own voice and it doesn't sound like my real voice at all.

"From what she told me Kayla felt somewhat responsible for visiting him because she was the only one left in Chicago with him," Mack says softly but it doesn't matter. My heart is breaking even as I sit here staring at Mack like what he said is the most shocking thing ever, which it kind of is. Kayla doesn't want or even like children she's told everyone often.

"She visited my son?" I whisper choke the tears back as best as I can.

"Yes. I don't know how often, and the only reason I know is because she called me to tell me she saw you at his gravesite in the rain looking very sad. She called to let me know you were sitting on the grass against his tombstone without an umbrella getting soaked, and she thought you maybe needed to talk to someone about how you were feeling. And basically she knew not to tell Suzanne, so she told me instead, in case you needed to talk about it. But you never did."

"Why didn't you say anything?" I ask again barely above a whisper.

"Because it's not my place to say anything. I may be your best friend, and now your therapist, but if you didn't want to discuss visiting your son with me, it's not my place to bring it up. That's between you and Thomas, and indirectly Suzanne as well."

"She knows?" I gasp shocked. "She never said anything about it, or even hinted she knew."

"Yes, she knows. And she didn't say anything because you didn't. She was respecting your privacy as well."

"Did Kayla tell her?"

"No. I did actually."

"Why? You just said it wasn't your place to talk about it."

"She thought you were cheating on her." What? There goes my air again. *Christ!* My head is spinning. "And though I may have overstepped, it was as your friend not as a therapist at the time."

"Why did she think that? When she couldn't reach me?"

"That and the fact that it was usually the same day every month, which naturally meant you were having a *torrid* love affair on a set date," Mack smirks at a typical Suzanne expression.

"Was she mad?"

"Not at all. She was sad for you. She actually cried her eyes out thinking of how hard it was for you being away from your son. She wanted to figure out a way to bring you two back together. She even discussed maybe moving back to Chicago, or somehow bringing Thomas here for you."

"She cried?"

"Z, she's not a monster. She-"

"I *KNOW* that," I snap. "That wasn't what I meant."

"She cried for your heartache, and for Thomas."

"Because she feels something for him?" I ask already knowing the answer I'm going to get. I don't even need to see Mack's face to know what he's going to say.

We are US...

"No. Not as her own loss, but as yours, certainly. It absolutely breaks her heart that you suffered- suffer over Thomas."

"But she still feels nothing for our son?"

"Not like you do, no."

Before I can stop myself, the ever present word bursts from my mouth, "*Why?*"

"Because she can't feel him, Z. Not like you do, or always will."

"I know that, but *why* didn't she love him?"

Exhaling, Mack seems to have been waiting to have this talk with me because we never have before. We've skated around the issue, and talked briefly about Thomas and Suzanne, but we've never really talked about Thomas and the pregnancy, and Suzanne's lack of feelings toward it all. But I think I need to know now.

"I think I'm finally ready to hear the answer, Mack. I need to know why she feels the way she does, or rather *doesn't* feel love for Thomas," I croak again from my upset and nervous tension waiting for the explanation I don't really want to hear but finally should.

"From a physiological standpoint there are many reasons- some easy, and some very complex. But I know that isn't what you want to hear. So I'll tell you the long and the short of it in very basic terms if you really want to understand."

"I do," I nod because I really do want to understand Suzanne's reaction to Thomas, even knowing this will probably be very painful for me.

"Well, essentially Suzanne felt raped by you when you forced her to carry a baby she didn't want."

"*What?*" I almost throw up from the term rape and Suzanne in the same sentence regarding me.

"Z, she wasn't ready to have a child, I think we can all agree on that." When I nod he continues. "And emotionally she had just woken from a horrific accident scarred physically and psychologically damaged. She was confused after the memory loss and gain, and then she suddenly found herself not only expecting a child, but expected to *want* to carry the child."

"But why would she feel raped?" I barely say the word out loud.

"Well, something was done to her body-"

"With consent!" I yell at Mack because he has to know I would never hurt her like that.

"Yes, the sex was consensual, Z, but the pregnancy wasn't."

"But it was an accident."

"For you. For her it was a violation against her body that she didn't choose again. Someone, *you*, got her pregnant against her will, and then you forced her to carry the baby she didn't want. Basically, in her mind you forced something on her body like they did, and you made her keep it when she wanted to make it go away."

"But..." Barely breathing, I don't even know how to defend myself.

"You wanted the answer, Z. And that's the answer. Add in the fact that she has next to no self-worth, she thinks she's a horrible person, and therefore was going to be an even worse mother to a baby she didn't even want but was forced to have, and you have a recipe for an emotional disaster."

"But what could I do? Let her kill my son?"

"Of course not. You were in a no win situation. Either allow an abortion and spend your life hating her, or force her to carry your baby and potentially cause her to hate *you* forever. Z, that was one of the hardest decisions I've ever had to witness in my life. So please, don't *ever* think there is a judgment being made against you for any of it. Suzanne doesn't even resent you for that now. When she's strong, she knows exactly how hard a decision that was for you, and how awful she made your life then. She still can't forgive herself for anything that happened between you, Thomas, and even herself."

"What can't she forgive?"

"Killing him," Mack says simply as the air explodes from my chest.

Gasping, I feel like I did the night she decided to die. Struggling for breath, my hands start shaking immediately as I look at Mack a little panicked.

"Z, breathe slowly."

"Fuck off! How could you say that? She didn't kill him!" I yell trying to breathe through the anger and upset raging through my body. "She didn't *kill* him."

"She thinks she did."

"She didn't. Everyone knows that."

"Except Suzanne," Mack says gently, and I see everything a little clearer suddenly.

"All the tests said it was just one of those rare things that happens to like one in ninety thousand or something. It wasn't anything she did."

"I agree. Suzanne *doesn't* agree with us though. Because of her shit

life, and her shit thinking patterns she believes she somehow killed him. She didn't want him, and she hated having to carry him and then he died. Therefore to her she killed *your* baby. Did you know she paid an exorbitant amount of money to have every single genetics test available?"
 "Um, no."
 "Well, she did. She almost passed out from all the fingertip blood samples she had to take and send away, but she did it. In her mind she can't believe you still actually want to be with her when she's a murderer, and because you being with her makes no sense to her whatsoever she wanted to find the reason she killed Thomas. She was actually looking for one single reason, or a genetic marker, or just *something* so she could tell you how she killed him," Mack exhales shaking his head, even as I shake my own head to clear it.
 "Why does she want me to think she's a murderer?"
 "So you won't love her anymore."
 Oh. Holy *fuck!* That wasn't what I expected to hear. And actually it pisses me off as usual.
 "Let me guess. Because me loving her doesn't make sense to anyone, least of all Suzanne?"
 "You got it," Mack agrees without sounding happy about it in the least.

After another long silence while I think of all the ways I've told her I love her, I realize once again she'll never believe me or understand my feelings toward her.
 "But she still doesn't actually love him."
 "I don't think so. Not like you do. She loves him as your son. A son you love, which makes her love him for *you*, but not for herself," Mack finishes looking so pained for her I don't know what to say to him.
 Mumbling, I barely hear my own voice so I don't think Mack hears what I'm saying. "I don't think... Can she ever love?"
 Wow. The was way too heavy a question, and yet one I'm struggling with every day that we're apart.
 Looking at Mack who seems to be waiting for eye contact, he nods and says sadly, "Yes, she can love. She loves *you*."
 "But it's not enough," I whisper again knowing it's the truth between us.
 Leaning forward again, Mack asks, "Not enough for who?"
 "Both of us, I think. I love her but she doesn't believe me. And she says

she loves me, but I don't believe she actually can love. Oh, fuck..." I moan as reality smacks me in the face again. "I don't think we're going to work, Mack," I admit as I feel everything turn dark inside me again.

"Z, just take a deep breath and reel it in a little. It's too soon to be over, and it's not soon enough to have all the answers. Okay?"

"Uh huh," I nod completely numb. "I have to go, Mack. I'm fucked right now," I moan already standing for the door.

"Z! I want you to think of all the ways you lie to Suzanne, for good reasons and for bad. I want you to really think about what you do to make everything okay for her, even if it's not okay for you. Can you do that for me? *Will* you do that?"

"Sure." Walking out the door I don't even notice the ugly waiting room with my retreat.

Christ! All the ways I lie to her to make things better clearly didn't work. She's still fucked in the head, and now she's made me fucked too.

Nothing I did worked. I wasn't enough, and Suzanne needs more than I can give. And though there's nothing left for me to give her it still wasn't enough.

Shaking, I walk the miles to my truck in a trance and leave Mercy for the sudden comfort I hope to find in my awful hotel suite.

We are US...

CHAPTER 17
SUZANNE & Z

Almost skipping I keep laughing at what a loser I am. Honestly. But I don't even care. I made it and I love it, and I can't wait to give it to Kayla for Christmas.

Knocking on Mack's door, I wait not so patiently for him until he calls out, 'who is it?'

"It's me! And I'm coming in!" I laugh throwing the door open grinning.

When I see Mack stand from behind his desk I hide my Kayla gift until smiling I look and see Z standing to the side of Mack's desk as well.

Oh *Shit*.

Gasping my shock, I can't do anything but look down. I haven't seen Z in 7 weeks and I feel everything for him instantly, and nothing at all.

I don't know what to do. And I don't know what to feel. And I don't know-

"Hi, Suzanne," he says in his dark chocolate voice as I melt in place. I almost forgot his voice though I didn't at all because I hear his voice in my dreams all the time.

"Hi. Sorry. I'll, um, go."

"Suzanne, Z was just leaving, and you're an hour early," Mack says more like only a statement than an angry accusation.

"Sorry." Spinning on the spot, I attempt to rip the door open until Z's hand lands on my cast freezing me in place.

"Stay, love." *Love?* "I was just leaving," he says quietly stepping closer to my side to get to the door.

"I'm sorry," I moan and I don't know what I mean anymore.

Shit. Mack would ask 'what are you sorry for?' And I'd have to tell him the reason I think I'm sorry. But this time, like this, I have so many sorry's inside me I can't tell what any of them are specifically.

"Why are you here, Suzanne?" Mack again asks gently and I want to scream. My chest is killing me and my mind is blank, and I can actually smell Z. But for real this time. "Suzanne?"

"Ah, I made your Kayla a gift," I whisper suddenly embarrassed.

Scrunching up the folded scarf in my hands, I don't want to show him anymore. I don't want Z to know I'm officially the crazy knitting lady, and I don't want him to see me excited *about* being the crazy knitting lady.

"What did you make?" Z asks quietly beside me and all I can do is shake my head. "Ah, come on... Tell me what it is," he asks with his smile-voice and I almost weep from the sound of it.

Still looking towards the door, I don't make eye contact but I at least raise my head a little. "I made Kayla a scarf," I admit totally humiliated.

"Did you? Can I see it?" Z asks like he's afraid I won't show him. He sounds nervous, or like I could actually deny him anything. But I don't want to deny him anything as simple as this, considering all the life I have already denied him by being with him.

Turning toward Z, I don't look at his face, but I hold up the stupid purple and black scarf for Kayla as he takes it from me gently and unfolds it to inspect my work.

"Is this your first attempt?"

"Um, no. I made you one first, but it wasn't quite as good, and it had a few holes in it, and it was really misshapen," I again admit looking at the wall behind him because I feel like an idiot suddenly.

"You knit me a scarf?"

"Yes. But it wasn't as good as this one," I mumble blushing.

"Well, thank you."

Looking up because of his sweet voice, I notice the scarf hanging in front of him and finally see what I made. Like totally see it without the giddy blinders I was clearly wearing when I made it.

Oh, crap. There are tons of holes in it, and it looks skinnier on one side and the color change doesn't blend right near the top against the edge like it should. It looks kind of like a stupid joke gift actually.

Looking up at Z quickly, his eyes are so shiny I can tell he's trying not to laugh, desperately holding it in, and that look of Z's pretty much does me in.

Bursting out laughing, I grab the scarf from him and hold it up to see right through the holes to Mack, for Christ's sake.

"Shit!" I howl with laughter as Z finally barks a quick laugh. "I thought it was so good this time. *Way* better than yours."

"It doesn't look that bad," Z tries. But he's full of shit, and we both know it.

"God dammit. I'm not even a *good* crazy knitting lady," I giggle again.

Okay, this sucks. I need to get out of here, and I need to burn this pathetic attempt at a scarf. Oh, crap! I'm not allowed any flammables I suddenly remember which sets me off laughing again.

"I'm going to go. Sorry I interrupted you. Please don't tell Kayla about the scarf I'll *never* give her, okay?" I ask grinning at a remarkably quiet Mack.

"Can I have *my* scarf?" Z asks barely above a whisper but I shake my head immediately.

"Not a chance. If I thought this one was great, I'm sure you can imagine what yours actually looks like," I laugh again.

"I don't care, Suzanne. I'd love it, because it's from you," Z says so seriously suddenly the air in the room changes from my embarrassed stupid, to sad and desperate in a millisecond.

"I can't. It's shitty, and I want you to have a perfect one."

"I don't care about perfect, Suzanne. I never have," he whispers as I nod.

"I know. And that's the problem," I admit to our collective silence. "I have to go," I almost plead as I walk out just shy of a run with my stupid holey scarf and my sad desperation on the surface of my face.

"I'll see you in an hour, Suzanne," Mack calls out behind me but I can't acknowledge him. I need to get the hell away from Z.

It would be so easy to just beg Z to love me anyway. Even though I'm not perfect and he doesn't care about perfect, but I can't. I won't do it to him anymore. I'll never again beg him for anything, because Z can't say no to me even though he should, and deep down probably wishes he could. I'm not going to ask, so he doesn't feel obligated to give in to me and the life he shouldn't live *with* me.

Pausing in the hallway a few corridors from my room, I breathe out my disappointed want and upset. I want him so badly, but I'll never again ask him to love me. I'll never again beg him for more. And I'll never again hope for more.

I am however going to start the proceedings for a divorce.

ႶႶႶႶႶ

"She looks terrible, Mack," I admit painfully. "How much weight has she lost?"

"I don't know. Not that much, Z. Not enough to harm her."

Falling into the chair with a huff, I beg, "Are you sure? Her face looked so gaunt and pale, and just too skinny."

I think I was almost more shocked by Suzanne's appearance than by the fact that I was actually seeing her for the first time in forever. Okay, not true. I couldn't believe I was actually seeing her, and after the initial shock we seemed almost normal together, or like there hadn't been nearly 7 weeks missing between us.

"Yes, I'm sure," Mack says again breaking me away from my thoughts. "Her physical health is fine, Z. And she actually feels better about herself now that she's lost a little weight," Mack says like a fucking idiot.

"Well, she shouldn't feel good about it."

"Why's that?" Mack asks too calmly for the anger I'm suddenly feeling.

"Because she isn't meant to be that skinny."

"Why's that?"

"Because it just not her. She's supposed to be curvy and soft."

"According to whom?"

"Me!" I yell then stop the second I realize what a dick I sound like. "Shit..."

I didn't realize I felt that way. I always thought I was too good for those kind of thoughts about women. I thought I loved them all shapes and sizes, but I suddenly realize I definitely have a preference. Suzanne.

I like big breasts to fondle, and a nice ass to squeeze, and I even like curvy hips to hold. I like a woman shaped like a woman should be... according to *me* apparently.

"Ah, next session?" I bark another quick laugh.

"Yup," Mack says with humor. "There's that arrogant dickhead I mentioned."

"Too often," I grin and shake my own head before asking, "Is it really so bad to like my wife curvy?"

"Not at all. You like what you like in a woman's appearance. It's only a problem when you tell her to look a certain way, or expect her to stay a certain way *because* you like it."

Nodding, I understand. "I would never tell Suzanne what to do with her own body."

"That's good, because she has severe body issues, Z. And if she thought you didn't like something about her body she'd spiral downward again, just from the rejection or thoughts of rejection from you alone."

"I could never reject her," I whisper sadly. "I miss her," I huff before shaking my head again.

I always sound like a fucking pussy now with Mack. I can hide it at work, and even around Marty, but there's something about Mack that just makes me spew up all the pussy inside me.

"And I sound like a pussy all the time."

"And an arrogant dickhead," Mack adds again for the hundredth time as I nod my head. "Z, you don't sound like a pussy. You sound like a man who loves a woman, is confused by a woman and doesn't know how to understand the woman. You're just a man, Z. And you need to start realizing that."

"I know I'm a man, Mack," I snap irritated.

Laughing, Mack shakes his head at me again. "Not like that, Z. We both know you're a man, you idiot. What I mean is, you're a man in a marriage who is struggling. Who for the first time in his life is lost."

"I'm not lost."

"Yes, you are. You're not Suzanne's caregiver anymore, and before her you were always someone's caregiver. That's what you do, or *did*. You were always Z, with either the answers, the money, or the strength, physical and emotional to help people to always get by. But now?"

"Now, I can't help," I exhale again. Christ, Mack's annoyingly bang on.

"Yes. So you feel lost."

Grinning as I stand to walk to the door again, I admit, "I'm not so good with lost, Mack," even as he nods sympathetically. "I'll see you on Thursday."

Opening the door, I half expect to see Suzanne crying in the hallway, or waiting behind a corner to get a glimpse of me again. She usually would be, and I know she did that at our condo frequently. If she hadn't seen me in a while or I was away all day, even after I returned home I would notice Suzanne watching me from corners, or just watching me in general.

But I never understood if it was because she liked looking at me, needed the comfort of seeing me knowing I was home to protect her, or if it was straight up insecurity on her part making sure I was still there and hadn't left her. I always wanted to ask why she would watch me quietly from a corner while I sat there aware of her presence but not

We are US...

acknowledging it because she clearly didn't want me to know. But I never did ask.

   Thinking about all those secret watching's I'll admit I used to just hope it was because she loved me and simply wanted to look at me without me knowing. Not for all the other negative insecure reasons she probably was.

   Looking around the last corridor before the elevators to the security check and my freedom, I feel the very absence of Suzanne and I'm instantly aware of missing her eyes on me, until it's another goddamn pain sitting on my chest.

ϘϘϘϘϘ

   Walking into Mack's office just under an hour later, I'm awesome. I haven't cried, and I haven't freaked out. Yes, finally seeing Z was a shock, but I handled myself well and I left before he could see me weak.

   "Hi, Suzanne," Mack smiles as he motions to the chair in front of his desk.

   "Hi... Um, I don't want to sit, okay?" I ask and Mack immediately nods as he sits down at his desk. I know why he sat anyway, and I appreciate it. I still hate being over-heighted, except with Z.

   "What's going on?" He raises an eyebrow waiting for me to speak.

   Exhaling on a huff, I lean beside his opened door to keep my drama in check. I don't want to be dramatic Suzanne, and I would die if people actually heard my conversations. So talking with the door open feels like the perfect way to keep myself calm.

   "Um, 2 things."

   "Hit me," he grins.

   "I want to get out of here tomorrow because I'm ready. I know it and I feel it. So I'm going home tomorrow," I say as a statement instead of a question he can argue with.

   "And the second?"

   "I want a divorce from Z. And I, ah, want you to be there when I tell him," I whisper on another long exhale.

See? I'm strong enough to leave. I just said something I never thought I would, and I didn't freak out or cry, or anything. I'm much better and I think Mack finally knows it.

"A divorce?" Mack asks calmly.

"Yes. It's time I think."

Remaining remarkably calm as he usually does, Mack barely shows any emotion when he pauses before speaking. "Why do you want to get a divorce? Why now?"

"You know why," I mumble.

"Actually, I don't. So why don't you explain to me why you want a divorce."

I'm not going to get in shit, I know. And I probably should explain this so Mack understands, but this is hard to talk to Mack about. "First, will you agree that I'm ready to leave?"

"Yes... Though if you're getting a divorce where will you go?"

"I hope our home for now. But maybe we can sell it quickly so Z and I can move on."

"Move on?"

Huffing, I see Mack is going to play the word game with me, and I'm really not in the mood. "Look, do you agree I'm ready to be released or not?"

"I already said yes," he answers still calm though there's a bit of an edge to him.

"Good. Because I'm ready to leave. I'm strong enough and I'm making a decision for myself here without freaking out or losing it. I want to leave and I want a divorce."

Nodding, Mack says, "I understand what you said. I'm just trying to understand what it means."

"What what means? A divorce? Well, it's the ending of a marriage, Mack," I reply sarcastically.

"I'm well aware, Suzanne. There's no need to be a smartass," Mack says with the first sign of disapproval I think. "What I would like to know is *why* you want a divorce and what you hope a divorce will accomplish."

Exhaling again, pressed against the wall, I cross my arms to hold myself together. "I don't want to be married to Z anymore. And I'd like to move on. Out of here, and out of my marriage."

"Understood. But why?" Mack pushes again.

"Because I'm not happy, okay?"

We are US...

"With Z? Did he do anything to make you unhappy, Suzanne?"
"Nope. He's perfect," I growl.
Smirking, Mack asks, "Is he?"
"Yup."
"Yup?" Mack repeats annoying me further.
"Okay. I'm done. You don't have to listen to me or even agree, that's up to you. But I've made my decision. And whether you support me or not, my decision isn't going to change."
"I understand," he nods gravely.
"So my only questions are will you sign off on my release, and will you be there when I tell Z I want a divorce?"
"Yes. You've finally asked and admitted you were well enough to handle getting out of here, so I will absolutely set up your release paperwork."
"Thank you," I exhale. But before I can turn to leave, Mack continues like I knew he would.
"Z is going to be here Thursday afternoon for a session. So I'd like to tell him about the divorce then. Does that work for you? You can tell him here with me present. My only request is you wait for your release until after your meeting."
"But-"
"That's only one extra day, Suzanne. Tomorrow is Wednesday. That also gives me time to ask Z if he'll agree to a joint session with you."
"What about tomorrow?" I beg. Shit, I don't want to prolong this.
"On such short notice? Z may have plans."
"More important than me?" I ask surprised. Z would typically drop whatever he was doing for me. Wow, I kinda sound like a spoiled brat.
"Suzanne, Z will be out of town tomorrow," Mack says in a way that suggests I'm being an idiot.
"Why?" Where's he going? He never goes out of town, unless for "Thomas..." I exhale the quick pain with my breath.
"Yes."
"Okay. No problem. If he's available, I'll see him in your office Thursday," I again turn to leave before I *do* actually feel emotional.
"Our session isn't over. And we still have one tomorrow, Suzanne."
"Actually, this session *is* over. But I'll see you tomorrow. Bye, Mack," I say quickly walking right out the door before he can speak again.
I know what I want and I know what I need. I also know if I spend any

more time with Mack he'll try to either talk me out of it entirely, or try to make me think about this decision more. He'll think it's in my best interest, and he'll act like he cares about my decision, which I'm sure he actually does. I just don't know if he can separate his lifelong friendship with Z this time to ever agree with me or support me in *my* decision.

  Walking quickly away, I'm not giving Mack the opportunity to change my mind this time where Z is concerned.

We are US...

CHAPTER 18
SUZANNE

Walking down the corridor to Mack's office, I feel good. I dressed nicely, as opposed to my yoga pants, and I washed and dried my hair, even putting it up in a messy kind of sexy updo. My makeup is good, all the scars are covered with my thick makeup and my hair, and I'm barely shaking.

Blowing off Mack yesterday was hard though. He didn't like it, but when I explained I would explain everything today, he really had no argument to force a session. Plus, he did sign off on my release for later tonight, so there wasn't much he could do. I know he was both hurt and disappointed in me for canceling our session, but I also didn't care at the time.

I'm making my own decisions, and I'm starting again. Again.

I've had enough of me, and I want to make some serious changes. Living a half-life either faking happiness or waiting for the unhappiness to return isn't what I want anymore. I don't want to wait for more bad, and I'd really like to move on past the bad I've already suffered, because I think it's finally time for me now.

I also think no one will support me this time with my decision. And really, why would they? Mack is on Z's side, whether through their friendship, or just because he thinks I'm wrong. Kayla will side with her husband, and Chicago Kayla, though a bit of a wildcard will probably choose Z because he's helped her move and settle into New York during my absence, Mack told me. Plus, I swear she secretly has a thing for him, and really, why wouldn't she? Z is Z.

Knocking on Mack's door, I don't even need to breathe. I'm as ready as I'll ever be, and I know no matter how bad today goes, I've been through worse, which somehow I handled, albeit usually poorly. But hey, I'm still alive, reasonably well, and, well, that's about it. But it's still something.

When the door opens to Mack, I'm a little surprised he met me at the door instead of calling me in. Then again I pissed him off yesterday by

We are US...

canceling our session so maybe he's going to be more formal with me than usual.

"Hello, Suzanne. Z's running 10 minutes late," he smiles. "Would you like to wait with me inside or wait in the hall until we begun?" When he asks almost as though we're strangers I feel really shitty suddenly. It's amazing how quickly that rejection can settle into my chest.

"Oh, the hallway will be fine," I nod already trying to get away from Mack's irritation with me.

Shaking a little for the first time in 2 days, I plaster my best smile on my face and walk the few feet back to the waiting room of people.

Looking at my hands, I notice of course the one dark scar from the accident, and the pale pink nails I painted last night in my boredom after my cast was finally removed a week ago. I also notice my index and thumb polish is totally messed up because I couldn't wait to start knitting before the polish was dry.

I was damned and determined last night to make the best goddamn scarf possible, and I will. It's like my new obsession- making a hole-less scarf for someone. I know who I keep thinking it's for, but I'm not going there anymore.

"Suzanne?" Z breathes and my physical reaction is immediate. Oh *god*. Seeing and hearing Z is always the same for me. Soul-consuming, numbing, and just light. Z is a light for me, almost like a nightlight I turn on way too frequently to keep me company in the dark.

"You're a night light," I whisper before catching myself again.

"To keep you company in your darkness," Z whispers back like he already knows. Somehow I can almost hear myself telling him that before in one of my sad but happy with Z moods.

"Why are you out here?" He asks squatting down in front of me. Looking at me, I could almost kiss him, or cry, or like beg him to hug me. But I can't now, and I won't ever again. But it's just so hard to stop myself when he's like this with me, so loving and soft and caring, and just beautiful to me always.

"I was waiting for you," I whisper with agony clearly heard in my voice.

"I'm sorry I'm late. The traffic was brutal and the parking lot-"

"Is always full," I smile sadly. "I remember from my Phillips visits." Wow. Maybe next we can casually talk about the weather next?

Smiling, almost like he knew the sarcasm I was thinking, Z stands back up, stretches his hand out to me and asks, "Shall we?" But once again

I'm stuck.
 If I take his hand, I'll lean into his arm and smell his cologne. I'll probably even rub up against his warmth and fall right back into the Z trap. The one I love like an addiction, but know I must kick like a habit.
 I can't fall back into Z because it's just too hard to climb back out of his love and affection.
 Waiting out my pause, Z slowly lowers his hand and smiles before walking toward Mack's door. I think he understands how hard touching would be for me, at least I hope he did so his feelings weren't hurt.
 Jumping up quickly, I just reach the door when Z walks in and takes what I consider my chair in front of Mack. Well, this is awkward. Is it weird to ask Z to move so I can have the chair to the side so my face has more coverage? Probably.
 Almost laughing, I don't know where to sit. *Shit.* Apparently, I can add OCD to my lengthy list of issues as well.
 "What's wrong?" Z asks while I stand to the side trying to figure out how I do this in the wrong chair.
 "Nothing." Walking a foot, I slump down into the wrong chair and feel nothing short of irritation and discomfort. I'm totally uncomfortable in this chair because Z is staring right at my scars. Ah, how do I talk to him if I'm staring at the opposite wall because I can't look in his direction?
 "I think I understand," Z suddenly says rising. "Here, love. Take this seat," he smiles gesturing with his hand.
 "Thank you," I whisper diving for the right chair. He knew! He always knows. If ever there was a man perfect for me, I'm pretty sure Z is it. "And I'll never find this again with anyone."
 "What won't you find?" Z asks. When I panic, I look at a very somber Mack who is watching us but not participating at all.
 Almost begging Mack with his eyes, he shakes his head no to me very slightly. The *bastard!* He's actually going to make me do this by myself, which I know I should, even though I don't want to. I need Mack's help with this, but I'm fairly sure he's going to make me do it alone.
 "Okay, why are we here? Not that I mind. It's lovely to see you again, Suzanne."
 "Ah, you too," I choke trying to figure out how I start.
 Turning in his chair a little, Z looks right at me before he says, "You look as beautiful as always, Suzanne." Ha! No, I don't. I'm a scarred mess I almost snap but just hold it in.

We are US...

Z hates when I talk like that. He always stops me, or tells me off, or waits until I've calmed down before telling me again close to my face without actually touching it that he thinks I'm beautiful. But it's not true.

"You're a liar," I say loudly. But this time I think I meant to say it out loud.

Watching Z jolt in his chair, I'm okay with it. He and I need to be honest I think, and if that means I have to start the conversation then I will.

"I'm a liar?" Z asks with his infamous raised eyebrow as I nod. "How so?"

Taking a deep breath I go for it. "Every time you tell me I'm beautiful you're lying. And every time you say I'm lovely you're lying. And, um, every time you said you couldn't live without me you were lying!" I yell at the end which totally killed the calm atmosphere I was going for.

"I *can't* live without you," Z says calmly to my growing anger.

"Well, you look alive and well to me. So I guess that was a little Z drama for once, *not* mine."

"Really? Would you like to know how I've been living, Suzanne?" He asks as I stare. "Not all that well, actually. I go to work miserably, and afterward I go back to a hotel miserably. I have a drink, eat something, watch tv, then crash on the couch, just to do the same thing the next day. That's how I've been living. I do nothing else, and I don't want to do anything else. So yes, I'm *physically* living but I'm far from *actually* living without you."

"Why are you doing that? You could be out with anyone. You should be out getting laid and having fun being Z." Yes, that sentence actually killed me to say, but it's true. Z should be with someone normal.

"*Should* I? When the woman I love is in the hospital ignoring me and making me suffer, so I have to wait to see when she's coming back to me? I should cheat on the woman I've loved and lived with for years now who doesn't think I'm enough apparently? I should go out and party while the beautiful woman I'm in love with struggles to-"

"You're such a liar!" I cut him off angrily. I don't want to hear any more of all this flowery shit from Z. I don't care, and I hate hearing it.

In a voice that oozes anger Z says, "Do *not* call me a liar, Suzanne."

"Why not? You *are*. Everything you've said to me has been lies. All of it. And I finally woke up."

"Did you? How exactly did you wake up? No! Better yet, how am I a liar?"

"Because I'm not beautiful!" I scream totally frustrated with Z and his bullshit lies.

"You are to me!" Z yells right back.

"Then you're fucking blind! And I'm sick of all your bullshit all the time!"

"Really? And what bullshit is that?"

"*You*," I exhale.

Jesus *Christ!* I can't believe how angry I feel suddenly. I want to scream and rage and tell him to fuck off! I want to slap him and hurt him like he hurts me every single time he lies to me to pacify me.

Looking at me like I've hurt him, which I know I have, Z asks simply, "*Me*?" And all the fight leaves me at once.

Shit, I don't dislike Z. I love him, I know that. I'm just frustrated and pissed, and tired of being with him. But it's not his fault I'm like this. It's all me. As usual.

"What else do I do that's so bad?" Z asks quietly as I breathe deeply. His deep dark eyes are staring at my face waiting, and I feel nothing but sad.

"Nothing... I'm sorry. You're not the problem here. I am," I exhale again as all the anger fades from my body completely. "I'm sorry..."

"Don't do that, Suzanne. If you're angry tell me why. If I've pissed you off in some way, tell me that too. You don't have to be sorry for feeling angry if you are, but please tell me *why* you are. Because I honestly don't understand what I did to make you angry with me."

"You've done nothing, Z. I'm sorry," I moan because I'm always sorry with Z.

Looking away from a strangely silent Mack and a desperate sounding Z, I know what I have to do. I think all this anger is simply misplaced sadness because I don't want to do in my heart what I know in my mind is the right thing to do for both of us. It's the right thing for us, it just sucks.

Pulling up my big girl panties, I finally turn to Z and say it. "Z, I want-"

"Wait!" He barks quickly cutting me off as I jump in my chair. What the fuck? Ahhhh... Holy buzz kill. "I have to talk to Mack for a minute. *Alone.*"

"What? *Why?*"

"It's personal," he says shaking his head. *Personal?* Because our impending divorce isn't personal? I giggle stunned.

"Personal?" I ask softly like I don't know what the word means. Z never does 'it's personal' with me, only I do it with him. Well, this is new.

We are US...

   Nodding, he says yes as I stare at him like a moron. Do I stand up? Do I leave? "Do you want some privacy?"
   "Yes, please. I'm sorry, Suzanne. But I really need to talk to Mack for a minute. Is that okay?"
   "Ah, sure."
   Standing, I feel so awkward and confused by the sudden change in Mack's office I don't know where to go or what to do. It's like I've forgotten how to walk or something.
   "Um, do you want me in the hallway, or like in my room? How long will you be?"
   Turning back to me as he stands, Z reaches out his hand to my face slowly like he's in pain. He has a look that screams something is wrong and I desperately wish I knew what was happening. Waiting, I can't even breathe until he makes contact with me and naturally I turn right into the hand against my face. God, I miss him.
   "Can I hug you?" Z asks like he never would've before. Well, sometimes he asks if I'm freaking out, but usually we both just walk into each other without thought because he needs to hug and I need to be hugged.
   "Yes," I whisper as he hugs me tightly with a low, sad groan.
   Oh *god*... He's just as warm and strong as he always was. His body though way bigger than mine fits me so well. We're like puzzle pieces the way we fit together. Exhaling, I rest my head against his chest and breathe him into me. For the last time, I think.
   Oh *god*... My heart is breaking with the realization that this is probably the last time he'll ever hug me, and I can't stand the pain everywhere inside me suddenly.
   Pulling away slowly, Z whispers against my hair, "I'm sorry," and I don't know what he means. He shouldn't ever be sorry to me. He is too good for a sorry to me.
   "You never have to be sorry, Z. You've been everything for far too long to ever say sorry to me for anything between us," I moan pulling away completely to walk toward the door.
   Opening the door quickly, I realize I don't know how I'm going to get back in. I don't know if they'll come get me, or if I'm just supposed to wait in the hall until they open the door again. I don't know anything right now but the feel of Z and the awful sadness surrounding us.
   I do know walking away from Z is such a physical pain within me, I feel totally broken inside again.

CHAPTER 19
Z

"Z. Sit," Mack says firmly as I fight my whole body from reaching for the closed door to stop Suzanne's sadness. I have to physically lock myself in place to actually listen to him as I turn around.

I wanted to go after her so badly, but I knew I couldn't. I think I know where she's headed with us, and I need to have everything out before she does. I need to be honest about the biggest lie I've ever told before she changes things forever.

"I knew her," I admit on a gasp as the emotion threatens to strangle me.

My throat is tight and my heart is pounding so hard in my chest I need to hold it so I don't have a heart attack from the fear and pain. I don't know what's happening to me but I even feel a little nauseous which is another first for me in years.

Leaning forward, Mack asks absolutely everything in only 2 words. "From *before*?"

"Yes..."

Fuck! Between my pounding heart and Mack's shocked face, I don't know what to say as I finally fall into the closest chair. I don't know how to start, and I don't know what to do. I've held this lie for so long, I feel sick with this secret.

Shaking his head, Mack looks as fucked up as I feel. Leaning forward in his chair nearly across his desk, I don't think he can even speak. I don't think he knows *how* to speak until he suddenly does.

"What do you mean?" He asks in a voice filled with such emotion between us I feel the betrayal of what I'm going to say to Mack so strongly I'm afraid I'm going to lose them both over this. "Z?"

Taking a deep breath, staring at the sad eyes of my best friend, I say what I should have admitted to both of them years ago but couldn't.

"Ah, what Suzanne doesn't know or understand is it's always been about her eyes for me. Her beautiful, nearly clear, pale blue eyes."

"Yes," Mack moans nodding.

He knows. Everyone knows what her eyes can do to us. They make us smile, and they make us weep for her. Every feeling she's ever felt shows in her beautiful eyes.

"Suzanne's eyes are the eyes of my dreams, Mack. But sometimes they're the eyes of my nightmares, too. Um, I have always known her eyes, even before I knew her."

"Oh *fuck*, Z. Tell me," Mack moans again breathing hard.

"What you don't know is I saw her once. I saw her years before, but I didn't know how to tell you when she was fucked up in New York with me the first time, and then it was too late to admit to it when she and I worked everything out the night before her accident. So, I didn't tell either of you after she woke up from the accident because we weren't together, and then we were together again and it seemed too late, and I've just been holding it in since then."

"When did you see her?" Mack asks cutting me off a little angrily, which I expected.

Bracing myself, I finally tell it all.

"Years before, when I stumbled upon my father's sick fucking other life, I saw her. I know I lied when she asked if I ever saw a picture of her when she was little. I know I said I saw a young brunette in my father's office when I realized what he was, which was true."

"But?"

"But I saw a young, tortured Suzanne, too," I say quickly like the speed of me admitting it will soften the blow or something.

Standing to lean against his back window, Mack pauses for only seconds before asking, "You *saw* her? *When?*"

"That day in my father's office. When I was rummaging through his desk for his extra golf cart keys, I saw the link for 'Graphic'."

"*Graphic*?" Mack says like it's the most disgusting word he's ever heard, which in this situation it truly is.

"Yes. That's all the file said. But I honestly didn't think it meant graphic like it was *graphic* images. I thought it had to do with the new graphics for the wineries. I was curious, and even annoyed that he didn't include me in the final say of the new graphics we were going to use on the new wine label from California. So I opened the file pissed that he was going behind my back, and then I was sick," I moan remembering the picture I saw first. "Right there on his goddamn computer. A computer me or my mother could have used at any moment, on any given day. The file was right there..." I whisper remembering that day so clearly.

"What did you see?" Mack asks in a voice that sounds so far from me and my memories I barely hear him as I struggle with my memories.

"Ah, I saw- Um, on the screen there was a little brunette being raped by a much older man. She was maybe 12 years old if a day, and I was so shocked at the image and so sick so quickly I had to keep swallowing the bile that formed in my throat. I think unconsciously, or maybe I just didn't know what I was doing, I don't know, but I scrolled over one more picture and I was absolutely winded. I was so stunned and nauseous, I remember puking right in my father's garbage can under his desk."

Feeling the memory of that day so clearly, I actually feel the bile rise up my throat again. Over fifteen years older, and a man, and not a twenty something punk doesn't matter. I feel exactly what I felt that day.

I feel horror.

Walking around his desk, Mack actually squats in front of me so I can look at his face. Feeling like I'm drowning in the memory of that day, I grab hold of Mack's eyes to help center me in this horrible moment of my past.

"What did you see?" Mack asks looking level with me to give me extra support I think.

"I saw her that day," I choke out barely above a whisper. Shaking my head, I continue before Mack has to ask. "But I didn't know it was Suzanne Beaumont, and I didn't know I would ever see that little girl again. Our parents may have travelled in the same circles, but I didn't know who she was, until I did years later. At the time I didn't know if the pictures were old or new, and I didn't know what happened to that little girl. Mack, I didn't know anything except horror. And blue eyes," I finally exhale as my strangled throat gasps a groan of agony from my chest.

"It was so bad, Mack," I cry out. "The picture was torture. You could actually *see* the torture. She was held down by someone at her back and someone was raping her from behind, but all I could see was her face turned to the camera. She was screaming I think because her mouth was open, but it was her eyes. The picture was black and white, Mack. It was black and white, and all you could see where her wide eyes staring at the camera. And her eyes looked almost entirely white because the blue was just gone in the black and white of the picture. But they held me captive, and I was beyond anything even close to stunned. I didn't know anything but those fucking eyes of this tiny little girl being raped and abused and tortured and-"

"Z."

"No," I shake my head so he stops speaking. "I didn't know her. And I didn't know what to do. I don't even know how long I sat there staring at her. What I do know is I sat in my father's chair and I stared at the little helpless girl on the screen of my father's computer in my parents' condo in the best part of Manhattan and I was absolutely destroyed," I admit as the first tear falls down my cheek before I can brush it away quickly.

Staring at Mack, I know I need something. I don't know what, but I'm desperate for him to say or do something to help me because I feel like I'm dying inside suddenly remembering Suzanne like that.

"Did you know it was her when you first met each other at the hotel outside Chicago?" Mack asks as I shake my head no.

"I didn't *know* until she lost it in my apartment with you. When she admitted everything about Mr. Williams. When she said my father's name it was then that I put it together that my father hurt her, I think. Actually, I think I may have known unconsciously because of the way I felt about her when we started talking."

"In what way?" Mack asks standing and walking back to his chair.

"Everything was just so intense between us right from the beginning. I mean one phone call and I wanted to help her, and then when I looked up her profile picture, I wanted her. I wanted to *help* her with her job, and Marcus, and with just *everything*. It was an insta-love feeling neither of us could ever explain. And it wasn't something I did, or even felt before her. It made no sense to me at the time why I felt as strongly for her as I did. But then that night in my apartment when she was having her breakdown and losing it and telling us her secrets and when she said my father's name, I remembered the picture. Hearing her say Mr. Williams was such a shock, and the horror of my memories and everything I was feeling that night just became too much for me to process fully. And then she was in the tub dying, and she tried to kill herself in my bathroom using a prescription some woman left at my place accidentally, and then..." I shrug.

Mack knows the rest. He was there for her and for me, and then for us. Mack knows everything except how I felt.

"It was the most horrifying picture I've ever seen in my life, even if it hadn't been Suzanne. But it *was* Suzanne, and that just makes it so much worse. And I never did know if it was my father raping her at the time because the man's face was bent over her like he was grunting or something. But *her* face, Mack- she was in agony, and so scared, and just so young," I cry, finally bursting into the tears I was trying to hold in. "She was just a little girl and her eyes were screaming for someone to help her. But no one did. They just hurt her and photographed it. And I can't stand it anymore," I sob as Mack watches with tears in his eyes too.

"Z, *you* didn't-"

"Wait. *Please*?" I beg trying to get it together. Wiping my cheeks with my palms I need to explain what happened.

"That's when I confronted him and went after my father that day. I did, Mack. I waited for him to get home, and I took him to his office and I pointed at the screen and asked what the fuck he was looking at. But he was just so blasé about it. He lied and said a friend sent him those pictures and he hadn't looked at them yet so it was no big deal. And then he deleted them right in front of me. But honestly, I didn't believe him. I had never heard or seen my father do *anything* pornographic, or with children, or even with woman. As far as I knew he and my mother were very much a loving couple, so I had no basis for not believing his story, but I just didn't. For whatever reason, I think maybe the way he blew it off, or maybe *because* he didn't look at the picture shocked like I did, I think that was the tell I needed to not believe him anymore. I think his calm delete of the pictures told me everything I needed to know and that was it. I actually shoved him hard as I passed him for the door and I told him I thought he was a fucking pig. Then I walked out of their house for my own apartment and I never looked back as you know."

"I do. Your explanation for cutting off your parents made no sense to me and Marty at the time. 'My dad went behind my back on some contracts, so I'm never speaking to him again?' Even for you that was a little dramatic. But you insisted so we let it go, especially after a few months and all the desperate calls from your mom to try to understand what was going on between you and your father."

"I couldn't talk to her either because I swear she knew, Mack. She would have to. They were too married, and too close, so she had to know what a sick fuck he was, which means she was a sick fuck too. So that was it for them with me. And I never spoke to them again."

"And then they died," Mack adds like he finally understands as I nod.

"And I was relieved," I admit like a bastard though it's the truth. I *was* relieved. "I thought if he was dead, then there was one less perv in the world looking at horrific pictures of child porn, or maybe even participating in it. But I didn't know if he was an active participant, or a child rapist, or anything else until Suzanne told us that night," I exhale again as the memories of the night with her at my apartment swamp my mind again.

"So you didn't tell me because?"

Looking at Mack I admit the truth of everything. "I was afraid you would think I was a pig like him."

"I would *never* have thought that, Z. Try again," Mack pushes shaking his head at me.

"I *was* afraid of that. But also I didn't want Suzanne to know because she would have never been able to separate me from my father. And I loved her by then, and I was too scared to admit to anything that may have pushed her further away from me. So I didn't tell either of you because I wanted her in my life."

Exhaling, the silence between us is so thick I can't understand it. I don't know if Mack is disgusted with me, hates me, or just thinks I'm a lying douchebag.

"I understand why you didn't tell her. But this is huge, Z."

"I know."

"No, you don't. This is absolutely everything for Suzanne. She has told me hundreds of times how grateful she is you never saw her like that. She used to cry and feel such relief that you only *knew* what happened to her but never actually saw any of the pictures because she can't have you see her that way."

"But I don't," I cry out desperately.

"Yes you do, remember? It's all about her eyes. The eyes of your dreams and the eyes of your nightmares."

"But it's not like that," I try again, though I see what he means and I know where this is headed.

"It's exactly like that, Z. And to Suzanne it will mean the absolute end to you together. She hates you seeing her physical scars alone knowing what caused them. But *this*? This is absolutely everything she will never be able to handle- you actually seeing her abused as a little girl," Mack exhales hard right from his stomach I think. "Knowing you actually saw her raped will kill her because she wants to be a woman to you, not *her*," he exhales again covering his face with his hands.

"I do see her as a woman," I plead but Mack doesn't even acknowledge me. "Mack! She *is* a woman to me. She's my wife, and lover, and my beautiful Suzanne."

"It won't matter, Z. For being horribly weak, ironically, Suzanne can be a stubborn pain in the ass," he huffs a quick laugh. "But this will absolutely break her when she finds out. I know her, Z. She hates everything about herself. *Everything*, Z. And I've worked so hard for years now to build her up to make her see herself as the woman she is now. And sometimes she slides backwards like what just happened to her 2 months ago. But overall she has moved past her childhood remarkably well. And you helped. A lot actually," Mack nods at me.

"I tried to."

"I know, but it wasn't what you did. It was who you were with her. You were just a man to her. A man who may have known what she went through but you didn't see it, so she could move past it with you enough to have as normal a life, a married life, and a *sex* life with you as she possibly could. She even knows I saw some of the photos and brings it up sometimes with such self-loathing, I have to spend an entire session trying to convince her that I don't remember the pictures or what I saw. Sometimes I blatantly lie and say I only looked quick but didn't really see anything that I remember so she lets it go for a few months. But with you-"

"I actually saw her like that," I exhale again the gravity of this situation. "What do I do?" I ask unsure of anything anymore. The truth has not set me free as it were. Or maybe as I hoped. I don't have a fucking clue what to think any more about anything actually.

"I don't know. I mean let's be real here. Of course you're supposed to tell her the truth. You're supposed to have no more lies between you, and you're supposed to move forward, together or apart, but..." Mack shakes his head.

"But lying- or rather not telling her this is better for everyone involved," I say knowing it is.

"Can you live with that though? Can you try to forget the little girl you saw with the eyes that still haunt you?"

"Yes. For her I can. I did for years. I finally just told you because I thought I had to. You told me to think of any other lies I've told her, or anything I hide from her and this was my one thing since she already knew about my monthly visits to Chicago. I thought I was supposed to tell you, but I can forget it and keep it inside and move on. I *will* move on."

"Z, you were just sobbing, and you're still haunted and shaken by it."

"It doesn't matter. Suzanne matters. And with all the shit she's gone through, lived through and had to deal with, I can keep this one thing to myself for her. Even saying it like that changes the way I feel about it. It's just one thing *I* have to deal with versus the thousands of things she struggles with every day of her life."

"But it won't always be that easy. And at the end of the day it's still actually a lie, Z. A pertinent piece of information about her childhood that you're keeping from her."

"*For* her," I say with conviction. "That's the bottom line for me, Mack. Suzanne has nothing to gain from knowing I saw a horrific picture of her when she was little. And I have everything to gain by keeping it within this room. So that's it as far as I'm concerned."

"You're sure?" Mack asks again like he's not sure of anything between us anymore.

"Yes. It's done. I have one nightmare from an otherwise fairly charmed life to keep secret, and I will. But can you?"

"Yes," Mack nods and I know he will.

"Okay. Done. I talked to my shrink and told him my deepest darkest, and he made me feel better and now we can both move on. Got it?"

"Yes," Mack exhales again and I feel better already about everything while we sit for minutes thinking silently.

"Okay, let me go get her so she can tell me she's getting out of here tomorrow," I grin knowing she was going to dramatically announce she was able to come home with me tomorrow. Like I didn't already know as her next of kin.

"Z, there's more," Mack says seriously and I could almost laugh at his serious expression as I stand for the door.

"Of course there is, Mack. Suzanne doesn't do anything easily. So let's get this over with," I laugh opening the door as Mack calls out to me again louder.

CHAPTER 20
SUZANNE & Z

Walking down the corridor I see Suzanne on a little bench actually knitting. Damn, she's cute. Even as the crazy knitting lady.

When she sees me, her blush almost makes me laugh when she quickly whips her knitting to her side like she could hide it from me, which she actually does in an honest to Christ knitting bag. Huh. Not that sexy, but adorable anyway.

"Hey, love," I smile as she stands awkwardly. "We're ready for you to come in now," I gesture behind me to Mack's office as she nods gravely.

Watching her pick up her knitting bag, almost using it as a shield against her chest, I barely hold in my grin. I'm so used to her little dramas and physical insecurities, I don't get half as stressed or pissed about them anymore. They're kind of endearing to me now.

Like the way if she ever has an opinion, or wants to argue with me she gets scared I'll be mad at her or not love her anymore. But she couldn't be more wrong if she tried. I love her standing up for herself, and I love it when she stands up to me. It means she's getting stronger, and I want her strong.

"After you," I smile when she enters Mack's office looking too pale and skinny but kind of sure of herself, too. It's a strange look for Suzanne and one I also find endearing.

"Ah, please sit, Z. *Wherever* you want," she adds like she knows I should be able to choose whichever chair I want, regardless if it stresses her out or not. So naturally, I sit in the chair that'll make her less uncomfortable. Watching I can see her relief when she sits in the chair that hides her face from me and I know I chose well.

"Suzanne? How are you feeling? Would you like to speak with me privately before you talk to Z?" Mack asks like they have a secret from me, but it doesn't bother me this time. If she needs to talk to Mack first she can. I did for Christ's sake.

"No. I'm ready," Suzanne says in her fake, louder than usual voice. I also know that voice of hers well. It's the one she uses when she's trying to hide she's scared shitless, which naturally makes me want to hold her hand right now for support.

"If you're sure, please go ahead," Mack prompts again and I could kill him for pushing her even though I want her to get on with it myself.

Turning to me visibly inhaling, Suzanne makes eye contact in a way that looks both weird from her and too intense for anyone. I hate when she struggles to speak to me.

"I would like a divorce, Z."

Okay, not what I was expecting. Neither is the grin I can't help from spreading across my face.

"Try again, love," I smirk turning my whole body to face her.

Staring at me, Suzanne actually works up the nerve to continue her bullshit. "Um, I'm serious, Z. I've thought about it, I really have, and I've decided I would like us to get a divorce." When Suzanne says it again I actually laugh as her face pales and her eyes look quickly to Mack for help I assume. Well, she's not getting any help from him this time.

"That's not happening, Suzanne," I say standing with the most purpose I've felt in 2 fucking months. Turning to Suzanne as she pushes back in her chair a little, I don't care that she looks like she feels threatened suddenly. If she actually feels threatened by me physically, I'm gonna tell her off for that, too.

"We're not getting a divorce. Period."

"But-"

Leaning right into her face with my hands on the chair arms, Suzanne's eyes widen in alarm, but I don't give a shit.

"Are you leaving tonight or tomorrow morning?" I ask to surprise on her face. "Of course I know about your release. Do you really think there's anything I don't know about you?"

"Um..." she actually gulps like I've confused her again.

"Today. Or. Tomorrow?"

"Tomorrow morning," she whispers.

"Fine. I'll be here at 9:00 to pick you up."

"But I want a divorce," she squeaks pathetically.

"And I said that's not going to happen. So cut the shit, Suzanne. You've taken your moment. Another long goddamn moment that excluded me. A moment that was 2 fucking months long, and I'm done waiting around for you," I smile sadistically as she shakes a little below me.

"I wasn't taking a moment, Z. I was trying to get better."
"Yes, trying to get better. And when you couldn't figure out how to deal with anything, you decided to push away the one thing, the one *person* offering you happiness. And I won't have it. I'm not allowing it again."
"I wasn't doing that," she shakes her head.
"You were. And it's not going to happen. We're not getting a divorce, and you're not pushing me away again. You owe me this, Suzanne."
"I owe you everything," she nearly cries which breaks my heart again. But I'm not getting distracted this time by her sadness and insecurities.
"That's not what I meant. You owe me a chance at this marriage that I love, because I've given you a hundred chances to not fuck us over with all your shit- even though you keep trying to," I actually growl closer to her face. "And it stops today."
Panicking a little, Suzanne tries to look around me for Mack until I move to block him from her view. Mack's a smart man though, and he's not helping or jumping in, which is good. Because right now I feel pretty pissed at everything and I don't want to go after him in my frustration.
"I wasn't trying to fuck anything up. I'm trying to do the opposite," she actually cries. "I want you to *not* have a fucked up life, Z."
"Really? Well, as I said, then stop the shit. Do you love me?"
"Yes, but-"
"Nope. There's no but. You love me, and I love you, and I've had enough Suzanne shit for a goddamn lifetime. So this time you're going to do something for me. *You* are going to give back to me all the love and patience I've always given to you. Understood?" I ask like a total threat. But again, I don't care if I sound too aggressive. I need her to get me this time.
"Ah..." she moans confused I think. Fine, I'll help her confusion.
"Suzanne. I'm picking you up at 9:00 tomorrow morning and we're going home together for the first time in 2 months. I've never asked you for anything," I say fiercely as she unconsciously nods. "And I'm not asking you for this. I'm *telling* you. I *am* picking you up at 9:00 tomorrow morning, and you *are* coming home with me."
Gasping, she tries again. "But you should have a good life!"
"I do have a good life with you. But I'm not naive. I know we'll probably fight and struggle until we figure this shit out, and I'm prepared for that. Fuck, we may even fall madly in love with each other again if we're given the chance."

"Z..." she begs crying.

"I don't give a shit what happens, but we're doing it together. That's all there is now. You and me. Your fucked up past doesn't exist in our marriage, it exists in your old life. And our marriage has nothing to do with your past. It's always been about the future we want together. Am I right?"

"Yes, but-"

Shaking my head I cut her off again. "Tomorrow morning I'm picking you up, because I'm making a decision for us for once. You don't get to make all the decisions, and you don't get to decide when we're over. I get a say in our life together and I get to make some decisions between us. Do you understand?"

"Yes," she whispers looking freaked out still.

Leaning into her slowly, I kiss her lips as she gasps against me taking the air right from my lungs as my arms shake holding me up.

"You are coming home with me tomorrow morning, and we are NOT getting a divorce," I growl against her lips.

Waiting, Suzanne actually leans into my lips harder and whispers *okay* against my mouth as I expel the breath I've been holding tightly in my chest for the last 2 months.

"Done." Pulling away from her quickly, the shocked look on her face makes me bark a quick laugh, but I still don't care. "You're not pulling this shit with me anymore. I love you, and I have been by your side through all the nightmares, but it's time to give me something back now, Suzanne. You."

"But-"

Smiling, I'm through listening to all the reasons she thinks I'm better off without her. "And don't do anything stupid before tomorrow morning, love, or I'll just drag your ass out of here kicking and screaming. Got it?"

Nodding, with her eyes wide and her hands shaking she whispers, "Yes," and that's all I need.

"Good," I nod firmly so she understands I'm not fucking around. "I love you and I'll see you in the morning," I grin before walking around her chair for the door. "See you in the morning, Mack," I turn to see him covering his own grin with his hand before I finally walk out the door abruptly.

Jesus *Christ!* The adrenaline pumping through my veins is making me so fucking light-headed I feel like I need to hop on a tread mill or something. Actually, I just need to run off all the anxiety, and pressure, and relief, and the adrenaline spiking through me all at once.

Zipping my jacket, I throw open the door to the crisp New York air and I just start running. I'm sure I'll quit way before I make it to the hotel but I don't give a flying fuck. I'll cab it back to my SUV later. I need this right now. I need to run all this shit away.

I need to run from the picture I'll never forget of the beautiful little girl who tortures my nightmares. I need to run far away from her past and my father's place in it, and I need to run from the divorce Suzanne will *never* get from me.

She's fucking delusional if she actually thought I would agree with her. She's fucked up, and delusional, and stubborn, and really pretty fucking exhausting. But she's *my* Suzanne and I will never let her go, no matter how hard she fights us.

"Fuck *that*," I exhale on a laugh before picking up my pace to run away from our past to start our lives again. Again.

ααααα

Um... Holy *shit!* Giggling, I feel like I'm going to throw up when Z closes the door behind him with a snap.

Whipping my head back toward Mack I ask, "What the hell just happened?" Before I burst out laughing.

"Well, Suzanne, I believe you just had your ass handed to you by Z," he grins as I laugh again. "How did that feel?"

"Shocking? I don't know. Um..." Wow, I'm just stunned. "Who the hell *was* that?"

Grinning, Mack says simply, "That was Z- no holds barred. I think he finally realized like I did some time ago that you don't respond well to coddling. So I believe he may have tried a more direct approach with you," Mack tries to say seriously, but his eyes are dancing with laughter.

"No shit." I giggle shaking my head again.

We are US...

I have NO idea what just happened, or what the hell Z did to me. I was so sure of my decision to get a divorce before, but now I think I may have been wrong. Well, obviously I was wrong. But wow. *That* Z was hot. And scary. And sexy. And like, oh! "Dominant much?" I say out loud laughing again at my stupidity.

"He can be," Mack agrees. "Did it bother you?"

Thinking about it, yes he scared me a little but not in the physical way I'm usually afraid of people. Z isn't like that for me. Z is more just scary when he's so serious, and I can't really fight it, and really, I don't think I want to. I think I like Z taking the pressure away from me sometimes.

"No. I mean obviously he was a little intense but I kind of liked it. It made me feel like he really loves me," I admit as all these realities start making sense to me suddenly.

"Because he really *does* love you. Fiercely. And intensely. And completely, Suzanne. Z loves you exactly like you say you want to be loved, but fight at every turn."

"I don't *fight* it," I defend.

"Yes, you do. At every single turn you fight Z's love. And you better start thinking about your actions and words with him now, Suzanne, because he won't stay patient forever. Z has never had to work for anything in his life. He had the money, and the creativity, and the knowledge to succeed. He had the looks, and the women," he continues even as I glare at him.

"He has had everything, not necessarily handed to him, but certainly in a way that was easy for him to succeed. But you are always hard, and not easy, and to top it off you say things like he's not enough, and you make him feel guilt he shouldn't feel because *you* think you're unattractive. You even punish him because other women flirt with him, which he has never reciprocated, I promise you."

"I don't mean to-"

"Make him feel like shit?" Mack asks a little angrily as I nod. "Then stop doing it. He has never, and will never cheat on you, but you still wait for it. You don't trust him at all though he is the most loyal friend, husband, and lover you could ever ask for. You constantly put yourself down to him, so he feels almost bad for being attractive, even though he finds you stunning, Suzanne."

When I scowl, Mack pushes right on. "That's the look. Right there. You can do it to me like what I said is bullshit because I don't love you like Z does. But every single time you do it to Z it's like a little slap. You're saying 1) he's lying to you which Z doesn't do, and 2) that you think he has a problem thinking you're attractive. And yet you're so insecure about everything about yourself, he tries to tell you how attractive you actually are but you get mad at him. So essentially, Suzanne, you've created a situation where Z is fucked if he does and fucked if he doesn't. And that is *all* you."

Shaking my head, I need Mack to understand my perspective. "I don't mean to do that to him. It's just hard seeing what I see but hearing what he says because they aren't the same thing."

"To *you*, Suzanne. But to Z they're exactly the same thing. He loved you before the scars, and he loves you after. You're the only one who doesn't love you or think you're attractive anymore," Mack finally exhales like he either needs a break from me, or maybe is simply giving me a break to absorb all he just said. Regardless, I appreciate the break while my head spins.

Leaning across his desk, Mack eventually continues. "Suzanne, my point is this. Z loves you. He even loves the bad, shitty Suzanne. But *you* have hurt him repeatedly. Through all your insecurity and fear of him *maybe* hurting you one day, which I guarantee he would never do willingly, you have hurt him instead. Badly."

"I didn't mean to, it's just hard."

"No more excuses, Suzanne. Your past is your past. And your past will always creep up to hurt you. But we're talking about Z now. And there is NO excuse for you hurting him. He is amazing, Suzanne, as your friend, your protector, your lover, and your husband. He really is. And it appears everyone else sees that but you. So you have some decisions to make, and I hope you make them before it's too late for the 2 of you."

Sitting closer to Mack's desk, I need to know. "What are my decisions?"

Exhaling, Mack looks at me like he thinks I'm an idiot, which I know I am right now. But I want to get this right suddenly so badly, almost like my life depends on it, which it actually does I realize.

"You have to decide if you want to love Z back, or if you want to punish him for your past. Because until this moment, that's what you've been doing. You've been punishing the wrong man and making him insecure and unsure of himself when he shouldn't be. He has been amazing for and *to* you, but you've been kind of an asshole to him," Mack finally says without the humor that statement would normally cause between us.

Slumping back in my chair, I see what he's saying with a clarity I've never experienced in my life. And he's totally right. Every single time Z said I was attractive or beautiful I gave him a dirty look or dismissed him because *I* couldn't see past all my ugliness. So I did essentially call him a liar, and I did negate his feelings for me because I couldn't see past my own ugly feelings. *Shit.*

"Wow," I sigh. "I've got many apologies to make," I mumble to Mack shaking his head at me.

"You've missed the point again. As usual, Suzanne," Mack says sounding totally frustrated with me. "You don't have to apologize. Up until today, Z accepted all your Suzanne shit so he's not looking for apologies. You, however, have to change today. Because one day you may wake up and Z is just gone. You can only love someone one-sided for so long without either fading away completely which I doubt he would ever do, or growing a set and walking away, which I think he will absolutely do if you don't wake the hell up now. You have a really good man, Suzanne. So enjoy him, and live with him, and love him finally. Before it's too late for you."

"Okay," I whisper as my brain continues to spin.

I don't think I can even move as I try to understand what I've never understood before. I mean I know Z loves me, but I didn't think it was like Mack said, or maybe it's more I didn't realize how little I actually gave back to Z for his love. I think that's more the reality I'm struggling with. I thought I trusted him to love me enough, but I really didn't.

"I still wait for Z to turn on me so I don't give everything to him so he can't hurt me when he finally leaves me."

"Has he ever left you, or said he was leaving? Has he *ever* given you a reason to not trust him?"

"*No...*" I exhale everything. "Shit."

"Shit is right," Mack finally grins and I think Mack and I will be okay after this.

"I've fucked up, Mack. Again," I whisper as he nods. Not even trying to placate me, Mack agrees with my wrongs to Z. "Shit."

Waiting out my potential brain hemorrhage from over-thinking, I keep having little epiphanies that either make me huff or giggle as I try to grasp everything I've learned on this totally fucked up, amazing day.

And then it hits me.

"Can I use your phone?"
"Of course," Mack agrees standing.
"You don't have to leave. You're always a part of this, Mack. You're always part of the Suzanne and Z love story," I smile as he does.
Reaching over the desk, I dial Z's cell and wait out only 1 ring.
Gasping like he's running or something Z speaks before I can. "Did she freak the fuck out after I left? Is she okay?"
Grinning, I answer quickly. "Yes, she did. But she's okay."
"Oh. Ah, hi," he seems to stop breathing.
"I wanted you to know I love you. And I can't wait to go home with you. And I can't wait to *go* home. I would ask you to come get me tonight but I haven't had a proper razor in 2 months, and that's just hairy and gross. So I'm going to go to sleep tonight with thoughts of you, and I'm going to wake up to thoughts of you. Then I hope I see you at 9:00 sharp so we can go home together. Is that okay?"
"God, yes," he whispers as I smile at Mack.
"I'm sorry for all the times I hurt you. I was such an asshole," I grin as he laughs. "But I'm going to try my hardest to never be an asshole to you again. I'm going to try very hard Z so you finally understand that to me you have always been everything in every moment between us."
"Suzanne, you're killing me here. I'm like a total pansy trying not to cry on a goddamn busy street in Manhattan at rush hour," he says so seriously I just catch myself before I laugh.
"You can be a total pansy with me tomorrow, okay? And I'll hold *you* for a change. Sound good?"
"Yes," he moans, which kind of hurts my heart. Almost like he's been waiting for me to say that to him for years.
"I'm going to go. I'll see you in the morning."
"Okay."
"I love you," I grin when he moans again- his sexy Z moan.

Hanging up I slump back in my chair and just stare at the window for a minute in silence.
"Um, you're so awesome, Mack," I whisper still staring at the window.
"I know," he agrees just like I knew he would as I grin.
"I should go. I have to pack up my room, and I feel like knitting," I giggle.
"And you have lots to think about."

"Yes."

"Suzanne? I just want to say one more thing before you leave, okay?"

"Sure," I finally turn to look at my Mack.

"It's not always going to feel this good. And the depression will probably come back, and life won't always feel this hopeful."

"I know. But I wrote stuff down this time, like triggers and feelings and things that started getting messed up in my head before I realized what was happening. And I'm going to show Z the list this time so he knows when I'm losing it. I want him to know when I'm feeling messed up and confused so he doesn't get hurt like he was this time."

"That's an excellent idea. I'm surprised I didn't think of it myself," Mack says with a grin I return.

"I'll let you read it, too. Okay?"

"Please. I'd love to understand your mind a little better," he says and I can't tell if he's joking or not until he continues. "Honestly. I'd love to see what you see. And I need to understand how you feel so I can help you fight your demons quicker, Suzanne."

"I'm going to go. Um, for the five thousandth time, thank you Mack. For everything, always."

"You're welcome," he smiles before rising for our customary good bye hug.

"I feel so weird Mack," I whisper against his chest.

"Good weird, or bad weird?"

"Really good weird."

"That's really good, Suzanne," he says squeezing me a little tighter.

"Ugh... I have lots to think about, and a scarf to butcher," I grin as he laughs.

"Have a great evening, and I'll see you in the morning with all the paperwork at 8:30." Opening the door, I nod one last time to my Mack.

Walking back to my room with my knitting bag, I feel so giddy, I can't stop smiling at walls and giggling at nothing. I'm pretty sure once the monitors pick up my mood Mack'll have to explain I'm just happy and not suffering another mental snap of sorts to the monitoring doctors, which is too funny to not laugh at as I skip for my room.

CHAPTER 21
SUZANNE

Gathering all my stuff, Mack knocks and enters my room when I yell come in. After the worst night's sleep ever, I'm ready to just get today over with. I don't know how I'm going home, well, I know Z's picking me up, but I don't know *how* that's going to work.

"Good morning, Suzanne. How are you?" Mack smiles as he enters.

Lifting my luggage on the bed, I state the obvious. "Good morning to you, and I'm scared shitless."

"Are you?" He smirks knowing I am. "Shall we sign all the forms to get them out of the way before we talk?"

"Yes, please," I nod walking to the little table and chairs near the window.

Mindlessly, I sign everywhere Mack points as he flips through pages. Without hearing a word he's saying, I sign after explanations and moments of pause. Thinking of nothing specific, but more a jumble of multiple thoughts, I sign until Mack finally squeezes my hand and then we're done.

"Breathe, Suzanne," he suddenly says and I gasp a quick breath when I'm told to. "What's the biggest feeling taking you over right now?"

"Um, nervous, I think. I don't know," I shake my head to clear it.

"That's normal. And I guarantee Z is nervous as well. So calmly be nervous together, okay?"

"Okay," I exhale and walk back to my bed to grab my one luggage of clothes, my knitting bag, and my purse.

Turning to Mack, I need to know one very little, basic, strangely obvious thing that I really can't figure out on my own. "Ah, Mack? Um, what do we do? Like how do we leave here?"

"Hand in hand," he says so simply everything suddenly clears for me on a whoosh of breath.

"I can do that," I smile.

We are US...

Joining Z in the hallway outside Mack's office, just the sight of him makes me smile and blush again. Like I always have, and probably always will, Z always brings out my smiles and blushes.

"Good morning, Suzanne," he says honestly sounding as nervous as I feel which eases me immediately.

"Good morning, Z. Do you need to talk to Mack at all before we leave?"

"No," he shakes his head. "I signed the papers an hour ago, and I've just been waiting for you to finish up," he seems almost embarrassed that he was here so early for me.

Looking at Z waiting for me to get my shit together, I say everything I can to start this life over again with Z. "Okay. Then let's go home."

And before he can question if I'm really ready, or mentally well, or a list of a thousand other questions he probably wants to ask because he's always like that with me, I take his hand and turn for the hallway we leave the ward from.

"I'll call you tomorrow, Mack," I smile not looking at him as I tug Z's hand down the hall before he takes my luggage from me and silently wheels it beside us as we leave for our home.

At the truck, I just jump in. I don't wait for Z to open my door, and I don't wait for him to speak. I need no questions about my emotional well-being, and I don't want to explain anything right now. I just want to go home. With Z.

"Please take me home," I whisper when he sits in the truck beside me.

"Okay."

During the drive, I notice the silence is heavy but somewhat comfortable. I think we're both reeling, and I *know* there's no music intentionally. Z didn't turn it on, and I wouldn't dare. I mean why tempt fate at this point? Plus, about the only type of music that doesn't cause a trigger of some sort for me is rap, and I just don't think Z's the type to blast rap in his black SUV while driving through Manhattan, I almost giggle.

Honestly, sometimes, I'm so deranged it's really pretty funny to me.

Sarah Ann Walker

When we're nearing our home I know if I don't say something soon to Z, or tell him what I feel I'll start to cry from the pressure, which I know will give him the wrong idea about my silence and tears. I know the way he thinks, but he isn't always right about the way I think. So I need to give him something before he assumes the worst.

"I've missed you very much, Z," I finally whisper within our silence. Turning to look at his beautiful profile, there is so, so much more I want to say. There are thousands of words and endless feelings, and a multitude of emotions I need him to hear and understand. There are even endless apologies I need to make, but I don't know where to start and I don't know what to say anymore.

"Don't look at me, okay? Just keep driving so this is easier," I laugh as he smiles at me quickly then turns away with a nod.

"Um, you are everything to me, Z. And I know I say that, and I know it doesn't really tell you anything, but it really is the truth for me. You are the best husband, and friend, and even lover," I smile as I see his quick grin, "I have ever had or known. You are just *everything*. And I wish there was something better than that, or better words than those, but I don't really have them. I just kind of feel it inside me," I whisper again unconsciously raising my hand to my chest.

"I feel you always inside me because I love you so much. And I know it's a good love, I *do* know that even if I don't always act like I know it. But I do know you are healthy and good for me, and just everything I could ever want or need, even though I said you weren't enough when I was struggling. But I didn't mean that at the time. I've never meant that. I just didn't know how to express how deep my sadness was, and how heavy my depression was without making it somehow about you, which it wasn't. I know that," I exhale hard fighting the tears that want to burst from my chest when I think of how much I've hurt Z.

"Actually, I think I've always known you were enough, it was just everything else I couldn't understand at the time. I'm not done, okay? Just give me a minute," I ask trying to gather my thoughts as Z nods once beside me but doesn't look at me or acknowledge my pause and deep breathing. Driving us minutes from home, Z does as I ask like I know he always will for me.

"God, you're like the best man in the world, Z. You deserve a medal, and awards, and I don't know, some kind of party or something for your awesomeness," I giggle at my stupid as he grins again. "Can I tell you

something?" I barely whisper.
 Turning his head to me quickly, but looking back at the road just as quickly he breathes a nearly silent, 'please...' and I finally tear up.
 "I honestly don't feel like I deserve you."
 "Suzanne-" he interrupts, but I cut him off.
 "Just listen," I try again and he silences with another nod. "I don't feel like I deserve you because I think I'm shit," I say as he flinches and looks at me anyway before turning back to the busy roads and traffic around us.
 "I do. That's just the way I feel about myself all the time. It's how I've always felt. When I was just a kid, as a teenager, when I was married to Marcus, and sadly even when I was with you. I wish I didn't and I wish I could stop the feeling of being shit from choking me, but it's always there, Z. No matter what you, or Mack, or the Kaylas say, I don't feel anything but shit about myself which feels really shitty," I finally laugh at my pathetic explanation. "Wait," I quickly add while still laughing a little so he doesn't interrupt me yet. For Christ's sake, Suzanne, get to the friggin' point I giggle again sounding a little mental. Ugh...
 "Okay. I think we both just thought everything would magically get better. Or like because we loved each other my past would go away and not hurt me anymore. I know *I* thought that, and I'm sure you did too because you're used to fixing people and things and just everything around you. But that didn't happen. My past didn't just go away with your love. So the more I struggled, the harder it was for you to accept I was struggling. And I felt like I shouldn't struggle because you should've been enough to make me all better. But that isn't reality, or even logical. I know that now, and I think you do as well," I ask almost as a question until he nods slightly.
 "So, even though we were together and you loved me, I still felt like shit all the time about myself, while you're like the anti-shit. You're Z who everyone knows and loves, and wants, and admires. You've been described as New York's *former* bachelor extraordinaire, you're in magazines and newspapers because of your wineries and charities, and yeah, you're just Z Zinfandel who is amazing. So what am I beside you? I'm the shit wife. The ugly, scarred, nasty wife with the even nastier past. I'm shit beside you, and with you, and that hurts me all the time. I feel like shit anyway about myself, but knowing the world, or at least New York thinks I'm shit as well really hurts. And sometimes..."

Shit. Here it is. Okay, just say it.

"Sometimes?" Z questions me staring ahead until I realize we're parked in his spot in the underground of our building. Wow, I'm so oblivious to my surroundings it's a miracle I can get from the mall to home without getting lost most days. "Sometimes?" Z actually begs bringing me back to our reality.

"Sometimes, I've wished I never met you so I was just Suzanne Anderson in Chicago. I wished I was completely unknown, and just a woman without a past who no one knew or looked at or read about or even cared about. I sometimes wished I was back before you, blissfully ignorant of my past, and my family, and everything else that's so awful. I wished I was the old Suzanne who was good at her job, professional, emotionally detached and sure of the boring, unfulfilled, mediocre little life she lived then."

When Z turns his head to look out his window I know he's hurt. I know my words have hurt him, but that wasn't my intention. Shit. Finish this!

"But only sometimes. Like when I'm really sad and depressed, and just looking for anything to be an excuse for why I feel so shitty. But most of the time, I thank god for you, Z. *Honestly*," I whisper touching his leg until his hand reaches to cover mine though he still doesn't look at me.

"Kayla says I'm fabulous," I grin as he does briefly. "But of course I don't feel fabulous. I feel insignificant, and ugly, and just so goddamn insecure and paranoid all the time I can't really ever let myself *be* fabulous with anyone, but especially with you. But I want to be. I really want to be fabulous with you like you are with me so I can finally feel like I deserve you. I don't want to *think* I'm shit anymore so I don't *feel* like shit anymore. I really do want to be fabulous, Z. But I need your help."

"You have it," he says quickly before closing down again.

"I'm so sorry for all the things I've put you through. I'm so sorry, Z," I cry gently. "I never meant to make our life together worse, and I didn't realize I was making it worse until everything happened again. Then I didn't know how to fix it, and that's why I wanted to kill myself."

"Suzanne..." Z chokes, but I continue anyway.

"I know you've wanted to really understand why I felt that way, and why I wanted to do that to myself, and that's why. I knew I was screwing us up, but I didn't know how to stop myself until all I thought about was stopping everything. I guess I didn't want you to finally realize I was shit, too," I exhale and wipe the tears sliding down my cheeks.

"I've never thought you were shit, Suzanne. Not ever."

"I know you didn't, but I did. So it didn't matter what you said or did. I couldn't get past thinking the way I think, which just made me turn everything bad onto you. But again, I really didn't mean to hurt you. I just didn't believe you could actually like me, or want me, or even love me. It has never made sense to me, so I never truly believed anything you said to me," I admit finally.

"And now?" He asks quietly.

"Now, I believe you," I whisper as more tears start falling.

"Why now?" He asks in a tone that sounds both confused and somewhat disbelieving.

"Um, because you're here. For whatever reason, you keep coming back. After all I've done and said and put you through, the fact that you showed up at the hospital demanding to take me home, made me believe you finally. For whatever reason, I believe you love me and I want you to love me as much as I love you."

"But you still think you're shit," he says like now he doesn't believe me.

"Yes, but I'm trying to see the woman you see, and I'm trying really hard to believe she's the woman you love. It's like, if the famous, amazing, sweet, kind, sexy as hell Z can think I'm not shit, then maybe I'm not. Maybe I'm just a screwed up woman with a shitty past, who isn't actually shitty herself. Maybe..."

"Definitely," he exhales squeezing my hand tighter on his thigh.

"I'm going to try so hard this time, Z. But I'll try for both of us this time, because I hate being without you more than I struggle with my past now. And that was the biggest difference this time when I was in the hospital. Before, my past was bigger than me, or you, or both of us combined. But this time my past felt smaller than the loss of you in my life. So as Mack would say, I finally woke up to my reality *now* and what's actually important within it."

Winding down, I think I'm finally at the point I'm trying to make to Z. "Look, I know I'm never going to be completely stable. I think we both know that. But statistically, the fact that I'm not a junkie, or an alcoholic, or even worse, a whore because of my sexually abusive past and lack of self-worth says something good about me. And I want it to say that I'm stronger than I thought I was."

"You've always been strong," Z says turning to me.

"Again, you always said that, but I didn't believe you at the time because I didn't *feel* strong. Now though, I believe it because I'm starting to think it's true, too," I admit with a little smile as Z watches my face closely. "Um, I don't think I'm as shit as I thought, and I want to live with you and love you as best as I can now," I whisper as Z tears up beside me.

In the darkened underground within the darker windows of his truck, Z and I watch each other for long, intense minutes until he finally nods.

Squeezing my hand, Z leans across the front seat and hugs me so quickly I gasp at the movement until I just exhale in his arms. Holding me tighter than necessary and longer than usual, Z doesn't move or speak, and I don't want to. His scent and his warmth and his everything makes me suddenly feel totally grounded and loved.

Pulling away slightly, Z kisses my lips softly before he says the sweetest words I've ever heard in my life. "You are *everything* to me, Suzanne. And if or *when* you feel like you're shit, you just tell me, and I'll love you harder until you don't feel like shit anymore. You just tell me when the shitty feeling hits, and I'll love it right out of you. Okay?" He whispers kissing me again softly.

"Okay," I whisper back with a little cry of relief.

"Let's go home, love," Z smiles his beautiful Z smile, and even as my tears falls harder, I nod.

ααααα

Walking to our front door, both Z and I are grinning and kind of moving awkwardly. We're still holding hands, but as we walk down the hall we aren't in step with each other so my arm pulls, or his leg pauses to wait for my leg to move to catch up. It's really awkward, but thankfully as I giggle he huffs a quick laugh.

"*Losers?*" He smirks.

"Totally," I laugh as we reach our door.

"Come on then, loser. I want to hug you," Z smiles opening the door to the home I wasn't sure I would ever enter again.

We are US...

Looking around, everything is exactly as I remember leaving it, with the exception of the beautiful bouquet of flowers sitting on the coffee table. Walking to them, I lift the card and open it to find Z's handwriting with only 'I love you' written inside and nothing else.
"I didn't know what to say, and they don't have cards along the lines of 'Welcome home from the nuthouse, ya crazy psycho' so..." he says so deadpan with a shrug I burst out laughing as he grins.
"They're beautiful and the card is perfect, Z," I smile until the awkward hits us again.
Looking at each other, I don't know what to do, and clearly neither does Z. I mean really, what the hell do we do now? Talk, cry, laugh, sleep? Actually, I'd like any or all of those options with him.
"I'm just going to take my things to our room if that's okay?" I ask awkwardly.
"It's your home, Suzanne. Do whatever you'd like. I'll stay here so you can have a moment if you'd like," Z says almost as a question.
"I don't need a moment. I'm tired but a little hyper as well. Um, would you lay down with me?" I ask sure of my question, but unsure of his reaction.
"Of course. I've slept horribly without you, and I need to hold you Suzanne," Z admits so sadly, I walk right back to him still near the door and take his hand. Not even pausing, I pull him with me to our room as he wheels my luggage behind him.
Walking straight to my room pulling Z, I kick off my heels, drop inches lower to the floor, and continue pulling him as I crawl up our bed. Pulling his hand, I don't wait for him to climb up before I'm against the headboard making him fall into my side and partially on my chest as I wrap my arms around his shoulders.
Holding him tightly against *my* chest for once, I want to weep with the sadness and the happiness, and the overwhelming sense of right in this room with Z. This is where I should be, and where I want to be, and where I'll always be from now on.
"I'm never going to screw us up again," I whisper against his head as he snuggles into my chest harder. Nearly squeezing the breath from my lungs, Z doesn't speak, and I don't need words. I need this- *me* holding Z for a change.
Threading my fingers through his hair, I breathe Z into me and find the strength I need to tell him our last unanswered.

"I have to tell you something before I can listen to anything you want to say, and before I can finally move on with you. I'm going to be very honest and I want you to listen and believe me, okay?"

"Okay," he moves pulling away from my chest to lie on his side beside me.

Turning to my side as well, I sit up quickly to pull my favorite throw blanket over the 2 of us before settling back down on my side. Staring at Z's beautiful face waiting for me I know what I have to do and I know what he needs to hear.

Inhaling deeply as he waits, I smile quickly before speaking. "I do love Thomas, Z. I always have," I whisper as he jolts beside me.

Burying his face in our bed I hear him moan, 'oh fuck, Suzanne,' and I immediately reach for him. Throwing my leg over his hip, I tug him into my chest as I feel him moan under me. Wrapping my arms tightly around him he moans nearly silently against our bed, and I feel like I need to protect him this time. From me, from our past, and from the pain I wish he didn't always feel so he can finally move on.

"Listen to me," I whisper against the side of his face. "I do love Thomas. I think I always did, but then he died and it hurt me so much to see you in so much pain, I just shoved my own feelings of loss aside so that you could have his loss as your own. I didn't want to take that away from you, or make it about me. So instead I made myself feel nothing. But I did feel his loss, and I still do. And I hate what happened, and I hate that we lost him. I hate that you lost your beautiful son because of me," I whisper choke.

"You didn't," he struggles to sit up but I hold him tighter so he won't look at me.

"Come on, Z. At the end of the day, for whatever reason, it was *my* body that wasn't enough for him and he died. So that's my burden to carry, and that's why I didn't want to act like I cared or loved him. I didn't want you to have to split your pain, or have to do or feel anything for me as well. I wanted you to feel his loss however you needed. I know you see him and that's why when I found out you were still visiting him once a month I didn't say anything to you. Because I didn't want you to have to add the Suzanne to your feelings for him."

"Mack just told me you known for a while now," he mumbles under us.

"I know he did. He told me he told you I knew."

"I'm sorry I hid that from you."

We are US...

"*Never* be sorry for anything you do for him. Thomas was going to be your son, so you can handle that however you need. And that's why I left it for you alone. Not because I didn't feel sadness, and not because I didn't love him, Z. I pretended I didn't care, so you were free to care however you needed to by keeping all the dramatic Suzanne shit out of it."

"But-" Z tries to lift away from me, but I pull him tighter to me again.

"I have the picture," I whisper as Z jolts beneath me again. "Mack told me about it when I found out and I asked to see it. I *know*, Z. And Mack made me a copy when I asked, and it's in my wallet, and sometimes I look at it and I just cry. I know it's the only picture you have of him, and I know when I was in recovery after the C-section Mack took the picture for you. I also know you have it in your wallet as well. I *know*, Z..." I whisper as the pain threatens to crush me. But I push through my sadness for Z.

"That picture of you holding our little baby boy in your arms, so gently, is the most beautiful, heart-breaking picture I've ever seen in my life. It's so sad, and lovely, and just *heart*-breaking, Z. And when I see his little face poking out of the blanket, I can't believe he's dead, and I can't believe the look of love and sadness on your face as you hold him. And I can't believe how badly I wish everything about that day was different for both of us. But I can't change the fact that he died, so all I can do is try to never forget him, or how much you wanted him in your life. And that's what I do. I remember him with sadness and regret, and with almost a promise now that I won't ever cause you that much pain again."

"But you didn't kill him, Suzanne. It just happened," he moans, finally pulling free of my death grip to turn to his side as I resettle. "I've never blamed you for even one second for what happened to him."

"I know you haven't. And I love you so much for that. So, so much, I want to try to make it up to you one day," I admit with the implication of my sentence hanging all around us and all over our bodies. It's just there in our silence and I know Z understands, and I know Z finally feels hope for our future.

"One day...?" He questions as I nod.

"2 more things," I say as he huffs like he's had enough for today, which naturally makes me grin. "I promise I'm almost done my shit," I smile as he does. "I'd like to go with you next month on the second anniversary of Thomas' death, and I'd like to make a copy of that picture so I can

frame it and put it in our atrium, if that's okay?"
 Pausing again, Z seems to think before he answers me. Inhaling deeply, he says, "Of course you can come with me, I'd love that. And that picture framed I'd love, too. I've always wanted one but I thought I was hiding it from you," he smirks. "But why the atrium?"
 "Because that's the place I thought of ending it all. Where I made my decisions, and wrote my letters, and where I saw the end of me so clearly. I think I need a picture of what could've been to remind me of what might one day be again, in a different little version. But the atrium is kind of about death for me, so somehow the picture of you and Thomas feels like it might make it about life for me. Or something," I fade out when my words make less sense than the emotions behind them.
 "Okay," Z says gently, moving on our bed to lean back against all the pillows like he always does. Pulling me up on his chest and side, everything suddenly feels like it should between us.
 "I know I'm not normal, Z. But I'm going to try to be."
 "Suzanne. Shut up now," Z says with his smile-voice and I stop speaking immediately with a grin. "You're so beautiful," he whispers pulling me up against his lips. And for the first time I appreciate his words and I accept them from him.
 "Thank you for saying that," I whisper against his mouth as he huffs an agonized sounding cry. Leaning his forehead against my own, Z exhales and I feel the smile on my face I should've had all along when he tells me I'm beautiful.
 "You aren't normal, and I'm not perfect. But this right here is what we are. We are US, Suzanne. And I love us," Z exhales all the tension and sadness for both of us as I'm pulled back down his chest to snuggle into his warmth and love.

We are US...

Sarah Ann Walker

BREATHE

We are US...

CHAPTER 22

"Holy *shit!* You're a psycho," Kayla starts laughing as Z pauses beside her shaking his head with a grin.
Turning around quickly to glare at her I defend myself immediately. "I'm not a- okay, I am. But not about this," I growl as she hands me a pumpkin pie she swore she was going to bake herself, but clearly didn't from the packaging. "Nice pie, Kayla," I glare again.
"Whatever. I burned my real attempt, so I bought one to make up for it. Honestly, how tall is it?" She stares up at the ceiling.
"At least 18 feet," Z adds not so helpfully with a cough laugh.
"And how tall are your ceilings, Z?"
"16 feet, I believe," Z says again just barely holding in his laughter.
"You know what? Both of you can piss off!" I growl. "It's going to look beautiful when it's finished." Laughing as I walk toward our kitchen I still hear the 2 of them laughing at my back. The assholes.
I've been out of the hospital for 2 amazing months, and thankfully after a heavy conversation with each Kayla, they seemed to forgive my actions and the choices I almost made. Kayla Lefferts even still comes to our house frequently though she has her own cool apartment just 2 1/2 blocks away from us now.
And we're all really good. Mack still councils me and Z, together and individually, and though it's hard for him sometimes to keep the shrink out of it when we're out of his office, somehow he manages for us which we appreciate.
After the hospital I stopped seeing Dr. Phillips completely, and I seem so much better. I *am* so much better, but neither Z and I are naive, nor do we think the darkness will always stay behind us. We do however talk more about the dark things when they bother me.
I even keep a journal now, which though a little high schoolish, has been remarkably helpful for us. I write almost every night before bed, or when the mood strikes, or when I've had a 'thing' throughout the day. And every morning Z reads the previous day's entry with his coffee

We are US...

before work, so he can see where I'm at, and it seems to be working.

Amazingly, I don't lie or alter the truth knowing Z's going to read it, and he doesn't react poorly or pissed off if I write something negative. Sometimes, he even talks about the negative with me and I either see his side, or he sees mine, and we both feel better. I know I could just tell him at the time what I'm feeling which is ideal, but it's not ideal for me. I still have a hard time expressing what it is I'm feeling exactly when or how I feel it, but by writing everything down I seem more able to express my thoughts clearly for Z, which he loves.

Some mornings when he's up reading, I hear his laughter from the kitchen over something I write, and some mornings I feel him crawl back into bed beside me to reaffirm how much he loves me in his life if I was insecure the day before.

And for those few days when the feelings of being shit overwhelmed me and I wrote about it, Z snuggled right in, morning breath and all, and he loved the shit feeling right out of me like he promised he would do. Quite well, actually.

"You're not mad at me, are you?" Kayla asks from the kitchen doorway.

"Not at all. I know the tree is huge, but I picture it so beautiful when it's finished, I couldn't stop myself from buying it. I love Christmas trees, and my parents always had one proper tree that their staff decorated, and Marcus didn't think it was practical to have one because it was just the 2 of us. And though last year's tree was nice it just didn't feel as special as I wanted. Anyway, I bought the biggest tree I could find, to decorate it the way I want. So laugh about the height all you want, it's going to be fabulous when I'm done," I grin as she does.

"But how are you going to get to the top? You're like a little person," she grins as I burst out laughing.

"5'3 isn't a little person, ya asshole. And Z says maintenance has a huge ladder for me to borrow. So I'm telling you by next week I'll have the most beautiful Christmas tree in New York."

"I can't wait to see it," she smiles as she lifts the lid off the gravy and dunks a little bun into it before I can stop her. "I'm starving," she wiggles her eyebrows when I stop to lean against the counter.

Crossing my arms, I'm dying to know. "Who?"

Wiping her mouth after moaning over my delicious gravy, she grins blushing. BLUSHING! "Ah, Marty. But don't tell anyone!" She yells as I

screech and cover my mouth. "We're just casual so we're not telling anyone, and he's going to totally ignore me today and act like we weren't just screwing 4 hours ago. And I swear to god if you tell Z I'll kill you."
"I won't! But oh my god, how was it? Is it? Like how often is casual?"
"I don't know, a dozen or so times," she mumbles as I jump in.
"A dozen? That's not casual for you, Kayla. That's almost a relationship."
"No, it's not!" She yells back until we both quiet down looking nervously at the kitchen door for Z.
"Have you gone out for dinner? To the movies? Anywhere besides your bedrooms?"
"Yeah..." She moans looking mortified.
"Well, Kayla, here's a news flash for you. You're dating," I laugh as she flinches and looks so uncomfortable I reach to hug her.
"Shit," she mumbles again as I laugh at her look of almost fear.
Pulling away, I'm dying to know. "So? Is he more than a test drive? Do you, ah, like his stick shift?" I giggle when she looks at me like I'm pathetic.
"Ugh, that soooo doesn't work for you. But yes, his stick shift is just fine. Awesome, actually. And I can work it and ride it all night. Which I did actually," she bursts out laughing when I feel my own face heat up redder and redder the longer she speaks. "Fuck, you're funny. As if you don't ride your own sexy as hell stick shift every chance you get," she laughs again as I cover my smile and blush with my hand.
"What are you girls talking about?" Z asks as we both spin and yell *nothing* at the same time. Okay, we're totally busted, and I'm cringing because Z always gets the truth out of me with just a look.
"Z. This isn't Suzanne's, so you can't force it out of her. It's *my* secret. So just leave her alone," Kayla says stepping a foot toward Z like she's actually protecting me from him which is too funny.
"Understood," Z nods gravely, but when she quickly turns back to look at me like we're safe, he winks letting me know he's gonna get it out of me later. *Shit.*

"Hello?" Mack's calls from the living room as Z spins out of the kitchen with a grin for me.
Walking out behind him, Kayla grabs my wrist and begs one last time, "Please don't tell anyone, Suzanne. I'm not ready, and I don't think

We are US...

Marty is, and we're not a couple or anything, and I don't want anyone to get the wrong idea, okay?" Begging me all panicky, it's kind of refreshing to see on her usually composed, cool, almost arctic face for a change.

"I would never tell, Kayla. I promise." After she exhales a nod back with a thanks thrown in we leave the kitchen.

"Hi." Grabbing Mack for a hug Z takes Kayla's coat from her.

"Hi back, Suzanne. It smells delicious in here." Looking quickly at my unadorned gigantic tree I can see Mack wants to engage me, so I jump in first.

"I'm not crazy. I just wanted the biggest, most beautiful Christmas tree in New York *outside* of Rockefeller Square anyway, so I bought it. I'm going to take off the last few branches so it doesn't actually bend against the ceiling, and it's going to be beautiful," I add before he can.

"I have no doubt it'll be beautiful Suzanne," Mack smiles. Ha! I love him more than anyone but Z as I turn and smirk at Kayla who rolls her eyes and mumbles 'he's just hungry' making us all laugh but his Kayla.

"Take these," Kayla groans handing me bowls of turnip and squash, I think. "Quickly," she adds before dashing to my kitchen with me and Kayla following.

"Ahhh, what's-"

"Wait." Fanning her face leaning against the counter Kayla ignores us. Watching her breathe deeply I can't help but grin at (formally) Chicago Kayla who rolls her eyes again. "I'm-"

"Pregnant," both Kayla and I join her as she moans the word.

"What? How did you know? Did Mack tell you?" She asks furiously.

Placing the bowls on the counter, I smile and shake my head no. But before I can speak, Kayla jumps in.

"You're like the *worst!* At Macy's a few weeks ago you had the stomach flu. Then last week at Marty's restaurant you had food poisoning when you 2 left before the main course. And the week before that, you declined Chinese when we all came back here after Z's speech, and-"

"Okay, I get it," Kayla whines. "I was trying to get through the first trimester without making it obvious."

"By barfing everywhere, or looking like you were going to barf, or by moaning about barfing every time we saw you for the last 2 months?" Kayla adds helpfully as I grin silently.

"Ah, yeah. This pregnancy sucks," Kayla huffs a laugh finally.

"I'm so, so happy for you both," I choke up as I hug her. "You're going to be an amazing mom, Kayla. I know it," I whisper as she hugs me tighter.

"Thanks, Suzanne," she whispers on a long exhale.

Pulling out our hug, Kayla steps in for one of her own, and I'm happy. We're all doing well, and nothing seems bad, well, except for all the nausea. But hey, it's not me barfing this time, so I'm cool with it.

"It's been bad, huh?" Kayla asks as Kayla nods.

"Fuck- *frigging* brutal," Kayla corrects as I laugh. "I'm trying to watch my language now so I don't traumatized this kid with an f-bomb every few minutes of his or her little life," she grins as I laugh again.

"No worries.. With a Shrink for a dad, I'm sure the kid will be screwed up anyway," Kayla adds as Kayla howls with laughter. "Oh! Can I have Mack's Porsche now?"

"What? *Why?*"

"Don't you have to buy a minivan or something equally as responsible? Won't it look weird driving a Porsche with a baby in the back?"

Grinning as Kayla thinks, I realize from her wrinkled forehead she hasn't thought about Mack's car yet. "Um, there isn't even a backseat, so..." she shrugs. "Shit. My beetle is too small, too. Oh, crap. Mack and I have to go buy a car now. I never thought about it," she says sounding panicky.

"You have lots of time. Relax, Kayla," I try to soothe as she exhales again. Jeez, talk about mood swings.

"What are you girls taking about?" Z asks from the doorway, as both Kayla and I yell *nothing* again like losers.

Laughing at the two of us, Kayla says softly, "I'm pregnant, Z," almost like she's afraid that might hurt him but it doesn't. The smile she receives is so beautiful my heart nearly bursts as I watch his face light up.

Walking to her, Z takes Kayla into his arms so sweetly, she snuggles in deep and exhales again. When he whispers something in her ear which I'm dying to know, Kayla immediately tears up and pulls away to look at his face again with a smile. Kissing his cheek briefly, Kayla whispers 'thank you', and I find my own eyes filling up.

She looks so happy, and Z looks so beautiful at her I realize if it was me who was having his baby he would always look at me like that. Z would look at me with such sweetness, my heart would actually swell in my chest.

"Are you okay?" Mack leans into my side to ask quietly.

We are US...

Turning to him, "I'm so okay. And I'm really happy for you both. Oh! And I'm going to knit a blanket for your baby!" I yell as everyone looks at me like I'm a little bit mental, which I'm not. I'm just happy.

"I'd love a baby blanket," Kayla adds stepping away from Z to take Mack's hand.

"Wow. I'm going to be kind of an aunt," I add with awe in my voice. "I never thought I would be. Well, actually it was impossible as an only child, but now I am kind of, which is very cool. Aunt Suzanne," I say but I don't really like it. It seems too formal or something. "Aunt Suzie?" I question no one in particular. "Auntie Sue?" Huh. I've got nothing.

"I like Aunt Suzie," Mack says before Kayla adds a 'Q'.

"Yeah. Aunt Suzie-Q is cute for sure," Kayla laughs at my wrinkled nose. "And I'll just be it's fabulous Aunt Kayla," she adds nodding like it's a done deal.

"I don't want to be Suzie-Q," I whine as Z laughs at me taking my hand.

"What about Aunt Tommy," he says as I gasp. "It *is* your actual name, love," he adds with a little smile.

"Oh my god! Like Grama Tommy, but Aunt instead. Oh, I love it. Can I be Aunt Tommy?" I turn to a teary-eyed Kayla.

"I think Aunt Tommy is perfect," Mack says softly as I feel my own tears well up again.

"Wow. Talk about growth, huh?" I question as both Z and Mack laugh at my expression.

"Yup. You're doing good, Suzanne."

"Thanks, Mack." Turning from him back to the stove, I don't want to get heavy, and I don't want to make this about me at all. This isn't my news, and it's not my day, so I'm going to leave all the Suzanne shit out of it for everyone. "Why don't you all go back to the living room while I finish up. Dinner should be ready in about 20 minutes, so grab drinks while you wait." With my back turned to everyone I hear the mumbled okays as they leave me in the kitchen.

"Suzanne?"

Jumping right in, I have to be sure. "Are *you* okay with hearing the name Tommy all the time?" I turn to Z leaning against the counter watching me for any upset.

"Yes. He's Thomas to me. I never think of him as Tommy, and it wouldn't matter anyway. He was named after you. A charming name I love for the beautiful little blue-eyed, strawberry blonde love of my life.

So Aunt Tommy is cool with me," Z says so sweetly again, I laugh cry before leaning into his chest.
　Wiping my few tears, I whisper, "You're good, Mr. Zinfandel," as he laughs. "And now I wish we were alone for an hour or two," I pull away with my own attempt at a naughty eyebrow wiggle, which I doubt I pulled off but has Z smiling anyway when he leans down to my ear.
　"You. Me. Sex-couch. Tonight, love. So be prepared," he growls sexily in my ear as I shiver. Oh, I'll be prepared alright. Though I better watch all the turkey I eat so I don't fall into a tryptophan coma like everyone tends to do after Thanksgiving.
　"Don't eat too much Turkey, Z. I want you wide awake with me alllll night," I rub up against him suggestively. Groaning, Z mumbles, 'fuck me, Suzanne,' and I can't stop myself. "I plan on it," slips out and as I blush he growls again before shaking his head and stepping away from me.
　"Watch yourself, Suzanne, because I don't care half as much about dinner as I do about getting inside you," he threatens as I gasp again. What a dirty bugger! "Come out here and have a drink with me while we wait for Marty," he takes my hand with a dirty boy smirk, like he knows his words just totally turned me on, which they totally did.

　Sitting on the love-seat beside Z, he and Mack talk about a Giants game vs. some other team I could care less about when the door knocks signaling Marty. Practically bouncing in my chair my head whips over to Kayla who actually ducks her head quickly with another goddamn blush as she smiles at her glass of wine. Holy *shit!* This is gonna to be awesome.
　"Good afternoon, everyone," Marty smiles handing Z a huge platter of his famous honeyed ham.
　"Hey handsome,' Mack's Kayla smiles as he leans in to kiss her cheek quickly. But when Z starts walking to our kitchen with the ham I reach for his pant leg to stop him.
　Pausing for a second to look down at me I tilt my head quickly to Kayla and just as he looks, Marty walks right up to her, lifts her off the couch by her hands and plants the biggest, oh *wow*, sexiest kiss on her lips as she moans and leans into his body.
　Watching them kiss, I look quickly at Kayla and Mack and almost burst out laughing. Mack is wide-eyed, and Kayla is grinning from ear to ear while bouncing a little on the couch across from them. Kayla even leans

to the side to get a better view of their kiss which finally does me in.

Giggling, Marty finally breaks off their kiss, wipes his mouth casually and smiles at me with a quick wink.

"Um..." Kayla moans blushing again, and I swear to god, we're all mesmerized by her blushing discomfort.

"I've missed you, Kayla. What's it been, 5 hours since I was last in your bed?" Marty asks with such a sexy voice *I* almost feel it, so I can only imagine what Kayla's feeling.

"Holy shit! Shoot! *Whatever*. That was hot!" Kayla yells as Mack laughs beside her. "5 hours?" She grins as Kayla still stands speechless.

"Yup. And much too long for me. Let's not go that long without seeing each other, alright?" Marty asks a nodding Kayla who doesn't seem able to speak. "Good," he says kissing her lips quickly before she plops back down on the couch.

Still holding Z's pant leg, I finally let go and look at him laughing at me as I grin. Now he can't torture me later.

"Nice potential tree, Suzanne. Once you remove those few extra branches up top, I bet you have the most beautiful tree outside of Rockefeller," Marty says my exact argument to the others, making me smile immediately in triumph.

"That's the plan. Would you like a drink," I ask rising as Z finally takes the ham to the kitchen.

"I'd love one. Kayla?" He turns back to ask a still silent Kayla who only lifts her half glass of wine in the air. As an aside to me, Marty whispers, "I think I'm in trouble," as he grins a very Z-like grin.

"Yup. You're dead meat when she gets you alone," I whisper back as he gives a charming little shrug.

Walking to the far end of our living room, Marty lifts the scotch decanter and as he adds ice cubes to his glass I'm just dying to ask him anything, and everything, and just, yeah... I'm dying to know what's going on between them from *his* perceptive.

"I'm crazy about her, Suzanne," Marty says staring at his glass. When I hear myself gasp he turns to me with a beautiful smile.

Leaning into Marty, I just hug him. I don't feel weird, and everything feels so right suddenly I hug him as he squeezes me back. Resting against his chest, I whisper, "Good. She needs someone who is crazy about her."

"I know."

"Um, but she's going to fight you and be bitchy and act like-"
"She doesn't give a shit? I know that, too," he smiles and I suddenly realize he does know, and he doesn't care.
"Okay. Good," I finish as he nods our understanding. "Ah, would you please help me get everything ready at the same time? I can cook decent enough, but having multiple dishes ready at the same time isn't my strong suit. And seeing as you're a famous chef I'm assuming you'd be a big help right about now for me," I beg as he nods.
"Yup. Cooking and *patience* are my strong suits. Lead the way, Suzanne," he motions as we walk to my kitchen to a waiting Z in the doorway.
"Nice entrance," Z smirks.
"Uh huh. I learned from the best," Marty counters as I laugh. That *was* such a sexy Z thing to do.
"She's going to kill you for that later."
"I know. So I'll quickly get her into bed until she's exhausted and forgets she's mad at me," Marty smiles and I see why Kayla is attracted to him. He's charming as hell, good looking, successful, and really just so like Mack and Z it's like they really are the brothers they basically are for each other in life.
"I can't even imagine what the 3 of you were like as teenagers, or even in college. The girls must have been so in love with the 3 of you," I add looking between Z and Marty who is already stirring my gravy before opening my double oven.
"We did okay," Marty says with a little laugh pulling out my broccoli casserole to check the temperature.
"Uh huh. Something tells me you did more than okay," I grin to Z smiling at me. "Who had the most *followers*?" I ask with a smirk.
"Mack," they both reply and I'm stunned.
"Really?" I gasp. "I though Z for sure, no offense Marty, then you, then Mack. I didn't think... *Really?*"
"Yup," Z smiles as Marty nods.
"Why? I mean he's really good looking, and sweet, and so kind, and just awesome, but... *Oh.*"
"Pretty much," Marty laughs. "Let's see... Z was the sexy, rich, dark, bossy one," he nods his head at a grinning Z. "I was the good looking, funny one, who used my skills in the kitchen to get them into the bedroom," he says so seriously I blush laugh. "But Mack was like all of

the above. He was good looking, funny, and serious. Plus he was going to be a doctor, and he was sensitive, and he listened to women talk, and he was so understanding women just fell over themselves for him. Right?"

"Yup," Z adds still smiling at my shocked face. Suddenly, I can totally see it, but he's just been so good to me and kind of like never sexual that I didn't think he was like that. "Suzanne, stop over-thinking. Whereas Marty was a love em and leave em kind, and I was a love em a little kind, Mack wasn't a pig, no matter how many women wanted him. He was very respectful, and he had relationships not one night stands. So don't worry, he's still the saint you imagine," he smirks as Marty laughs.

"Okay. But wow. I just assumed you 2 got all the chicks," I admit stupidly as they both laugh at me.

"Oh, Z and I did alright," Marty adds as I growl at him.

"Enough, Marty. You've never met my crazily possessive, jealous as hell little wife here, and I'd much rather you didn't," Z finishes by kissing my lips gently. "Forever in the past, love. You are *it* for me," he whispers against my lips as I lean into his chest exhaling the quick thoughts of Z and other women.

Standing on my tiptoes I breathe against his ear, "You. Me. Sex-couch tonight. So be prepared, Z," and as he moans against me I turn for the counter toward all the food Marty keeps touching, testing, and moving back and forth to the ovens or stove top.

ααααα

During dinner, the atmosphere is so warm and wonderful, I catch myself smiling often and tearing up sometimes. I'm never sad though, and nothing bad surfaces. I feel such happiness in my new life with my new family, I enjoy my new everything. It's a happiness I've truly never known, and a happiness I would have never thought was out there waiting for me.

"I'm really happy," I mumble out loud as Z takes my hand quickly on the table and squeezes it. Looking at him, I smile my best smile and continue eating the best Thanksgiving dinner I've ever had in my life, surrounded by tales of the 3 men, Kayla tales from Chicago, and even a few New York Kayla tales of being a gangly 6 foot teenager which she hated.

And throughout I listen and laugh and smile. I don't have any stories of my own, and no one even tries to ask me. I mean, they all know my life wasn't something you discuss over a happy Thanksgiving meal, and that's okay. I take in their pasts and enjoy our present together.

"Come here, Love," Z growls as I exit the bathroom. Pausing for only one second, I've been waiting for him to love me all night. Christ, I was almost anxious to get dessert over with so everyone would get the hell out I wanted him so badly.

"Where do you want me, Mr. Zinfandel," I ask shyly, and I swear I saw his arousal climb just from my words alone.

"Sit on the couch, Suzanne," he growls again until I move. Stepping around him, I make sure to brush against his naked side before sitting demurely in the middle of our special little sex couch. "Take off your nightgown, Suzanne."

Watching his eyes darken as his eyelashes lower on his cheeks, I do as I'm told. Lifting my black nightie overhead, I don't even have time to toss it aside before Z is on his knees in front of me. Spreading my legs wide, he pushes between them with his hips taking my face in his hands for a deep kiss.

"I love you, Suzanne. And I had a wonderful time today. You pulled off the best Thanksgiving dinner I've ever been to, and you made everyone love you a little more with your sweetness today."

"Thank you," I whisper against his lips wrapping my arms around his shoulders to pull him closer to me.

Moaning, I move against his body trying to get more of him. I need him so badly, and I want to feel him inside me so deeply I beg, 'please' before I can stop myself.

"Please, what?" He teases like a little shit, and I want to growl at him.

"Please, please me," I squeak feeling embarrassed but not really caring either.

Pulling away from my face, resting on his heels with his hands on my spread thighs, Z asks softly, "Don't I always, love?"

Exhaling with a little shiver at his dark, delicious voice I moan, "Yes," as he looks down at my naked body. Wanting to quickly close my legs, I fight the urge and I'm rewarded by Z slowly moving his hands further up my thighs to lightly touch me. Staring at my eyes, Z touches me until I seem to move into his touch.

When Z's thumbs open my body to his sight I moan before he does. Wanting so much and nearly begging for more, Z smiles at me before entering me slowly with a finger.

"Oh, *please*..." I whine as my left leg starts shaking on the floor.

"Lift your feet on the couch Suzanne, and lean back," he breathes as I moan again.

Lifting my feet, I know what he sees. I know he sees everything, and still he stares like my body is beautiful to him. He stares at my opened body and the look he holds releases me once again from the horror of my past.

Moving closer, Z bends until touching me with his tongue we both gasp and moan together at the sensation. Feeling his mouth and fingers inside me, while feeling the tense buildup to all I've ever wanted with Z, I wait out my release. Crying and groaning with the pleasure, Z keeps me on the edge until my begging sounds more like a chant in our room.

Forever it seems I move and moan to Z's mouth taking me. Pushing against him, pulling him deeper inside me, I'm almost there when he suddenly pulls away to enter me slowly with his body leaning over me for a kiss as I suddenly release.

Grunting and moving awkwardly against him, Z holds my hips in place as he continues his slow impalement through the shudders wracking my body. Kissing the breath from my lungs, he speeds up his movements as my own slow down until we match rhythms. Slow and securely we move against each other as I open my eyes to his dark eyes watching me always.

"I love you," I groan as he kisses me again, and then I have no more words.

Lifting my right thigh around his back, Z continues to enter me deeper as I speed up our rhythm with my own. I need to feel him inside me, and I need to feel his release.

I want all of Z tonight. I want everything he can give me deep inside me to keep me surrounded and protected by his love.

"Come inside me, Z," I whisper as he speeds up his movements again. Pushing the back of my thighs up against my chest with his hands, Z thrusts into me everything I know of his love. He is here and I am free, and there's nothing between us anymore.

There is only us in our room and in our marriage now. There is nothing but this love between us.

"Are you ready, love?" Z groans as he thrusts into me harder and deeper.

"Always," I smile as I push faster against his movement.

This is where we go together. Z touches me and I know the build and the climb, and the end to all I've ever wanted. I know the plans and the future, and I know the life and love we're going to share together.

We are US... and I love us.

"Look. At. Me," he grunts with each thrust. And just as my eyes focus on him, the wave washes over me into Z as he returns the tide back into my body. We are free floating and I never want to resurface. I am floating in a sea of Z and I never want to reach the surface without him.

Leaning his forehead against mine as we both breathe our recovery, I wrap my weak arms around him and pull him down to my chest.

"Just stay with me like this," I beg as Z exhales on me.

"This is where I'll always be, Suzanne," he whispers.

Holding him tighter to my chest, I return the only words I have left for Z. "I believe you."

And that's all there is between us in this moment. Z's words and my acceptance of his life and love in my arms, always.

Sarah Ann Walker

CHAPTER 23

"Suzanne..." Kayla moans when I open the door. "I'm sorry, but-" running for the bathroom, I just catch the tray she was handing me before Mack starts to follow.

"Here," I push the tray back at him. "Let me," I squeeze his arm as he huffs a nod.

Following closely behind Kayla she just makes the toilet in my master bath before throwing up. Again. For like the 10 thousandth time in the last 4 months. Trying desperately to hold in my own gag, I realize once again I could never be a nurse.

God, everything bodily grosses me right out, and I have NO idea how doctors and nurses handle sickness all the time.

"What can I do, Kayla?" I ask gently behind her as she stretches right out beside my toilet.

"Nothing," she cries which breaks my heart. Grabbing a facecloth to wet with cool water, I drop down beside her and take her into my arms for a hug.

"Um, you look lovely," I try for anything.

"*Seriously?* I'm still Barfy McWhatthefuck? And I'm dying here. Plus, it's official. I have hyperemesis gravidarum, or severe morning sickness in layman's terms which means I have to take medication and be monitored closely because I'm so dehydrated from this little bastard."

"It's not actually a bastard, Kayla, considering you were married when you got knocked up," I grin as she laughs then lifts quickly for the toilet again.

Bracing myself behind her, I rub her back and fight my own gags with each horrible wrenching sound she makes. God, her pregnancy is ugly. "Thank god I was in a coma for the early stages of mine," I say out loud before realizing it and that's it. Kayla calls me a lucky bitch and starts gag-laughing into the echo of my toilet bowl.

"What can I do?" Mack asks behind us and as we turn, Kayla's eyes fill with tears. "Please, Kayla? Let me take you home," Mack begs but she still shakes her head no.

"Do you want to lie down on my bed for a few minutes? It's nothing. No one's even here yet. And who gives a shit anyway?"

"You don't mind?" She asks with the saddest voice ever, and I actually laugh a little.

"Are you kidding me? After all you've done for me, you really think lying on my bed is a big deal? Pu-lease..." I say in her tragic accent and as she smiles we both start to slowly move to stand up. Leaning into me, Kayla uses Mack's outstretched hand and my side for support.

Turning to the mirror, she sees her pale, make-up smeared face but before the upset can hit her, I flip up my hair from my scars, and whisper, "I still beat you," as she smiles sadly with a nod before scrubbing her face and hands in the sink.

Collapsing on my bed, Mack crawls in beside her and takes her into his arms so gently, I flip a throw blanket over them and stand mesmerized by their love.

When I hear Kayla whisper she's sorry for ruining dinner to Mack his voice is calm and beautiful when he shushes her before whispering, 'Never be sorry for carrying my baby inside you as best as you can.'

Nearly crying, they are so sweet together, and that was such a private moment between them, I will never forget seeing their love as long as I live. So walking away and quietly closing the door, I leave them to their struggle together.

"Is she really bad?" Kayla asks as I nod and try to blink away my tears.

"She's pretty sick but Mack's with her, so we'll see if they join us later or not. She may just need to rest a little."

"Okay. Merry almost Christmas, Suzanne. You look gorgeous. And dinner smells amazing and I'm *starving*," she smiles with a dirty grin and I know immediately why she's starving. *Marty.*

"Where is your stud anyway?"

"At the restaurant. He promised he wouldn't be long, but most of his staff took Christmas Eve off, and surprisingly there were more customers than he thought or planned for. He said we could start without him though and he'd get here as soon as he could."

"Sounds good. What do you want to drink?"

"Anything. Where's Z?"

"The kitchen I think," I turn surprised myself Z isn't entertaining Kayla.

"He's not actually. I started for the kitchen first," she grins pointing to a plate with some roast beef on it.
"You ate some roast?" I laugh shocked as I start pouring her a drink.
"I told you I was hungry."

Calling Z ten minutes later, I can't understand where he would possibly go. Everything is ready, except for our guests at this point, Kayla just keeps helping herself to dinner, and Mack and Kayla are still in my bedroom.
"Hi, love. I'll be back in 10 minutes."
"But where did you go?"
"Christmas..." He says with his smile-voice. Oh.
"Can I have a hint?"
"Not a chance. I'll see you in 10 minutes. How is everyone?"
"Well, the MacDonald's are still hiding in our room, Marty hasn't arrived yet, and Kayla's stuffing her face with dinner," I grin as she flips me off.
"Huh. Sorry I snuck out but it'll be worth it, I promise. Love you," he says sounding excited which naturally excites me more. I'm dying to know what made him leave, and I'm almost bouncing with the need to know what his surprise for me is.

"What's he up to?" Kayla asks walking back to my kitchen for more food.
Following her, I laugh when she just jumps up on the counter beside the warming grills. "I have *no* idea, but he's excited, so I think it's gonna be good," I giggle. "Christ Kayla, stop picking and just make a plate already. Dinner is kind of off anyway so you may as well fill a plate for yourself."
"Join me?" She begs already hopping off the counter to make a full plate.
"Sure, but can we at least sit at my dining room table? Did you see how beautiful it is? I spent hours decorating the table to match the world's best Christmas tree, outside Rockefeller, of course," I laugh as she does.

Sitting down at my table, Kayla switches out the name tags so we can sit beside each other but I don't really care anymore. The formality of my Christmas Eve dinner is off anyway, and at this point I'm so hungry I wish I could just throw on my yoga pants and dig in.
"Can I have my present?" She asks with a mouthful of potatoes.

"Sure." Already running for my tree I practically throw myself under it towards the back. Sliding out her 2 beautifully wrapped boxes I dance back to her laughing at my excitement.

"Yay! I *love* presents!" Ignoring the bows and perfect wrapping completely she tears them open quickly. Ugh... If she only knew how long I spent making her gifts look perfect.

Opening the smallest box, she smiles when she sees the jewelry box until she opens it and honest to god, gasps. Yay! Pulling out the necklace, I lift my own from my chest so she understands what I had made.

"Oh, *Suzanne*..."

"So the middle black diamond circle is me, and you are the diamond circle on the side, and I made one for Kayla, as well. Um, the 3 circles are linked together, like my darkness and both of your light, or like me in the middle in my black," I smirk, "And you two in your white around me, or something like that," I fade out feeling a little embarrassed.

Lifting her hair quick, she practically yells at me to put it on her, which I do jumping from my chair. Once on, Kayla pulls away and grabs me in a hug so tight, I can't breathe, and I don't want to. This is the best kind of suffocation, I giggle.

"Suze... This is the most beautiful, thoughtful, best present I've ever received. It's just awesome. Thank you," she says choking up which makes me choke up until we both just laugh at each other. "You made one for Kayla?"

"Yes. Um, you two are very special to me," I mumble as she takes my hand for a little squeeze.

"Right back atcha. Holy shit! I *love* getting diamonds," she yells making me laugh.

Turning when we hear Z walking in, he shakes his head at me. "You couldn't wait?" He smiles knowing I've been dying to give my Kaylas their gifts for the last 2 days.

"She begged me," I defend myself lamely as she nods.

"Hey handsome. Merry Christmas," Kayla jumps up as Z joins us. "Isn't it beautiful?" Kayla asks lifting her necklace up to Z.

"It is. I couldn't have designed it better myself," he laughs like an arrogant bastard. When I told him what I wanted to do 2 weeks ago, he pulled out the Mr. Zinfandel card at the Jewelers to make sure the 3 necklaces would be finished before Christmas for me.

"Where were you?" She asks with a glare.
"Out. How was dinner?" He pushes her back.
"Good. But it isn't half as good as Thanksgiving was," she laughs returning to the table.
"Well, if people stopped messing with my wife's dinner plans, it would've been perfect, I'm sure," he leans down to kiss my head. "Are you going to open the other gift?" Z smirks at me as I swat his ass for teasing me still.
Smiling, Kayla quickly rips open the second box to find the scarf and mittens I knit her. Hot pink and black, and exactly what she would love, she holds them up and actually sticks her finger through the ONE hole at the side of the scarf that couldn't be helped. Bursting out laughing, I shrug at my almost perfect scarf for her.
"Much better, Suzanne," she grins wrapping the scarf around her neck, but making sure the necklace isn't hidden. "Thank you so much for everything."
"You're welcome," I kiss her head rising to pull Z into the kitchen by his hand.

Once inside, I push Z against the counter, stand on my tiptoes, and growl, "Spill, Mr. Zinfandel."
"Can we wait?" He kisses my lips quickly.
"Do we have to?" I counter kissing his lips just as quickly.
Smiling against my mouth, Z nods. "It would be better if we did, just for a little while so you don't have to explain yet," he says so cryptically, I'm dying to know what the hell he's talking about.
"Argh... Fine. Do you want dinner now? There's really no point waiting for Marty."
"Please," he agrees already reaching around me for a plate. "You?"
"I'm full. Kayla made me eat with her. Everything?"
"Yes, please."

Walking out of our kitchen just minutes later, Kayla is lounging on the couch, moaning loudly, whining about over-eating as I laugh at her and sit beside Z. Smiling at her, Z digs in with his own moan which I love.
"Don't moan like that," I whisper as he grins his dirty sexy grin.
"Why? You don't like it when I moan?"
Blushing, I actually play along. "I *love* it when you moan, but this isn't

the time or place for those kind of moans, Z." Waiting for his dirty reply, I continue. "Do you have any idea how dark and delicious you are?"

"Dark and delicious?"

"Yes. You're very dark, and everything about you is delicious," I whisper looking down at his pants like a dirty girl suddenly.

Leaning into me, Z asks, "Would you like to see how dark and delicious I can be against the bathroom counter for a quickie, Suzanne?" And as I gasp, he takes the opportunity to kiss me hard, wiping the shock off my face with another moan.

"Gross. At the table?" Kayla asks holding Mack's hand as they walk toward us.

Giggling, Z and I pull away with the promise of 'later' unspoken but felt in the heat between us.

"How are you?" Z asks concerned as he rises to hug her.

"I'm good. And I'm craving potatoes and buns with gravy, and some corn I think."

"Take it easy," Mack says gently but Kayla looks totally irritated at him.

"I will, Mack. But I'm starving," she whines pulling away as I jump up to follow her to the kitchen.

Grabbing a plate, she piles on half the potatoes I had made for everyone. More than half. Actually, if Z, Kayla and I hadn't already eaten I'd be panicking about not having enough suddenly.

"Smells good, Suzanne. And thank you for the bed. I'm exhausted all the time, and this little bastard is killing me."

Watching her pour the gravy to the point of almost spilling over the edge of her plate, I just barely hold in the flinch. Shit. Her plate looks like a sloppy, nasty, mess.

"Ah, are you sure you have enough gravy?" I just barely hold in my laugh as she growls at me and walks out of the kitchen with a 'humph.'

"Oh, wow," Chicago Kayla says before I can give her a quick head shake behind Kayla's back.

"Fuck off, Kayla. I'm starving, and this kid is killing me. And I'll just barf it up in 10 minutes anyway so I won't get fat either. Where's Marty?" She asks shoveling mashed potatoes in her mouth as Mack leaves for the kitchen with Z, presumably for his own plate of whatever is left after Kayla was finished.

"Would you like your gift?" I ask to ease any Kayla vs. Kayla tension.

"Uh huh," she smiles a nasty potato teeth smile which makes me laugh as I dive for my huge tree again.

Bouncing, I hand Kayla the same perfectly wrapped, ribboned together 2 boxes I gave Chicago Kayla who is smiling wide with excitement as well. Kayla is even holding and hiding the necklace and pendant in her hand waiting.

Opening the bigger box first, I almost groan and Kayla *does* groan her irritation, but Kayla ignores us to unwrap her black and purple scarf and mittens.

"Oh, they're adorable. And barely holey," she laughs poking her fingernail through the ONE tiny hole in the left mitten. The bitch.

"Don't put the scarf on," Kayla helps but I glare at her for being too obvious.

"*Okay...*"

Unwrapping the small obvious necklace box, Kayla is grinning before she even lifts the lid. "I love your gifts, Suzanne," she smiles before finally, painfully slowly opening the little snap. "Oh! It's beautiful," she says as both Kayla and I practically assault her leaning in to show her our matching necklaces. "Oh!" She gasps looking between the two of us and her gift.

"Suzanne designed it and had them made special for us. She's the black diamonds in the middle, and you and I are the *fabulous* white diamond circles entwined with her!" Kayla yells before I even have a chance to explain. The bitch!

"Oh, Suzanne..." Kayla chokes up immediately. Yay! Practically clapping, I smile and giggle at her reaction. "God, it's just so beautiful, and lovely, and so, so thoughtful, and *MACK*!" She suddenly screams making me jump.

"*What?!*" Mack bursts through the kitchen door with Z right on his heels spilling his drink in the doorway.

"Look! Look what she made for us! Oh my *god,*" she says before bursting into tears. Ugh. Now I feel a little bad. I mean I wanted her to appreciate it and maybe choke up a little, but I didn't plan on her bawling her eyes out, or scaring the shit out of Mack. Ummm...

When Mack drops to his knees in front of her taking the necklace to look at it, his smile is so sweet at Kayla, I feel their love again. "Suzanne-"

"It's her in the middle, the black circle, and Kayla and me holding her- like linked arms or something. Right?" She asks wiping her nose on my Christmassy linen napkin, and that's it. I can't stand it anymore, I start

We are US...

howling with laughter.

This has been the strangest, most dysfunctional Christmas Eve dinner I could have *never* imagined in my craziest moments.

"Basically," I laugh as she stops crying to look at me like I'm mental. "Nope. *I'm* fine. You however are Crazy Kay again, and I LOVE it!" I laugh as Mack fights laughing to put the necklace on her.

"Whatever. I'm pregnant, not crazy. That's different," she glares as thankfully Mack jumps in.

"It IS different, Suzanne," he says sounding angry until I see his smile start. "But not by much."

"*Anywayyyyy*... It's absolutely perfect, and beautiful, and I can't believe you bought us diamonds. Our gift absolutely sucks now," she pouts.

"It doesn't matter. I wanted you and Kayla to know how special you are to me. So I made them. And that's it. No more crying, okay? Just eat as much as you can before you start throwing up again."

"Okay," she mumbles already eating before I even finish speaking.

When Z joins us after wiping the floor in the doorway, he hands Mack his plate. Sitting in the chair beside Kayla, smiling often, Mack actually lifts my necklace again to take a closer look.

Watching them, I feel so happy again, I realize all the stress of pulling off a perfect dinner is stupid. This is like the worst dinner ever planned, but perfect anyway.

Finding myself awkwardly standing over Mack, I look at Z and just sit in the Marty chair as he follows to sit beside me.

"Marty's here," Kayla adds dropping her phone in her purse before her excitement makes the four of us grin at her when she waits by the door for him. Turning on the security monitor, Kayla actually giggles when she sees Marty stepping into the elevator.

"She's pathetic," Kayla says and before anyone can speak, Kayla lifts her hand in the air to flip her off silently from the opened doorway before walking out to meet Marty. "Do you have cameras in the hallway? I want to see them make out," she adds as Z laughs.

"We do. But *I* don't want to see that," he chuckles with Mack nodding in agreement.

"Hey everyone. I'm so sorry I'm late. The restaurant was a mess, but we left it so everyone could get home to their families tonight," he says walking over to shake hands with Z and Mack, followed by a kiss on

Kayla's still eating head, and a quick little touch on my forearm.
"It's no problem. Dinner has been very strange tonight anyway. Did you eat?"
"No, I was too busy."
"Well, come get some food before Kayla finishes it all off," I tease squeezing her shoulder as I pass her.
"Cute, Suzanne," she mumbles still eating anyway.

In the kitchen, Marty fills a plate, and compliments me often. He's very nice and appreciative, and though we're not as close as everyone else is, it doesn't feel uncomfortable for me. It feels good, and almost like we'll be better friends over time. Especially if he and Kayla keep dating, which I hope they do.
"Here's a drink," Z hands it over as Marty sits at what should have been Z's original spot.
Digging in Marty moans which makes me quickly look at a smirking Z, and then he tells me everything is delicious. He even asks what spice I used in the yams and I'm thrilled a professional New York chef likes my cooking enough to ask.

Looking around at everyone, I stand awkwardly, deciding on an impromptu toast like a friggin' moron actually. It's not the right time, and we're all knee deep in food or conversations, but I just couldn't stop myself from standing. Suddenly finding myself with all eyes on me I realize what I loser I still am. Honestly.
"Sorry," I giggle. "Okay. Totally wrong time I know, but I wanted to make a toast to you all. Um, thank you Mack for saving my life- multiple times. Thank you Kaylas for loving me and wanting me to think I'm as fabulous as you both are. Ah, thank you Marty for forgiving me when I hurt your best friend. Wait!" I say quickly when Marty almost interrupts. "And thank you Z for loving me so good the bad stays in the background now. I know I'm never going to be completely okay, but that actually seems okay now. I have a really bad past, but it feels like it really is in the past now. And I want that. I want to live like that. And I am I guess. So thank you everyone for being my friend and for thinking I'm not as shit as I was always lead to believe I was. Um, thank you so much for this wonderful life of mine. Merry Christmas," I add as the first tears fill my eyes when I raise my wine glass to everyone joining me in my pathetic

We are US...

toast.

"Sorry for that. Toast over. I'll go get dessert started," I giggle embarrassed as Mack actually laughs at me knowing what a loser I am.

Stumbling for the kitchen, the silence in our dining room is too much, so I yell, "Keep eating and talking! And don't follow me," while I close the kitchen door.

Honest to god. Sappy Suzanne? Buzzkill Psycho? Dinner Ruiner? Laughing, I realize these little speech like outbursts of mine seem to be forever in my future. Usually either totally inappropriate, or just completely the wrong time, I swear I have NO ability to stop them when I'm overcome with my situation.

"Would you like some help?" Marty asks in the doorway.

"Yes, please. Sorry for that," I nod toward the dining room. "I probably should have made my speech later but it just hit me. And before I knew it I was spewing," I laugh as he does.

Pulling ice cream from my freezer Marty shrugs like my speech wasn't a big deal. "It was a lovely speech, Suzanne. And no one thinks you're any weirder than normal," he grins as I laugh. "But I need to say one thing to you if that's alright?"

Turning to lean against the counter, I knew this was coming. I knew whoever followed me to the kitchen had something to say, even though I asked them all to stay put.

"Of course, Marty," I nod waiting for hopefully not something too bad.

"I didn't forgive you, Suzanne, because there was nothing to forgive. I knew there was something serious between you two so I let my anger go for all the times I saw Z struggle because of you, and especially after everything happened."

"When Thomas died," I whisper as he nods.

"Yeah. And then you two were back together and Z was so happy, and I was told a little more about everything, and I saw myself what Z felt for you which made me like you- actually like you myself, not because Z loved you. But it was hard for me to just forget everything you had put him through at first."

"I know, I'm sorry," I almost beg but keep it in.

"Don't be sorry. You owe me no explanations for anything you did, and Z is happy with you which makes me very happy with you, not that that should matter."

"But it does matter. *You* matter to Z, so I want you to like me," I admit

like a totally insecure idiot. "Sorry." Oh, shit. I'm going backward here and this isn't good.
"Suzanne, I'm really sorry. I didn't mean to upset you. I was actually trying to make you happy here. I don't have to forgive you because there's nothing for *me* to forgive. And you make Z very, very happy, which makes me happy. And I just want you to know that I think you're great," he says gently squeezing my forearm for a second before turning for the oven to pull out the pie.
"Thank you," I whisper just as Z walks in with his calm, but could get pissed in a second face.
"Marty," Z almost threatens so I quickly jump in.
"Is helping me get dessert, and everything is really good. Go sit. We'll be out in a minute, Z." Nodding my head toward the door, Z watches me and actually gives in.
"He was never like that with anyone else, you know?" Marty asks leaning into my side.
"Like what?"
"*That*. Possessive. Ready to kill me or anyone else who upset you. It's weird to see, but it's cool, too. It definitely lets me know how much he loves you."
"Oh... Well, just so you know, I love him that much also. I will do anything for that man, and I will do *everything* for that man. He really is absolutely everything to me," I exhale as he looks at my face and nods.
Turning for the desserts, Marty seems to finally understand what everyone else has always known between me and Z. There is just a thing that binds us together no matter what shit we deal with.

Finishing my delicious desserts with coffee, Kayla actually manages to hold in dinner to climb on our huge couch only 15 feet from the table, but still close enough to be part of the conversations.
"Your turn," Z whispers pulling a box from his pants I didn't notice before.
"Now?" I giggle as Kayla sits up to look from the couch while everyone else stares.
"Yup. Because now it makes sense. You'll see," he grins handing me the jewelry box.
Quickly opening it, I love Z gifts. I never received any as a child, except from my grandparents. And Marcus thought gifts were stupid between

We are US...

two adults. Whatever. I give many gifts, and I like getting them too, I'm not gonna lie.

"Oh!" I gasp as he starts to explain my new ring.

"The round black diamond is you," he smirks again. "Surrounded by a circle of garnets. I know they're red, but they're my birthstone, and they're not too red, so I thought they'd be okay."

"They're okay, Z."

"And then they're surrounded by white diamonds around you and me for our light, as you always say," Z winds down looking a little nervous suddenly.

"Did you design this?" I whisper holding up the ring.

"Yes. After your necklaces, I thought you should have a ring that kind of matched, and it's you and me together. And I like you wearing something that's you and me," he finishes attempting to put the ring on my shaking right hand index finger.

"I absolutely love it. It's so special, and beautiful, and just perfect for us. I like love, *love* it, Z. Thank you," I lean in to kiss him gently.

Pulling away from his kiss, I just stare at my new ring. It's even better than my engagement ring. It's better than any ring, really. Grabbing Z, I fight crying and just about a thousand different emotions I'm suddenly feeling staring at my hand, and I don't know what to do. I'm in a trance staring at my ring, and no one else is speaking, and I just feel overwhelmed by how beautiful and loving my ring is. Z made it special for me, and it IS special. It's perfect, and the red doesn't even bother me at all. It's like the red is okay because it's all about Z surrounding me.

"Wow..." I whisper to no one until Kayla whines across the room, 'Let. Me. *See*...." making me finally move from my trance.

Nearly tripping to get to her, Kayla takes my hand and says wow as well. Turning my hand this way and that, she stares at my ring with awe. "It's perfect," she agrees as I nod. I swear to god I'm speechless. "You did good, Z. Take some pointers from him, Mr. MacDonald," she throws in finally breaking me from my ring spell.

"Will do," Mack nods.

"We have to go, okay? Dinner was delicious, and I'm stuffed for a change, but I doubt this barfy reprieve is gonna last. So I'd like to go now. But I'll see you Boxing Day for all the sales?"

"Of course. Have a wonderful Christmas, Kayla," I lean in to hug her.

"Thank you for my necklace, Suzanne. You did good, too, Mrs.

Zinfandel."

"Why, thank you," I grin as she slowly tries to stand.

"We're going to go too," Other Kayla adds. "Thanks for the necklace, and the food, and for an awesome Christmas Eve. I'll pick you up at 10:00 for our marathon, okay?"

"Absolutely. Wear comfy shoes, Kayla," I turn to her already being helped into her big, warm, prego coat by Z.

"Of course. And *don't* start, Mack. I'll stop when I'm tired, and eat when I'm hungry. But this is our boxing day tradition, and I'm not breaking tradition for this little bastard inside me," she growls again.

"You really have to start calling it a baby or something. Otherwise we'll all be referring to him or her as Little Bastard when it's born," Z smiles squeezing her shoulders.

"I know. My mother will have a fit which is almost worth it."

"Bye, Suzanne. Thank you for dinner, it was delicious," Marty extends his hand but I lean in for a little hug instead. Just a little one, but enough to let him know I'm okay.

After a round of multiple hugs, thank you's, and handshakes, Z finally closes the door with a huffed exhale.

"Let's go lie down."

"But-"

"Our house is destroyed, there's shit everywhere, and food on every surface Kayla touched. But I don't care. I want to lie down with you, Suzanne. Please? We have all day tomorrow to clean up. Please, love?"

"Thank you for my ring, Z. It's the most special gift I've ever received in my life," I lean into his arms as he hugs me tightly.

"You're welcome. Bed?"

"God, yes..."

After undressing, removing all my makeup, and using the washroom, I'm exhausted. I swear to god, I don't know how my mother did this every friggin' weekend of my life. She was so frail and seemed too weak to pull this shit off all the time. It's weird when I think of her as she was because she makes no sense to me, then or now. She's an anomaly. She's an evil frail little anomaly, and I hate her.

"What's wrong?" Z asks leaning against our headboard, and just as quickly as my mother entered my thoughts, she's gone.

"Nothing at all," I climb into bed as Z pulls me to his chest. "Thank you for the best Christmas I've ever had. It was way better than last year's formal affair I threw."

"It was," he smiles down at me before kissing my lips. "Now go to sleep, Suzanne. Santa's coming," he says so sternly I giggle and snuggle in.

CHAPTER 24

Turning quickly to Z storming into our atrium, I jump but recover quicker than he approaches.

"Okay, Suzanne. I've had enough. You're freaking out, you're not telling me why, and I'm about to go postal if you don't tell me soon what's hurting you."

"Nothing's hurting me!" I cry shaking as he stares down at me with his hands on the arms of my chair. "I'm, ah, I have to tell you something, and I'm scared."

"Of me?"

"No, not of you. But of, well, you're going to get mad at me, so I don't know what to do."

"So tell me and we'll handle it together. Come on Suzanne, no more secrets, lies, or hiding. Remember? We've been great for 5 months now, so just tell me. I'll help you with anything, and so will Mack. But you have to tell me, love, so I *can* help you," Z says trying to calm his voice when he squats down in front of me instead of towering over me.

Inhaling deeply, I try to say the words, but they just won't come out.

"Suzanne, please?" Looking at Z looking at me with such concern I know this won't be good, but I just need like a day or 2.

"Do you trust me?" I ask knowing the answer.

"Implicitly. Completely. Totally. Do *you* trust me?" He counters with his calm, be reasonable for Suzanne voice, and I almost giggle. Shit.

"Will you trust me to talk to you tomorrow night?"

"*What*?" He asks like what I just said is tantamount to murder or something which makes me laugh because my nerves are totally shot.

"I need you to trust me tonight, and I promise to tell you everything tomorrow. I was going to tell you tomorrow before you burst in here like a friggin' bull. And I *will* tell you tomorrow night. I just ask that you give me one more day."

"Is this why you're going to Chicago?" Pausing, the fact that Z knows my travel plans does surprise me a little. I thought I had it all figured out and I thought I hid everything from him this time. But again, he always seems to know everything.

"How did you know about Chicago?" I ask feeling both surprised and a little irritated.

"Tony called to ask if I was joining you and if we'd be staying overnight."

"Oh..." Huh. A stupid Suzanne move. I didn't want to cab it to the airport, but I didn't think the driving service would actually call Z. *Why would they call Z?* "Do they always call you when I book them?" I ask as suspicion inches down my spine. Watching Z, I realize he looks guilty suddenly and I have my answer. Wow, it never occurred to me. "Okay. *Why* do they call you?"

"Because I like to know where you go," he says like he's not a psycho, which really, he kind of is. New topic for Mack on Thursday? I'm thinking yes.

"So you always know where I go when I use them?" I think he finally senses my shock and he wants to fix it. But honestly, I'm not sure he can. "Because you don't trust me?" I squeak.

"Never that. I trust you totally. I just don't trust other people anymore with you. After learning about what your mother attempted to do to you, and about the driver, and the letters you still get, and... I just want to make sure you're okay. That's all. I don't give a shit where you go, or with whom. But it makes me feel better if I know where the drivers take you."

"Why? No one wants to hurt me I don't think." Do they? Well, the creepy letters suggest otherwise, but I've always received them.

"The fact that people still find your email addresses somehow, or make it through our mail, or find our unlisted number way too often concerns me, and it always will, Suzanne. So yes, I ask the driving service to let me know where you go so *I* feel a little better about your safety. That's all it is, I promise." Leaning away from me, I find I feel bothered and irritated by Z hiding this.

"You didn't tell me. And I thought we were telling each other everything now."

"We are. This is nothing."

Standing to walk into our room, I feel Z following me. I don't even need to look behind me because I feel his presence right against me. "It's something," I mumble.

"Okay. Then why are you going to Chicago, and why didn't you tell me?" He counters and he's absolutely got me. I'm screwed actually. I *was* keeping a secret, and I did know he'd lose his shit if he knew about it beforehand. So now I either tell him and we fight, or I don't tell him and I'm a hypocrite. Shit. "Well played, Z."

"I'm not playing, love. You asked a question and I answered honestly. I've also asked a question, and you're evading. So why not just tell me and I'll let it go."

"Because we're about to have a huge fight if I tell you. And we haven't fought since I got out of the hospital, and I don't want to fight."

Exhaling as he leans against my dresser with his arms crossed on his bare chest, I know I've lost. Raising his eyebrow, I also know I'm screwed. Now he won't let this go, and inevitably, he won't let *me* go.

"I'll wait forever, Suzanne. You may be stubborn, but so am I. And I have nowhere to go tomorrow, but apparently *you* do. So you may as well tell me what's going on," he says with a smug smile. The bastard.

I. Am. So. Screwed. "Um..." Shit, he's gonna lose it, and I actually fear this one a little. Not him of course, but I fear how big this fight is going to be and how big it's going to get between us.

"Just say it, love," he pushes again in his soothing voice but it doesn't work. I'm not soothed, and I don't want to talk.

"Tomorrow night-"

"Now."

"No, I promise to tell you everything tomorrow."

"You won't be going to Chicago without me if you don't tell me, so you may as well tell me now."

"I won't be going to Chicago if I *do* tell you," I moan defeated.

"I'm not a control freak, Suzanne. Of course you can go wherever you want. Chicago included. I just want to know *why* you're going to Chicago."

"To visit my mother," I whisper and after Z jumps against my dresser actually rattling my Jewelry box, he doesn't move again. There is nothing in our room but Z silently still with me watching. I don't even think he's breathing, he's so still.

Moaning, I barely hear his words, but I feel them. "No. Fucking. Way."

Shaking his head as if to clear it, he stares at me like I'm insane again, which I'm not at all actually. "No. *Fucking*. Way," he says again just above a whisper, but I know better than to try right now. He's in shock, or pissed, or just stunned maybe. I don't know, but I do know as he tries to process what I said, it's best to give him a moment.

We are US...

Waiting out the silence, I sit slowly on our bed and just watch him. From his suddenly pumping chest, to his constant head shakes, I think this one is pretty big between us. I think this is maybe the biggest yet, at least when I'm rational, which maybe he needs to know.

"I'm sane, Z. This-"

"No, you're not!" He yells so loudly, I flinch. Shiiiiiit.

"I am. I *swear!* Look, she sent me a letter," I yell jumping to run for the atrium quickly. Ripping open a drawer, it comes right off the track into my hand so I just drop it to run back to a still fuming, breathing hard, looking somewhat pale Z. "Here. Read it, Z. Then maybe you'll understand."

"Never," he breathes on almost a gasp.

"But-"

"Fucking *never,* Suzanne. I will never read anything that fucking bitch has to say. I don't understand what she's doing, but I do know you are NOT seeing her. Period." Oh, really? Well, this isn't going well, I almost laugh. "You are *never* seeing her again. I'll fucking-"

"What?" I yell standing in front of him suddenly. "What will you do? *Forbid* me? Ground me?"

"If I have to," he growls like an asshole.

"Piss *off!* You can't forbid me, Z. I'm not a child, and I won't be told what I can and can't do by anyone. Not even by you!" I yell stepping closer to him.

"Yes, you-"

"*Never* again, Z. By no one. So you can shove that alpha, dominant bullshit right up your ass for all I care. But I'm going whether you like it or not!"

Grabbing my upper arms Z scares me for a second, growling in my face as he continues. "You are not going to see that bitch. And if I have to call Mack, or lock you up again I will."

"*What?*" Gasping, I fight his hold as he releases me immediately. Pulling at his own hair he growls again, and if I wasn't so shocked by his threat I might care that he looks so messed up suddenly. But I don't care.

"I can't believe you just threatened me with that because I won't obey you," I spit at him as I turn to leave our room.

"Suzanne!" He yells again as he steps up to me to stop my retreat.

"*DON'T* touch me!" I scream in his face making him flinch before I run for our bathroom.

Slamming and locking the door I'm just stunned. I mean, I knew- I *knew* he'd be pissed and scared and maybe even slightly irrational. But to threaten to lock me up because I won't do as he says? That is *way* beyond anything I could've ever imagined.

"Suzanne... Please come talk to me," he says through the door but I'm not doing it. He's pissed? Well, screw him. I'm *more* than pissed. I'm hurt and shocked, and just wow. What a dick! "Suzanne, please? Just talk to me," he tries again.

"Not on your life," I growl back. "Go away. I'm not talking to you tonight, or tomorrow, or for a long goddamn time, Z. So go away!" I yell banging my hand against the door.

"I'm sorry, Suzanne. I didn't mean to say that to you. I was just shocked and I reacted like an asshole. I really don't want you to see that woman. And I don't understand what you're doing this time," he mumbles through the door still.

Shit, even though I'm reeling with my own anger and shock at his threat, I feel myself thawing a little as his desperation to talk to me climbs. "Can you talk to me? *Please?*"

"No."

"Please, love? I won't yell anymore, I promise. I just don't understand why you would even entertain seeing her. Could you please explain it to me. Because I really can't understand why you would do this, or want to, or even think about doing this. This makes NO sense to me after everything she put you through. And after how far you've come, and how happy you seem, I don't understand why you would hurt yourself this way. I can't see what you'd gain from this because *I* see nothing. She's a fucking psycho who tortured you and nearly broke you and she's just-"

"My mother," I whisper through the door.

Sliding down the door, my head bangs against it as I raise my knees to my chest. "Good or bad, Z, she IS my mother. And I want to know why or how she did what she did to me. I don't think I'll get answers, but I'd like to know if she *is* willing to talk to me, which she says she is."

"What does it matter?" He asks quietly and I swear as insane as this is, I feel his hand resting on the door next to my head.

"It just does. Maybe she'll hurt me one last time, and I can say goodbye finally. Or maybe she'll explain her actions and I can finally say goodbye. Whatever happens though I feel like I need to see her for the last time so

We are US...

I *can* say goodbye to her and to my past finally."

"But you have said goodbye."

"I haven't, Z. I've moved past it certainly, but I haven't said good bye to her or my childhood. It's still there all the time, and I feel like I need a goodbye so I can start my entire future with you."

"We've started our future. It's all around us, Suzanne. It's everything we do each and every day we're together. It's right here," he mumbles a little louder like he's desperately trying to make me see his point. And I do see it. I know what he's saying, but he doesn't understand that it's not over for me yet.

"We have started, Z. I know that. But I want to have a baby with you one day," I whisper hoping he heard me, but not wanting to repeat it if he didn't. It's too hard, and too intense, and it's just everything left between us unspoken.

"Open the door, Suzanne. Please..." he moans, and I can't deny him any longer.

Reaching up I flick the lock and move just to the side of the door as he turns the knob and slowly enters the bathroom beside me.

Waiting for something, Z enters fully and slides down the wall staring at me. Bending his legs up with his hands dangling over his knees, Z looks absolutely exhausted suddenly. When he lowers his chin to his chest, I want to go to him but I don't know how.

"Explain what you're thinking. Make me understand the logic. Because I don't see it, Suzanne."

"Um, I want to say good bye to her so I can move on. I want to see her as either the demon she is, or as the fucked up mother of my past. Whatever happens though, I need to say goodbye so I can forget she was ever my mother."

"You'll never forget that no matter what happens tomorrow," he says raising his eyes to look at me.

"I know. But after I've said my goodbye, I don't have to think of her as my mother anymore. She can just be the demon of my childhood and youth, so *I* can be the mother I want to be without her as my example. I feel like she needs to no longer be thought of as a mother, so I don't think of her as the mother I know. Ah, I know it probably doesn't make sense to you, but I swear it does in my head."

"Come here," Z says opening his arms for me to crawl into. Actually lifting me, Z places me right in his lap with his bent knees holding me up against his chest as I finally exhale.

"A baby?" He whispers as I nod. My heart rate just spiked and I feel nauseous as hell, but I'm very sure of my decision.

"Yes. Your baby. But I need to say good bye to her for some reason I can't fully explain. I just know I have to do this, so I can be a good mother."

Nodding, leaning his head against my forehead he breathes a nearly silent 'okay' as I exhale again.

"But I can't go with you, and I can't see what she does to you. Please don't ask me to be a part of this, and please don't resent me for not being able to be a part of this. Because I can't, Suzanne. I'll wait at home for you to return, and I'll help you if you need me when you get home. But I can't do this with you. I *won't* do this with you. I hate her, and everything to do with her, and I really hate that you want to willingly put yourself through this."

"I know you do. And I actually understand where you're coming from. I didn't want to put you through this with me which is the only reason I didn't tell you before."

"Okay. So you do this fucked up thing, and I'll wait for you to return. Should we call Mack?"

"He knows, and he disagrees with me as well," I smirk as he huffs. "But he also reminded me that he's my speed dial." Which was Mack's way of saying what Z did. They both disagree with my decision, but both will be there for me after I do this stupid thing.

"So you're leaving at 8?" He questions already knowing the answer.

"Yes."

"Okay. One more thing, love, then bed. I really am sorry I threatened you like that. I was just shocked and pissed and I went for a low blow out of desperation. I would never do anything like that to you again. I couldn't, unless you were in serious trouble like before. I'm not a big enough dick to do that to you just because you won't listen to me. That was a shitty thing to say, and I didn't mean it at all. I just freaked out," he explains again staring hard at my eyes until I nod.

"I know. But please don't ever threaten me like that again. No matter what, okay? Because it makes me not want to trust you, and I always want to trust you."

"Understood," he nods again. "Will you come to bed with me now? I have a feeling things are going to be bad for you after tomorrow and I want to be with you while you're still happy."

Ugh. What a shitty thing to say and an even shittier thing to acknowledge because he's probably right. It's like he knows I'm about to freak the hell out and he wants to be with me when I'm still me, for right now anyway.

"I'm so sorry for this, but I have to go. And somehow I don't think this is going to set me back." When he suddenly looks at me like I'm delusional, I continue. "I really don't, Z. Seeing her one last time feels like exactly what I need to do to make things okay for me and our future."

"Okay," he says not believing me at all as he lifts me off his lap and stands to rise.

Taking my hand, Z walks us to bed and crawls in from my side to pull me in with him. He doesn't touch me, or fondle me, or even want me sexually I can tell. He just wants to hold me which though sweet, makes me fear tomorrow even more.

"Good night, Suzanne. I love you very much," he says sounding scared and I can't stand it.

"I promise everything will be okay. I promise I won't have a setback, Z. Trust me..." I beg as he nods against my head.

Quietly, we lay in silence awake. For hours.

Sarah Ann Walker

CHAPTER 25

Walking into the prison, I'm surprised by how many entrances and doors and buzzers I have to go through to see her. I've signed my name and shown ID twice already, and I've even gone through 2 different metal detectors and one body imaging scan. In my nervousness after the scan I almost started laughing thinking of my underwear totally grateful they weren't big granny panties in case the guy could actually see them through the scan.

Buzzing into another room with a few chairs facing glass, almost like half stalls I realize I'm in the dangerous section where they don't allow visitors to have physical access to the convicts which is good. Because I'll admit, I kept wondering what I would do if she ever reached for me. Actually, I knew what I'd do. I'd freak the fuck out. Thankfully, that's not an option for her though.

When there's another loud buzz I almost jump out of my seat. Pulling my hair across my face and smoothing down my black pencil skirt in my uncomfortable plastic chair, I'm shaking with my anxiety. This is the first time I've see her in 4 years. This is the first time I've been close to her in what feels like a lifetime, which it really is if you consider my life finally started in New York with Z.

"Suzanne. It's lovely to see you," she says sitting down with her nasty voice and I cringe immediately.

Somehow I forgot how much I hated her soft, deadly voice. I mean I remembered it but not with the same intensity as it is to hear her actual voice in person. Ugh. It's just so scary sounding.

"Hello..." Mother? Mrs. Beaumont? Shit. I never thought of what I'd actually call her face to face.

"How's your husband?" She asks with her fake smile, and I'm jumpy instantly.

"He's fine. Why?"

We are US...

"I was just curious if you were still together?"
"Why wouldn't we be?" Shit. My heart is pounding already.
"I was merely curious Suzanne. I was making conversation only."
"Why am I here?"
"So we can talk, and maybe get to know each other again."
"Why?" I ask feeling panic settling deep in my stomach.

This was a mistake, a *huge* mistake I know now with certainty. Looking at her smiling at me I find I'm simply waiting for the evil to surface. I can actually feel it coming, but like a car crash I can't seem to look away from her face.

"Why get to know each other? Well, Suzanne, because I'd like to know what your life is like now. I'd like to know about your husband, and what you're doing with yourself now that you have no financial worries," she says with her scarily calm voice.

"*Financial* worries? What does the mean?"

"It means, darling, that I know you received all my father's money before he's even passed, though I do hear the should be any day now," she grins. "I know your father changed his will to give you everything instead of me," she sneers again as I shake my head. "And I know that husband of yours is quite wealthy, so as I said, you've married very well. Therefore I know you have no financial worries."

"I don't use any of grandfather's money. And I don't want *his* money."
"Whose? Your father's?"
"No. Your *husband's* money," I say trying to stay calm. What the hell is she doing?

Smiling again like what I said is exactly what she wanted to hear, she leans forward a little to ask, "Oh? So you live off your husband's money only?"

"No! Well, yes, but he's not like that. What's his is mine, and..." I shrug trying to end this. What the hell is her angle here? And why does she care about all the money?

Reigning in my confusion, I decide to just ask the question. "Why am I here? You said you wanted to talk to me because it was very important. Actually, you said what you had to tell me was life or death because you needed to tell me some things I didn't know. So talk, please."

Looking at me with her very pissed off face, I doubt she liked me talking back or demanding anything of her because that's not really our thing. Actually that's never been our thing. As far as I remember I never spoke to her or questioned her when she was my mother, except over my long hair which she hated back then. And that was the only fight she ever lost with me.

"I have some questions for *you*, Suzanne," she says in her deadly calm voice, and I know what's coming. She's about to slaughter me.

Exhaling and leaning a little further away in my chair, I know somehow she's about to hurt me in this game. I can see it and even feel it. I *remember* that tone of hers before she would hurt me.

Knowing what's coming, I go for broke. What do I have to lose? Well, other than my sanity, I smile to myself as she watches me.

"And I have some questions for you as well," I add knowing what's coming but almost comfortable with it because I'm not going to be caught off guard.

Smiling back at me, she continues the game. "Really? Like what?" Leaning back in her chair to mirror my posture she folds her hands together casually and waits.

Looking at me like I'm a piece of shit again, I find I can't really speak, or ask, or even think clearly. But she's still just waiting triumphantly for me to ask what we both know I'm going to ask her inevitably.

Pulling in a big breath, the only word that leaves my mouth is "Why?"

"Why what, darling?" She grins knowing I can't get the words out.

"Why did you do that stuff to me?" There. Holy *shit*! I asked it.

"What 'stuff', Suzanne?" She smirks quoting me as I begin shaking. In the silence between us I can see her absolute pleasure at where I'm headed. She's trying to mindfuck me, and she's going to win again as usual. She's doing her calm I hate you thing, and I feel her hatred in my chest so suddenly, my breathing is getting labored and my hands are shaking. Really, I feel like a total piece of shit again she's so good at this game.

"Never mind," I gasp. Oh shit. I'm not doing this. I took an extra pill before walking in here to keep me calm. I wrote everything down, and I said goodbye to Z this morning promising to not let her hurt me. I promised Z.

"Never mind?" She grins her evil grin, and as I watch her hands separate I see them as they always were. White, bony, evil skeleton hands.

Tapping on the table her nails are much longer than she used to have the perfectly manicured French tipped nails of my childhood. Staring at her hands, they look so much worse than I remember.

We are US...

   Her hands not only look like they could strangle me slowly, but they look like they could actually rip my skin open now too. Her hands look like I remember but so much worse.
   Standing up quickly, I actually make enough noise with my chair to have a guard stand to look at me. But it doesn't matter. I'm totally done.
   "I'm done with you."
   "Nice face, Suzanne. How does your husband stand looking at you?" She laughs as everything stops around us.
   Slumping back in my chair I hear no voices and I feel no air. There is nothing but her laughter and her mean face staring at me in silence.
   "Answer me!" She growls leaning up to the glass closely and I almost jump backward. Almost. But the glass is there and I know she can't touch me. I know it though every part of me wants to flee from her before she can wrap her hands around my throat again.
   "You're so stupid, Suzanne. Stupid, simple, fat little Suzanne. You are *nothing* but only an ass to fuck and a mouth to suck. And I think you should thank me, darling," she laughs again.
   Even as I hear her, I'm stunned into asking what I thought I never would ask in my life. "Why would I thank you?" I groan as the shaking takes me fully.
   Tapping the glass with her nails to get my attention, she smiles so evilly I shiver before I even hear her answer.
   "Well darling, because I taught you how to suck and fuck, and with a body like that, and a face as hideous as yours, your bedroom kills must be the *only* thing keeping your husband around. Am I right?"
   "No," I moan. "Z loves me!" I yell smacking the glass with my palm.
   Shaking her head at me, she actually makes her disgusting tsking noise and breathes an obnoxious, "Okay, darling," as I watch in horror.
   "He does love me. And I'm not stupid. I NEVER WAS!" I scream before I can stop myself, but it's too late. The guard is already at my side speaking to me in calm tones words I can't understand.
   Laughing at me, my mother actually raises her skinny, skeleton hand and scratches a fingernail down her cheek where my scars are. Staring at my stunned face, she even rubs her fingers tighter signaling money before laughing so loudly the visitor 2 chairs down from me stands to take a look at her.
   Gasping in shock I feel a hand on my arm, and before I lose it totally, I say everything.

"You're wrong about me. I'm not a whore, and I'm not shit. My husband loves me, and I have money of my own if I need it, but I don't. I'm beautiful and fabulous- scars and all." Speaking past her crazy sounding laugh, I finish us forever. "You're an evil bitch! Goodbye, Elizabeth. You're finally dead to me."

Stepping to my side, I actually grab onto the guard's arm for a moment, which though totally strange and unlike me is all I can do to get away.

I don't think my feet will work on their own, and I can barely breathe. Everything feels so unreal to me, I hold onto his arm even as he tries to push me off him like maybe I'm a threat. Oh! *Shit.* Just like I'm a threat.

"I'm sorry," I mumble letting him go quickly as another guard bares down on me. "I have to go now. Please help me out of here," I beg desperately.

Not touching me at all, the prison guard walks quickly toward the huge metal door which suddenly buzzes open drowning out her laughter behind me.

And then I'm out.

Crying, I'm escorted out by a different guard ignoring me completely. Walking through another loud buzzer and more doors, I'm walked down another goddamn corridor. Walking we even pass a prison gift shop. *Really?* I finally start laughing. Okay, that's like the only time in my life I haven't wanted to go shopping, I giggle-cry still walking as quickly as I can for anywhere but here.

Waiting in a line of 4 other people to collect my things, I have to walk back out through metal detectors. Screaming inside I want to ask *why?* I don't understand why we'd leave with weapons we didn't have before.

God, I'm so desperate for air. I'm losing it, but slowly, which is the best kind of losing it for me. It's not quick and sudden, making me lose all control. It's slow, so I can manage a little control before I lose it totally in private.

Gasping while ripping off my name tag and handing over my driver's license again, I'm bouncing to get out while a guard slowly pulls my purse and coat from an orange bin on a shelf behind him.

"Please hurry," I moan as he hands me my stuff before making me sign a sheet of contents. Crying, "I don't care! Take it all. I just need my phone for Christ's sake," he ignores me completely.

I need my phone so badly I actually dump my purse right there on the

We are US...

floor. And. I. Don't. Give. A. Shit. People are looking and watching me, but it doesn't matter what they think. I *need* my goddamn phone.

Tapping in the 4 number code, Z's picture fills my screen and I suddenly laugh. He's so good looking it's unbelievable. Christ, even on a phone he's hot as hell.

Waiting for just one ring I jump in before he can. "Z! I'm sorry. And you were right! I'm done and I need to see you, and please just-"

"Suzanne, listen-"

"She's such a cunt, Z," I say pausing before I burst out laughing. Holy *SHIT!* "Wow... I just said the baddest bad word ever and I don't even feel bad. Because she is, Z. She's a total *cunt,*" I say again laugh-crying nervously. I can't believe I said that word. But it's so true. She's just so nasty and evil and seriously, why the hell did she want me here?

"Walk out the doors, baby." What? *Baby?* Ummmm... I kinda like that name sometimes, and it doesn't really feel dirty or like a bad name when Z says it to me.

"What?" I pause trying to get all my scattered purse contents and even my scattered thoughts together to understand what he means.

"Walk out the fucking door, Suzanne. *Now,*" he growls as I breathe slowly. Grabbing my purse stuff my feet start walking to the main doors and my freedom from the evil bitch now known as the Cunt, I laugh again.

Throwing open the door, I see him. Standing there with his phone to his ear, he turns to me to walk so quickly I stare with my phone still at my ear. "Oh, *god...*"

Being lifted right into his arms, Z turns me against a wall and bends down low in my face to stare at me. Staring, he wipes my face, and leans his forehead against mine until I finally just drop the phone from my ear to the ground.

"You came anyway." I choke up as he does. "You came anyway. Oh, god. Thank you so much. I love you so much. I'm so sorry," I cry between gasps as he tries to shush me quiet. "I can't believe you came anyway," I burst into tears wrapping my hands around his shoulders so tightly I have to move my face to the side to breathe.

"I did," he whispers as I hold on tighter exhaling my upset to breathe him into me deeply. His scent and his warmth once again ground me in a way that I've never known before him.

"I said good bye. It's done. She's exactly the same, and I don't know what was so important. She didn't tell me anything. She just insulted me and talked a lot about money. Oh! Am I a gold digger?" I ask pushing my head against the wall so he has to look at me.

"I'm sorry?" He actually shakes his head. "A gold digger?"

"We only use your money to live, and I don't contribute anything, or even have a paying job."

"We use all your trust fund money for our charities, Suzanne. We don't *live* on it, but we spend it, which is the same thing as pooling our money and spending it jointly on living expenses and charities and donations. We use both our money jointly, Suzanne. Mine to live on, and yours to donate."

"Oh..." Okay. He's right, but I didn't think that clearly when she was accusing me of marrying well.

"For some reason everything was about money with her. My grandfather's, her husband's which apparently I'm getting when he dies, and even yours. She only wanted to talk about money and how ugly I am," I fade out turning my head to the side to look beyond the parking lot. "She still hates me, and she blames me and I'm still shit to her."

"To *only* her, love. And coming from the most evil *cunt* I've ever heard of, it doesn't matter what she thinks of you. It has never, and *will* never matter. Her opinion doesn't matter for anything," Z pushes turning my face back to look at him.

Pushing Z away from me gently I mumble, "I need a moment," as he nods stepping back from me immediately. Crossing his arms over his chest, he leans back against the wall and watches me without speaking.

"Maybe she has financial troubles, Z?"

"She does. She's spent much of her money on lawyers, and she had to pay restriction to you."

"She did?" *Really?*

"Yes. It went into your trust fund, and she was barred from writing her story in a book when she attempted to. There was an injunction put into place, and she was told all monies made on a book deal would have to go to her victim anyway, which is you."

"Oh," I nod. That makes sense, kind of. I mean if my grandfather cut her off, and she and my father are no longer together, and Marcus isn't around to invest their money, and she used tons and had to give me tons, then maybe. "How broke is she?" I ask almost laughing at the thought.

We are US...

Money is everything to her. It's the only thing she ever cared about. Money and her social standing which she also lost.

"Well, she still has enough money to be wealthy to normal people," Z grins. "But for her, a last 2 million would seem like poverty, I think."

"But what can she spend it on? She's in jail? Oh! There *was* a gift shop," I burst out laughing again.

Hunching over my own knees, I feel insane but not at all. I'm like giggly because everything is so messed up, but I'm not giggly because *I'm* messed up. And somehow that makes a big difference to me.

Touching my shoulder until I stand again, Z says simply, "I don't think it matters if she can spend it. It only matters to her that she has it." And I know he's right. My mother was obsessed with money always.

"She told me before she only had me to secure her place in my grandfather's fortune. She said she never wanted me but had to have me. She said I was just a necessity she never wanted or loved because I was nothing to her. And I'm still nothing to her."

"Does it matter?" Z asks gently. "Does it really matter why she had you, or how she hurt you, or what she thinks of you still? No one else thinks like she does and no one else feels like she does. She's just fucked in the head, Suzanne. And *clearly* she's been for years."

"I know she is."

Leaning in closer to me, Z looks almost desperate when he speaks. "Please don't make her matter anymore. You came, you saw, and now it's done, I hope."

"It is," I nod walking back into his arms for a little quiet. "Guess what else she said?" I ask leaning into him tighter.

"I don't want to. Can we just forget her?"

"Last thing I promise. I just have to say it so I see your reaction, so I know it's not true. Okay?"

"Okay..." Z breathes stepping away to look at my face intensely. I think he wants to give me the right answer so I'll let this all go for both of us now. And I want that.

"Um, she said I should thank her," I whisper as Z jolts in front of me but doesn't speak. "She said I've only kept you because she taught me how to fuck and suck and how to keep a man," I moan as the nausea threatens to take me. Holding my stomach and swallowing quickly, I barely hold the bile in. "Um, because I'm so stupid and ugly and scarred, it's only because I have an ass made for fucking and a mouth made for sucking that-"

"Jesus Christ, Suzanne! *Enough!*" Z yells, pulling me back into his arms. "That's not true, love. At all. Have I ever touched you there or taken your..." he doesn't finish the sentence which I really appreciate. Because just the thought of anal sex right now makes me gag and swallow harder and want to scratch my own skin off with the filthy memories of being little and scared and hurt and used so badly.

He has never taken me back there, and I don't think he ever would. He knows I can't. And he knows I couldn't get past it.

"No, you haven't," I moan. "And I don't really suck you with my mouth enough to keep you, right?" I suddenly burst out laughing at the absurdity of my statement.

Laughing against his chest, Z doesn't laugh with me but he does hold me tighter as I have a tiny, little breakdown.

She's wrong. She taught me nothing but agony, and I don't use any 'skills' she claims I have with Z. Whenever I've done that to Z with my mouth it was because *I* wanted to, not because he asked or wanted it himself. He has never tried to touch my ass, and he's never wanted to use my mouth. Z knows I can't.

"You know me so well."

"I do," he nods against my head.

"I'm sorry I didn't listen to you about this. But I had to say good bye."

"And did you?" Z asks squatting lower in front of me to look at my eyes.

"I did. She's dead and buried like Marcus, and I can move on now. I don't have a mother, and really, I never did. She wasn't a mother, Z. And I will never be like her. Ever."

"I know you won't. *Everyone* knows you won't, Suzanne. You are nothing like her. You are good, and sweet, and so beautiful no matter what life has done, and I couldn't love you more if I tried. You are *nothing* like her, Suzanne. And-"

Reaching up, I stop his rambling with a little kiss. Just a light kiss, but as he exhales a huff in my mouth I know he needed my kiss. I know he needed me to be okay, and I know he needed *us* to be okay.

"When is your return flight?"

"The same as yours," he smirks.

"You knew I'd need to be with you?"

"I had hoped you'd need to be with me."

"I'll always need to be with you, Z."

"Good," he smiles before giving me another quick kiss. "We have 3 hours to kill, would you like to grab something to eat?"

"I'd like to see Thomas," I exhale knowing Thomas is exactly what I need right now.

Looking at Z breathing deeply, he takes my hand without words and walks us to a rental car, I assume. Unlocking and helping me inside, he leans into me and asks exactly what I knew he would. "How are you feeling, Suzanne?"

"I'm honestly okay this time. I don't think she'll ever hurt me again, no matter what she does, or what I learn. She's hurt me in a way that can never be trumped, I think. And I don't want to care anymore."

ΩΩΩΩΩ

Walking hand in hand to Thomas' grave, I ask for a minute which Z gives me. Sitting on a bench not far from Thomas, I lean into Z, kiss his lips gently, touch his head with my hand, and walk to my son.

My 'son' still feels so weird to say but it's true, and I feel it, and I know it's true now. Thomas is my son, and it's about time I acknowledge him as my son.

"Hi, baby," I start while resting on my knees in the snow beside his gravestone. "I'm your mom, and I know I've really sucked at it. I was very messed up when I was carrying you, and I didn't love you like I should've, and I'm very sorry for that. You'll never understand what I was like then, and I can't explain it or say sorry enough. And even though it's a little stupid, I made you something," I whisper pulling from my bag a baby blue blanket.

Lying it over where I think his little body would be resting in the ground, I feel so sad but kind of good too when the blanket is laid out perfectly. I wish I had been able to keep him warm in life, but I couldn't. Now I can warm him a little bit here in death I hope.

"Um, it's the only perfect blanket I've ever made," I smile at the ground. "There isn't even one hole, and the colors blended perfectly on the edges, and it's really good. Well, it's good for me anyway, because I can't seem to get this knitting thing down yet," I giggle a little feeling stupid talking about my lack of knitting skills to his grave.

"I'm sorry I didn't love you enough to keep you alive when I should've, but I promise I didn't mean to hurt you. I *never* meant to hurt you, and I never wanted you to die," I whisper as the first tear slides down my cheek. "I really wanted you to live, and I wanted you and your daddy to be very happy together, but I just didn't love you enough to keep you alive, and for that I'll always be sorry. I'll always know what a horrible mother I was to you, but I promise I didn't mean to be."

"Suzanne," Z says sitting down beside me in the snow. "You didn't do anything wrong, love."

Shaking my head, I'm a little mad Z interrupted me, so as I turn to his face I ask him to be quiet. "This is between us," I whisper pointing to the baby blanket as Z nods sadly.

"Anyway, I think I'm going to try to have another baby with your dad, but I want you to know that if I succeed and have a little brother or sister for you, I'm never going to not love them enough, or good enough, or best enough to keep them happy. And alive," I choke up again. "I won't, Thomas. I'll be a good mom, and I'll love them the way I should've loved you."

Crying hard in a quick burst, nothing feels good, and I'm sad as I lean down on his blanket clutching my own chest. I'm aching and so devastated, the memories of his little face poking out of the hospital blanket are all I know in this moment.

"I'm so sorry, baby. But I do love you. I love you so much, and I really want you to know that. Okay?" Choking, I cry and wipe my cold face on his blanket. "I love you Thomas, and I always will. Please forgive me," I beg as the sobs spill from my heart to seep into the frozen earth that surrounds him. "*Please...?*"

"He forgives you, Suzanne," Z whispers before lying down against me and wrapping me in his arms. "He told me he loved you and forgave you in a dream I had. He loves you and he forgives you, I promise."

"Oh, *god*... He does?" I cry into his baby blanket. Clutching him to my chest I weep for the little baby boy I didn't know how to love.

"He does..." Z whispers then silences as I let the pain take my body.

This is the goodbye I never had, and these are the words I never said. This is the love I never showed my Thomas. But it's right here all around us together. And I can finally start my life with Z now.

We are US...

"Let's go, Suzanne. Let me help you," Z whispers sadly.

Lifting me right off the ground, Z makes sure my heels are stable as he wipes the snow off my body. Wrapping his arm around my waist Z kisses my forehead before we walk away slowly.

Turning only once, I see Thomas' gravestone and his blanket, and though I feel sadness making me cry again, I feel a little peace as well.

"I finally warmed my baby boy, Z."

"I know you did. And I know he feels it," Z moans kissing my lips softly.

Entering our apartment hours later, I'm exhausted. Z and I didn't speak much on the plane, but we really didn't have to. We know where I'm at, and we know where I want to be.

And I'm going to get there.

"I'm going to shower and go to sleep, okay?"

"You haven't eaten," Z pushes.

"I'm not hungry. I'm sad and tired, and I want to sleep away these goodbyes, so I can start again tomorrow."

"Okay," he smiles and I know he's scared but willing to let me have my time.

"Thank you for everything. I love you, Z," I kiss his lips softly before walking to our room.

Looking at my face, I see what he's seen for hours, and I suddenly just don't care. My scars are totally visible, and though I'm hideous it seems so insignificant now I actually don't care.

I mean I'll still cover them up as best as I can, but if Z can still hold me and love me and not even notice them, then I'll try not to notice them as much either.

These scars are me, and they have made me the person Z loves. The ones on my body and inside my soul are the scars that brought me to this place finally. So I'm done hiding now.

And I'm finally ready for life.

Sarah Ann Walker

LIVE

We are US...

CHAPTER 26

Walking up to Z in the living room I'm scared shitless and excited but yeah, totally scared shitless. *He's* not going to be though which is comforting.

"Hey, showering at 4:00? You either want me, or you need to wash away something bad. Do you want to talk about it?" He asks putting down his papers and turning to look at me with his sexy intensity that I love.

"It's one and not the other," I grin.

"Oh?" Under the circumstances I feel like being silly. Jumping over the arm of the couch I almost knock him out getting into his arms as he humphs my sudden weight on his chest.

"I did something 2 months ago I should've told you about, but didn't. Not because I was lying or hiding, but because I didn't want to excite you too soon if it wasn't going to happen soon. But then it did happen soon, and now I have to tell you what I did."

"Okay," he says calmly, pulling away a little to rest more sideways on the armrest so he can look at me closely. "Spill."

Giggling, I'm all nerves. I'm scared and excited and ready. But I probably should've told him first.

"Ah, I had my IUD removed after we saw Thomas, and, um, I'm pretty sure you knocked me up, Z," I giggle nervously again.

"*What*?" Z whispers so quietly I laugh. He always looks adorable when he's stunned.

"Well, I assume we had agreed we *would* have another baby, so I had my Mirena removed because it can take up to 6 months to get pregnant afterward, and I didn't want to tell you right away in case I didn't get pregnant when we started officially trying. But then it didn't take 6 months, it only took like a month and a half I think because I just felt like I was pregnant even though I don't feel bad at all, and I don't even know what feeling pregnant feels like, but I took a test anyway, and wait!"

Struggling to get off him, almost fighting his death grip, I laugh again as I run for our bathroom. I probably should've had it with me when I told him, but I didn't think I'd tell him so soon. Then I just couldn't wait when I saw him sitting there looking all yummy after work. So-

"Oh!" I gasp when he's suddenly standing right behind me in the doorway. "I didn't see you. Here!" I shove the pregnancy test at him before he walks slowly toward me to take it from my hand.

"Maybe it's a false positive, Suzanne. Maybe-"

Shaking my head I burst out laughing when I pull open the 3rd drawer on my side. "Look!" I giggle as he watches me, stepping closer to the drawer to look inside making him suddenly laugh too. Actually, he starts howling at me looking inside the drawer.

"Wow. That's a lot of tests, Suzanne. When, um, how did you have that much pee?" He asks stupidly and just the sight of his reaction and the sound of his laughter makes me laugh even harder.

"I've drank *tons* of water since yesterday. And *really*? Like I wouldn't obsess over this?" I giggle again watching him move the tests around, lifting a few to see the double lines, or plus signs, or even the pink line versus the 2 blue lines.

"You're pregnant," he whispers after the laughter fades when I nod. "Holy *shit*... You're pregnant," he says again sounding a little less happy than I thought, or maybe hoped.

"Are you happy?" I beg unsure suddenly of what I've done.

Jolting beside me again, Z doesn't speak. Taking my hand he leads me to our room and lies down against the headboard to pull me into his side and chest as always. Rubbing my back, he begs quietly, "Just give me a second."

Staying quiet I'm not going to freak out, and I'm not going to fear the worst. I did this yesterday after the first test, and then I did this all day and night and even today after every other positive test. I freaked and needed a minute, so he can have one too. I am NOT going to freak out. But he better hurry the hell up, because my resolve can only last so long.

"Z..." I whisper as the shaking starts. "I didn't think this was a mistake. I thought you wanted this and I thought I was finally giving something back to you. I thought you'd be happy."

"Don't, Suzanne. I am so unbelievably happy about this. I'm just surprised, but I'm beyond thrilled. I am so happy you're pregnant- that *we're* pregnant. I'm just nervous because we hadn't really agreed or talked about it, or decided officially. I'm shocked, baby. That's all. So I need a minute to process, okay?"

"Okay," I smile and relax a little in his arms. He's *beyond* happy, so I can wait for days if I have to. I can wait until he's ready to talk. I can wait-

"Okay. I've processed," he suddenly barks making me jump from my thoughts. "Holy *shit,* love. You've made me speechless here," he huffs moving me flat on the bed. Crawling between my legs, Z holds himself up by his elbows staring at my eyes until I grin. "How do you feel?"

"Fine so far. But I'm nervous I'll be like Kayla and I *really* don't want to be like Kayla," I moan as he shakes his head.

"Okay. But how are you mentally? Are you scared? Freaked out? Losing your shit a little? It's okay to be. We'll deal with it together."

"I'm not actually. Not yet anyway," I say holding his hands holding my face. "Maybe because I did this, or chose it, or set it in motion makes the difference. I don't know, but I feel good about this. Like it's something *I* did for you and for us. I wanted to do this, and now that I have I don't feel freaked out. Much," I giggle as he smiles down at me. "I didn't even lose my shit when the first test was positive. Oh, actually I did a little which explains running back to the pharmacy and buying 20 other tests. I actually bought 20 and left only 2 on the shelves for everyone else. But I really wanted to make sure before I told you. So now I'm sure."

Smiling down at me, Z leans in for a kiss. Gentle at first, then harder by the seconds, and before I even know what's happening we're breathing heavy and reaching for clothes.

"I need you naked, Suzanne. *Now,*" he growls as I tear at my own clothes to get them off.

Leaning up, Z strips off his shirt quickly while I pull my cami overhead. Watching him unzip and lower his pants as his legs thrash to get them off, I actually moan a little as I lift my own butt to pull down my yoga pants.

"Suzanne..." He whispers and I can't stop the emotion that surfaces. He looks so happy, though still kind of stunned making me realize I want this so badly with him. "A baby," he breathes against my lips as tears fill my eyes. "I don't know what to do," he says sounding confused and I suddenly mirror his confused expression.

"About what?"

"Is sex okay this soon? Should we wait to make sure everything's okay?"

"God, no," I groan as I rub my body suggestively against him.

Leaning back away from me while looking down at my face, Z seems totally conflicted. "No, I think we should wait. I don't know if penetration is okay when it's still so new and I don't want to hurt it."

"We're fine, Z. Everyone has sex when they're pregnant."

"Yes, but this early?"

"I think so," I moan frustrated. Shit, I really *don't* know. I haven't read the books yet, or asked Kayla, or, huh... I really don't know anything about being newly pregnant yet.

"Let's wait okay? Just a little bit to make sure everything is okay. We'll set up an appointment first thing tomorrow to make sure your medication is okay when pregnant, and to get the go ahead before we have sex again. I, I'm not comfortable with this yet until I know if it's okay for you."

"But-"

"Please, love. I need to be sure, and then we can. I'm nervous about this so soon," he practically begs and I understand where he's coming from. After what happened to Thomas, I'm sure he'll be anxious about many things. "Let me please you without penetration. I need to feel you, but I don't want to risk anything until we know for sure," Z says so painfully, my sexual need instantly vanishes to be replaced with the need to comfort him.

"Come here." Tugging at his arms he falls on my chest and side. "Let's just lie here like this for now. I didn't need to have sex, but you got me naked which always makes me want sex with you," I grin as he nods against my chest.

"I'm sorry," he says with his smile-voice.

"Wanna have dinner in bed?"

"Very much so. I just can't believe- I'm so happy Suzanne. Honestly," he says kissing the side of my breast, while putting his warm hand across my lower belly flub.

CHAPTER 27

"We can't tell anyone for the first 3 months, Z. And you look way to friggin happy all the time. So cut the smiley shit, okay?" I ask laughing at his goofy grin. "Seriously. Kayla's baby is due in a month, and soon after that I should be out of the danger zone, and then we can tell people. So let's just let her have this time okay?"

"I've said okay a hundred times, Suzanne. I've told no one and I won't." But then the stupid grin of his reappears as I laugh at him.

"You're hopeless."

Walking to the kitchen and our Easter dinner, which somehow again is my job, I check on all the food. Not that I mind, but seriously, can't a Kayla cook? Just once? If Z hadn't insisted on taking me out for my birthday dinner, I swear everyone would've assumed I was throwing my own dinner, which I would've actually. Thankfully though we ended up at Marty's restaurant and I could relax and enjoy myself.

"Z!"

"What?" He asks smirking at me in the doorway.

"I think we conceived on my birthday. Remember that night when we-"

"Oh, I remember," he wiggles his eyebrows and I almost jump him in our kitchen. I want him so badly, but other than a little touching he won't have sex with me. He's offered to pleasure me, but it's not the same thing. I don't want to get off alone, I want to be with him. "Don't look at me like that, Suzanne," he moans as I do.

"But I miss you. And I *want* you, Z. Badly. I'm like super horny and I want to have sex. *Please?*" I whine completely aware of the irony of me begging for sex.

"*Super* horny?" He laughs as I nod. "Soon, love. Just a few more weeks, okay?"

"But we've been given the clear."

"No, we weren't. We were told it should be fine. *Should* be. But I'm not willing to risk should be with you. I can't, Suzanne," he says no longer teasing and I sober instantly to his mood.

We are US...

I know he's scared to death I'll lose this baby somehow. I know it though he hasn't come right out and said it, but it's always there between us. I know he's asked the doctor if its normal for me to have next to no nausea, and I know he fears all the time I'm doing so well because somehow the baby died inside me. I also know I get extra exams because Z begged our OBGYN to watch me very carefully.
I know Z's very excited, but very nervous and almost cautious of his excitement as well. He won't discuss the nursery yet, and he hasn't taken me shopping for any baby things yet. He's scared to death, and I need to be strong for him this time.
"I'm sorry," I whisper before he pulls me in for a tight hug.
"Never be sorry for being super horny for me, Suzanne," he pinches my butt as I giggle. "I'm just not ready yet. But when I am, watch out, love. I'm going to love you until you beg me to stop."
"Okay."

ϘϘϘϘϘ

Watching Kayla eat her way through 2 dinners, I'm stunned she's not running for the bathroom yet because her pregnancy is the stuff horror stories are made of. She has intense continuous morning sickness, gestational diabetes, she's the size of a house, and she's so swollen everywhere she needs to lie down for hours a day to alleviate some of the swelling. But she's still so happy, it's amazing to watch her.
She and Mack tease endlessly, and they seem to have such a handle on all the medical stuff she's dealing with, they just do their thing with each other until the baby is born I think.
"Oh, we found out what it is by mistake," Kayla grins between bites as we all silence. "I was snooping at my records and found out, so Mack wanted to know, and now we both know. Wanna know?" Kayla asks as both Kayla and I scream *yes* together. Honestly, for two opposite women, Kayla and I speak way to similar sometimes which makes Z laugh *and* cringe at us.
"Drum roll, please," she teases and Mack and Marty drum on my table

immediately. "Well, you two bitches are going to be Aunts to a little baby... *boy,*" she smiles as I gasp clapping my hands together.

"A boy? Well, that sucks," Kayla growls as we all pause stunned to look at her. "What? I wanted you to name your baby after me and now you can't," she pouts as Mack actually bursts out laughing, thank god.

"*Kayla?* Really? We never know who the hell we're all talking about now with 2 Kaylas. As if we'd throw in a third one," Mack laughs.

"Doesn't matter anyway, it's a boy," Kayla still pouts until I shake my head.

"I can't wait. Do you have a name?"

"Nope. We're fighting over names. Mack likes all generic, boring names, and I like funkier sounding names to make him special. I mean really, *Matthew*? How boring. Plus, Mack, Marty, *Marvin,*" she laughs at Z's dirty look, "and Matthew? Too many M men around here I think."

"I agree. At least you have a month to decide," I squeeze her hand tightly.

"Ah, I think I'm going... Yup. *Shit,*" she moans moving to the bathroom with Mack following holding her arm and back as she waddles away.

"Remind me *never* to get pregnant. You'd have to be a fucking idiot to put yourself through all that just for a kid," Kayla scowls and I almost start laughing. I mean it's right there and if I make eye contact with Z I'll start for sure, so naturally I turn my head and rise for the kitchen for coffee and dessert.

"Could you please help me?" I ask touching Z's shoulder and he rises to follow immediately.

Closing the door behind us, Z's smile is so big I finally start to laugh. "How are you doing, you fucking idiot?" He asks so seriously I laugh even harder. "She's such an ass sometimes," Z adds pulling me in for a big hug.

"I know. But she doesn't know about me, *obviously,* or she wouldn't have said that. So it's just funny, Z. You know she'll be excited when she finds out, especially if she thinks I'll name a friggin girl after her."

"Which will NEVER happen," he adds as I nod. "I can't even imagine having a Kayla for a daughter," he smiles and my heart almost stops. Just the word daughter coming from Z can make me start hyperventilating until I force myself past it so he doesn't know where I'm at.

"Ya know, we're going to have some serious issues with the last name

We are US...

Zinfandel. I'm thinking we should probably start arguing now about names," I lean up to kiss him quick, as he gently swats my butt when I turn for the fridge.

"They're leaving," Kayla pipes up with her head in the door.

"Already? Z just grab the whole almond torte and give it to her."

"But-"

"Really, Kayla? You want to strip her of a dessert when she's suffering like that?"

"Oh, piss off, Suzanne. You're getting really good at guilt trips," she snarls leaving the kitchen in a huff as we follow.

"I'm sorry, Suzanne. Dinner was delicious, but I feel horrible suddenly. And I just want to crawl in bed."

"No worries. Take some dessert and relax. You lasted 2 whole hours without throwing up which I think is a record," I tease.

"I agree," Mack adds bending to kiss my cheek goodbye. "See you Wednesday."

"Good night," Z kisses Kayla's forehead as she turns quickly to leave.

"Wow. I would hate feeling like that," Kayla grabs for her coat. "We're gonna split too. Thanks for dinner, it was delicious," she adds with a hug.

"You're welcome. Do you want to take the chocolate pie with you? I know it's your second favorite."

"Yes, please," she grins as Z walks back to the kitchen for the pie.

Standing close to me, Marty leans in for our customary half hug with a 'thanks for dinner' as I smile at him. He's so funny, and he makes all my dinners such a fun affair I love having him around. And clearly by the way Kayla holds his hand all the time, she likes having him around too.

Handing Kaylas her pie after another round of goodbyes, they're gone.

Turning into Z I mumble, "Done. Holy shit, I'm tired," as he flips on the security and locks the door behind us.

"Let's lie down on the couch. You must be exhausted," he smiles tugging me to the couch where I collapse beside him.

"The dishes and table-"

"Can wait til tomorrow," he finishes turning on the news as I snuggle into his chest.

ααααα

"Suzanne? Suze...?"
"Yeah?" I mumble still half asleep on the couch.
"Look at the tv, love. Um, your grandfather died this morning," Z whispers waking me fully. Like a jolt, I flip to my other side and stare at the last seconds of the story about the great American Industrialist Edward Montgomery who passed away surrounded by family and friends at his estate in DC.
"What family?" I whisper to the tv, but there's no answer before CNN moves on to a story about a shooting in El Paso.
"Are you okay?" Z pulls me tighter to him.
"Yes... I said my goodbye to him over 2 years ago. And it's not like he ever tried to reach me again. So his death is just the complete end to what was already over. And I'm fine," I whisper into Z's forearm that rests across my chest.

When the phone rings some time later Z jumps up before I have a chance to think or wake fully again. I hoped this wouldn't start tonight, but it always does. Whenever there's a thing involving my family or past, the creepy calls begin from everyone looking for a quote, or for a scoop from me.
"We have to go, Suzanne. Kayla's in labor and Mack's freaking out because it's too soon. Apparently they didn't even make it home before she was crying over the labor pains."
Gasping, I jump up way too quickly and as the dizziness hits hard my hand just reaches the wall to steady me before Z has his arm wrapped around my waist.
"What's wrong?" He yells, but I need a second. Shaking my head, I breathe through the quick spins and lean into him for a second until everything slows back down for me.
"I stood up too quickly I think. That all. Everything else feels fine though," I steady my voice as he stares hard at my face again. "Honestly, it's already passing. Just let me sit for a second," I beg plopping back down on the couch. "Can you get my purse and jacket?"
"Should we go to the hospital for you? Should we have you checked out? This could be serious, and you were on your feet all day, and you shouldn't have made Easter dinner. I should've stopped you and said-"
"Stop," I wave my hand in the air and he stops immediately. "I'm okay. I wouldn't risk anything, Z. I literally got dizzy from jumping up after lying

down for a while. That's all it was. I can tell because I feel perfectly fine now. So please don't freak. Just get me my purse and coat and I'll stand slowly and walk even slower to the door. Everything is fine, Z. Trust me," I stare back at him squatting in front of my face until he exhales.

"Sorry."

"Don't be. I get why you'd be scared, but there's no reason to be. Not about this. It's already passed."

"Okay," he whispers like he only half believes me, but it's enough to get him out of my face so I can stop fake smiling and exhale myself. Shit, that sucked.

Standing as Z rushes back to help, I really do feel perfectly fine again. And I let him know as he pulls my jacket over my arms, everything *is* fine. I know it this time.

"Let's go. Kayla must be so scared, and Mack needs you," I take his hand as he nods.

Walking into the maternity ward, I spot Laura and almost groan. I mean obviously she'd be here, but she not my favorite person and dealing with her always sucks.

"Suzanne!" Mrs. Rinaldi yells jumping up to hug me. Looking over my shoulder at Z he shrugs before looking around for Mack. "She almost lost him. Kayla almost lost him, but they got him out with an emergency C-section and he's in neo-natal with Mack," she actually cries hugging me again.

"What happened?" Z leans into Mrs. Rinaldi as I pull away just enough to see her trying to speak.

"We don't really know. Mack called to say she was in early labor, but by the time we got here the doctors informed us she was in surgery and Mack was with the baby. We don't know anything else," she cries again until I hug her. Looking over her shoulder at Laura I see she's bawling her eyes out in her chair talking on the phone, and I suddenly realize this could be very bad.

"But we just saw her a few hours ago." Like that matters. Holy random thought, Suzanne.

"I know," Mrs. Rinaldi actually pouts. "She prefers having all her holiday dinners at your house now, Suzanne. So I think you need to start inviting me for dinner so I can see my daughter and grandson on the holidays."

"But what about Laura and Paola?" I grin. "And I am NOT inviting them as well. You can forget that idea. So really, you have to have dinners still otherwise they'd have nowhere to go," I tease as she smiles.

"Good point. But can't you give up Kayla just once or twice a year? Like we'll switch out Easter or Thanksgiving every year?"

"Okay. We'll try to set up a visitation schedule. Good?"

"Yes. Thank you, dear," she smiles looking much calmer than only minutes ago.

Turning to Z, Mrs. Rinaldi squeezes the hand he offers her, and leaning in she whispers, "You're looking as handsome as ever, Mr. Zinfandel," right in front of me which makes me laugh when Z actually blushes.

"Oh my god. *Please*..." I giggle as she smiles her own cheeky grin and walks back to sit beside Laura.

Feeling Z's breath on my cheek, he whispers, "You did good calming her. And wow, that was awkward," he groans as I turn to him.

"Face it, Mr. Zinfandel, wherever we go women are going to flirt with you. Just don't flirt back and I can handle it," I warn as he nods pulling me to the chairs beside the Rinaldi's.

Shaking Mr. Rinaldi's hand we all discuss what we know which isn't much. We talk about Easter, and wanting to see the baby, and we all just soothe each other as best as we can until Laura suddenly snaps maybe my cooking caused whatever happened to Kayla. But after a quick flinch from me before Z can defend me which I know he was about to do, Mrs. Rinaldi tells Laura to apologize immediately, which she does, begrudgingly. And then we all wait some more in silence.

Eventually, I curl up in a chair against Z as I feel sleep pulling at me, Kayla and Marty walk in to join us seconds before Paola arrives. And by 12:15 we all settle in, wrapping our jackets around our knees to keep us warm, snuggling into each other to fight off the hospital waiting room chill.

"Hey..." Mack says behind us as everyone jumps awake. Z and Mr. Rinaldi stand before I can even process I'm looking at Mack. "Here's what we know," he says calmly before the Rinaldi's can start yell asking their questions. "My unnamed son is perfect," he smiles so brightly Mrs. Rinaldi cries out before covering her mouth. "And my beautiful wife is in recovery. She had a partially ruptured placenta, so they performed an emergency C-section to get him out quickly, and she had internal bleeding which they've found and repaired," he nods at Mrs. Rinaldi

We are US...

again.

"Kayla can still have children, though I'm sure we won't. I'm never going to risk a detached placenta again, and hopefully Kayla will be reasonable," he grins as we all do. "And hopefully she won't make me force the issue in the future now that our Little Bastard is born healthy," he finally huffs a little laugh as Kayla and Marty grin at him.

"Little Bastard weighs 6 pounds 10 ounces which is a healthy weight, and he appears to have fully developed lungs though he'll be monitored closely for the next week. Kayla will also be monitored closely, and hopefully she'll be able to leave in a week herself. So, that's where we're at," Mack finally winds down before sitting in a chair across from our whole group.

"Can I see her?" Mrs. Rinaldi asks quietly but Mack shakes his head.

"Tomorrow morning. She'll be in recovery for at least a few more hours and by the time she can have visitors it'll be morning anyway. So why don't you all go home, rest up, and meet back here at 8:00 for visiting hours. I'll even take each of you in to meet my boy," he says so sweetly I move before I even realize it.

Sitting in the chair beside him I squeeze him with all I have. Kissing his neck as he side hugs me, I whisper, "They'll be fine. And you did good, Mack. I can't wait to meet my little nephew," I grin as he smiles warmly at me.

"He's beautiful, Suzanne," Mack breathes with awe in his voice.

"Of course he is. Have you *seen* his parents?" I add as he exhales.

"Oh, Mack," Mrs. Rinaldi moans joining us on his other side. "I'm so happy for you both, and I'm so happy Little Bastard," she says with a grin, "is going to be okay. I just love you both so much. Thank you for my first grandbaby," she cries until Mack pulls from me to hug her closely.

"You're welcome. But go home now. Rest up, and come back in the morning, okay? Kayla's going to be a mess when she wakes up, and I have a feeling she's going to want her mom with her," Mack says again so sweetly Mrs. Rinaldi chokes up even more. Nodding against his shoulder, he said the words that'll put her in action. She's a mom, and she's going to be a mom to her daughter, no matter how old her daughter is.

"I'll be back right at 8. You just tell Kayla to hold on until then and I'll be back for her. I love you, Mack," she smiles before kissing his cheek as he leans in for another hug from her.

"Thank you," he exhales as the first heavy looking emotion settles in deep. I see it and I know everyone else does as well. Mack is fighting not crying, and he looks just exhausted suddenly.

"Everything is going to be fine now," I whisper as he nods beside me.

"I know. Okay," pulling away from Mrs. Rinaldi who stands to walk back to her husband, "Everyone go home. There are no visitors tonight anyway, so there's nothing to do here. I'm going to sleep in Kayla's room when she's moved, and hopefully the baby will be moved into her room within a few days."

"What do you need?" Z steps forward and as Mack contemplates his question, they seem to share something so heavy between each other, I just stare at my 2 men in awe. They are so like brothers, I know they're almost silently communicating all the pain and fear and upset Mack must've felt tonight.

"Ah, clothes?" Mack says finally to Z replying done. Hugging Mack tightly, Z whispers something in his ear and Mack nods with a smile. Whatever he said took all the pain off Mack's face, and Z seems so calm I know he gave Mack something he needed to hear. Everything is going to be okay now, I can actually feel it.

"We'll be back before visiting hours with some clothes for you," I cuddle into Mack's side for one last hug.

Looking at me closely, Mack whispers in my ear, "Are you okay?" And as I pull away thinking he means about Kayla and their baby, he adds softly against my cheek, "I'm sorry to hear about your grandfather. Do you need to talk about it?" Wow. Even *now* he offers to be there for me? Honestly, this guy is too much.

"I'm perfectly okay. I'm just happy my *real* family is going to be okay. Okay?" I grin as he does.

"Okay. We'll see you in the morning?"

"With clothes and food, and presents, too," I giggle. "You have a baby, Mack. And I'm so happy for both of you."

"Thank you." Shaking his head a little, Mack seems overwhelmed but happy. "Um, I'm going to go back in, so I'll see you all tomorrow," Mack smiles again at everyone watching our exchange before turning to leave us for the ward doors.

"See you all tomorrow," Z reaches for my hand to leave. "Let's go, love. You need to sleep a little," he grins down at me so I understand his implication without saying anything everyone else will understand.

We are US...

"We should go to their apartment first so we can sleep as long as possible before coming back."

"Sounds good," Z agrees before saying goodbyes to everyone else as we leave the hospital for Mack's home and eventually our own bed.

Arriving home, I'm exhausted. Between throwing the Easter dinner and this little baby inside me, I need sleep so badly, I almost hop in bed without even taking off all my makeup.

Turning to Z in the doorway while brushing my teeth, I smile a white foaming at the mouth smile as he laughs at me.

"You haven't mentioned your grandfather at all," he says softly joining me at the sink reaching for this own toothbrush.

Looking at his face through the mirror, I make sure to keep eye contact so he knows I'm telling the truth. "Because I'm okay, Z. Besides wondering who the family was by his side, I just hope he didn't die completely alone. But other than that, I don't feel much of anything. I mean I guess I'm sad he's dead, but I don't feel sad about my *grandfather* being dead. He was just someone I used to know at this point."

"When the papers find out how much more you're going to inherit, everything's going to start up again for a while. And I'd like to put security back in place until it dies down. I need to protect-"

Leaning into his side, I cut him off before he starts freaking out. "Okay. Whatever makes you comfortable, Z."

There is NO way I'm fighting this. Not with a baby inside me, and not when I know he's right. Bring out my name in the papers, and the perverts and threats start up again. "You'll get the lawyers on standby?"

"I already called Humphrey," he grins like a bugger.

"Of course you did," I swap his butt as he laughs.

Taking my hand, he kisses it softly on the palm, which is one of his sweetest gestures before he walks us to our bed.

"Come here," he pulls me on top of him and just as I snuggle in, barely fighting my closing eyes, Z whispers, "I love you," making my smile the last thing I remember before sleep takes me for a few hours before we meet my new nephew.

CHAPTER 28

"I still can't believe you named him Matthew," I giggle as sweet little Matthew holds onto my finger with his tiny little baby fist.
"He was the Little Bastard for 2 weeks and I finally just caved when my mother threatened to name him herself," Kayla laughs.
"Well, he suits Matty," Kayla pipes up and I couldn't agree more. Matty is beautiful and sweet, and getting so big. I can't believe he's 2 months old and so alert. He's just my most favorite thing these days.
Shopping has been so much fun for me because there's a whole new little world I knew nothing about, and the ideas I'm getting for my own baby are making my head spin. Every day I think of a new nursery theme and every day I buy something that sits in the spare room unopened and waiting. But still Z doesn't engage.
Almost crying suddenly, I barely hold it in, but Chicago Kayla sees it and raises an eyebrow to talk until I gently shake my head no before other Kayla sees me.
I think she thinks I'm having a hard time with Matthew as a baby, but she couldn't be more wrong. Matthew doesn't feel like my Thomas, or remind me of what I've lost at all. He's just this special little person who I love separately from anything in my own life or past. And I adore him way beyond anything I could've ever imagined I'd like, or even love about a baby.
He also gives me hope for my own baby because I never felt awkward with Matthew, even days after he was born. Somehow, I just knew how to hold him and I adored him immediately. He's so pretty really, and every day I swear he changes to looks more like Mack, or more like Kayla until he changes again.
Matthew makes me feel good when I'm around him, so I have hope that I'll feel if not the same, hopefully even more when I have my own child months from now.

We are US...

Listening to the Kaylas talk about nothing special, I think of my own special and just spill. I figure I'm safe now, so why not?

"I'm pregnant," I exhale with a grin as Matthew's hands move awkwardly around my face.

"*What?*" They both yell like I knew they would.

Grinning at my Kaylas, I nod again as they stare. Standing with Matthew, I pull my black empire waist shirt tightly against my stomach so they can finally see the little bump I've been hiding.

"I'm about 4 1/2 months now, and the due date is around December 6th, though we're best guessing based on my measurements."

"How?" Kayla squeaks. "I mean, I thought you were protected and didn't want..." she kind of leaves hanging in the air around us.

"I was then I wasn't. And I want," I exhale as New York Kayla smiles warmly at me. "I didn't say anything because I didn't want to take away from your own pregnancy. And also because Z's so freaked out something bad is going to happen he isn't even really enjoying it yet. But now that I'm in the second trimester, I hope he'll start to relax a little."

Thinking about Z I realize he's really disappointed me with this baby. I remember how tenderly he looked at Kayla when she announced she was expecting in our kitchen, and I remember how much he fought me for Thomas. I remember thinking he was going to be so happy and loving and just so sweet about us having a baby, but he hasn't been. He's been almost distant about it.

Crying softly, I only realize I'm crying when I see a tear drip on Matthew's little onesie. Shit. Looking up at my best friends I know they're going to misread my upset if I don't explain quickly.

"I want this. This was my choice and my decision, and I *really* want this baby. I'm not sad or freaked or panicking about being a mother at all anymore. I *want* to be a mom, and seeing this little thing," I smile down at Matthew, "makes me feel good about being a mom finally. I, ah, don't really think I'll be shit at it anymore, because I don't really feel like *I'm* shit anymore."

"Then what wrong, Suzanne? Why are you crying?" Kayla leans into my side as I pass over Matthew to Chicago Kayla.

"It's Z," I moan finally bursting into tears. Crying my eyes out, I can't hold it in anymore. I'm disappointed and sad, and just so angry with Z for this.

"What did he do?" Kayla whispers.

Gasping, I say everything in one word, "Nothing."
"Like?"
"Like actually *nothing*. He was so happy the first 5 minutes I told him, and then that's it. He won't have sex with me or touch me unless he thinks *I* need to get off. He won't talk about the nursery, he won't look at the baby clothes or the stuffed animals I've bought. He has done nothing, but he won't *do* anything either."
"He's just scared, Suzanne," Chicago Kayla adds not so helpfully, and I snap.
"I *know* he's scared. Like I'm not?! Every goddamn day I'm scared this baby is going to die, or be born sick, or just... *die*. I'm afraid I'll lose my shit soon because I haven't at all about this pregnancy which is weird. And I'm scared post-partum depression will make me a mess, or crazy again. I don't know, but everything has been almost too good. I don't get sick, I'm not half as big as I was the last time, and I even like the feeling of being pregnant. But I'm scared too. And I'm freaking out that I actually *will* be a shit mom."
"Suzanne-"
"No! Just listen," I cry as they both silence. "I'm scared I *will* be shit and maybe I'm just fooling myself right now into thinking I won't be. But not really, because Matthew helped actually. I love him and I like holding him, and when you were still too sore to do much in the beginning and I came over every day to help, I loved it. Matthew is like special to me, and he's not even mine. So I hope I'll be good with a baby that *is* mine."
"You will be, Suzanne," Kayla says turning right into my face to slow down my upset.
"I hope so. But I don't want to do this alone. I couldn't even tell you two and I was dying to tell you, but Z is just so distant with me. No, not with me," I shake my head. "No, he still loves me and snuggles up and talks to me like he always did, but with this," I say pointing to my stomach, "with this he doesn't seem to care. But I know he does. How couldn't he, right? I mean look at the way he feels about our Thomas. So of course he cares about this one. I know he does. But I'm just so scared and kind of lonely with this and I'm mad at him I think for not looking at me the way he looked at you when you were pregnant, or for not loving me the way he used to when we made this baby happen. Um, this wasn't supposed to be a bad thing between us, it was supposed to be the *best* thing between us. And I'm sad..." I eventually fade out.

We are US...

Pulling in a big breath, I look to make sure Matthew wasn't upset by my yelling but he seems to be sleeping soundly in Kayla's arms.

"Look, hormones make women-"

"Oh, piss off, Kayla. This isn't hormones," I snap shutting her up instantly. "I've had no sickness, a few dizzy spells, and nausea once or twice. This isn't hormones, this is about me having a baby with a husband I love more than anything else in the world, *alone*. I barely talk about the pregnancy unless it's about appointments which we have many of. And I don't tell him the funny or even gross stuff about pregnancy because he just nods and acts like I'm boring him or something."

"So explain this to him. Tell him how you feel," she pushes as other Kayla nods quietly.

"I can't," I moan. "If he *is* just scared this baby will die then I can't fault him for not wanting to get attached to it. And if it *is* something more, like maybe I made a mistake and he wasn't ready or didn't even want another baby with me yet, then I don't want to know that either."

"But maybe if you talk to him he'll understand what he's doing."

Shaking my head I cry where I'm at. "I'm scared I made a mistake and finally trapped Z like I always feared I did. Maybe he was only excited about Thomas because it was an accident, but this baby was on purpose and maybe he doesn't want it or even want me anymore," I whisper as the pain hits me hard.

Lying my face on Kayla's cold glass table, I try to rationally handle all the fear and upset I've been holding onto alone for months now. "What if *he* thinks I'll be a shit mom and didn't want to tell me, and now it's too late?"

"He doesn't think that, Suzanne. I know Z, and I know he doesn't. He may be an idiot right now out of fear, but he loves you very much. I also know he wants a baby with you and there is NO way anything has changed about that. It didn't change, Suzanne. He's just being a fucking idiot," she grins as I huff a little laugh against her table. "But you need to tell him everything you just said to us. You have to. Write it in the book you share if you can't actually say it to him. But he has to know," Kayla leans in to kiss my cheek before I start crying all over again.

Shit. What a mess. I never cry like this anymore, or I do so infrequently I kinda thought I had cried my fill for a lifetime and there weren't any more tears left inside me.

"What else? Ask me or tell me," Kayla adds as I sit up slowly from her nice, cold table.

"Um, I'm super horny," I giggle embarrassed as other Kayla bursts out laughing almost waking Matthew. "Is that normal?"

Grinning Kayla admits, "It wasn't for me. But I was so sick in the beginning I couldn't stand the thought of sex, then when the hornies hit when I was around 6 months I was so fat and swollen and just so gross, Mack and I only tried a few times," she bursts out laughing as I grin at her. "We must've looked so funny trying all these angles while lifting legs and moving strangely, until I finally just told him to forget it," she shakes her head as I blush at the visuals. "We were like virgins trying to be porn stars, and it didn't work. Then I was over it until the next day when we did the same thing and I called it quits again."

"Poor Mack," Kayla whispers as I laugh.

"Yup, blue balls for sure," she howls with Kayla. "Honest to god, when we finally had sex just last week for the first time in months, we laughed the whole time. I wanted it and so did he, but he didn't want to go off quickly, and I wanted to prolong it for him. Eventually we both just laughed and had a quickie which was a relief- for both of us, trust me. Afterward though we made up for it, and everything seems to be back the way it was," she says with a dirty little grin.

"Just jump him! That's what I do with Marty," Kayla adds as I giggle at both of them nodding.

"Ah, Z's afraid he'll hurt the baby, or maybe like hit my uterus or something."

"Wow," Kayla teases. "As if he's that big," she laughs but as I blush and look down she gasps. "He is, isn't he? He's got a huge dick? I *knew* it," she continues as I die embarrassed. "Tell me. He does, right?"

"Ah, I can't tell you that. He's my husband, Kayla."

"*So!* Tell me. Come on, Suzanne, I'm dying to know. Come on, tell me. Tell me. Tell me," she continues chanting until I give in.

"Yes. Okay?" God, I'm like purple I'm blushing so bad.

"You are one lucky bitch, you know that?" She laughs as I finally make eye contact with her. "Along with all his other pluses, he's got a huge dick, too?" Shaking her head like she can't believe my luck, I can't believe it either most days.

"What about Marty?" Kayla asks taking the heat off me thankfully.

"Marty? His is about average, but he's really good with it, so I have no

complaints," she moans making me blush again. "Mack?"
 Quickly covering my ears, I hear them both start laughing again, but I don't care. I cannot think of Mack's penis. Like ever. As far as I'm able to handle he doesn't even have one.
 "We're done," Kayla tugs at my hand. Looking at them they're both grinning from ear to ear when I tell them they're perverts.
 "Can I lie him down?" I ask reaching for Matthew when Kayla says of course.
 Lifting him from Kayla, I walk slowly to his nursery inhaling and taking in everything Matthew. From his little weight, to his baby smell, I hold him close to my chest. He is just so beautiful to me, I never thought it was possible to love a baby so much, especially if he wasn't my own. But once again I'm wrong about something in life, I smirk to myself.

ΩΩΩΩΩ

 Returning home, I throw on my comfies and start writing to Z. Without holding back I tell him everything I said to my friends today, and I even add more personal stuff I couldn't say. I explain how lonely I feel, and I explain how I'm starting to get the shitty feeling inside me because I'm not sure if he wants me anymore. I explain my sadness, confusion, and even my own fears about this baby maybe dying.
 And finally, I explain that if this was a mistake, I'll leave Z alone if that's what he wants. I don't offer to make our baby go away, because I couldn't possibly. But I do offer to leave Z alone if he wants nothing to do with this decision I selfishly made without him.
 And after I write everything down I'm left with two issues that scream the loudest in my head.
 If I lose this baby I don't want to regret never experiencing the happiness of carrying it or of making it with Z. And if I don't lose this baby I don't want to regret not enjoying my pregnancy or the experience of being pregnant with Z. But I know now if he can't get on board, I will absolutely make *myself* enjoy this experience no matter how it turns out for me and Z.

Placing our nightly notebook on the living room table, I know he'll spot the book immediately when he comes home. I also know I don't want to be around him when he reads the page and a half of random, sad thoughts I left for him. And not just because I may feel embarrassed, but because I want him to have his own moment when he realizes where I'm at, and what I want from him with this baby.

Walking to our room, I'm absolutely exhausted again. I know my own little bastard makes me tired, but I think the sadness weighing me down mixed with the tears I shed at Kayla's has me struggling. So without fighting it anymore, I climb in for a little rest knowing I have at least 3 hours until Z comes home.

ϘϘϘϘϘ

I know I'm in a dream. I *am* in a dream and I know it. It's the kind of dream where you want to get out and you know you will eventually, but it's just too real and too heavy to pull yourself out of quickly.

Watching the little girl scream in agony as the man touches her, I smash my hands against the glass screaming with her. Screaming and smashing the glass wall, I can't get in and I can't break through. I'm trapped in glass watching a little dark haired girl bend her back in a painful arch as the movement behind her begins.

To watch and not be able to stop him is torture. To bleed all over the glass as my knuckles try to break through is a nightmare. Watching her mouth open in agonized screams, I can't look away from her horror.

"Look at *me*, baby!" I scream for her, but she never looks at me or sees me trying to help her. She doesn't know I'm here, and she doesn't know I'm trying to stop her pain. She doesn't know anything but her agony as he pulls her hair, and bruises her hip with his huge man hands all over her little body. She doesn't know I'm here trying so hard to get to her.

"Stop! Don't fucking touch her!' I scream to silence in my glass prison. But he isn't stopping, and she's growing weak. I can see and feel her weakness as her arms start to shake and her head hangs low. She isn't even screaming anymore.

"No! *Fight* him! I'm going to save you this time!" I scream and scratch and kick at the glass preventing me from saving her.

And then it happens.

A tiny crack. A little splinter in the glass and I have my in. Slamming my fists, punching with the side of my hands, thrashing and kicking, I watch the tiny splinter spider web into a hole I can scratch my fingers through. Ripping and tugging at the glass the hole widens as the noises grow louder around me.

Oh, *god*... I hear him. Grunting into her little body, he continues. Banging into her little body he thrusts his evil into her broken little soul.

He's a fucking monster. And I'm going to kill him.

Breaking my way through, I feel the glass tear my clothes and rip my shoulders as I force myself through. Landing on my bleeding hands, my legs tear apart from the glass ripping down my thighs. Fighting, I finally make it through as she whimpers one last time.

Landing on her cheek, her body is held up only by his hands on her hips as I struggle to get to her.

"*Mommy?*" She whispers opening her eyes and my whole world ends when I see her.

I have never known horror like this in my life.

Her dark hair surrounds her pale face, and her ice blue eyes no longer cry. She is a ghost of a little girl dead on the floor. She is my daughter, dead in the agony and filth he created.

And I'm going to fucking *kill* him.

Diving for his face I know no power greater than this. This is a mother and this is his death. He hurt her and I will not stop until he knows the pain of his death by my hands.

I will never stop. Until he does.

Sounds I didn't know I could make screech around the room masked only by the sound of his cries as I tear his flesh from his face and neck. Biting and ripping, and tearing him into chunks, his blood is all I know. His blood is the taste of the hatred I feel.

Quickly he's dying, and I look forward to watching him beg for his death.

"You are dead," I laugh as he fights against my raking nails and my vicious jaws. "You took my *life*!" I scream as I watch his fight slowly fade before me. He is losing, and I'm gaining the strength of the vicious.

"Suzanne! *Suzanne!* Wake *up!*"
No! I can't lose this fight and I can't let him live. I *won't* lose this time.
"Suzanne! Holy *fuck!* Wake up, baby! Wake. The. Fuck. *UP!*" He screams as everyone starts to fade around me.
Sitting away from the mess left of him, I stare at her blue eyes, opened but unseeing. She is gone, and I didn't save her in time. I wasn't saved in life, and I didn't save her in death.
"NO!" I thrash against the hands pulling me away from his death. "*No!* I have to finish him so she'll live!" I scream as she starts to fade into the floor.
Gasping, I cover my mouth and watch as her little body becomes more and more transparent as the seconds pass. Watching her hair fade out to clear, and her skin melt into the floor I reach for the nothing left of her soul.
"I'm so sorry, baby, but I tried. I tried so hard to protect you this time," I weep when she fades to nothing. Reaching for her I feel nothing but only her agonized tears glistening on the floor where she once cried for me.
But she's gone.
Before I even held her or knew her, she's been taken from me. She is a memory. She had dark skin and hair, with my see-through blue eyes. She was a beautiful girl who is now a faded death.
And I have to go with her.

"*Suzanne...?*"
"She's dead," I choke as the pain slices my heart from my chest. "I didn't save her. I *couldn't* save her even though I tried. But it was just too hard to get through the glass," I gasp again as the breath leaves my lungs for the very last time.
Crying, I can't fight the agony of my loss.
"I want to be with her now. It's my time..." I breathe my last words before the darkness takes me away.

We are US...

CHAPTER 29

"Suzanne...?" I hear him and I know I'm alive. Unlike all those other times I woke and wasn't sure, this time I know. Just the pain in my chest alone tells me I'm still alive.

Opening my eyes quickly to Z I look at his dark eyes and have to know. "Did you get her body? Did you bring her home to me?"

"Who, baby? *Whose* body?" He actually cries and I hate him for not bringing her to me.

Moaning, I push his chest and turn away from him as my hatred grows. Replaced only with the sadness of her death, I hate Z as much as I mourn her.

"Who Suzanne? Oh god... *talk* to me," he begs shaking my shoulder.

Willing myself to breathe, I hold my chest tight to ease the ache. "My daughter."

Flinching, I'm stunned silent by the agony all around me. Saying the word again, I can't stand the power it has over me. "My *daughter!*" I scream. Gasping awake my living nightmare I can't stand my heartache.

"I had a daughter. And she was beautiful, but now she's dead," I cry as the agony takes my breath away again.

"Suzanne. You don't have a daughter," Z whispers as I choke.

"I know. Because she's *dead*," I cry my loss.

"No, because you don't have a daughter. There is no daughter, Suzanne."

"Not anymore," I weep dying with her.

"Not *ever*. Listen to me," Z says sitting on my other side. "Listen! You haven't had a baby yet. You haven't had a daughter yet. There is no daughter, Suzanne," he says squeezing my shoulders into his chest so tightly, I don't even fight him. "There is no daughter yet. No one died, love. Can you understand me?"

But I can't understand because I saw her. I watched her raped, and I watched her slide to the floor before she died. I watched her horror and I heard her call my name.

"*Mommy?*" I whisper her word so powerful to me.
 Watching her scream, I know that pain. I know what that horror feels like, and I know the desperation that makes you wish you were dead. I know that agony, and I know that defeat.
 "She begged me, and I didn't save her."
 "Baby, listen. You're in our bed, and you had a panic attack. You don't have a daughter, now or before. Suzanne, you're safe, love. No one will get you here," Z pushes as the heavy weight of agony starts to lesson with his words.
 "But they *will* get her eventually," I moan as the pain crushes me once more.
 "They will *NEVER* get her, Suzanne."
 Suddenly throwing up on my bed as he moves quickly, I know the truth. I know it so clearly because I always did. *This* is why I didn't want to be a mother. "They'll get her, Z. They always do," I cry and gag before vomiting again.
 "Suzanne. Look at me. It's Mack." Pressing my hand against my chest to stop the pain, moaning on my bed to fight the vomit, I need Mack to save her.
 "Z doesn't understand," I beg reaching and squeezing Mack's arm. "He doesn't know what you know they did to me. But they'll get her Mack. They'll rape and torture and *kill* her."
 Bending low into my vision Mack shakes his head fiercely. "They will never get her, Suzanne," Mack pushes ignoring me like Z does.
 "He raped and killed my daughter while I watched. I couldn't save her, Mack. No one can because she's mine, and they always kill my daughter."
 "*Enough!*" Z yells at my side making me jump. "Feel your stomach. Feel it right now!" He yells again pushing my hand to my stomach. "The baby is still in there. You haven't had a baby yet. So no one died, and no one will. I'm telling you, she isn't here yet. Wake up now, Suzanne. Wake up and see your reality," Z yells again scaring me awake.
 "But it was so horrible," I cry more tears of agony. "She's beautiful, Z. She looks dark like you but she has my eyes," I choke. "Then they just stopped seeing. They stopped Z after she called my name. She *begged* me to help her but I couldn't stop him."
 Holding me again, Z shushes and soothes as I break down in his arms. He'll never understand what that was like to see and feel. And he'll

never understand what it's like to watch your child die. "You don't know what it's like to see her die," I weep.
"But you didn't, Suzanne. You had a bad dream. A very bad dream. But that's all it was- a very bad dream."
"But she died."
"In. A. Dream. Not in real life and never in my lifetime. No one will ever hurt our baby, Suzanne. Ever," he growls pulling me away to stare hard at me again. "*Never*. I'm telling you our child will be safe always."
"But-"
"There is NO but. Have you ever been touched or hurt since we've been together? Have you?"
"No."
"No. Because it will never happen again. And no child of mine will ever be hurt the way you were. *Ever,* Suzanne."
"But..." I whisper quietly as reality slides into place. Almost as quickly as I lost touch with reality, it's suddenly coming back to me. Staring at Z, smelling of vomit, scared and shaking, I'm here. I'm right here now with Mack only a foot from us watching in my bedroom as I come back to us.
"I'm sorry... But it was so real."
"It's okay, love. You had a bad dream you couldn't wake up from," Z soothes again. "But it wasn't real."
"It wasn't real," I agree slowly looking around my room at all our things. My dresser and Z's, and the glass door to the atrium, and the door to our bathroom beside his closet. Everything is real now, but the pain still feels so real.
"I feel like I'm still mourning her, Mack, and I don't know what to do."
"You just breathe Suzanne until the panic fades and the dream fades back from real to a nightmare. That's all you do. Breathe your way back to the present reality you have with Z."
"Um, I don't want to have a daughter," I whisper as Mack sits on my bed beside us.
Smiling, he actually shakes his head before speaking. "Well, that's not really up to you, and there's nothing you can do about it now. But *if* you have a daughter you'll learn to fight past the fear for her. You will, because as a parent that's all you can do."
"But I don't want her to ever be hurt. And she's so pretty, and men are so evil, and she's going to get hurt," I sit up so sure of myself. "I think this was a warning or something."

"No it wasn't, Suzanne."

"I didn't want to tell you, but I don't want to have a daughter. I'm afraid of a daughter. I really don't want one, and Z says son or *daughter* all the time and I almost cry I'm so afraid. I can't have one, Mack. And now I know what's going to happen to her if I do, and I won't survive it, Mack. I won't because I've seen what happens to her."

Leaning back into me, Mack takes my hand tightly and smiles softly as I try to breathe again. "It wasn't a vision Suzanne. You had a bad dream."

"But I saw what happens if I have a daughter." Just above a whisper I try to make Mack understand, "I *saw* it."

"Suzanne, that wasn't a vision of your future. That was a bad dream because you're stressed out and Z is being an asshole right now. You had a very bad dream only," Mack says as I actually startle at the Z's being an asshole part. "Let me ask you this- was Z in your dream with you?"

"No."

"And why is that? Why wasn't he there protecting your daughter?"

"I don't know," I admit as Z's head suddenly lowers beside me when I look at him.

"Could it be because he hasn't been there for you during this pregnancy? Maybe because you just wrote to him in your journal telling him how scared and alone you felt, you had a horrible nightmare and Z wasn't there to help you or to protect your daughter? Maybe because you don't feel like he's here for you now, you dreamt of him not being there for you then?" Oh.

"Um, maybe? I don't know. It just felt like I was supposed to see what was happening, and I was supposed to protect her, but I didn't because I couldn't get through the glass because I'm a bad mom. Just like I was with Thomas," I cry again as more upset shakes me. "I think I failed them both, Mack."

"You didn't fail Thomas- nature did when he was taken from you. He wasn't taken from you because of anything you did wrong. And your daughter wasn't taken from you because she's not here yet. You don't have a daughter to fail, and neither does Z."

"Oh..." Huh. Seeing everything the way Mack just said it makes me feel better suddenly. She's NOT here, so I didn't let her die, and maybe I won't fail her if I do have her one day. "Maybe I can protect her from bad men," I whisper to no one as Z grabs me quickly into his arms.

"I'm so sorry, Suzanne, but we *will* protect a daughter, I promise. Not one bad man will ever get to her, I swear. You never have to fear like that because it will never happen. We aren't your parents, and we aren't bad people who do bad things to children. We aren't like your parents or mine with sick fucking people around wanting to hurt children. Look at who our people are- our *safe* people. No one will ever do that to her. She won't have your life, baby. She will *never* have your life or past. Believe me. *Please*," Z begs and I do believe him. Looking at him speaking so fiercely to me, I believe him totally.

"I believe you. But I still don't want a daughter, Z. And I don't think I'll handle it very well if I do. And I'm scared I'm going to have an episode if I do, and I really don't want a daughter." Looking at Mack, I know he gets this. I know he understands. "A daughter will be a mistake, Mack."

"Not a *mistake*, Suzanne. It'll be a challenge for you. But you've had challenges before and survived them. And if you hold a daughter in your arms, I guarantee you'll fight to deal with that challenge as well. Because as Z said, you are surrounded by safe people who will protect your daughter to the end."

"But what if they can't?" I whisper my biggest fear desperately.

"They *can,* Suzanne. And we will. No one could get past Z, Marty or me to your daughter. And can you even imagine what your Kaylas would do to someone even *thinking* of hurting your daughter?" Faking a shiver, I almost laugh at his face until he ends this for me finally. "She will *never* be you Suzanne. And if you have ever believed a single word I've said to you, then believe that. *If* you have a daughter, Suzanne, she will never be *her.*"

Oh, god. That's it. I don't want my daughter to be *HER*. Ever.

"I was HER... But she doesn't have to be," I whisper my reality to no one but myself as the silence suddenly clears my mind. "I need to shower," I jump up so quickly I almost smash my head on Z's chin.

"Suzanne?"

"It's just a shower to clean away the vomit. I'm okay. Thank you, Mack. Again. Always," I fake smile as he nods. "It's just a shower Z, and I'll clean up the bed later. I'll talk to you about everything tomorrow, Mack, I promise." Turning, I close and lock the bathroom door before I cry again in front of them.

I know it was a bad dream now. I get that totally. It mean, it was so real, and her face was exactly as I imagined that it's hard to suddenly turn off the upset, but it *is* fading.

We are US...

God, she was *exactly* as I imagined she would be though. Oh. Maybe because it was my imagination creating the dream. Wow. Okay, that makes so much sense I feel way better now.

Stepping into the shower, I realize even if they say they could protect a girl I still really hope I have a boy so I don't fear his life as much as I would hers. Because honestly, if I do ever have a daughter and she gets hurt like I was, I don't know that anyone would survive it, least of all me.

ooooo

Walking out of the bathroom however long later I stop to watch Z just finish smoothing down the comforter I don't like as much as our normal one on our bed. Then again, barfers can't be choosers so...

"Thank you. I was going to change the sheets after my shower."

"It's no problem," Z says stopping with the pillow under his chin for the pillow case shimmy. "How are you feeling? Are you still freaked out by the dream?"

"No. It kind of faded away when reality surfaced. Is Mack still here?"

"No. He wanted to get home to Matthew," Z smiles and I understand totally. I'd want to go home to my baby too if I had one.

Looking at the clock, I realize it's only 5:15 which surprises me. It feels so much later, and Z doesn't usually get home till 5:30.

"Why did you come home early?" Walking over to the throw blanket on the chaise, I fold it up to lie at the end of our bed where it belongs.

"Today's Tuesday," he says not looking at me as he finishes the pillow.

"Yeah. Oh, you were at your session with Mack."

"Yes," he nods sitting on the side of our bed suddenly. "Your best friend called my best friend to tell him what an asshole I was, and my best friend told me off for being an insensitive asshole to you," Z says softly with just a little grin that fades quickly.

Shit. I feel really bad suddenly. Almost like I betrayed him or something when I talked to Kayla which was not my intention earlier.

"I wish she hadn't done that, Z. I just needed to talk to a friend, and I never expected her to run to Mack or for him to confront you."

"Suzanne, it's okay to talk to your friends. And it's okay for them to tell me off when I'm an asshole. That's what friends do."

"I know, but during a session is different. That time isn't about friends or our issues. It's about your time to talk to your doctor," I huff feeling a little pissed at both Kayla and Mack suddenly.

Turning to me Z motions to sit beside him, which I do. "To be fair, Mack waited until after our official session, then he let me have it in the hallway," Z laughs. "It's okay, Suzanne. I didn't really see everything clearly, and I didn't understand how my upset was affecting you, though I absolutely should've. And I'm very sorry for that."

Leaning into his shoulder I nudge him and whisper, 'It's okay', as he takes my hand and kisses my forehead.

"Can I tell you something?"

"Of course."

"Losing Thomas was brutal for me. But *almost* losing you time and time again has been the worst feeling in my life. There has been nothing that comes even close, except for Thomas. And though I'm passed the initial hurt, I'm still stunned by how it all went down. And now that you're pregnant, I'm just scared, Suzanne. Like totally fucking scared shitless something bad is going to happen again."

"I know. I feel the same."

"But boy or *girl,* Suzanne, I want this and I want you." Doing his intense stare at my eyes thing he finishes this. "And you *both* will always be protected from bad people. I promise you."

"I believe you."

Inhaling deeply, Z shakes his head before confessing. "I read your journal before I realized you were having a nightmare. Mack was here to talk to both of us, but I saw your journal and I read it first while he waited silently in the den. And you know, it was your last 2 sentences that woke me up and pulled my head out of my ass, because you're right. I don't want to not care about this pregnancy if we lose this baby, and I don't want to not care if we don't lose the baby. I was so scared of feeling what I felt before and experiencing the disappointment and mourning I suffered before, I was too weak to enjoy this one. But you were totally bang on with me, and I'm really sorry for that. I'm sorry it took you

We are US...

telling me what I was doing to you and us to understand what I was really doing to this baby, too."

"It's okay, Z. But I don't want to just live day to day feeling nothing in case something bad happens because then I'll have no memories good or bad. And I've already done that once. This baby is special to me and I want to love it and enjoy it and spoil it before it's even here. But if you don't want this-"

"Stop," Z cuts me off abruptly. "I read that shit in your journal too. And to be honest, I was kinda pissed at you for that. *Really,* Suzanne? I may be freaked out about the baby not surviving but I'm not freaked that we're *having* one. And I sure as hell want a baby with you. I never want you to leave. And *really?*" He glares at me suddenly. "'I'll leave if you don't want me or this baby?' What kind of bullshit was that?" He snaps angrily.

"Um, I didn't know. I was just giving you options I guess, in case I trapped you with this because I didn't ask you first. Look, I thought I'd surprise you and I wanted to give this to you, but I didn't even think about asking you first, so-"

"You assumed the worst of me again. And actually entertained for even one minute that I'd want to be apart from not only you, but our baby as well. What kind of bullshit is that?"

"I didn't know!" I gasp at his anger.

"Well, do you now?"

"Yes."

"Good. Now kiss me!" Z yells and after a split second pause of confusion, I finally just burst out laughing. We really are a pair of whack jobs. Honestly. "Kiss me, Suzanne. I need to feel you," Z says so sadly I lean into him for a kiss.

Soft and sweetly, Z holds the good side of my face with his hand and reaches around my hip to pull me over his lap. Stretching the bottom of my long nightgown to straddle his thighs we kiss. Kissing, we are slow and beautiful, and everything ugly fades between us as it always does when we kiss.

Against my lips he moans he's sorry again as I pull him tighter to me in forgiveness. I know he's sorry, and I know he wouldn't hurt me intentionally. I know we're just trying to get through the big things as best as we can.

When I feel him start trying to inch up my nightgown I panic. "I haven't shaved my legs."

"I don't care," he growls.

"No, like in a while," I giggle embarrassed. "You haven't wanted me and I was tired, and my legs are really hairy, Z," I hide my face in his shoulder mortified.

"Suzanne," he grins turning my face to him. "You threw up on me an hour ago, so hairy legs is nothing," he smirks as I laugh again.

Nodding at his attempt at humor, I lean back in for a kiss. Kissing, Z continues with the rise of my nightgown, and though I think of my nasty legs again, I really don't care. I need him and I want him.

"It's been so long," I moan out loud when he turns us so I'm on my back on our bed. "I've missed you," I tear up a little when he lowers his head to kiss my chest.

Feeling his hands touch me softly, I revel in everything Z. He is so warm against my skin I breathe him into me. Waiting for him to suck my nipples in deep, Z just makes contact when I nearly jump off the bed.

Watching him raise his head as my hand grabs my own nipple, I'm shocked by the pain. "Ah, I'm not sure-"

"Sensitive, love?" He grins and I realize I am. Huh. It's not like I play with my own nipples, so I didn't know.

"Apparently," I smile as he lowers again to nip my hand away before taking my nipple again a little softer. Oh, I feel the difference. Moaning, I can't stop myself as his hand slides down my hip to my thigh and back up, pulling my nightgown with his hand.

Ignoring my hairy legs completely, Z opens me up as he inches further down my body. Kissing my Thomas scar like he always does, he spends a little more time on my belly kissing and mumbling words I can't hear or understand to my bump.

"Off," he growls moving down my body onto his knees as my hips lift instantly for him to pull my nightgown off. Ripping it overhead as I wait, Z stares at my naked body like he always does, and I actually feel my arousal climb in seconds.

Leaning back on our pillows, I watch Z watching me as he raises my good leg over his shoulder to kiss me where I'm desperate to be kissed. Working his way lower, I feel the gentle insertion of a finger just as I feel his tongue lick me all the way up my middle to my clit. Pausing, Z moans at my eyes and begins flicking me with his tongue so quickly, I gasp and arch to the thrill of his mouth.

"Oh, *god*..." I cry unaware of anything but the pleasure, and his eyes watching me. "*Please*..." I whine until he starts pleasing me to the point of agony.

Writhing and groaning the building inside, I'm unaware of anything but Z. I smell his scent, and I feel his slow torture. I know his sounds, and I need him harder. "*Please*," I cry again as everything fades away but his mouth on me.

Waiting, I seem to be stuck, but I want more. I need this release, and I want this pleasure with Z. Feeling myself stretched by more fingers, I'm dying inside. But it's a good death. It's the kind of death you hope to experience over and over in your lifetime. It's the death of everything evil, replaced with a beautiful peace inside.

"Oh. *Um?*" Crying out, my release hits hard and fast. Nearly flipping on the bed again, Z holds my hips in place as he moves back up my body with sweet kisses and the gentle weight of his body keeping me grounded.

"Suzanne..." He moans before kissing my lips softly as I gasp my taste on his lips and his tongue bringing me back to him. I never get tired of this, and it never feels the same. Every time with Z is so different, I feel like I'll never know it again. But I always do. "Love?" He asks as a question until I open my eyes and smile at him.

Moving my own legs, I open wider for his entry. "I need you, Z. So badly," I finally cry as my tears fall. "Hurry up," I grin as he laughs against my mouth.

And then he enters me. Slowly and without the hard, fast need I feel for him, Z enters me, rocking into me until he finally settles in deep and exhales against my mouth again.

"I've missed you so much," he whispers before I attack his mouth with my own.

Moving my hips, I speed up his enter retreat until nearly pounding against each other, I know no sounds but our breath in our room.

"Please," I cry as he thrusts harder inside me. Harder and faster, I beg and pull at him. I need this. "I want this!" I cry when he lifts my legs around his waist to enter me deeper.

"Suzanne?" He slows a little, but I'm not having it.

"Sex is fine! Sex is good. I'm *supposed* to have sex," I gasp as he stops moving completely.

"*Supposed* to?" He grins rising on his hands looking down at me.

"Um, yeah. I think I read that somewhere. It's good for me, I think. Oh, who gives a shit?" I laugh as he does before he starts moving again.

Slower, he changes the pace from sex to make love in an instant and my whole body feels the difference. Z wants me but he wants to love me, and I know that matters to him. This is his apology and his desperate attempt to make me love and trust him. He is making love to me, and I know nothing but his love all around me.

Turning us to our side, lifting my thigh over his hip, Z continues his slow impalement, wrapping me in his arms, staring at my face as we move.

Sideways always feels so different. Almost like looking and watching each other makes all the difference. There is a calm and a peace that takes over the act, and I always feel his love so much stronger when he watches me watching him.

"Ready, love?" he smiles his dirty grin as I huff my yes with a nod.

Feeling his hand reach between us, I gasp again at the feeling of him touching me where we're joined. It's such an intimate feeling, and it always takes me over completely.

Moaning, my orgasm is softer than the first and it feels lighter in my stomach. I don't scream and arch, but as my eyes close and my hips move against his, I feel his own slow release quickly followed by a low moan. Feeling him inside me release our waiting and need for each other makes everything else fade away.

We're alone here in this place, and no one has ever known me or loved me the way Z has.

"I know you'll protect us," I breathe as he kisses my lips softly.

"Dinner in bed?" He asks my nearly comatose body after we finish our quick rinse off shower.

Wrapping my towel tighter, I can't even handle getting dressed I'm so exhausted. Looking in my bathroom closet, I figure, *what the hell* and actually walk to my bed undressed. If Z notices he doesn't mention it, and if Z is surprised he acts unconcerned.

"Crawl in and I'll make us something to eat," he smiles and kisses my forehead as I pull the comforter around my damp towel. "Take this off." Pulling the towel from under me, Z keeps me covered in blankets, but strips me of my last guard of nudity. And I just don't care anymore.

I mean really? Z has seen everything. The scars and the marks, and just all the hairy, gross that is me. But he's still here, and he doesn't ever seem to care. So I'm not going to struggle with myself anymore.

"I'm getting better," I whisper to no one but Z hears my confession to myself.

"I know you are," he kisses my naked back before leaving me to rest.

CHAPTER 30

"Is tonight my baby shower?" Turning to me quickly, Z looks guilty as hell and I know I have my answer. Shit.

"No. Why?" Walking away from me he doesn't make eye contact, and well, he's walking away from me which means I'm right. Pulling his arm in the kitchen doorway he stops moving. "How did you know?" He exhales long and slow.

"You suck at lying to me. And pushing me to go to Marty's when I told you I was exhausted today, and moody, and kind of grumpy actually? Normally, as soon as I say I'm tired you drop everything and make me lie down, but today-"

"I basically told you to suck it up and get dressed because we're going out for dinner whether you're tired or not," Z laughs as I do.

"Basically."

"*Please* act surprised. The Kaylas have been calling me and torturing me over this baby shower for weeks. I've received more calls from them in the past 2 weeks than I have in all the years I've known them. Kayla even threatened my balls if I told you."

Shivering like he's actually afraid for his balls, I have to know, "Which Kayla?"

"Does it matter?" Z replies deadpan until his eyes light up with humor.

"Ah, not really I guess. Okay, I'll act surprised. When does it start?"

"7:00."

"7:00 on a Wednesday?"

"Marty's slowest evening. They were so sure you wouldn't suspect anything if it was held at his restaurant, instead of at one of their homes since you rarely go out now," Z says sounding a little upset.

"What's wrong?" Leaning against the wall I wait for him to speak. Z suddenly looks almost unhappy about something, and we've been perfect for months, almost too perfect. Huh. "Are we too happy?" I moan out loud without meaning to as usual.

We are US...

"Never." Leaning down to my face, Z kisses me so softly, I instinctively move into his arms until he stops me from going further. "There is no such thing as too happy between us, Suzanne. There is not happy enough for you though. And I know you've been struggling this last month."

"No, I haven't. I've been fine." And there's the word. Suddenly realizing I've said 'fine' thousands of times in the last month, once again negates the 'I'm fine' argument I use way too often when I'm not fine. "Shit."

"Please talk to me. I'm going out of my mind with this, and so is Mack actually. But you won't talk to either of us, and you keep saying I'm fine which is killing me, Suzanne."

Leaning into Z, I try to figure out what the problem actually is so I can explain. But again, strangely enough I do actually feel fine. "Okay, this is all I've got." When Z pulls away to watch me closely again, I say my stupid. "My lack of problems is what *feels* like a problem, which is just warped really."

"How so?"

"Ah, I don't feel depressed at all. Actually, I haven't for so long now I'm scared it's coming even though I don't feel anything bad coming. I've been out of the hospital for a year now and I still feel good."

"That's good."

"Is it? I don't know if it is and that's what scares me. I have 3 weeks to go and I'm, ah, closer than I was before. Saying what I'm saying without saying it is hard, Z. But I just don't want to say his name in case I get upset and maybe jinx *this* baby which is stupid, I know. But I'm getting nervous the closer I get to the end."

"And?"

"And I'm still scared I'm going to have a girl, which I don't really want which is a horrible thing to say, I know. But I can't help it. No matter what you and Mack say, or what I even believe I'm scared to have a little girl, in case..."

"Baby, there is no in case. I cannot express enough that you're worrying about something *we* would never allow. A daughter will be as safe as any son we have, Suzanne. I swear on my life."

"I know that logically, Z. I do. It's just hard thinking of a little girl of ours getting hurt."

"Then don't think about it, because she will never be hurt like that. And if we do have a girl, I know you're going to love her and care for her just as much as you would if it was a boy. You're going to handle this Suzanne. I know you will, okay?"

"Okay."

"What else?" Z leans closer to me to take my hand as I think about what's bothering me.

"I think that's it. It's like I'm in the home stretch now, and I'm scared. Next week is Thanksgiving and then I have 2 weeks to go to just wait."

"I understand, love. I really do," Z exhales. "If it helps, I'm getting very nervous myself. But maybe we can just be happily nervous together? Could you try?"

"Of course."

"As for the other things you're feeling, or NOT feeling I guess, I don't know what to say other than why not just enjoy not being sad right now, instead of being weirded out that you're not sad. Maybe try to be happy that you're not sad."

Looking at Z, I once again know he's right. And logical. And sane. And like all positive and shit. Whatever. I've never been one of those annoyingly positive people. Though I am much better than I used to be.

"I'll try. But I have to tell you *not* having a problem is kind of freaking me out," I grin. "Maybe we could have a huge fight later so I feel unhappy and more like myself?"

"Or maybe I could just love the shit out of you later until you forget you're nervous and not unhappy?"

"Okay. I like your idea *way* better than mine, Z."

ΩΩΩΩΩ

Walking into Marty's I feel as awesome as I can tonight. I'm dressed in a black coat as usual, but it has little faux fur embellishments around the wrists and collar to change things up a bit. Even my dress underneath is a perfect fitting crisscross bodice, knee length swing dress in black with a midnight blue sash above my huge belly which is adorable. So overall, I feel pretty attractive for having a gigantic beach ball out front of me.

We are US...

"I can't wait to untie your dress when we get home," Z whispers in my ear just as he opens the door to Marty's restaurant for me.

"I can't wait for you to untie this dress either. I miss you."

"Since last week?" He grins his dirty sexy grin.

"Always."

"Good answer. Now stop procrastinating and show me those acting skills you *think* you have," Z adds like a total smartass just as the hostess Maya walks up to us.

"Hello, Maya. It's just the two of us this evening," Z says in his sexy voice, and I want him even more now.

"Certainly. If you'll follow me," she smiles politely at me even grabbing 2 menus to make it believable.

"Where are-"

"*SURPRISE!*"

Jumping with a little scream, I know I was totally believable because Kayla actually did scare the shit out of me. Grabbing my chest as my heartbeat pounds, I know I look the part suddenly.

"What are you doing?" I ask with shock still heard in my voice from the sudden surprise yell I wasn't expecting.

Being pulled into a huge hug by New York Kayla, she's smiling like she just pulled off the biggest surprise ever. Joining us, Chicago Kayla hugs me too and laughs like she's awesome. Which she kind of is. Jesus *Christ!* Does she ever look like shit?

"Welcome to your baby shower," she smiles so brightly I hug her again with a thanks as Z suddenly strips me of my coat from behind.

Whispering in my ear, Z concedes, "Okay, *that* deserved the academy award you want so bad." Turning to smirk at his smartass comment I see Mack and Marty standing a few tables away.

Looking around, I didn't ask Z who would be here because it would've sounded sad, but I really didn't know who would be at my baby shower besides my 2 Kaylas. I mean really, it's not like I have any family, or any other friends. But unbelievably there are 5 other woman, and Mack and Marty waiting for me.

Smiling at Dee my most favorite hairdresser, and Mrs. Rinaldi (awww), and Tonia (yay!) and Veronica (awkward) and LUCIA? What the fuck? I'm kind of super stunned now. What the hell? And *why?*

"Ha! I love it when Suzanne's speechless. It keeps all the crazy in check," Kayla grins and I finally just laugh.

"Wow. Um, thank you for this, and thank you for coming. And, ah, wow..." I fade out like a loser until Mack saves me thank god.

Walking up to me, I steal Matthew right from his arms when he leans in for a Mack/Suzanne hug. "Sorry. But you've totally been replaced," I giggle as Matthew touches my mouth with his little hands. "Hi sweetpea," I smile at my favorite little person in the world. "What are you up to tonight?" I ask a baby smiling Matthew who dips his fingers actually into my mouth as I giggle before I can pull away.

Hooking him above my stomach he's just able to hold himself against me, kind of leaning into me and I can't stop staring at him. God, I love this little boy.

"Ah, we boys are on our way out. We'll see you in a few hours though," Mack attempts to take him from me, but Matthew snuggles in and as I hold his back with my hand pulling him closer to me, I really don't want to let him go. He's not only a shield for me against the woman I'm nervous being around, but he's like my own little angel these days who always keeps everything bad away. Wow, Matthew is always a shield for me I suddenly realize.

Tearing up when Matthew lies his head back down on my chest, I'm messed up. I don't know what's wrong, but I feel sad and I don't want to let him go. Ever.

"Suzanne... ?" Z whispers but I can't speak. Crying, I feel totally stressed, and embarrassed, and unhappy. And I really don't want to give Matthew back to Mack.

Shit.

Handing over Matthew quickly, I turn for the back room we've been in a few times to talk to Marty. Walking, I can't look at anyone and I'm afraid I've ruined everything again. Goddammit.

"Stop," Z says as I push open Marty's office door, but I can't stop. I have to keep going until I'm totally inside hiding for a minute. Waiting for Z I don't turn around until Mack surprises me by speaking first.

"What is it, Suzanne? Talk to me, or us, or just me. Whatever you need."

"I love Matthew," I moan as a sob breaks from my chest.

"And?"

"That's it I think. But I also want to keep him. I didn't want to give him back to you because I actually want to keep him Mack. Like a kidnapper," I sob even harder. Holy shit! I'm so screwed if Mack gets scared of me being with his son. Turning to a silent Mack, I actually beg, "Please don't take him away from me?"

When Mack starts grinning, I'm not only shocked but nervous of his grin. I can't tell if he's going to take Matthew away or maybe lock me up.

"Like a kidnapper, Suzanne?" He starts laughing. "Could you actually take my son away from his mom and me?"

"No. But-"

"You want to?" He asks as I nod. "Good. Because there's no one Kayla and I think would love and care for our baby more than you," he whispers as I choke up again.

"I don't understand."

"You love our son. And we love you loving our son. And Matthew absolutely adores his Aunt Tommy. So where's the problem?"

"I want to keep him," I cry so he understands.

"But would you?"

Looking at Mack I realize what he's asking, and I know the honest answer he wants. "No."

"So again I'll ask, where's the problem? Loving a baby is normal. And loving the only baby you've ever known is normal. And loving a baby who is by all definitions your nephew is normal. Even wanting to steal him is normal, otherwise every aunt and grandmother on the planet would be locked up, Suzanne."

"Oh." That calmed me down significantly. "I thought it was wrong to love him and want to hold him and not want to give him back to you. Like out there, I didn't want to give him back to you. I wanted to keep holding him so he'd keep all the sad away. *Oh.*"

"When he was a snuggled into your chest, completely content to rest on your belly? Why *would* you want to give him back? Some days I almost cry when he's sleeping on my chest and I have to go to work. All I want to do is hold him and snuggle in and smell his little baby smell."

"But he's your son."

"And he's your nephew. And you love him."

"I do," I nod as reality starts sinking in again. "You don't think I'm a freak for wanting to kidnap him?"

"No, because you would never hurt him. And kidnapping Matthew from his parents would hurt him, right?"

"Of course."

"Then there's no problem."

Looking at Z resting against the wall silently, I feel kind of bad for this upset. "I didn't mean to ruin my party, Z, but I felt weird."
Nodding he smiles but doesn't speak. Turning back to Mack, I exhale again and try to calm down fully.
"Suzanne, I think your biggest issue is the fact that you actually *love* my son- who is a baby. And you didn't know how you felt about it because you've never experienced it before. Am I right?"
"I think so."
"What else?"
"That's it I think. Oh, I'm also scared my own baby is going to die any day now and I won't have one to love, so I want to be with Matthew so I know what it's like to love a baby."
Holy. *Shit.*
Watching Z's head lower I whisper 'I'm sorry' but he doesn't speak or acknowledge me.
"That was the most honest thing you've ever said without prompting, and I'm proud of you. I'm also very sorry you feel that way. But here's where you're at, Suzanne... Your baby is alive and well and ready to be born within weeks now. So at this point you have to just have a little faith that everything will be fine. There is absolutely nothing else you can do. And if something bad happens, you'll deal with it. Sadly, you have before and you will be forced to again. But I really don't think that'll happen this time, and I have faith that in a few weeks you're going to be handing me my very own niece or nephew to love and want to kidnap as well." Listening to Mack's own smile-voice as I watch Z, I feel so much better.
"If something bad does happen you have an entire support system for you. But I don't believe that will be needed this time. I really believe everything is going to be okay, and I really want you to believe that too. Could you try? For just a few more weeks- the *last* few weeks. Could you try to be excited and happy and as ready as possible? Because I don't want you to miss a thing when this little one is born."
Walking to me Mack doesn't even pause before he hugs me tightly to his chest. Exhaling for the last time, I snuggle in, thank him, and just wait out the seconds until I'm well enough to pull away.
"I'm sorry, Z," I moan as Mack stays beside me with his hand on my back.
Looking so sad, Z replies, "Don't be. I've felt and thought all the same

We are US...

things, Suzanne. I've talked to Mack about it all as well," he finishes as Mack nods beside me. "We're just going to have to believe everything will be okay as Mack said because I'm tired of being afraid of this little bugger," he adds huffing and I totally get what he means.

This little bugger has been torturing us for months and I wish it would just come out already so I can hold him or her.

"Ah, what do I do now?"

Holding out my purse to me, Z says simply. "You fix your makeup and get the hell out there before the Kaylas start a riot in Marty's restaurant. The men are leaving for 2 hours, and then I'll be back to get you and all the presents for home. And that's it. No one expects anything of you, they just wanted to be here for you."

"Lucia?" I kind of moan embarrassed.

"Loves me, and since you two spoke last year, she thinks you're great. Plus I love you, so she would love you anyway."

"Why is she here though? She didn't fly all the way here just for this, did she?" God, I hope not. What a colossal disappointment for her if she did.

"Not entirely. She and Stephano wanted to come back to the US anyway for a trip, so she made a side trip here for your shower."

"Ugh. No pressure though," I giggle uncomfortably.

"She's only met you twice love. And both times you freaked out, so I'm thinking she's just going to assume you're a nutter and get over it. She *is* Italian, Suzanne, so she knows a little something about drama," he laughs as I do.

10 minutes later I finally make my way back to my baby shower. Remake-upped and as stable as I can be, I slide in behind my 2 Kayla's talking to the others and hug their necks from behind. Whispering I'm sorry, Kayla shakes her head, and other Kayla squeezes my hand around her neck.

"Thank you for my party."

"You're welcome. Now come get some cheesecake before that one eats it all," Chicago Kayla points her fork at Tonia who laughs with a mouthful.

"Um, thank you all for coming. This was a wonderful surprise though my entry suggests otherwise," I giggle. "And thank you Lucia for side tripping it to New York for this. I can't even imagine what you're thinking of me. Again," I smirk as she claps her hands with a quick laugh. "But I really appreciate you coming."

"I'm happy to be here, Suzanne. Stephano wanted to see the Christmas of New York and I want to shop of course," she beams as I nod. God, she's nice and friggin gorgeous.

"We soooo get that," I smile at my nodding Kaylas. "So what do we do?" I plop down between Kayla and her mom Mrs. Rinaldi.

"Well, Kayla had stupid games for you to play," she continues past Kayla's 'hey!' "But I figure we could just open presents and eat. Open mine first!" Chicago yells hopping up and I relax totally when Tonia pushes the cheesecake at me grinning and Mrs. Rinaldi hands over a plate.

"Thank you all for being here. Truly. I really didn't know who would be here but these 2, so you just made my baby shower very special for me."

Smiling at Veronica, I force myself to *not* think of what her husband witnessed, or of what she must really think of me. I mean she's here right? So unless Kayla threatened her, which she would totally do, Veronica chose to be here anyway for me which is very kind.

After opening Kayla's thousands of gifts, ranging from baby clothes and tons of baby paraphernalia, she finished my gifts with an awesome carseat baby buggy in multiple pastel colors. Sitting back looking at all the gifts from her I'm stunned she spent so much money on me. Then again, she's had months of shopping so I can totally see her over doing it.

Veronica's gift is a beautiful frame for 'Mommy's first picture with me', and more generic, genderless clothing. Dee's gift is a gift certificate to her hair salon, and after Kayla pipes up I'm gonna need it after the baby, everyone laughs and starts talking about how hard it is to even get a shower in with a new baby, never mind actually having time to do your hair.

"Here you go *not* so little one anymore," Lucia leans forward making me laugh. God, between her accent and her beautiful clothing she makes me wonder if all Z's relatives in Italy are as gorgeous as she and Z are.

"Are all the Marvinelli's gorgeous?" I ask like a moron.

"Si," she laughs. "We were blessed with some of good genes. My Zia Carmella, Z's mother, was beautiful and I think that's why Peter stole her away to America when she was so young," she adds smiling but everything changes instantly around me. I can even sense the Kaylas understand.

"*Open* your gift, Suzanne," Kayla says heavily beside me snapping me out of where my thoughts were going to go too quickly to stop them without medication.

Slowly unwrapping what looks like a bracelet box, my mind is spinning. I want to know so badly how young Z's mother was when Peter found her. I want to know if he was a pig with her. I want to know what he did to her. But I hold it in for another time. *Barely.*

"Oh! It's beautiful." Holding up and admiring my gold charm bracelet, I see the letters Z and S, and in between a blank spot for the baby I'm assuming. Wow. It's like the thickest, heaviest gold bracelet I've ever seen in my life.

"You have no name I was told?" When I nod she continues. "When you having the baby you just call me with the name and I'll send the other charm. Yes?"

"Oh, I will. Thank you, Lucia. It's absolutely beautiful." Turning to Kayla I ask her to put it on me which she does quickly after admiring the weight and gold.

Smiling once again at Lucia, I actually lean over the table and squeeze her hand in thank you. It's a beautiful bracelet and I can't wait to add the third charm suddenly I wish this little bugger would just get here already.

"So… names?" Tonia asks and everyone nods.

Grinning, I know I'm going to piss everyone off with this. "Ah, Z likes Michael, and I like Macklan, but-"

"Mack!" Kayla gasps and claps like I knew she would. "Baby Mack is sooo cute. And it's another M for the boys in our family," she says making me tear up. Whenever I hear these 'our family' references I'm always emotional still. To think I actually have a family is just bizarre, but to experience it is amazing.

"I don't like it," other Kayla pouts as we all laugh.

Leaning over me to her, Kayla laughs, "You're not even married to Marty, so you can't be offended that she's naming her baby after *my* husband."

"Yes, I can. Marty loves them, too," Kayla Lefferts actually whines making me giggle at her face.

"Um, Macklan Martin Zinfandel?" I say squeezing her hand. "But don't tell them so it's a surprise."

"Oh, *that'll* do," Kayla agrees and I'm glad she's over it quickly.

"And for a girl?" Veronica asks excited as I flinch slightly. I kinda hoped they wouldn't go there, but naturally they do.

"Ah, we haven't decided."

"But maybes?"

"None yet," I squeak leaning over to grab the next gift while burying my face under the table for a second to stop panicking.

Z and I almost fought over not even entertaining a girl's name, but I just couldn't do it. I explained again I hoped I had a boy, and Z huffed his frustration but gave in when I started panicking that day. Now though, I think I maybe should at least think about it so he doesn't just name her something weird if I do actually have a girl.

"What is it?" I laugh stunned at the weird looking gift from Mrs. Rinaldi. "Oh, a breast pump?" I stare at it through the box. Jesus, it's pretty freaky looking actually. Really, it looks more like a boob torture device. Yikes.

"You have to start using it right away dear. Even if you're going to breast feed you have to use it daily so your body gets used to it. Trust me, you don't want to be the only boob available always. Right?" She asks Kayla who nods. "Plus, that way you have milk for me when I babysit. Which I'm going to do. Often," she smiles squeezing my hand. "My other 2 daughters have been a total fail," she adds as we all laugh at her terminology. "So I'm taking on your baby as an adoptive grandchild. Okay?" Oh, wow. Um...

"Why?" I moan as the tears start up again.

"Because I love you, dear. And I need more grandchildren, and I *want* yours."

Shaking my head to clear it, I whisper okay as the happiness shocks me a little. "Thank you. I don't have anyone else," I cry sadly when she leans in to hug me.

"Yes, you do, Suzanne. Plus I'm the perfect person to call with all the crazy baby questions. I had 3 daughters in 5 years. Right, Kay?"

"Yup. Like, why does he always wait to pee in the air as soon as the fresh diaper is ready? Or why does he only scream bloody murder when Mack and I start to get a little sexy with each other? What does he have, *radar?*" She asks sounding a little sexually frustrated as I giggle. "Well,

you'll see, Suzanne."
 "I can't wait to ask all these questions. And thank you so much Mrs. Rinaldi. You are very sweet to me, and Laura and Paola are going to be totally pissed that I gave you a grandbaby before they did. So yay, for me!" I burst out laughing as she does.
 Looking at all my stuff on the table and floor all around us I realize I'm set for like a year maybe. Or maybe not. Actually, I have no friggin' clue how much stuff a baby uses in their first year.
 "I can't give you my gift yet. I'm sorry, Suzanne. But it's a little gender specific so Mack and I have to wait for the baby first. I hope you don't mind?"
 "Of course not."

 Talking and laughing and sharing pregnancy horror stories, which thankfully I have none of with this one, I wait for Z and the men to arrive. I'm feeling exhausted suddenly, almost bone weary and somewhat sad though I have absolutely no reason to be.
 With only a few minor incidents, I've enjoyed my party and the women here. Tonia and Veronica and Lucia have fit right in with the Kaylas and everyone is loud and funny, and really fairly sarcastic and smartassy with each other, which always cracks me up. Jeez... even Mrs. Rinaldi gets in a few shots at Chicago Kayla who thankfully pisses herself laughing instead of going for Mrs. Rinaldi's jugular.
 And then I see him. Carrying Matthew in his arms, Z walks into the restaurant and I swear the air vanishes from the room. Even the 2 other tables across the room of diners stop what they're doing or eating or saying to look at Z walk in with baby Matthew, Mack and Marty and I know what they're thinking, Shit, that man is hot.
 And here come the hornies again, as Kayla would say.
 Leaning down to kiss me gently, Z smiles against my lips. "Hi, love. How was your night?" When Kayla scoops her baby from Z I almost moan because I missed my chance to hold him. "Suzanne?"
 Turning from Matthew, I finally speak. "My night was amazing. And we have so much stuff, thank god you have an SUV. Look at my bracelet from Lucia," I hold up my wrist as he inspects it.
 Turning to a beaming Lucia, Z shakes his head. "It's beautiful Lucia. And there's nothing like Italian gold, right?"

"Not in America," she teases as he laughs. 'I will also send the charm of the baby's name when it is born."

Nodding, Z actually bows a little to Lucia saying 'Grazi' as she nods back with a gorgeous smile.

Getting in closer, Z asks if I'd like to go, and I whisper yes as quiet as possible while everyone talks and gushes over Matthew who is passed around among them.

"Thank you all for coming, and for being here for Suzanne's baby shower. And thank you Kaylas for putting on her shower. And don't either of you ever call me again," he says so seriously, I burst out laughing before everyone else realizes he's kidding. Jeez people... lighten up.

"We'll help," Mack offers picking up multiple bags and the breast pump box which mortifies me. But other than looking at it quickly, it goes right under his arm as he heads out of the restaurant with Marty and Z in tow.

Standing, I ask for Matthew and Veronica hands him over.

"I have to go sweetpea, but I'll see you on Sunday for Thanksgiving. Ow... you little bugger," I giggle as he tugs the hair against my cheek. Resting his head on the top on my chest, I melt in place again. Holding his little head in my hand I make little weird sounds I don't know where the hell I get them from, but he always seems to love them.

"Don't put him to sleep, Suzanne. I have to nurse him first. And whenever he's lying on your boobs he falls asleep," she laughs when Mrs. Rinaldi says 'like a total man'.

"Bye baby," I whisper kissing his head.

Handing him over, Kayla does the quick flip blanket boob not even exposed thing she's a pro at and suddenly he's hidden from me and I almost pout.

"Are you ready?" Z stands behind me.

Nodding I turn to everyone, some standing and some still sitting. "Thank you again for coming and for throwing me this awesome baby shower. You have no idea what it means to me that you would actually come and celebrate this little one with me and Z. So without getting sappy again, thank you. Sincerely," I close out just shy of tears.

Hugging Tonia and Veronica briefly, Dee holds me way longer. Telling me I look as beautiful as always, she says she can't wait for me to bring the baby to the salon. She even makes Z promise to call her when the baby's born.

We are US...

When Lucia stands I'm instantly insecure. Watching as she approaches I'm nervous she thinks I'm not good enough for Z, or better yet, I'm a complete psycho, rightfully so. I just hope she doesn't say anything mean because Z will freak on her.

"I do hope we get a telephone call when the baby is born as well?" She asks.

"Of course. Thank you again for the beautiful gift, and if you and Stephano are ever in the States again, please feel free to visit us."

"We will. Take care of yourself," she touches my stomach briefly. "And keep making Z happy with whatever it is you do that keeps him smiling like that," she says with her own eyebrow wiggle.

Laughing, I have to know. "Is that strictly an Italian thing, or Marvinelli sexy thing you've got with those looks?"

"Marvinelli. *And* Italian, I'm sure. I don't think you Americans can pull off the sexy looks like we can. You're much too uptight in America," she laughs again.

"Don't encourage her, love. Lucia has always been trouble," Z says so affectionately, Lucia jumps in his arms for a huge hug.

"Do you need a ride to your hotel?"

"No, this one Tonia and I are going out for a drink before I meet with Stephano."

"Be good, Lucia," Z scowls as she laughs like they're teenagers still.

"I don't know this word in English," she smirks before kissing both my cheeks to walk back to the table.

"Ready?"

"Very."

"We're leaving. Thank you again everyone. Drinks are on us tonight, so have fun."

After final hugs from everyone, lots of kisses, and thank you's all around I'm finally done.

Waving, Z walks me out of the restaurant with his hand on my back snuggled into his side.

"Tired?"

"Exhausted."

Sitting in the dark of the SUV, the silence is lulling me asleep until I think of Carmella suddenly.

"How old was your mother when they married, Z?"

After a long moment of silence, Z finally breathes, "I really don't know. I know she was younger, but I don't think by much. Why?"

"Just something Lucia said. I think you should try to figure it out, Z. I think she was pretty young, and if she was maybe she didn't know or understand about him. Or know what to do. Maybe..." I fade out when I realize Z is deathly still beside me. "Sorry," I lean over to take his hand.

"Look, whether she was young or not when they got together, she wasn't young when I found out about him. So to me it makes no difference. If she knew, she was old enough to stop him, Suzanne. And nothing changes that," he says in his scarily calm voice so I let it go.

Walking into our condo, I want to wait for Z to bring up all the gifts but I'm too exhausted.

After washing all my makeup off and hoping in the shower for a quick rinse off, I think about my sexy black lacy pregnancy nighties but decide on my huge prego pants and a cami instead.

"I'm going to bed!" I yell before crawling in without even turning the overhead lights off. I can't get back up, and I don't care. Pulling the pillow over my head, I know Z will be in any second to kiss me goodnight anyway, so I'm done.

We are US...

CHAPTER 31

"Suzanne... Wake up, love. It's time to go," Z whispers wrapped all over my huge body. Moaning, I move my ass against him trying to stay warm in bed. "Baby, please. We have to be at the hospital in an hour and a half, and I know how weird you're going to get," he says with his smile-voice as I giggle.

"I've changed my mind about all this. Let's just stay in bed and forget about a baby, K?"

Snuggling in even closer, I wiggle against him again until he growls. "Do you really want to be this fat forever?"

"What?" I gasp shoving his chest as he laughs.

"Just kidding. You still look amazing. But I really want to get this little bugger out of you today because today feels like a good day to have a baby. And I really want to hold my baby today. So, ah, get your ass out of bed before I pull you out of the covers and into the shower clothed. Understood?"

You're mean..." I whine pulling the covers over my head one last time before he actually does rip all the covers off me right onto the floor.

"Let's go have a baby!" Z laughs as I kick at him playfully.

"You're ugly," I say fiercely making us both burst out laughing. Yeah, right... Z's ugly my fat ass, I laugh again finally sitting up with Z's help.

"And *you* are stunning, Suzanne."

Turning to look at his beautiful eyes, I whisper, "And *you* are still good, Mr. Zinfandel."

"I know." Jumping off our bed Z's so excited he's practically bouncing around our bedroom. "I've already showered and only slept for about 5 minutes so I'm just waiting for you. The traffic looks good, and the snowplows have already been out. So it should be smooth sailing to the hospital *if* you ever get out of bed," he huffs anxiously.

"Okay..."

We are US...

    Driving in Z's Escalade, I keep looking at the car seat already strapped in behind us, and it just looks so weird. Good weird, but weird. We've been just the two of us for so long now, I can't believe soon it's going to be not us anymore.
    After my mid-pregnancy freak out, and Z's sad confessions we both changed drastically. Together we embraced this pregnancy, and each other for the last half of it. We shopped and laughed and bought everything we could find to give this baby the life we hope will make it as happy as we are.
    We made love often and we prepared for this little bugger together. Really, we just became a couple madly in love, desperate for this little baby to be born healthy for us to love. And it's been amazing.

"Promise you'll still love me and *want* me even when I look like shit, wear the same clothes for 2 days in a row and only shower 3 times a week?"
"Yup," he says again smiling at my stupid.
"Because from what everyone tells me, I'm going to look like shit for a while and I'll even have to schedule bathroom breaks. Kayla told me she actually called Mack at the hospital once crying to beg him to come home so she could pee and shower because she couldn't get away from Matthew for even 10 minutes."
"And did Mack go home?"
"Of course."
"And would I come home?"
"Of course..." I smile knowing he would in a heartbeat. "Okay, I feel better."
"Good. Are you just rambling because you're nervous?"
"Yup," I answer as he takes my hand to squeeze it.

    Walking into Mercy for my scheduled C-Section, Z fills out all the paperwork while I sit breathing like I'm in actual labor. Deep breathing is all I can do at the moment though to calm the hell down because in less than a half hour I'm supposed to have a friggin' baby. A baby! *Shiiiiit.*
"Ready to be wheeled in? I guess they take you first and prep you then I get to come in for the fun stuff. Will you be okay in there alone?"
"Of course I will."

"I'll be in the minute they allow me."
"Okay."
Seconds later a nurse introduces herself and walks up to me with a wheelchair. I can walk I want to argue but slump in the chair anyway. Looking up at Z, he smiles and squats in front of me like he always does to calm me.
Holding my hands he leans in for a very soft, sweet little kiss. "I'll be right there beside you, I promise."
"I know."
"Ya know what else? You really are fabulous, Suzanne. And you've got this."
Smiling at the fabulous comment I exhale again. "Thank you, Z. But I'm good. And I'm so ready for this."
"I love you," he whisper-kisses against my lips before standing.

"How we doing?" Nurse something asks as she navigates another turn.
"Ah, good, I guess. For someone whose going to be cut open in a few minutes, I'm great," I huff as she laughs at me.
"You won't feel a thing. And they don't use chainsaws anymore, so it's much less messy than it used to be."
Turning to look at her smiling, I have to know. "Do you know Kayla Rinaldi-MacDonald?"
"Yeah, she trained me."
"Figures..." I groan when we push through a door to the surgical room.
"Can you get out of the chair?"
"Sure." Struggling to get up, nurse whatever helps me stand. Turning to hand me an ugly ass hospital gown, I cringe at the stripy blue and white.
"Do you need any help changing?"
"No, I'm okay."
"Well then, I'll give you some privacy and Dr. Modair, Dr. Keaton and I will be in in a few minutes. Did you eat or drink anything after 10:00 last night?"
"No."
"Good. I'll be back in 5," she smiles and though I kind of like her type of smartass, I don't like her because I'm nervous and I don't want to do any of this suddenly even though I really want to meet this little bugger I've been cooking forever.

We are US...

Lifting my sweater I hear the door suddenly push open as I freeze in the gown just over my head to yell 'hey!' in a panic.

"Nice boobs, Suzanne." *Kayla!*

Pulling the gown down quickly over my yoga pants still, I gasp looking at Kayla standing in the doorway.

"What are you doing here?"

Walking to me, she hugs me. Tightly and with tons of emotion, Kayla hugs me and I'm totally calm all of a sudden.

"Mack and I pulled out all the favors we could, and though I'm not a labor and delivery nurse, I was allowed to be here to assist."

"*Really?*"

"Yup. I'm here for you and I can't wait to see your little bugger. Surprise!" She laughs at my stunned face.

Croaking a very heavy, "Thank you," I'm relieved.

"I wanted to be here with you guys, and I'm sure you could use the extra support this morning."

"I could. I met your smartass prodigy by the way, but she just wasn't the same as you. Ah, where's Matthew?"

"With Mack," she looks at me like that was a dumb question, which I guess it was. "They'll be here in a little over an hour to meet your new baby though."

"Oh, wow. That soon, huh?"

"Yup, and once you're prepped everything moves very quickly. Plus you feel no pain after the spinal just anxiety waiting for your baby. But enough talk. Finish getting changed so Dr. Modair can start, okay?"

Changing quickly, everything does move very fast. I'm on the bed with an IV as the 2 doctors move all around the room preparing everything, while Kayla stays beside me talking about everything and nothing to distract me.

After a painful spinal that Kayla held my hand through I'm laid back down and suddenly everything begins. Z pushes through the door quickly in scrubs and cap and booties, and even like that he looks hot, I giggle nervously when he takes my hand.

"Really, Z? You have to look hot even in that outfit?"

"Sorry, love," he grins a very cute lop-sided grin that's new for him. "Grasping for anything?" He smirks.

"Totally."

"I am so ready for this, Suzanne. I want to meet our baby so badly my heart is pounding in my chest. Feel."
Taking my palm he leans down to kiss it sweetly before placing it on his chest, and I *can* actually feel his heartbeat pounding. "Okay, that makes me feel better."
Suddenly leaning back down, Z takes my whole head in his hands and rests his forehead against mine, burying me in Z. This moment feels so intense and emotional without any words or sounds except for the room around us beeping and humming with activity I need to pull away before my nerves make me loopy.
"Kayla's here," I nod to our left when he rises smiling instantly as she walks to us.
"You figured out a way," he laughs.
"Mack had to preform sexual favors on a few doctors for me, but it worked," she attempts a Z eyebrow wiggle and I finally exhale my tension with a quick laugh at the 2 of them.
With Z side-hugging Kayla, she takes my hand and raises it over my head as she walks to my other side without letting go. "Here we go..." she whispers.
"Are you ready to meet this little one, Suzanne?" Dr. Modair asks over the screen covering my stomach and as I exhale deeply again I nod yes.
"You may feel a little pressure, but no real pain. And in under 5 minutes you'll hear your baby screaming bloody murder."
"I can't wait."
"Would you like a play by play?"
"God no," I huff. "I don't like medical stuff or anything about this, so can you please just do it? I'm ready."
"Understood. Let's begin."

Zoning out I feel Z squeezing my hand too hard, and Kayla rubbing my other hand gently. No one speaks, and though I hear almost a weird slurping sound and the 2 doctors mumbling quietly to each other, I try to ignore it. I don't like the sounds in the room at all and slowly I'm feeling my anxiety growing to nearly unmanageable until Z looks back down at me and everything stops.
With his dark eyes holding my own, the panic recedes. His long eyelashes, almost highlighted by the light blue cap he has to wear makes me calm. His eyes are holding me here and now, and I love him.

We are US...

"We are us," I whisper.

"Always," he replies softly until he suddenly jolts and looks at my stomach when we're pulled from our moment by bloody curdling screams.

Oh, *god*... This is it!

"What is it!?" I cry out crazily.

"You have a beautiful baby girl, Suzanne," Dr. Modair says as I burst out laughing.

"Jesus *Christ!* A *girl*?" I laugh as Kayla leans down to me. "I *knew* it. Holy shit. A girl?" I continue yelling and laughing sounding almost crazed, but I'm not insane. I'm resigned. And I think I always knew. And of course it's a girl, because why wouldn't it be? I'm friggin' Suzanne.

"Suzanne?" Kayla whispers as Z does something behind the screen.

"A *girl*?" I laugh as she watches me closely.

Squeezing my hand hard Kayla gets right in my face and growls, "Focus, Suzanne. You have a beautiful daughter, and nothing changes. You're going to love her more than you love my Matthew, and you're going to keep her safe always. *Understood*?" She glares at me angrily, which actually kind of snaps me out of my head just as Z leans to me with my friggin' daughter.

With tears streaming down his face Z looks so overcome with emotion, I jolt back to my present again. I need to get back to Z and this moment between us.

"Look, love. *Look* at her," he moan cries making me look at her.

Taking in the baby in his arms he's holding her so carefully, everything changes for me in a millisecond. There *is* nothing but this millisecond.

Staring at the tiny baby in Z's arms, filthy and gross, I feel her so suddenly, I actually hear myself gasp.

"Oh my *god*... She's beautiful," I cry touching her cheek with a shaking hand when Z leans her against my chest. Kissing my lips Z expels a hard cry in my mouth.

Watching Z breakdown in front of me with this little baby not even crying anymore against my chest, I know nothing but this moment between the three of us.

And that's when I understand everything I'm witnessing. I've had a baby without incident, or death. Z is sobbing his relief and happiness, and I can hear her squeak a little sound against my chest.

This is it.

I can finally exhale the stress of the last 9 months of my life. My daughter is alive, Z is an emotional pansy as he says, and I've carried and had our daughter safely.

"I have a daughter," I moan as Z rises again to lift her to my face closer. Looking as he watches me I give into my sudden reality. "I have a daughter. And she's so pretty."

"She's beautiful, Suzanne. And so perfect, and thank you," he cries again kissing my lips.

When the baby starts crying, I'm scared and nervous and desperate with the need to do something for her.

"Wow. She's like, I don't know. So beautiful and *loud*, actually," I giggle as Z moves her closer to my mouth so I can kiss her nasty head while she screams bloody murder.

When Kayla whispers she needs to take her for a second, Z slowly, so gently hands over our daughter to her. Kissing Z right on the lips, Kayla's so happy she doesn't even refrain from her own Italian emotion.

"She's just perfect, Suzanne. And you're right. What a set of lungs on this one. She's like a friggin' Rinaldi," she smiles before taking my baby to the side of the room to a different doctor.

Huh. My baby. My *daughter*. That still sounds so weird in my head.

"What are they doing?" I ask.

"With you, or her?"

"Both, I guess. Is she okay?"

"Kayla's cleaning her up, and the doctor is just measuring her and weighing her I think. And you," Z looks behind the sheet, "Are getting closed up."

"Is it gross?"

"Very," Z nods as I laugh quickly. Leaning back down to my face Z whispers a very emotional, "Are you okay?"

"Emotionally or physically?"

"Both."

"Physically, I feel discomfort, like cramps or something, but no pain. And emotionally, I'm better than I thought I'd be. I think I always knew it would be a girl so I tried to get all the freaking out out of the way when I was pregnant so I'd be better when she was born, I think."

"And?" He asks looking over at Kayla and the doctor touching our baby.

"I'm scared, but kind of okay. Man it totally figures I'd have a girl though. It's not like my life ever goes the way I want," I kind of giggle sadly until Z looks down at me strangely until I understand. "Oh, except with you, and our friends, and my new life." Oh. "Okay, I see. I'm sorry. My life is actually pretty awesome now. Even with a daughter," I moan for a second as the emotion finally hits me hard.

Bursting into tears, I'm scared and happy and nervous but still mostly happy. I have a baby who is alive and I'm grateful for that. Soooo grateful, I need to remember that when the fear hits me. I also need to remember this man who loves me for whatever reason is still here watching out for me, holding my hand with him always.

"Thank you, Z."

"Thank *you*," he chokes up a little.

"No, not for the baby. For everything..." I cry so he understands.

"I love you, Suzanne," he says so fiercely against my lips, I exhale.

Looking down my body the screen is removed from my stomach and the sheets are in place. Dr. Modair even takes my hand and congratulates me and Z before stepping away.

"I have another delivery, Suzanne. But I'll be back to check in on you later."

"Thank you for this. For, ah, keeping her alive," I choke as she grins at me.

"I'm good, Suzanne, but not *that* good. This was all you, and I'm thrilled for you both," she smiles kindly before Z shakes her hand with another thank you of his own.

Looking at the side of the room, my daughter is still screaming with Kayla, but as I watch Kayla wrapping her tightly in a pink and white blanket she settles a little.

"Wow. A daughter," I say to no one but feel my hand squeezed tighter again by Z. "I hope she doesn't have my eyes," I admit a sad truth to no one again, but I think Z understands. "Did you see her eyes, Z? Are they like mine?"

When Kayla turns to us with my baby she's smiling so brightly, she takes some of my fear away.

"What color are her eyes, Kayla?"

"Very dark blue, like most newborns, but I think they'll darken up more." Oh, thank god.

I didn't realize how afraid I was of my eyes until the threat was suddenly gone. I couldn't possibly have looked at a little girl of my own with my eyes her whole life without thinking of *her* always.

Crying my relief, my arms feel heavy but I reach up for my baby anyway as Kayla places her awkwardly on my chest.

When Dr. Keaton starts explaining everything, my lack of leg movement, my pain, what I can expect to experience, what I'll need and when I can leave I see Z nodding. I know Z's paying attention so I don't have to, because quite frankly I hear nothing, but I *see* everything. And she really is beautiful.

"She doesn't even look like a newborn, frog ugly little thing does she Kayla?" I ask honestly stunned by how pretty my baby is.

"Nope. She came out beautiful. Then again, have you *seen* her parents?" Kayla smiles as I do. "So, she's 7 pounds- 2 ounces. She's 19 1/2 inches long which is good, and she is in perfect range on the Apgar scale. All her finger and toes are accounted for, and she has only a trace amount of jaundice, which is common and nothing to worry about. In other words, she's absolutely perfect, and beautiful, and I'm so, so happy for you both, I want to bawl my eyes out," Kayla actually says as tears spill from her eyes. "But you have to try to nurse now, Suzanne, while your colostrum and nutrients are concentrated."

"Of course." But I don't know what to do until Kayla just takes over. Pulling my gown down from my neck, naturally I flinch at the exposure but she doesn't even acknowledge me. Moving my baby to my breast, she does something weird to her cheek, lifting and moving her until she suddenly latches onto me as I gasp. Okay, different feeling that I'm used to I blush thinking of Z which seems totally wrong suddenly.

"I'm in nurse mode, Suzanne- not Suzanne's got a great rack mode. So don't be embarrassed."

When Z laughs beside me, I see him looking at my boob and my baby with a sweet smile making me relax as she takes from me what she needs.

Touching my daughter's little cheek while she feeds, I'm just stunned by her. She really is beautiful, so maybe there's way more Zinfandel in her than Beaumont.

"Do you have a name yet?"

"Ah, I couldn't really because-"

"Zoe?" Z interrupts before I get emotional but after a split second delay both Kayla and I start laughing at him.

We are US...

"Zoe? As in Z. Zinfandel? Pu-*lease*," she laughs as I do at her accent. Looking totally offended, I reach for Z's hand as he pouts.

"What's wrong with Zoe? I like it."

"You would," Kayla and I say together again laughing.

"I think I have the perfect name, but I have to ask Z first before you freak out, okay? So don't listen, Kayla."

Grinning, she plugs her ears and hums when Z leans down to my mouth. Taking the opportunity, I kiss his ear before whispering the secret name I thought of but couldn't acknowledge before this moment for my beautiful daughter.

"Oh. It's perfect," Z agrees tearing up a little as he pulls away. Waiting to be sure, he nods again. "Yes. That's perfect, love. And I think she suits it," Z touches our baby's cheek slightly.

"What *is* it?" Kayla yells turning to us. Nodding at me, I inhale before speaking the forbidden name I've loved all along for my daughter.

"Mackenzie Kayla Zinfandel," I flinch and grab my baby when Kayla actually screams and claps and dives for my face.

"I *LOVE* it! Oh, it's awesome. Baby Mack for a girl even. Ha! And with the Kayla middle name, Kayla can't be too pissed at the Marty exclusion," she laughs. "Oh, I just love it. And she does look like a little Mackenzie. Oh, Suzanne... Seriously, I just love you, and her, and you," she smiles at Z. "And this is just the best day. And I'm so happy I was here, and I have to call Mack and-"

"Let me tell him her name, okay?"

"Of course. I wouldn't dare. I know what my Mack means to you."

"Thank you. I'm glad you know what *my* Mack means to me," I smirk before she kisses me again on the forehead.

"Okay. I've got to take her to the ward, but we'll meet you when you're transferred to your room in about an hour. Why don't you two rest up for now. Z those chairs are comfy on purpose," she motions to the uglyass lounge chair in the corner. "I'll bring her back to you soon, and I won't place her name on the glass until you've told everyone her name. For now she'll just be 'baby girl Zinfandel'. Good?"

"Thank you. Um, will you be careful-" I stop looking at Kayla lifting Mackenzie from my chest lightly with a kiss on her head.

"Of course I will. She's my niece, Suzanne," she smiles making me tear up again. "Rest for a little bit until you're moved because once she's in your room and all yours, you'll never rest again. You'll see."

After the door closes quietly I find myself trying to process everything I've just been through, am going to go through, and just, yeah... my head is spinning.

"You know what, Suzanne?" Z asks leaning against my bed beside me. Actually lifting my head so it rests on his arm, Z removes his silly cap and exhales deeply. "As hard as this is for me to believe, I actually feel more in love with you than ever before." Kissing my lips as they part on a little gasp Z whispers, "I *am* more in love with you than before."

Burying his head in my neck I let everything take me as the exhaustion and nerves and panic and happiness take over. Bursting into tears, Z doesn't shush me or try to distract me like he usually does. He just lets me bawl my eyes out in his arms forever it seems.

Eventually pulling away to kiss me again, I see his own eyes red rimmed and shiny- like the beautiful marble eyes of my memories. Telling me to rest while I can, Z pulls up the uglyass lounge chair beside me, holds my hand to settle in while I take a quick rest.

"We did it, Z," I turn to him watching me.

"We did, love. And I've never been happier in my life."

"Me either..." I whisper stunned by my newest amazing reality.

We are US...

CHAPTER 32

Sitting in my raised bed, Z has helped me put on my normal clothes up top, and even held the mirror up to my face while I checked and reapplied my foundation. Smiling, giggling, and basically being stupid with each other, I'm nervous and excited Mackenzie is coming to my room any minute, followed by everyone else apparently.
"Do I look okay? Like covered up properly?" I ask when he puts my makeup bag back in my suitcase in the little closet.
"You look completely covered, lovely, and not like a woman who just had a baby an hour and a half ago. But how do you feel? Sore?"
Nodding, I really am. But it's like a full body sore somehow as all the numbness slowly fades. The pain doesn't seem concentrated on my nasty stomach like I thought I remembered from when I had Thomas. And actually...
"I'm sorry, but would you help me cover this up?" I ask blushing. This man has seen every one of my nooks and crannies, my scars, and even my insides at this point, yet asking him to look and cover my pee bag still makes me blush like a loser.
"Of course," he doesn't even pause. As usual.

Waiting patiently with Z holding my hand Kayla finally walks in pushing the plastic baby bassinette with my daughter. God, that still sounds really weird in my head.
"Are you ready for this little princess?" Kayla beams and I really am. "The picture guy will be around in a few minutes, so-"
"I've hired my own," Z says abruptly as both Kayla and I look at him. Shit. I understand what he's thinking so quickly, I'm almost winded trying to pull my baby closer to my bed.
"Pictures..."
Helping move my weak, still partially numb legs closer to the edge, Z nods. "Pictures are for us and our family and our *close* friends. So I'm not risking someone looking to make some money by selling her pictures

We are US...

without our consent." Spoken without emotion I see his hidden concern and even anger, but just before I continue the conversation Mackenzie starts crying and everything stops again.

Looking at her in her plastic little house, I beg, "What do I do?" as I start to panic a little.

"You hold her and nurse her often. She just wants some attention, Suzanne, that's all. She misses being with you every minutes of every day for the last 9 months."

"Oh." Wow, said like that, I'd probably cry to. "Can you hand her to me?"

Waiting, Kayla gently lifts her to me and as I settle Mackenzie on my chest those weird noises I can't explain that I make for baby Matthew take over, and they work. Jesus, they actually work and she stops crying almost immediately. As I hold her close I feel like I've got this.

"You should nurse her again Suzanne because the first time wasn't enough, and everyone is here dying to see her. Even Kayla took today off to be here all day with you."

"She did?" Kayla's a workaholic or a Martyoholic, so giving up a whole day NOT shopping, working, or doing Marty is pretty rare for her.

When Z holds Mackenzie to me, I try to learn the blanket toss, boob *not* exposed thing Kayla can do but instead get caught up in it, scare my baby and jump when she cries again. Okay. Calm down. It's just a boob, and Kayla is in semi-nurse mode, so I'll deal.

Trying again, I get Mackenzie where she needs to be when Kayla just goes for it again.

"Here, lift your boob to her mouth and kind of rub along her cheekbone to make her open- there. See, she gets it. And right now, she'll feed often but just for a few minutes then she'll fall asleep like all babies do."

"Thank you. I'm not sure about any of this. I did read all the books though," I admit like a bit of a loser but it's true. They tell to what to do, but it's not quite the same as actually doing it.

"As soon as she drifts off, I'll go get everyone when you're ready. In theory you're not supposed to have more than 2 visitors right after your surgery, but none of the nurses on duty will mess with me, so you're fine. I'll give you some privacy and be back with the troops, okay?"

Looking down at my sweet little baby who Z is watching like she's the most amazing thing he's ever seen, which she kind of is, I realize I want to see Mack desperately.

"Would everyone be offended if I just saw Mack first? Um, is that okay?"

Nodding, Kayla leans back down to me and hugs right over my baby and me as she says softly, "That's okay, Suzanne. And Mack has been dying to see you and meet this little angel all morning." Pulling away to wipe her tears as I choke up, she says, "Don't start your shit," making me gasp a little laugh.

"I'll bring him here in 10 minutes."

"K. And thank you for everything today."

"You're welcome. You did good, Suzanne," she squeezes my hand before hugging Z tightly when he stands up from the side of my bed. "You too, daddeo," she smiles before kissing his cheek.

In the sudden silence after the door closes, I realize I don't know what the hell to do next. Mackenzie seems like she's still nursing, kind of, but she's not moving or anything, and I don't know how long I do this for.

"Ah, what now?"

"I have *no* idea," Z smirks making me grin back. "Is she still feeding?"

"Not really. I mean I don't feel the little pulling anymore, so is she done?" Looking down at her, I don't know. "Yeah, I think she's done. Do I just pull her away?"

"Here let me," he says gently reaching for her as I quickly cover up my chest again with my ugly nursing bra and zip up black hoodie.

Walking to the window, Z's making little cooing noises rocking Mackenzie on his shoulder. Crunched all up close to his face her little bum is sticking out and it's the cutest thing I've ever seen in my life. With the light shining around him, and the air in my room lighter, I feel happiness. Plain and never so simple with me- happiness.

I may even feel something much greater than happiness, but I've never felt it before so I don't really know what the word for it is.

Minutes later there's the knock I've been waiting for, and as I yell my come in I see my angel step through the door looking both excited and as calm and handsome as always.

My Mack.

"Thank you," I whisper before realizing I spoke but it doesn't matter. Mack walks directly to me and gently scoops me up into his arms right on my bed. Even though I physically hurt from the movement, I'm so happy

We are US...

I don't care. I'm happy, and Mack did this for me. Time and time again.

Crying in his arms, he silently waits for me to finish. "You did this for me," I moan.

"I certainly *hope* not," Z suddenly says with a funny scowl and as I clue in to what he's implying I finally burst out laughing as Mack pulls away.

"This was all you, Suzanne. And I'm so happy and proud of you. Can I see her? I'm dying to meet this little one my wife can't stop gushing about."

When Z walks up to Mack and hands my baby to him, Mack is all emotion. Smiling, whispering, and almost babbling to her, Mack doesn't even attempt to hide his emotion from us.

God, I love him, and he deserves so many thank you's from me, thankfully, I have the biggest one to give him back for his love and support always. "I have a surprise for you."

"Oh, yeah?" He grins but doesn't look away from my baby. "And what's that?"

"Um, I'd like to introduce my *daughter* to you," I whisper and when he hears the inflection he finally turns to look at me. Nodding, he smiles and waits. "Her name is Mackenzie..." I tear up as he stares silently.

"Mackenzie?" Mack asks softly like he's surprised.

"Mackenzie *Kayla*," I grin, "Zinfandel. Or baby Mack as your wife calls her already."

Looking over at an emotionally silent Z, Mack nods something to him they understand between each other and then he just openly cry-smiles for me.

"I'm honored, and privileged, and I'm actually speechless which doesn't work well with my profession," he grins at me. "Thank you so much, Suzanne. And Z," he nods again at Z. "I have a namesake," he says almost to himself. "And she's beautiful."

Touching her cheek softly, Mack hugs her a little closer and I'm thrilled I could do this for him. This is the least I owe Mack for always bringing me back to my life and back to my present. Really, for just keeping me alive long enough to actually share this little baby with him.

"I love you, Mack. So, so much. And you've always been my angel, so I wanted her to be your little angel, too, if that's okay?"

Leaning into my side, Mack exhales a very powerful breath of emotion. He seems to almost shake with his feelings for me and Mackenzie. "I love you, too, Suzanne. And this is the best thank you you could've ever given me, and really, the cutest as well," he smiles down at baby Mack.

"We're coming in!" Chicago Kayla yells banging on the door but the spell *isn't* broken between me and Mack, it just changes. When Mack looks at me again with his knowing eyes, I finally understand everything he's saying to me holding my daughter and I smile back at him. I understand what his eyes said to me, and I know my daughter will always be safe with Mack watching over her as well.

"Let me seeeeee..." Kayla practically stomps her feet at the door until Z moves to open it for her.

Turning to give me back my daughter, Mack kisses my head, touches her cheek again then stands up wiping his eyes quickly with a grin as I laugh at the manly move.

And then there is a quiet chaos that takes over my room.

Kayla jumps into Z's arms, kisses his cheek, and practically tosses all 6'3 of him out of the way to get to me once she enters. Argh... Pulling Mackenzie in closer, Kayla is all over me in seconds.

"Congratulations, Suzanne! Let me see her," she whines, thankfully quietly so she doesn't wake my baby. Reaching in, I gently let her go to the force that is Kayla.

"Oh! Wow. She really *is* beautiful. Her face looks almost porcelain she's so pretty. What color is her hair?" She asks already pulling off the little pink bonnet to see just the little dark fluff on the back of her head. Dammit, I hadn't even looked at her hair yet. Actually, I haven't even seen what she looks like outside of her baby blanket yet.

"Hello, little baby... I'm Fabulous Aunt Kayla," she giggles at my sleeping baby. "And I'm going to spoil you rotten, and take you shopping, and babysit you all the time. And we're going to do things your parents don't approve of, and you'll tell me all your secrets, and I'll teach you all about boys because I know *all* about boys because I'm your favorite aunt," she continues as I laugh a little at her crazy babbling.

"What's her name? I'm dying to know," she whispers against her head once the bonnet is back in place.

"No yelling while holding her, okay? You'll scare the crap out of her and she's sleeping."

"Yeah, so pass her over," Kayla demands walking in as Chicago Kayla hands her off with a huff.

"Okay... So?"

"Mackenzie *Kayla* Zinfandel," I say quickly and jump like I knew I would when she screeches.

"*Kayla!?* After me, right?"

"Of course," I grin when other Kayla sticks her tongue out behind her back.

"Oh, she looks like a Mackenzie. Like a little baby Mack," she actually smiles at Mack understanding my intention. "I think it's perfect, which is lucky for you because I was going to raise hell if you picked some stupid sounding name like Zoe Zinfandel or something," she says with such repulsion on her face I can't hold it in. Gasping a quick breath, Kayla howls before I do.

"Zoe's not stupid sounding," Z defends which just makes me laugh harder. "It's not. But Mackenzie is better, certainly," he concedes finally laughing at Kayla MacDonald who is literally pissing herself I think until Z pulls my daughter from her arms with a piss off face.

"What?"

"Nothing," Kayla and I say together and thankfully Kayla drops it to stand up looking at my baby again in Z's arms.

"Um, Marty and the Rinaldi's are here, so I'm going to go get them."

"Really?" I look at Kayla who nods when Kayla leaves my room.

"Did you really think my mother would stay away, Suzanne?"

"I didn't know. I just thought-"

"Your daughter just got a set of grandparents to spoil her, so be prepared for drop ins to clean and cook, and drop ins when you need to shower. She's actually pretty great as a grandmother," Mack agrees beside her.

"Okay."

Looking at Z and Mackenzie, he seems so happy suddenly, I wish we were alone so we could talk. Then again, I guess we have all night and really forever to talk to each other about today. So though I want to be alone with Z, I want him to enjoy all this happiness and excitement on this very special day with our new baby.

Once Mrs. Rinaldi hands me flowers and introduces herself as Nonna Mary, she takes my baby and settles in the only chair in my room. Kissing and cooing, she keeps talking to Mr. Rinaldi, or Nonno Frank as he's called to Mackenzie while everyone makes conversation around me.

Joining in when questions are directed at me I watch my baby closely. Not that anyone would drop her or anything, but the fact that's she's so quiet is kind of freaking me out. I seem to recall being told newborns cry all the time, but mine has cried twice and quickly settled, which though awesome, is scary too.

"Is she okay? Is she breathing?" I suddenly yell at Marty who's holding her with Kayla by the window. "Is she alive?" I cry out as the silence around us almost strangles me until Z gets right in my face blocking Mackenzie from me.

"Don't, Z. Give her to me. Give her back to me Marty. *Now*!" I cry as I start to really panic.

When Marty hands her back to me quickly, I lay her on my lap and rip open her tight blanket to be sure. And when her arms do this spread out jump thing, I gasp a quick breath when she cries.

She's fine. And alive. And oh! Her sleeper is so cute, Kayla must've changed her into the 'Mommy's little Angel' sleeper in the nursery.

Oops.

"Sorry," I moan to everyone rocking Mackenzie on my shoulder. Shit.

"Suzanne?" Z begs leaning into my body to shield me from everyone.

"I'm sorry. But she wasn't crying like newborns should, and she was so quiet and I just thought maybe something was wrong. But she's breathing... and *alive*," I finally cry when she quiets again on my shoulder. "I'm sorry. I just thought maybe she died or something," I moan into Z's shoulder when he hugs us tightly.

"Kayla?" Z calls out like she has the answers I need.

"Suzanne, look at me," Kayla sits right on my bed as Z pulls away from his hug. "Mackenzie is alive and well, and not going to die. She's quiet because she's like 3 hours old, and because she's just a quiet baby, ya lucky bitch," she smirks at me as I huff a little laugh. "And even if something happened, which it wouldn't, you're in a *hospital*, Suzanne," she says all duh. "And even when you're home, you know what to do. Think about what you did when Matthew choked on that baby biscuit I gave him 2 weeks ago. *I* panicked, but you didn't. You just grabbed him from me and laid him on your lap and gently took it from his throat while I stood there panicking. Remember?"

"Yes," I exhale all the crazy. "Sorry. I just freaked a little."

"I know. And now that she's here *alive* and well, I can tell you all about my own freak outs. Which there are many of."

"Many, many of," Mack adds helpfully as Kayla laughs turning to him.

"I'm sorry everyone. Sorry I yelled at you Marty." Ugh... I feel like such

We are US...

an ass again.

"No problem, Suzanne. Kayla yells at me daily, so I can handle it," he flashes a cute grin at me and I feel better.

"We're bringing in all the stuff now," Chicago Kayla says walking out the door with Marty to ease the sudden tension around us I think.

Waiting only seconds, Kayla starts hauling in bouquet after bouquet and gifts and stuffed animals, and just about everything else shy of an entire Florist's shop. When Mrs. Rinaldi starts arranging all the flowers all over my room, I'm honestly stunned.

I had no idea this many people cared enough to send us flowers, and I had no idea I knew this many people. Well, that *Z* knew this many people.

When Mack hands me card after card, I gently hand Mackenzie back to Z, and everything seems so okay suddenly, I feel bad about my scare but good about everything and everyone around me.

This is going to be my life now I realize, and I want to live it.

Watching Z hold our daughter I'm captivated once again by him, and by Mackenzie, and by my whole life suddenly.

"Thank you..." I whisper to no one specific but to everyone specifically.

CHAPTER 33

When Z and I settle in after a yummy dinner he snuck into my room, I'm exhausted. It's after 8:30, everyone left a few hours ago to give us a rest, Mackenzie is sleeping soundly beside us, and Z looks like he's gonna drop any second now.
"Come here, Z. Come lie down with me," I whisper.
"How are you?" He asks sitting gently on the side of my bed.
"Sore and tired, but happy and excited. So kind of mental," I grin.
"Me too. Well, not the sore part- sorry," he says sweetly with a little grimace. "But I'm hyper and tired at the same time. This has been the best day of my life, and I'm just so happy I don't even think I can sleep yet," he grins as I snuggle up to his side. "Let me clean up and I'll crawl in with you," Z leans down and kisses my head before leaving me for the bathroom.

Watching Z quietly open the bathroom door I reach for his hand when there's suddenly another knock on our door. "Really?" I groan.
"Probably Kayla with another gift," Z passes me with a little kiss as I lean back in my bed.
"Hello?"
"May I come in, I'd like to speak with you?" I have no idea who this woman is, so naturally my hand goes on the edge of Mackenzie's little bed.
"What is this regarding?" Z smiles his charming smile as I roll my eyes at his back.
"May I come in, sir?" She pushes as Z steps back to allow entry. Watching her walk in, I'm stunned when she's followed by a Police Officer. "I'm Hillary Mason," she says lifting a badge from her chest. "I'm a social worker with the New York Child Protective Services Agency, and this-"
Gasping, I hear nothing else. Staring at Z looking ready to kill, my hand pulls Mackenzie right against my bed as I reach for her. Stunned, tears fill my eyes immediately as my heart pounds.

We are US...

"Please don't lift the infant, mam," the Officer says as I cringe. Oh my GOD.

Shaking his head to clear it I think, Z asks what I already know. "Why are you *here*?"

"There's been a report made about Mrs. Suzanne Zinfandel abusing her child, and with the history of her mental illness-"

"*What* report?! Mackenzie is like 12 hours old and we've never been alone with her, and Suzanne hasn't had even one minute alone with her!" Yelling, Z doesn't even hold back he's so pissed.

"That's anonymous sir. But again the complaint, collaborated with Mrs. Zinfandel's history of mental illness has given my department just cause to take Mackenzie Kayla Zinfandel into our care until an investigation and a final court decision is made regarding the health and safety of Mackenzie Kayla Zinfandel in the care of Mrs. Zinfandel."

"This is such bullshit," Z barks, but Ms. Mason looks totally unaffected. She actually ignores Z to look at the Police Officer instead. She even exhales like she's bored as I gasp another quick breath before my throat closes entirely.

"I'd like to speak with you outside for a moment if I may?" Z pours on the charm, and for once in our life together I'm glad she seems a little affected by Z. Maybe he can fix this. Or maybe he can change her mind. Or maybe he can *FIX* this.

"Suzanne, while I'm speaking with Ms. Mason I'd like you to call Mack and Stinson. Now, Suzanne," he growls to get me out of my head.

Looking at Z nod at me, my hand moves slowly to my purse beside me for my phone. Reaching, I keep my hand on Mackenzie's bed and pull my purse to my lap as the Officer watches my movements but doesn't speak.

Tearing through one-handed I just dump my purse for my phone I'm shaking so badly. Dialing, I'm not breathing or coherent or anything else but desperate as I hold Mackenzie as close to me as I can without touching her, like I'm not allowed apparently.

"What's up? How's that beautiful baby of yours," Kayla asks with her own smile-voice and I almost lose it.

Gasping, I say only, "*Mack*," before she switches the phone out quickly.

"What's wrong?" He asks calmly and I lose it. Bawling my eyes out I can barely say the words. "Suzanne... Talk to me," he pushes again.

"They're taking Mackenzie away."

"*Who* is?!"

"Child Protective Services. I'm not even allowed to touch her anymore," I cry between breaths.

"When did-"

"Mack! Please fix this. *Pleeeeease*. I need her, and I haven't hurt her and I wouldn't-"

"Suzanne, keep it together for me."

"But I-"

"*LISTEN* TO ME!" He yells louder than I've ever heard Mack yell before. Gasping my quick shock, I silence and my tears stop immediately. "Stay calm, Suzanne. *Think* about it. If you lose your shit, she'll write it down as an example of mental incompetence. Anything you do or say right now will be on record. So do NOT speak, lose it, or freak the fuck out. Got it?"

"Yes." Wow, do I ever. Mack literally just scared the crazy right out of me with his yelling and swearing.

"Kayla's parents have Matthew and we'll be at the hospital in about 15 minutes. Just stay put, don't speak, and where the hell is Z?"

"With the social worker in the hallway. Um, he's really mad, Mack."

"*Shit*. Go get him, Suzanne."

"But there's a Police Officer right here and I'm not allowed to touch Mackenzie, and I, ah don't want to leave him alone with her," I whisper.

"She brought the authorities?"

"Yes. He's right here."

"Go get Z, Suzanne, and make him stay with you. Do NOT cry, or freak out. Hold it in. Please trust me, Suzanne. I need you to hold it in until I get there. Can you do that for me?"

"Yes..."

"15 minutes. Have you called anyone else?"

"Z told me to call Stinson."

"Your probate lawyer?"

"Uh huh."

"No. I'll call Bradley in Family Law. Just stay put, get Z, and don't lose it."

"I'm scared Mack, and I didn't hurt her."

"I know," he says calmly before the phone hangs up.

Trying to get my legs to work, I look at the Officer watching silently in the middle of the room, then back down to Mackenzie. I know I'm only

We are US...

going to be about 20 feet from her, but just the thought of him being closer to her than I am makes me want to lose it, or like threaten him or something. Shit.

"Ah, I just have to talk to my husband. Um, please don't touch her," I beg as my eyes fill with tears again when the bastard doesn't acknowledge my request one way or the other.

Reaching for the wheel chair near my bed I almost fall out in my attempt to pull it towards me. Reaching desperately with my hand on my stomach like somehow that'll lesson the pain, I pull the chair closer.

How the fuck do I get in it? Jesus Christ my heart is pounding and I feel myself so close to losing it, I basically just throw myself sideways into the wheel chair and hold on to the bed as my numb legs crash to the ground before I scream. Oh my *god*... I swear everything inside me just ripped wide open.

Positioning my legs on the foot rests I frantically wheel my way to the door already hearing Z's angry voice as I approach.

"...her problems have *nothing* to do with our baby. They're about her past..."

"And can you guarantee she won't hurt the child in her custody if she has another mental breakdown as she has a lengthy history of- as recently as even 16 months ago our records indicate."

Holding my hand on the door I'm scared motionless while I wait for his answer. I hope he says the right thing, and I hope he knows I would never hurt her. I hope- turning back to Mackenzie the Officer hasn't moved closer to her, but I can't seem to move toward Z either.

"Well, *I'm* not crazy. I have no history of mental illness, and she's *my* daughter. She's going home with me, and *I'm* going to care for her." Oh... Huh.

"Mr. Zinfandel, you didn't answer my question. Do you believe your wife is emotionally stable enough to care for a new born?"

Oh god, *please*...

"Yes, I do." Thank *fuck!* "But should she ever have another episode I have contingency plans ready. I have a doctor on call 24-7, and I'm working from home for the immediate future to help care for my daughter." Wow, I didn't know any of that. A contingency plan? What the *fuck?* Like I'm some psycho who needs constant-

"As I said, Mrs. Mason, Mackenzie will be in my care, not solely my wife's, so there is no threat to my daughter." Oh. Ouch. Feeling my heart actually break, I finally find the strength to tug open the door.

Flinching at the sudden movement behind him, Z looks at me guilty as hell and I know he knows I heard him. But whatever. I'll kill him later for still thinking I'm a raging psycho.

"Mack and Kayla will be here any moment, Z," I barely hold the anger and feeling of betrayal from my voice. "And Mack has requested you stop speaking until he arrives."

Turning back to my daughter, I force myself to move emotionless and calm in the wheelchair. My insides are screaming from both the physical and emotional pain, but I'll fight it forever if it means I don't lose my baby. Because I *can't* lose my baby.

"Suzanne..." Z tries but I ignore him to lean against my bed where Mackenzie still sleeps oblivious to the fact that her brand new little life is about to change.

Ignoring the previous warnings, I lean forward and touch her little face anyway with my fingertips. Stroking my thumb gently along her little baby eyebrow, I feel such sorrow suddenly I can't help the tears that fall, though I do hold in the agony from cresting into a loud sob.

"I could never hurt you, baby. *Ever*," I whisper to Mackenzie's sleeping silence.

Waiting, Ms. Mason doesn't speak, and Z leans against the wall by the door, presumably for Mack. The silence around us is absolutely deafening, and I feel the slow building of panic trying to take me alive. Watching my hands slowly begin to shake, I casually try to hide them in Mackenzie's blankets. Looking at my purse contents still dumped on my bed, I see my anxiety pills and I know I need them, but I'm too afraid to show Ms. Mason I need them.

Mack told me to fight it, to stay calm, and to not speak. Mack told me what to do, so I'm doing it, but it *is* getting harder and harder by the second as time slows to not even existing anymore. Like my future apparently, I giggle.

Shit!

Changing my giggle into a cough as best as I can, I look up quickly at Z who death glares me silent. Oh, wow. That look is scary, but works. I feel no giggles, and I feel no crazy. I am breaking down in my head only and it's a silent breakdown I can hide for now.

We are US...

Throwing open my door, Mack doesn't even attempt niceties. "I'm Dr. Michael MacDonald, Suzanne's personal Physician and personal friend."

"Hello. I'm Hilary Mason, a social worker with the New York Child Protective Services agency."

"I'm aware. What I am unaware of however is why you're here so soon after the birth of Mrs. Zinfandel's child?"

"There was a complaint filed and references made to Mrs. Zinfandel's mental and emotional instability."

"I understand. What I'm asking is why are you here *now?* Not only is it after hours for your agency, but court mandated child removals take days to finalize, unless there is a specific incident called in by an authority such as a treating physician, or a police officer on scene." Ha! Good point, Mack. "Therefore, I ask again, why you are here when no such report has been made, it is after hours, and this child is 12 hours old- certainly not long enough to have a judge enforce an emergency removal."

"Look, Dr. MacDonald, I was given this file at around 4:00 this afternoon, and after reading the paperwork on Mrs. Zinfandel and setting up the police escort, I arrived here a half hour ago." Pulling out paperwork from her bag that I think I saw her give Z earlier, she hands it over to Mack. "Everything is in order, and the presiding judge signed and stamped all the paperwork at 3:30 this afternoon. I promise you I checked beforehand and everything *is* in order."

Watching Mack and Mrs. Mason try to fight each other, I can't look away. Staring at Mack, I realize everything that happens here is everything that can happen. There is no alternative, and unless he proves something I'm going to lose I think.

"When was the complaint made?" Mack asks what I think we're all dying to know.

"At approximately 2:00."

"Anonymously?"

"Yes."

"Okay, well I would like you to state for your records that I was in the company of *both* the Zinfandel's and their baby Mackenzie from a little after 10:30am this morning until 4:30 this evening when my wife and I left for dinner. And at NO point was Mackenzie abused or neglected by Mrs. Zinfandel. My wife, a nurse at this hospital, will also state for the record the same thing, along with a few other family members and friends who visited throughout the day. Both myself, a Physician at this very hospital, and my wife, also a nurse at this hospital were here for at least 6 hours without leaving this room within that time frame."

"I will note that, certainly."

"Make sure you do. I have the parking receipt showing when I arrived and also when we left."

"Understood."

"Where are you taking Mackenzie tonight?" **WHAT?!!**

Screaming out, I can't even hold it in. They're taking her anyway? "NO! No, no, nooooo... You're not taking her away from me."

"Suzanne, stop," Z barks, but it doesn't work this time. No. Fucking. *Way.*

Reaching quickly, I grab for Mackenzie before the cop can do anything about it. I don't fucking care what anyone says, they're not taking her.

"She was just born!" I scream. "She's even alive. And not a dead baby like Thomas. And you can't take her from me," I cry hysterically.

"Put the baby down, Mrs. Zinfandel," Mrs. Mason says in a calm voice that sounds weird in my head suddenly.

"Give her to me, Suzanne," Mack steps forward and I can't believe what I'm hearing. I can't believe he's actually trying to take her from me. "I'll make sure she's okay," Mack moans a little closer to me. Whispering as he leans down close to my face Mack says, "Don't do this. You have to trust me right now."

So I stop.

Nodding, I hand over my crying baby to Mack. Looking at me with the saddest eyes I've ever seen, Mack nods once and says, "We'll be back soon."

"Um, but I have to nurse her," I cry out as I feel my own breasts swell to nearly painful.

"We have formulas for newborns," the heartless fucking bitch says and I barely stop myself from attacking her.

"Can I please just feed her one more time? Um, it's really important that she gets all my nutrients in her. *Please?* I promise I won't be long, and I won't hurt her ever," I choke. I can't believe I actually had to say that to someone.

Waiting what seems like hours, Ms. Mason finally says, "Yes, you may. But the Officer and I must be present, and you have only 5 minutes."

"Fine!"

We are US...

Grabbing Mackenzie from Mack I don't even think. Within a second I just lift my hoodie up and unsnap the catch in my bra. I'm on autopilot, and I don't know what I'm doing, or seeing, or feeling except the need to feed my daughter. I don't even care that everyone can see my naked chest. I just care about feeding my baby.

Moving my ass in the wheelchair, I line her up and she latches instantly. Oh my *god*... This is it. This is the last time I'm ever going to care for her. This is the last time I'll ever hold her. This is the last time I'll ever *know* her.

Sobbing, I feel my nose drip, and my eyes pour. I know I'm breaking, but I can't stop it. There is nothing here for me but this beautiful little baby against my chest.

"I'm sorry, baby," I cry hearing Z cough cry across my room.

Forever I hold her little body in my arms and cry the most painful agony of my life. Nothing compares to this. Nothing I've known or felt or experienced in my life hurts me more than this moment. There is nothing left for me *but* this moment.

"I'm so sorry, Mackenzie..."

"Mrs. Zinfandel, we have to leave now. Please don't make this harder on her." *WHAT?!*

"You're the one making this hard on her. I'm just the person left holding *nothing*."

Walking to me, she doesn't acknowledge my words or even me. She merely takes Mackenzie from my arms as the Officer leans forward to help if needed, or to arrest me if warranted I guess. I don't know, but he doesn't speak, and Ms. Mason is a fucking bitch.

"I *hate* you," I moan before I can stop myself.

"I understand. But I'm just doing my job," she replies deadpan walking towards the door passing all the people who said they'd always help me.

"Wait! What about a carseat?"

"We have one."

"But what about her clothing? It's December and she's only in a sleeper and one blanket."

"Would you like to give me clothing to dress her in?"

Frantically wheeling over to our joint suitcase, I flip it and unzip it so quickly, it actually sounds like machine gun fire in my silent room. No one is speaking, and I don't see any movement in my peripheral. Tearing through our clothes, I grab the generic, genderless snowsuit of a white polar bear near the bottom and sob as I move past the pain of my body and my heart. Pushing Z's hand away when he tries to help me, I move to my baby one last time.

"Please keep her warm. I want this baby to always be warm. I can't have this baby always cold, too."

Gasping my agony, those are my last words for my daughter. That's all that's left of me. And that's the last of my sanity while my new reality destroys me.

♀♀♀♀♀

Watching the Fucking Bitch walk down the hall with the Officer, I want to scream and punch and kick and destroy everything around me. I want to stab people and gouge out their eyes with my fingernails. I want to destroy everyone like I've just been destroyed.

"Suzanne...?" Z touches my arm, but as I turn to him I seethe looking at his red eyes.

"Fuck. *You*," I moan wheeling back to my bed past his flinch and his silence, beyond Kayla stepping closer to me and Mack calling my name. "Get the fuck out of here. All of you."

"Baby, can I just-"

"If you don't get out of here Z, I'll fucking kill you. I'm not insane, and I'm not losing my shit. I'm perfectly fine. I'm perfectly enraged, and broken, and dying inside. But I'm sane, Z. So *fuck* you!"

"You're not mad at Z, Suzanne," Mack actually tries to defend him, and I barely stop myself from killing Mack first.

"No, I'm *not* mad at Z, I'm furious, Mack. And with *you*! You protected her for all of 12 hours, you piece of shit. 'Trust me, Suzanne'," I sneer. "Fuck you and your trust, and fuck him!" I point at Z.

"Suzanne, that's enough!" Kayla snaps as I laugh at her.

"You want in on this? *Really?* Who called Kayla? Who fucking told someone I hurt Mackenzie? *WHO?*"

"I don't know."

"Well, until you do, you can get out of here, too. Because for all I know

We are US...

it was you. I mean come on, Kay, we all know you're not supposed to have any more children, so maybe you thought you'd take mine-"

"THAT'S *ENOUGH!*" Z stops me as I laugh at his anger.

"Yes, it *is* enough. Go home Z. I'm done," I suddenly pick up my phone from my bed and whip it at him as he turns sideways. "You didn't protect me or Mackenzie like you said you would. You just stood and watched her taken away- to god knows where with god knows who so she can be brutalized. So fuck *you!*"

Walking to the door Kayla doesn't look back at me, and as Mack looks between me and her, his face is so pale I actually laugh.

"Go to your wife and *baby*, Mack. At least you have one, right?" I laugh like a crazy.

But I swear I don't feel crazy even though I sound like it. I feel anger and sadness and a numbing chill working its way to my heart. But I don't feel actual crazy this time.

"Z, please leave. I don't want to look at you, and clearly I'm not able to speak to you right now. So do us both a favor and get the fuck out!" I snap my point made quite well.

"Okay, love. I'll see you tomorrow," he adds like a dick as I laugh at him again.

"I doubt I'll want to see you then anyway, but maybe you can fix this for yourself in the meantime. I mean come *on*... As you said to the lovely Ms. Mason, 'you are sane, you have no mental health issues, and *you* were going to raise our daughter anyway', right?" I laugh as I use the dreaded finger quotes of our funny past with Mack.

Stepping towards me, Z tries again. "I was desperately lying to her to try to change the situation we were suddenly in."

"It doesn't matter. You fucked up, and now my daughter is gone."

"I didn't do this, Suzanne."

"Oh, I know. *I* did, of course."

"But I *will* fix it," he says so angrily I'm surprised he isn't yelling back. Not that it matters to me anymore.

"Whatever," I laugh suddenly turning my back on him as I wheel toward the window. Hearing Z walk closer I tense up but he quickly walks away again. Changed his mind about trying? Good.

"I'll see you tomorrow when you've calmed down," Mack says angrily, and I wish I cared, but I really don't.

I care about no one anymore but the baby I knew for only hours.

When the door closes presumably behind Mack and Z, I laugh again. Wow, I was the raging psycho I'm always accused of being and it felt good. Telling people to fuck off felt good, and hating people feels even better right now. Because without the hatred I'm left only with my devastation.

God, did I really think this would be easy? Did I honestly think I'd have a healthy, living baby and walk out of the hospital to all I've ever wanted with Z? Did I actually think my life would finally be happy?

Looking behind me I see Z placed my cracked iPhone on the table. Shattered beyond repair, when I try to turn it on I can't even see his beautiful face on my screen. Because he's gone, just like she is.

Screaming, I throw my arm across the table and clear it of my phone and a vase of flowers as everything crashes down around me.

Suddenly crying again, I feel my heart stutter once as I gasp, then break in my chest completely. "Did I really believe I could have a happily ever after? What a fucking idiot I am!" I scream to no one but myself as the pain and darkness take me.

We are US...

Sarah Ann Walker

LOVE

We are US...

Sarah Ann Walker

CHAPTER 34

2 days later after continually refusing Z and Mack, I'm ready to go home. All the nurses know what happened it's obvious by both the sympathy I get from some, and the glares I get from others. But I don't care anymore. I feel broken inside.

I was spoken to the day before by a social worker at the hospital and I told her the truth. I *was* mental in the past, but not about Mackenzie. I explained I was happy and mentally healthy, Z and I were very careful, and in no way did I hurt her or even *want* to. I told the truth as best as I could without crying and screaming the whole time, and she seemed satisfied.

Nodding and writing everything I said down, she actually had very few questions for me regarding my past mental health issues, or my current mental health issues, which are fairly obvious right now. And then she left informing me there would be a home visit to make sure our living arrangements for Mackenzie were suitable should we regain custody of her. Sadly, that's all I remember because I tuned out when she said I wasn't getting Mackenzie back before the emergency custody hearing on Friday.

After the social worker left I stopped taking my painkillers for my C-Section, and somehow feeling the physical pain of my stomach actually lessens the pain in my chest. At least minimally. Well, nothing actually helps relieve the pain in my heart and nothing stops my body from needing her with me. But sadly, I'm fairly resigned to the fact that this is my life now.

Dragging my suitcase to the nurses station, I request all my final paperwork. Waiting, I don't look up because I can't stand to see pregnant women or women with new babies. I can't stand anything anymore and I have nowhere to go.

"We're supposed to wheel you out," the first nurse and pathetic Kayla wannabe says behind me.

"I don't care. I can walk, and I'm leaving. So follow or don't but I'm walking out of here."

"I signed an affidavit yesterday about what I witnessed between you and your daughter."

Turning to her, I have nothing left. I can't even ask if she was pro Suzanne Zinfandel, or against. It doesn't seem to matter anyway because Mackenzie is still gone.

Walking away, she does actually follow me with the wheelchair, down the hall, down the elevators silently, and even to the front doors after what feels like an hour of walking in this shithole they call Mercy. And once again, the irony of being at Mercy when I've been shown none is not lost on me.

"Thanks," I barely acknowledge nurse whatever as I push open the doors to a blast of cold winter in my face.

Turning left and right, I know I have to walk for miles to get to any main road out of the exhausting parking lots of Mercy. So I begin, and quickly stop when the cold and wind get to me.

What the hell am I doing, and where the hell am I going?

Parking my suitcase, I sit down slowly on the little cement parking bump between cars and try to figure out what I do now. Blowing on my hands, nothing seems to warm me anymore and all drama aside, which is like the funniest statement *ever* coming from me, I really don't know what I'm doing or where I'm going anymore.

I thought I'd cab it to a hotel, or walk forever until I figured something out. But after 2 and a half days alone, and only walking for 10 minutes in this cold I have figured out nothing besides I was mean to the people I love because I had to hate someone for the situation I caused Z, Mackenzie, and me, whether intentionally or not.

Jesus Christ, it's cold.

Sniffing and laughing at myself, my stomach hurts so bad from shivering it seems a little just somehow. I probably should be punished for ruining Z's life, getting his daughter taken away, and then screaming horrible things at him because of it all. So yeah, I think a little physical pain is the least I deserve.

"Suzanne?" Wow. *Really?*

Turning I can't believe Z is walking toward me between parked cars. How the hell can he even see me? It's not like my head is even level with the goddamn cars I'm sitting between.

"Hi," I whisper casually wiping my nose on my frozen coat sleeve.
"What are you doing?"
"Sitting," I huff a laugh but he doesn't engage my stupid like he usually does.
"Why didn't you wait for me to pick you up? I told you I'd be there at 11:00."
"Ah, I didn't know if you really wanted to get me, or just felt obligated or something."
"Suzanne, let's go," Z says angrily. Looking up at him, I know why he's pissed at me but I don't know how to deal with it right now. "Stand up and let's go. My truck is only a few rows away." Again with the tone, and I still don't know how to move.
Staring up at Z, the shivering has taken hold of me so thoroughly, my teeth are chattering and my stomach is cramping it's so sore, but I still can't move.
Leaning down to my face, Z breathes the only words I've ever feared in my life. "If you don't get in my fucking truck right now I'll leave you here, Suzanne," he growls with the implication so obvious but unspoken, I gasp. "That's right. I'm sick of doing everything by myself when you snap, and I'm really fucking tired of your outbursts. So if you want to salvage anything between us, you'll stand up and get moving to my truck. Otherwise, I'm walking away and doing this by myself."
Placing my hand on the cement bump I've been sitting on to push myself up, I notice first Z isn't joking and second, he isn't helping me like he normally would. Once upright, I can't help flinch at the pain I'm in when my stomach pulls and the stitches threaten to tear from the cold.
God, my skin feels so brittle suddenly, but when Z simply walks away, I grab my luggage and follow like a puppy in trouble. Which really I am at this point, I laugh once nervously before he hears me.
Walking feet from the truck, I hear the door locks click open but still Z doesn't help me like he usually does. Opening the door, just the thought of lifting myself inside almost makes me panic so after placing my suitcase in the back, I grab hold of the handle and force myself in quickly with a loud humph and cry as I get in the seat. And he still doesn't acknowledge me.
Honesty, this is so unlike Z, not only with the lack of help, but without the questions concerning me. His silence is unlike anything I've ever experienced with him, no matter what I've done or said before. And I'm

We are US...

scared I've finally broken us completely.
 God, I remember when Mack explained pushing Z too far until he finally snaps and moves on. I remember hearing the words but not believing them fully. I was actually arrogant enough and so in love with *him* I didn't think I could push Z too far because I hadn't at that point. But here we are, and I'm suddenly scared to death he's already gone.
 "I'm really sor-"
 "Fuck. *You*, Suzanne," Z snarls as I silence immediately. Wow, that hurt my heart and my head and everything else inside me as well. Those words hurt like a knife slashing my skin. They were the same words I said to him, but he's never used them on me before so I didn't know how awful they felt. Stunned, I actually realize the power they hold suddenly.
 "I didn't mean-"
 "Don't speak. Don't apologize. Do *nothing,* Suzanne."
 "But-"
 Laughing like *he's* insane I shut my mouth when he starts shaking his head. His hands are squeezing the steering wheel, and he looks like he could crash the truck any second if I speak again. So I close my mouth and fight everything inside me wanting to spew my apologies and upset all over Z.
 Unsure of what to do besides being quiet, I make the mistake of looking behind me and when I see the empty carseat base, I can't believe the pain inside can actually feel stronger in my chest. She was supposed to be in this truck with us. And three days ago, I thought she would be. I actually believed we three would walk into our new lives together, but I was wrong again.
 God, I wish I knew what was happening to her, but I'm too afraid to ask.

Twenty minutes later pulling into the underground, Z finally turns to me with a look of pure hatred on his face. Internally flinching, I hold myself together for whatever he has to say.
 "Your *daughter* is doing well, Suzanne. *Not* that you asked about her," he sneers again before quickly throwing open his car door and slamming it with me stunned inside.
 Okay, not what I was expecting, but I'm grateful for the news regardless. Shit, I wanted to ask a hundred times. I was *going* to ask a hundred times, but he told me not to speak. So I didn't.
 Opening my door, I realize he's being pretty unfair suddenly, so I slam

my own door hoping to get his attention. "I wanted to ask, but you told me not to speak!" I yell at Z's back when he walks halfway toward the lower elevators already.

"Not good enough," he yells over his shoulder still walking.

"Hey! I *wanted* to ask. But you told me not to speak, Z."

"Whatever," he yells pushing the elevator button so hard I swear he broke his finger. *Whatever?* Not this time.

Running to Z, I hold my stomach with one hand and reach for his jacket to get his attention. "WHAT?!" He yells down at me and after my initial fear of his anger, I grow a set.

"I tried to apologize for-"

"Being a total bitch?!"

"No, for getting her taken away," I moan. "I was trying to say I was sorry she was taken away from you because of me. I've been thinking of nothing else but you and her and I wanted to say I was sorry for causing this. But you said fuck you, don't speak, don't apologize, and do nothing. *You* said that. So I didn't ask or speak. Not because I'm wasn't dying to know what's happening-"

"When you refused to speak to me or Mack for the last two days while you closed down and had another episode, leaving me alone and fucked scrambling to figure out what the hell I do to get us out of this mess!?" He yells again silencing me.

Shaking my head, I don't know what to say anymore. I mean this is everything right here and I'm scared I'm going to screw it up if I say the wrong thing.

"I wasn't having an episode, I was staying away so I could figure out what to do to fix this. And when you told me to keep quiet I did because I was respecting your right to hate my guts for ruining both your lives. It wasn't because I'm not dying to know what's happening to Mackenzie," I finally cry a little when he leans his head against the filthy elevator door that has already come and gone once. "How is she?" I whisper as he thaws enough to look down at me.

Moaning his words, he tells me all he can I think. "She seems good, for a 3 day old baby who doesn't have a goddamn clue what's happening around her. Kayla says she's fine, and being cared for properly," he moans so sadly, I burst into the tears I've been holding since he found me in the parking lot.

"Kayla sees her?" Nodding, Z doesn't speak. "Thank god..." I cry harder.

We are US...

    Pushing the button again Z still doesn't really acknowledge me, but when it opens he does step aside so I enter first which he used to do before he hated me.
    Standing beside each other silently, I have never felt so far from Z as I do in this sad moment destroying us.

    Opening the door to our condo, I'm assaulted by all things Mackenzie. From the flowers everywhere to the gifts on the dining room table, I'm assaulted and besieged by her horrible absence.
    "I didn't know what to do with all her stuff, and I didn't know where you wanted it, so," he shrugs walking into the kitchen away from me.
    Needing to use the bathroom anyway, I walk away to give Z some time to himself. Standing in my bedroom doorway suddenly I don't know what to do. I don't know if this is still my room, and I don't know if Z wants me in here. Exhaling, I turn for the crazily decorated room that used to be Kayla's and use her bathroom instead.
    Finishing up, I realize my stomach incision looks pretty red and actually has kind of a warmth to it I don't think is good, but when I hear Z yelling through the wall I quickly forget about my stomach and run for the living room.
    "What's happening?" I beg when Z tosses his cell on the coffee table.
    "Absolutely nothing."
    "What does that mean?"
    "It means *nothing* is happening. We've been rescheduled from the emergency custody hearing originally set for this afternoon until Monday and no one knows why. The judge bumped us and my lawyers can't understand what's happening."
    "Oh." I literally have nothing to add. "What happens Monday?"
    "We should win temporary custody of Mackenzie until a formal custody proceeding takes place in a few weeks."
    "But if we don't win on Monday?"
    "She stays at Cedardale in the custody of the State until an official custody hearing which could take weeks," Z admits so heavily I feel everything he isn't saying destroying him as I watch.
    "Is she safe there?" God, my head is suddenly spinning with what if's.
    "Yes," he says quickly, but I don't know how can he be sure.
    "Not to sound like an asshole or anything, but how the hell is this happening? I mean I get the *I'm insane* part, but with you it doesn't

make sense, does it?"

"How so?" Z asks sounding a little more curious then put out speaking to me.

"Well, you're Z Zinfandel of New York. You have influence and friends everywhere, never mind the money for the best lawyers. Christ, you could simply call the Times to explain your situation and just the sympathy and public pressure alone could get you Mackenzie back."

"We don't want publicity, Suzanne."

"Why?"

"So no one knows Mackenzie is there which is safer for her."

"Oh..." Okay, that quick fear just stabbed right through my chest again. God, I hope no one knows who she is.

"What about Glenn Rose?"

"He's already involved," Z states simply as I nod.

Shaking my head, I know there's more to this. I know it, I just can't see it. "A former D.A. of Chicago can't even pull some strings for you? Doesn't that seem weird? I mean just take me out of the equation, and you're the perfect parent for her. Oh!" Having a sudden epiphany, I see it all so clearly I can't believe he hasn't. "Z, take *me* out of the equation."

"Suzanne-"

"Wait! I'll move out. I'll leave for anywhere but here, and no judge would ever deny you your daughter back." Though this very conversation is tearing me to shreds inside, I know it's the only answer that makes sense right now. "Do it, Z. Tell whomever you have to that you've kicked me out so you could get your baby back."

"Our baby," he says softly, but it doesn't really matter anymore. *They* matter to me.

"Let me pack some things and I'll move out. Then you can get her back," I almost smile when the answer seem so simple but excruciating.

"Suzanne, we're not there yet."

Looking at Z trying to do the right thing for everyone, I know I need to help him for once. And this is the only way I can help at this point.

"I love you. And her. And *I'm* at that point now. Honestly, until you can think of something better, this is the best thing for Mackenzie and for you. Call your lawyers, Z. Tell them I've left. Tell everyone who'll listen that I'm out of the house so she'll be safe from her whackjob mother," I laugh a little in my agony. Shit this is hard, but it's the right thing to do. "This is the answer Z until you can come up with a better

We are US...

one, if you even want a better one."

"What the hell does that mean?" He asks standing over me.

"It means what it means. I said some horrible things I can't take back, things I doubt you'll ever forgive-"

"Suzanne-"

"No, it's okay. I'm not saying this to guilt trip you or anything, and I don't even blame you for being disgusted with me. I'm just seeing everything pretty clearly suddenly, and this is the right thing to do. Let me leave, and call your people so you can get Mackenzie back. She needs you," I whisper to his growing silence.

"She needs you, too," he says after forever, but I know its not true.

Touching Z's arm, I want him to listen to me and truly understand what I'm saying. "Thank you for saying that, but it's not the same thing. You're sane and normal and well respected, so you can get custody of her in a heartbeat. I can't though, and we both know it. So this is the best decision right now for you and her."

"I don't think I can," he says actually looking sad which feels good. But it honestly doesn't feel good enough when I think of her in that place.

"Yes, you can. For her you can, and so can I. For Mackenzie I can do anything, and you will too. Make the calls Z. I'm going to go pack."

"Wait," Z says pulling my arm as I turn from him. "This is just temporary, Suzanne. We're not over, love. And once I have her back, I'll get you back in her life as well."

"Okay," I smile my most beautiful fake academy award winning smile ever. "Give me 20 minutes and I'll be out of here so you can get her back."

"Where are you going to go? Ah, let me set you up in a hotel. Okay?"

"Sure. Sounds good," I finally turn away from his desperate broken sad eyes that are breaking my heart more than I thought possible after losing Mackenzie 3 days ago.

15 minutes later, I'm done. Grabbing everything and nothing, I've filled 2 large roller suitcases and one heavy over the shoulder travel bag. My entire body hurts and my heart is broken behind repair, but thankfully, my mind is functioning better than it has since if not forever, at least since the moment my daughter was taken from me.

"I'm ready. Ah, I have to know is Kayla like super pissed at me, or just pissed? And where's Mack at with me?"

Not even grinning at my ridiculous question Z goes right for the jugular, though I honestly don't think it's intentional. "Ah, Kayla is practically living at Cedardale to be with Mackenzie while her mother watches Matthew all day. But she's mentioned she doesn't think she can forgive you this time," he says sadly. Nodding my head, I hold in the scream I feel bubbling to the surface and wait for more. "And Mack is Mack. He's very angry with you, but if you needed him I know he wouldn't turn you away." Ouch. That almost hurts worse.
 "Got it. Thank you for telling me so I didn't call them too soon."
 "Suzanne, I appreciate what you're doing."
 "But you can't forgive me either, I know."
 "It's not because of Mackenzie though. It's because of what you said and did after she was taken. I needed you because our daughter was just taken from *us*. But instead of working on it together you trashed me, blamed me, said horrible things to me, and then shut me out completely, even when I forgave you enough to try again the next morning."
 "I understand, Z."
 "I don't think you do. When you continued your shit the next day something changed in me, like the sadness turned to anger and now I feel like I don't trust you or even really like you anymore." Oh my god... I'm *dying* here. "But I still love you if that makes sense."
 "I understand," I say again calmly. And I really do understand. God, I don't even really like me so why would Z?
 This is the worst moment besides 'I'm here to take your daughter away' I've ever experienced in my life.
 "I'm really very sorry for everything, Z. I never meant for any of this to happen, and it honestly didn't occur to me that it could."
 "I'm sorry, too," he says with tears in his eyes and I realize he basically just sealed the deal between us with his apology.
 Z finally said goodbye to me, and I don't know how to walk away. Leaning into him, I hug him around his middle and whisper the only thing I can- the only unselfish thing I've ever said or done in my life with Z.
 "Go get Mackenzie, Z. She needs you in her life."
 When Z nods against the top of my head, I know it's done.

We are US...

Pulling away, I keep the tears inside and the agony concealed. I hide my life ending and my world collapsing. I walk out the door of all I've ever wanted, to start again with nothing at all.

Z and I have finally ended.

And he's still everything to me in every moment between us. Even now, in this *final* moment between us it's Z's scent I smell and his voice I hear because it's Z I'm losing forever.

When I close the door behind me tugging up the heavy shoulder strap and wheeling my 2 luggage down the hallway to the elevator I know an agony and loneliness so dark it changes the color around me and the very air I breathe.

I've lost my daughter, my husband, and my 2 best friends in the course of three days.

And I am finally broken.

CHAPTER 35

It's been only 3 days in this hotel room but it feels like an eternity in hell. I can't eat or sleep and I'm always in intense pain now. I don't even know if I'm physically in pain or just emotionally destroyed but as my weak body paces the floors again and again I keep waiting for something to happen, some news, *something*.

Walking around this place, alone and exhausted I can honestly say I won't attempt suicide this time though, no matter how bad I'm feeling. I know I won't. I don't even feel like killing myself, because I already feel dead inside, which just makes a suicide a little redundant at this point.

Plus, I'm a mother to a child I'll never know but she'll know of me. So I can't have her knowing I was a weak-willed psychotic bitch who destroyed her life as a newborn then killed herself when I couldn't handle the fallout of my words and actions.

I won't kill myself or even attempt it. Because I'm already dead inside.

"Suzanne?" Gasping and spinning toward the door, I'm so lightheaded suddenly I grab for the wall to keep myself upright. Wow, what the hell was that? Laughing as the spins continue, I fall on my knees to stop listing to the side.

"Suzanne!" Kayla Lefferts bangs on the door, and I really wish I could get to her so she'd stop yelling. I wish I could call out to her, but my mouth is so dry it's like thick glue and my throat is so tight, swallowing is suddenly an issue.

"I know you're in there!" She screams and bangs again. "So open this goddamn door before I fucking kill you. And if you've killed yourself I'm going to fuck you up even worse," she says making me actually laugh as I stand back up and walk slowly to the door. Feeling nauseous, but kind of cold and sweaty, I'm fairly sure I'm getting sick.

"Open the door, Suzanne!"

"I'm- coming," I moan in my raspiest phone-sex voice yet. Reaching the door, I giggle when just raising my hand to the lock hurts my head. But slowly, I flip the lock and even flip open the catch in the bar slide lock.

"What are-"

"Ouch!" I cry stumbling backward when she pushes the door into my shoulder. Actually just falling right over into the wall, I laugh when she breathes close to my face.

"What's going on? Did you take pills?"

"Nope," I giggle until my throat closes again and my tongue actually sticks to the roof of my mouth.

"What's happening? Oh god, Suzanne. You look really bad. What did you do?"

"I didn't, I swear."

"What fucking pills did you take?" She yells at me searching for her phone. "What did you take, Suzanne? And don't fucking lie to me. You're pasty as shit, you smell pretty funky, and your eyes are all fucked up. What did you-"

"I didn't," I try again reaching for her phone but she just keeps yelling over me.

"What did you take, sweetie?" She slips a forbidden name but it doesn't really bother me right now which is good, I guess. "Suzanne, what did you take?"

"Sweetie isn't bad right now. Is that- weird?" I choke.

"What pills did you take?"

"Nothing. I'm a mom now, *was* a mom now- um, *then*. And you can't do that if you're a mom," I choke again.

"Please tell me, Suzanne?" She chokes up with me.

Finding whatever strength I have left I grab her arm to finally get her attention. "I did NOT take anything. I just don't feel well," I exhale a huff while she watches me closely.

"Um, I think- oh, *fuck*," she gags as I laugh at her face. Kayla never gags for real, just I do. "Found it, I think. Oh man, it's gross."

"What? What did you find?" I ask playfully until she lifts my shirt up. Flinching quickly, I look down and see what she sees which is pretty gag worthy for sure.

Looking at Kayla staring at my stomach I realize she's so beautiful always, and though her color palette is way too wild for me, she makes everything look stunning always. "Why do you always look good, Chicago?"

"How long has this looked like this? You're really hot to the touch and I think you have a bad fever or something. I don't know what we should do. What do I do, Suzanne? Do you want to go to the hospital by ambulance or can you walk to my car?"

"I can walk."

Fading out I'm so tired I feel like I can finally sleep a little with Kayla here. It's not as quiet or lonely with her here suddenly and I'm really tired.

"Can you stay here tonight so I can sleep?"

Sitting on a hospital gurney, the very absence of all my pain makes me grateful to be here for once. Whether because I'm actually medicated out of my mind or because everything is magically fixed I could care less. For this one moment in time I'm actually pain free, and I'll take it.

"Hey. How are you feeling?" I hear Kayla before I see her, and though I'm happy someone is here, I wish it would've been Z. "You scared the hell out of me earlier, Suze," she continues when I finally turn my head to her.

Exhaling, here come the apologies. "Sorry I scared you. But I didn't take anything."

"I know. I'm sorry I didn't believe you."

Shrugging, it makes sense. "It doesn't matter. I'm crazy Suzanne, right? So naturally you'd assume I did something like that."

I wish I could laugh. Christ, I wish I could even giggle crazily. But there's just nothing, and I feel nothing.

"What happened?"

"Um, my C-Section incision is infected and I became a little septic. The doctors didn't understand why I was so infected so fast being on antibiotics afterward until I told them I had stopped taking the medication."

"Not even pain killers?"

Shaking my head, "I stopped taking them after Mackenzie was taken away," I moan. "I guess there was an antibiotic with it and even an anti-inflammatory, but I didn't know that."

"Um, weren't you in a lot of pain? I mean both the ER Doc and Kayla said you must've been in agony." Kayla knows, but she's not here which tells me everything I need to know.

"Yeah, I was sore," I shrug again. "Why did you come to the hotel?"

We are US...

"Because you weren't answering your cell all weekend, and we were all worried about you."

"I broke it in the hospital," after Mackenzie was taken away from me I cry to myself.

"Okay, I'll grab you another one tonight."

"You don't have to." It's not like anyone will call me I want to say, but I hold in the self-pity for myself, because not only is it pathetic but I know it'll prompt Kayla to rip a piece out of me and I just can't handle her right now. "Thank you for bringing me here, Kayla."

"You're dismissing me? How very *Suzanne,* Suzanne. You do realize I'm the only person you have right now, right?"

"Yes, I realize. That's why I'm dismissing you, so I can't screw it up with you as well," I exhale again just exhausted.

"Why haven't you called Kayla to apologize for what you said to her? Which incidentally was one of your nastiest yet."

Huffing my annoyance, I look at her like she's an idiot. "Why do you think, Kayla? Because I know I was horrible, *everyone* knows I was horrible, and I don't want to hear Kayla tell me to fuck off for good. I'm kind of screwed up right now, what with losing my baby and my husband within days of each other. So the thought of being told I'm a piece of shit by my best friend wasn't really high on my list of priorities. Breathing and trying to live alone was."

"But you owe her a chance to tell you to fuck off. You owe her that, Suzanne. Kayla will yell at you, say horrible things, scream and carry on, and then she'll be done. You've seen the Rinaldi's, so you know that's what they do. They yell and scream, then the air is cleared and they move on. She wouldn't have told you to fuck off forever. She would've just told you to fuck off for now."

"I couldn't be sure, Kayla. And I can't handle anymore right now. I just can't," I finally cry a little as she watches me. "I can't handle anymore..."

"I know," she steps up to me. Actually taking my hand, Kayla plays the role of the sympathetic friend which isn't usually her thing, but I'll take it at the moment. "When I called everyone Z was in court with Mack, but Kayla was so concerned she called the ER to be told what was happening. She even choked up when she heard about your stomach, and the pain you must've been in. God, it was so gross," Kayla laughs shaking her head. "How the hell didn't you notice all the stuff stuck to your shirt and like oozing from-"

"*Ew.* Please stop," I gag a little as she laughs. "I didn't know. I was just kind of caught up in all the pain I guess."

"It looked really sore."

Shaking my head, I tell her the truth. "It wasn't *that* pain, Kayla, though physically it was bad. It was mostly everything else."

"Z won temporary custody of Mackenzie this afternoon," she smiles as I jolt.

Moaning, I'm so happy and sad and just so happy, I can't hold in the quick sob. Bursting from my chest, I realize the fear and stress I was consumed with all weekend when it finally lifts.

"Oh, thank god. Oh *god,*" I cry as she squeezes my hand tightly. "I hoped. I really wanted him to be with her. Is she- okay?"

"Yes, she's okay. Um, that's why he couldn't come here. He and Mack, plus his multiple lawyers left the court house and drove directly to Cedardale waiting to get her once the judge called in the order. Apparently he was just pacing out front, growling and moaning until he was finally allowed to enter to get her a few hours ago. Um, Mack texted me to say Z has Mackenzie and he's finally home with her."

"Good. That's really good..." I cry both relieved and heartbroken, but mostly relieved. "Do you know when I can leave here? Not for their home, but just out of the hospital?"

"In a few hours and after another bag of antibiotics I was told. You were so dehydrated when we got here the IV bag of fluids was practically sucked into your arm," she grins a little. "And I'd like you to come to my place so I can make sure you take care of yourself this time in case you don't remember to."

"Thank you," I smile kindly before turning my head to the ugly privacy curtains of another hospital. "But I really need to be alone right now. I have so much to think about and so many decisions to make, and I need to be alone to do it. I really appreciate the offer, but I need to get out of here for my own space. I don't think it's normal for one person to spend so much time in hospitals."

"It isn't normal, but neither are you," she says so seriously I laugh like I'm sure she intended.

"Thanks for visiting me this morning and for bringing me in," I add because I'm not sure what would've happened if she hasn't.

"I'm going to grab you a phone. But I'll be back in an hour."

"You don't have to."

We are US...

"I know I don't. But I will be," she squeezes my hand one more time before leaving me alone.
Totally alone.
But at least Z and Mackenzie are no longer alone, which is just about the happiest news I could get right now.

Once Kayla leaves and a nurse checks my IV and stomach again I'm happy to be feeling a little better. I'm going back to the hotel soon 4 1/2 blocks from Z and Mackenzie where I'll be close enough to always sense them, but far enough away to never see them. And that's okay.
Truly.
I know my life isn't meant to be happy, but I also know theirs is. And they *should* be happy. Z is an amazing person who deserves happiness, and Mackenzie will always know happiness and stability with him. They are meant for each other, and I'm okay with my place on the outside now because its where I've always belonged and where I'm most comfortable being anyway.
Experiencing moments of happiness in my life has never benefitted me long term, and I don't want to feel them anymore.
I'm Suzanne. And though maybe not *her* anymore, I'm not much more than the sad her of before and I'm slowly becoming okay with that.

ϘϘϘϘϘ

Entering my hotel room with Kayla a few hours later, I'm exhausted.
"I don't want to go, Suzanne. I want to stay for the night," Kayla lies.
"You've been an amazing friend today, but please go home.
"You're no trouble, Suzanne," she says seriously, but I laugh anyway.
"Said NO ONE ever. All I am is trouble Kayla," I grin. "But I need my own space. And I have to learn how to deal with all this by myself now."
"Tomorrow? Maybe I'll come back for dinner and we'll invite Kayla," she says softly but the effect is the same as a scream. Fear and sadness settle in deep thinking of New York Kayla. I don't want to end my

relationship with Kayla completely, so avoiding her at all costs feels like the only way I can ignore our friendship's official end.
 "I'm supposed to ask you if you want to deal with all the gifts and cards, or if you want Z to?"
 "I can do it. Just tell him to send them over. It's not like I have anything else to do," I smile but she doesn't play along.
 "Will you talk to Z? He misses you, Suzanne."
 "I will... Just not yet. I can't right now, Kayla. I need to be okay with not being together with Z anymore before I can be okay with being casual acquaintances with him at this point. Plus you'll give me Mackenzie updates which I'll love." And cry over, I don't add. "Bye, baby," I say like she does but not half as sexy or as flirty as she pulls off.

 Once I close the door on Kayla I know what I want to do, but I'll eat instead. I found out that Z rented me this suite with a full fridge and little kitchenette on purpose so I *would* eat. And though I forgot to eat this weekend, I won't do that again.
 Tidying up quickly, I make my way back down to the little deli mart half a block away to grab some food for my temporary home, and I'm kind of impressed with myself.
 I'm sane, relatively normal looking, and as functional as I need to be. I'm also ridiculously calm for walking into a store by myself with my hideous face showing.
 Smiling, I remember Mack always talking baby-steps. I remember even I used the term 'baby-steps' before. Though it's been quite a while for me, I seem to have picked up where I was before.
 Walking into the Deli-Mart alone is my first baby-step since I lost everything. It's also the first baby-step I have to make to handle everything.
 And I will.

ꀀꀀꀀꀀꀀ

We are US...

Grabbing my new phone without thinking, "Hello?"
"Hi." Oh no... Why is he calling me now? Unless...
"Is Mackenzie okay?" I cry out bracing for the worst.
"She's fine, Suzanne. Don't panic. She's sleeping beside me," he says softly as I exhale.
"Then why are you calling?" Oops. That sounded way ruder than I meant.
Waiting for a silent eternity, Z finally says simply, "I called to talk to you." *Why* sounds a little pathetic so I keep quiet. "I heard you were in the hospital yesterday because your incision was infected," he says sounding concerned, but at least it explains *why* he called me. "Are you still there?" He asks with his smile-voice making me want to cry.
"I'm here, and I'm fine. Are *you* okay?"
"Yes. Why did you answer this time?"
"I thought it was Kayla." Oh, ooops. Barking a quick laugh Z doesn't seem offended by what I accidentally said.
"Understood."
"Do you need something, Z?"
"No. I just wanted to talk to you, and Mackenzie is snuggled up beside me on the couch in her *almost* perfectly knitted baby blanket," he says again smiling I can hear. "So I wanted to call to let you know it's her favorite blanket."
"It is?" I grin happily until reality returns. "Um, are you teasing me? Because she's only 7 days old and it's not like she has a preference for anything at this point, so there's no way to know that, Z." Feeling irritated by his stupid joke, I shut down a little.
"I'm not teasing you. At all actually. She's a really calm baby overall. But when she *is* crying and I wrap her in your blanket she always settles immediately. It's like a trick I've figured out since yesterday," he says proudly.
Sitting on the couch I'm starting to believe him, and I have to know, "What else have you figured out?"
"Baby poop is disgusting," he moans as I laugh. "No, Suzanne, like *really* disgusting. Almost like wet Dijon mustard, and it gets everywhere if you don't get the diaper just right I learned the hard way. Incidentally, the throw blanket you love at the end of our bed is mustard poo-stained for life," he laughs. "I even had it under my thumb nail last night," Z groans making me laugh harder.

"Same thing for me with Matthew. When he was first born, I was stunned by the Dijon mustard, and so messed up scrubbing my hands when it got under my nails once. Even though I knew my hand was clean, I couldn't eat with my right hand for like a week," I laugh again remembering that day of poo. "Kayla thought I was hysterical when I used an SOS pad on my fingers."

"I used bathroom cleanser on my thumb," he adds as I smile.

"What's she like? I mean Kayla has given me updates, almost hourly, but what's she really like, Z?" Practically holding my breath, I know he's going to say the most perfect Z-ism ever and I'm dying to know but dreading hearing it as well.

"Ah, she's really boring actually." *WHAT?!* That was NOT a Z-ism, or what I ever expected him to say.

"*Boring?*"

"Yeah. Drink, poo, sleep. That's all there is to her. And to be honest I can't wait to have a little hockey player one day, because right now she's really boring to be around," he says seriously until I realize there is absolutely no way he is.

"Are you messing with me?"

"Yes..." He says again with his smile-voice and my relief is loud and long as I exhale. "Did you actually believe me for a second there?"

"Well, you sounded so serious and they kind of are boring when they're that new, so I thought maybe for a second. But I hoped not."

"*Very* not. She's just so sweet, Suzanne. Like always wrapped in my arms or on my chest or beside me. And I can make her fall asleep by just touching her little forehead with my thumb."

Moaning a little, I realize this is getting to dangerous territory suddenly. I feel the pain growing, and I know missing her is going to be an agony I won't be able to hide much longer from Z. The loneliness is going to start swallowing me up inside again, and I can't hold on much longer.

"I'm sorry," Z whispers. "I wasn't trying to be insensitive. I just wanted to talk about her to you so maybe you didn't miss her so much, and so maybe I didn't miss talking to you so much," he says again so sadly I'm at the absolute end of my calm.

It's time to hang up now before he hears me lose it.

"Thank you for telling me about her, Z. But I, ah, have to go out now."

"Where?" Shit, I've got nothing. "Why are you hanging up? Just tell me," he pushes before I start to cry. Ugh. "*Why*, Suzanne?"

We are US...

  Holding in the upset, I try to explain so he'll leave it alone. "Because thinking of you hurts and thinking of Mackenzie hurts worse. And I'm trying to be strong right now, but you're making me almost cry. And I can't keep crying all day, *every* day Z if I'm going to learn to live without you both. Okay?"
  "I'm still working on getting everything resolved Suzanne. I haven't stopped and I *won't* stop until you're in her life again." Wow, I heard that one clearly. *Her* life, not his.
  "Okay. Thank you. But I have to go, Z. Good night. Be safe, okay?"
  "Why wouldn't I be safe?"
  "I don't know. Nothing really feels safe anymore, does it?"
  "Suzanne-"
  "Good night, Z."
  Hanging up, I just stand when the tears start to win. Walking to my make-shift bedroom, I'm swamped by exhaustion and swallowed by pain. Collapsing on my bed to sleep, I miss them so much I feel nothing but a heart-breaking loss so deep it should've actually killed me by now.

CHAPTER 36

Opening the door, the delivery man hands me the huge box I was expecting. And after tipping him for taking the box to the table and locking the door behind him I'm ready. I also know this will be brutal, but I need to do *something* today.

After sleeping for almost a straight 9 hours last night, I can't stop picturing Z holding Mackenzie on his chest. I picture it so clearly it makes me smile *and* cry. I see his dark smooth chest, and her tiny little sweetness lying flat on his heart and the image is so beautiful, I almost hate it.

Thinking of them together like that doesn't make me feel good, and it doesn't make me feel calm. It makes me enraged that I'm missing everything. Because of my horrific past and my disgusting reactions to it, I am missing everything with the 2 people I love most in the world, and I'm so angry I could scream or punch something, though I don't. I hold in the anger until it changes back to the more manageable sadness I spend my days consumed with.

Tearing open the box, it's filled with way more cards than I remembered, and certainly more than I imagined. God, Z is popular, because these cards sure as hell aren't from my side of like 5 people who know or like me. Well, more like 2 people who still like me now.

Opening card after card, writing the sender's name for future thank you's or return cards should it be required, I suddenly gasp when I see her very distinctive handwriting on an envelope.

Looking perfectly generic almost like a card envelope from any gift shop anywhere, I drop it like it could poison me on contact. Holy *SHIT!* She sent me a card.

Shaking my head with the most incredulous huff ever, I pick it back up to see what she wrote. Slipping the boring, uninspired card of a little duck following the mother duck I assume, it says only 'Congratulations on the birth of your little duckling', and honest to Christ I burst out laughing.

We are US...

This is so not her, and so not her style, and holy *shit* this must've pained her so badly to purchase I can almost picture her pinched face of disgust.

Opening the cheesy card, there is only one sentence in the middle.

Don't get used to it, because I'm not done yet.

Don't get used to what?

Looking at her squiggly handwriting that she tried to unsquiggle a little, I remember tracing her name over and over again when I was little. I actually practiced this handwriting because I thought she'd like it if I wrote just like her.

Actually, I was just so desperate for her to like *anything* about me, I tried anything and everything all the time to get her approval. But it never worked, and she never stopped hating me.

Because I'm not done yet. With *what?* Torturing me? Abusing me? Yes you are, bitch!

Don't get used to it... To what? The money? My marriage? What shouldn't I get used to? Think like a psychotic bitch, Suzanne. *Think* like her. What shouldn't I get used to?

Oh. My. **God.** Like I can actually hear her voice sneering as she speaks to me, I understand.

Mackenzie...

Diving for the coffee table, I speed dial Z because there's no time to even think.

"Hi, how-"

"It was her that did it!" I scream.

"Suzanne, calm down. Who did what?"

"The *cunt*, Z!"

"At the hotel?" He yells snapping me back coherent. "What did she do!?" He yells again like he can't understand what I'm saying.

"I just opened a ridiculous card from her and she wrote 'Don't get used to it, because I'm not done yet.' Get it? Don't get used to the baby because she's not done yet?"

"Ah, maybe-"

"No. Listen to me, Z. I'm sure of this. I *know* her, and this is just like her to give a veiled threat. A threat that doesn't mean anything to anyone but the receiver."

"But she said don't get used to *it*, like a something, Suzanne, not your baby," he tries to reason with me.

"I know it looks like that. And that's actually what I thought first, like the money, or my marriage, or some kind of thing. The 'it' confused me until I realized she meant the baby was the it."

"How do you know?" Z asks now with more suspicion and less disbelief in his voice.

"Um, she used to call me the *It* Z," I moan quickly as my dark childhood memories flood my mind. "It used to sit quietly at the dinner table with her measured food, ignored and hated while It's 2 parents talked and laughed and pretended It was there."

"Suzanne, I need you to breathe slowly, love. You don't need to think about that anymore. You're not It, and you've never been It to me."

Shaking, Z's sad voice through the phone is enough to get me out of my head. I hate when he sounds sad like that. "I'm okay, Z. Please don't be sad. I was just trying to explain the *It* to you. But there's more."

"Are you okay?" He whispers and I love him. So much. So deeply. I hold in the upset to make everything right- or at least right*er*.

"I'm fine," I pause for a second to clear my head again. "When did these cards arrive?"

"I think that box was right from the hospital."

"Were any couriered? Like in an outside envelope?"

"Some, yes."

"Okay. Well, this envelope has no post mark and it looks totally pristine and unopened, but I knew her handwriting immediately. I used to want her to like me so I tried to be like her in any way I could so she didn't hurt me." When I hear Z moan again, I try to stop my train of thoughts from going back to my past. Kind of. "Never mind about that." Shit, head in the game, Suzanne. "Anyway, if this card came from Chicago when I was in the hospital, then she would've sent it for the due date without knowing what I had at the time. That's why it was an It and not a him or her. Well that, and she's a psycho who still likes to remind me of all the bad stuff whenever she can," I laugh cry quickly. Ugh. *Focus!* "People knew the date of my C-Section, right?"

"Yes," he says with his quiet anger. "Someone reported it after finding out at the hospital while snooping for a story. Stinson read it and let me know a few months ago," Z exhales and I swear I hear him actually shaking his head.

Wiping away those annoying tears that only fall from your eyes when you're frustrated or totally pissed, I try to explain what I'm thinking.

"So she didn't know what I was having when it was sent but she did know my due date was December 4th, and somehow she got a card couriered to us on my due date or within a day or two of it, right?" I cry sounding a little hysterical the more I speak. Shit.

"*Fuck...*" he moans thinking.

"No! Fuck *me*. I-"

"Maybe later, love. Try to focus, okay?" Z suddenly interrupts my growing anxiety and as his words sink in I burst out laughing. Like a crazy laugh which just about rips my stomach back open, but it feels so good to suddenly laugh I don't care about the collateral damage.

Winding down, I can still hear his smile-voice when he asks, "Can you be sure it was from her?"

"A thousand percent. Her writing is super squiggly and almost beautifully old fashioned. I know it's her writing, Z. And the judge-"

"The judge!" Z yells when he sees what I'm seeing. "That fuckhead put through the order late in the day when I couldn't get to court to either stop it or delay it- just like Mack said."

"And the anonymous phone call saying I hurt Mackenzie-"

"Could've come from *anywhere* anonymously. And from what I've learned an emergency removal with a police escort isn't common practice unless there is a medical report to substantiate the investigation and immediate danger or abuse to the child, or even a police witness to the abuse. Usually, there is if not a 2 visit investigation, there is at least *something* physical backing up the court's decision for an emergency removal of the child."

"Just like Mack said," I agree. "So I think the judge is the key here. The first judge when Mackenzie was born."

"Who was also the judge who delayed me over the weekend."

"He was?"

"Yes. Which my lawyers couldn't understand either. As a *prominent New York City business man and a well-known Philanthropist,*" Z says and I know he's smirking at the famous description of himself he hates, "Our lawyers couldn't understand how I was not only be denied custody of my own daughter, but pushed from the emergency hearing that was actually set up by Child Protective Services themselves to have this quickly settled. Even Hillary Mason attempted to have this rectified quickly when she saw no abuse to Mackenzie and after she spoke to the hospital staff the next day when you were still there. She wrote on record her findings of no abuse, and supplied Mack and Kayla's witness accounts and affidavits the day after that," he exhales like he's both angry and exhausted. "She believed you, Suzanne, she told my lawyer Brandon off the record." Oh.

  Shaking my head a little, the anxiety and strangeness of our situation has exhausted me. Thinking of what to do or say, I'm hit with the obvious so quickly I gasp my answer. "So find out how she knew him. Find out how much money she paid the judge, or how she knew him."

"Oh, I will."

"You have to be careful, Z."

"*Really*?" He asks not quite angrily, but more irritated that I think he would be careless.

"Not like that. I assume Mackenzie is protected?" I whisper words I hoped I'd never have to ask.

"Very," he exhales slowly.

"Thank you." God, that hurts thinking Mackenzie could ever be in physical trouble because of me. "Okay, here's what I'm thinking. You have lots of money and influence, but it was still hard for you to get her back or even to stop all this insanity from happening, right?"

"Yes."

"Okay. Well, my- um, *Elizabeth* had lots of money, but it was her influence that was everything to her. Think about what they all did for years without getting caught, or without tarnishing their perfect social standings and reputations until I remembered everything and came out. But her influence runs deeper than yours because it's like old school influence- influence and almost honor that runs deep. You know yourself, it's not the same as it used to be. You have many people you can influence or pull strings with, but only with your money. And I don't mean that bad!" I quickly throw in but he just says 'keep going', so I do. "This isn't the kind of generation that holds honor or secrets, or anything like her people did. *Obviously.* And overall your power lies in being popular because you donate lots of money and have your own charities and stuff. But people would take just as strongly to the next someone else throwing around money. Ugh... Not that you're doing that. Shit. I am *not* trying to offend you at all, Z. You're amazing and everyone loves you for a reason."

"But money talks."

"Yes. And she was one of America's *elite*, remember? So even though she's in prison and her money is probably almost gone, she was still elite, so-"
"She could still influence many friends and acquaintances from her generation."
"Yes. Find the original judge, and you'll find her."
"Tell me again the exact words from the card. I'm writing them down," he says already moving I can hear. "Go ahead, love," he whispers and I actually smile at his accidental affection.
"Don't get used to it, because I'm not done yet."
Growling, Z says everything. "Oh, she's done."

Waiting, neither speak and my head is spinning too rapidly between my past and my present to make sense of anything but this one fact in front of me. My mother is a fucking bitch who is *still* ruining my life.
"Where's Mackenzie?"
"Right here with Kayla." Oh!
"Which Kayla?" Wow, my heart is breaking again.
"Rinaldi-MacDonald," he says simply, probably waiting for me to lose it. But I'm not going to lose it- I'm grateful.
"That's good. Mackenzie needs a mother, and I'm happy she has Kayla."
"Suzanne, I'm going to fix this. And you'll see her soon, I promise. You did really good, love. I didn't make the connection to that bitch myself because I naively thought she was a non-issue in prison. But I should've thought-"
"You're not a psycho like we are, Z, so you couldn't have possibly thought like us. Plus I never told you I was It growing up."
"You're not an It, Suzanne. You've *never* been like that to me."
"Thank you," I smile to myself. "I'm going to go. Um, will you let me know what you find out? Maybe Glenn can pull some strings to get the judge's records or bank accounts or something subpoenaed? I don't actually know how any of this works," I giggle shaking my head thinking of t.v. detective shows suddenly.
"Oh, we will. And of course I'll let you know everything I find out as soon as I know it. Listen to me for a second, Suzanne," Z says seriously. "This isn't over. I told you that before, and I meant it. Just give me a little more time and I'm going to fix this for you so you can see and be with Mackenzie. But you have to trust me to fix this this time."

Crying softly before hanging up my final words burst from my chest when there's no stopping the desperation I feel. "I wish I could know you both again." Oh. *Ow.*

"Soon, love. I promise."

Hanging up quickly, I need those to be his last words to me today. He didn't say Mackenzie only, and he didn't say *not* him. He said soon.

Pulling up my big girl panties I decide I can hold out and wait for soon.

Moving back to the table I place the uglyass card to the side of all the others.

"I hate you..." I cry staring at the cheesy card from the evil bitch who ruined my life again.

Again.

We are US...

CHAPTER 37

2 days. To goddamn days! But nothing is fixed and I'm still without them. Mackenzie is 11 days old now, and I barely remember what she looks like. Well, I mean I do, but only in my pink blanket, hat wearing version of her newborn face. And yes, Kayla and Z have offered to send me pictures but I don't want one. A picture won't help me remember how she felt, and I can't stare at a picture all day until my eyes bleed to try to replace her with a copy, which I know I absolutely would do.

At least Z has called me 4 times since I explained my thoughts on the nasty bitch who birthed me. He has called with updates and excitement about where they're headed and what they're trying to find. He *has* updated me, but he hasn't fixed it yet. And I'm slowly going mental.

Kayla also calls me every few hours, which though nice, is a little too much Chicago Kayla for me. Between repeating everything she's heard, describing Mackenzie and trying to distract me with sexy tales of her and Marty, I want to kill myself, or *her* actually.

Like I need sexy visuals of her and Marty right now? I'd much rather stew silently waiting for something- *anything* to happen while my stomach finally heels and my heart slowly mends a little.

Soon.

God, I know I was right about this. I know she did something to make this all happen to me. I know it with such certainty, the purpose I feel destroying her is helping keep the heartache and loneliness away a little.

Jumping from the knock on the hotel room door, I nearly scream as I run for it. Please be Z. *Pleeeeease....* Resting my swimming head on the door jamb I'm dying to see him. "Hello?"

"Suzanne... It's me and Kayla and Matthew," Mack says softly as the air leaves my lungs on a gasp.

Crying out, I slide my hand to the lock but can't quite turn it. I want to see them so badly, and I need to hold Matthew. I miss my little angel so much, but I don't think I can do this with them yet. I can't see their hatred and anger right now because "I'm just hanging on to my last bits of sanity by a thread," I whisper unintentionally out loud.

"Open the door, Suzanne. We'd like to talk to you," Mack soothes and I almost unlock the door.

"Um, on a scale of 1 to 10 how much do you hate me?" I ask like the loser he knows so well.

Actually laughing a little Mack answers my stupid anyway. "I'm like a 2 now, and Kayla's hovering around 5, I think."

"Okay."

Slipping the bar lock open I think I can handle a 2 and 5. And even if I can't, what's the worst that can happen at this point? I cry, which they'll expect, or I break down which they wait for always. 2 and 5 seems almost too kind for what I said to them.

Stepping away, I take a big breath before opening the door to the kind eyes of Mack. Walking right in he doesn't pause or ask permission, he just hugs me his Mack hug, and my reaction is immediate. Like we both knew, I start crying in his arms while he holds me tightly.

"I'm so sorry. I *never* meant a word I said. I was just stunned and shocked and kind of broken when she was taken away."

"I know."

"I know you know, but I *really* need you to know. Honestly, Mack, I don't think for one second you would hurt me or Mackenzie and I didn't mean to make my sadness turn into anger at you. I didn't. And I don't. I just snapped from the pain, I think."

"I know, Suzanne," he soothes again as I bawl all over his coat.

"Please forgive me. *Please?*"

"I do," he nods against my head and my heartache seems so complete with his forgiveness I can't speak anymore. I have so many things to say, and so much to tell him, and I miss him so much, but I have no words left.

Pulling away after forever I finally step away from the door so Kayla can enter fully. Looking up at her eyes quickly, I see the anger, but I also see an emotion I'd forgotten she possesses in abundance- *compassion*.

"I, ah-"

"Look, I'm going to rip your face off later. Like rip it off until I feel better, but right now someone needs to see you. So I'm holding in ripping your face off for now. But later, the gloves are definitely coming off," she says so seriously I can't speak while she glares at me.

"Okay. I deserve it," I nod relieved she's even *willing* to rip my face off.

"Yes, you do. But later," she almost smiles. Like a tiny slight side grin that she quickly masks with her anger again. But it's something shy of pure hatred, so I'll take it.

Looking at Matthew in his blue super puffy snowsuit, I'm just dying to hold him. God, I can't believe I haven't seen him in 11 days either, and I miss him so much my heart is aching. I don't think 2 days went by when I didn't see him since he was born, and after 7 months with him keeping me happy and calm I need his sweetness to ease my broken heart desperately.

Waiting for something, Kayla moves right past me to the couch and sits down. "Come here," she says softly and I do immediately. God, I want to hold him but I wait until she turns him to me.

OH. MY. **GOD!!**

When she turns Matthew around I'm winded but manage a scream and a mouth-covering wail in my shock.

Laughing at me, Kayla says with a funny expression, "We switched them out. Matthew is with Z at your place."

"Wha- Oh my *god*..." I cry staring at Mackenzie because I'm unable to move.

"Suzanne, take her. She's okay, but she needs to get out of these clothes. We kind of bulked her up to look bigger than she is. We even put Z's socks in the feet and arms so they looked filled out when her little body looked too tiny and weird in Matthew's snowsuit."

Shaking my head, I beg, "I can touch her?"

"Of course you can. Z wanted you to see her and he begged us to switch out our babies," she smiles again sweetly with a little giggle at either the conspiracy or my still stunned face. "Take your baby, Suzanne. We're visiting for at least an hour."

Leaning forward I swear to god I don't know what to do. I can barely touch her my hands are shaking so badly, and I'm still so shocked looking at her I'm scared I'll do something wrong.

But then I do take her and everything falls into place.

Laying her on the uglyass hotel room couch, I start undressing her. Slipping the hood off I can't believe how badly I want to touch her.

Unzipping and removing her little arms out of the snowsuit is easy because her arms aren't even really in the arms of the coat at all, though the material feels heavy and full. Dripping tears all over Matthew's snowsuit, I'm almost done. So soon. God, she's right here, and I can

smell her already.
 When she suddenly wakes up with a tiny cry I'm dying to soothe her. Lifting her into my arms everything falls away but her little cries and the feel of her on my chest and shoulder.
 Oh god... This is everything.
 "Thank you," I weep holding my daughter finally.

 But her crying doesn't stop with me holding her like I always imagined it would. Magically, I always thought if I held her she wouldn't cry anymore. I believed my body holding her would always make her happy. But-
 Looking desperately at Kayla, she only smiles. "She's just hungry, Suzanne. Here," she says reaching for Matthew's diaper bag.
 "Can I nurse her? I've been pumping every day. Even when I was in the hospital the other day."
 "You have?" She asks as I nod. "You can try, but she may not take to you *only* because she's been on formula, Suzanne. Not because it's you," she adds quickly when I cry harder.
 "Can I try? Or maybe I shouldn't if she's been fed formula? What do I do? I don't want to mess her up if I'm not going to see her again," I cry out as the pain lashes my heart again.
 "Ah..." Kayla seems just as sad as I feel when she can't answer immediately letting me know the answer by her desperate hesitation.
 "It's okay. I don't want to make this bad for her." Even when I feel my own breasts heavy like they know she's near me, I can't do it. I won't hurt my baby, intentionally or not. "Do you have a bottle?" I ask past my own hurt and the sympathetic tears I see in Kayla's eyes.
 "Here," she hands me a little bottle from the bottle warmer thingy. "Do you want some privacy with her?"
 "You trust me?" I ask without thinking and I have my answer by her pissed off groan.
 "We're not the bad guys, Suzanne. And *we* know you didn't hurt her. So of course we trust you with her. Christ, would Z have begged us to bring her to you if *he* didn't trust you with his daughter?"
 "No, I'm sorry. I'm just nervous and sad and not really thinking clearly. Um, can I go to my room with her?"
 "Of course," she exhales turning to a totally silent Mack watching our exchange.

"Thank you."
Walking to my hotel bedroom, I gently bounce and carry my crying daughter to the bed. Sitting up and against the headboard, I know to use a pillow under my arm for support. When she settles into my chest still crying, I remember my weird noises for Matthew when I finally place the bottle against her sweet little lips.
Wow. Instant silence. Huh. Almost laughing, I'm surprised how she went from crying to total silence but for the little sucking sounds so quickly. Almost like a little baby switch she's in eating mode and she's just so sweet.
Watching her one hand move slightly, I manage to spread my fingers until her little fist closes on my pinkie. With her eyes still closed, she makes little mewing noises while she drinks and I'm just entralled by everything Mackenzie.
God, she's so pretty. She does seem porcelain like Kayla said when she was first born. Her little eyebrows are a soft brown, and her eyelashes are long like Z's though she seems pale like me.
Looking at the door, I hope this isn't too bad or creepy, but I'm just dying to know what color her eyes are now. So using my thumb gently against her eyebrow I pull up slightly as both her eyes flick open quickly before closing again. Quickly, but enough to make me cry out in relief.
Her eyes are dark, maybe even eventually brown like Z's which I love. Or maybe just a dark blue or hazel, even. It doesn't matter though what color in the end, as long as they aren't like my clear blue eyes.
"You're so beautiful, Mackenzie. And I love you more than I ever thought I could love a baby."

When she seems more asleep then eating I slip the tiny bottle from her lips, and though she makes one little sound of protest, she quiets just as quickly.
Moving her to my side, I slide down the bed gently and with the pillow at her back, I snuggle down on my side to hold her as she sleeps against me. Watching her, I take in everything I can hold always with me. I know this visit won't last much longer so I store every detail of her inside my heart for later.

Nearly crying when Kayla sits down beside Mackenzie on the bed, I know what this means and I want to beg Kayla to let her stay with me.

We are US...

"We have to go, Suze. Z's going out and we're supposed to come back to babysit *his* baby this evening," she smiles. "So we have to switch out babies now," she grins at their little game when I smile back.

Knowing this was only temporary, and knowing drama will only hurt Mackenzie I nod and prepare to NOT be upset by her leaving me again. I mean if they did this today, maybe they'll do it again for me once in a while.

"Will you ever bring her back?" I whisper with desperation lacing my raspy, sad voice.

"As soon as possible. And this isn't forever Suzanne, I promise. It's just for right now." Nodding, I try to believe her. Kayla has never lied to me before so I have to trust she isn't lying to me now.

"I know you're going to rip my face off still and I'm okay with that. But I have to say something today. Please?" Smiling sadly, Kayla nods before I continue. "Thank you for taking care of her. I know you were at Cedardale all the time when she was there, and I know you've been like a mother to her since she was taken from me," I barely manage to say without tears. "Thank you for being the best person I've ever known to be with her when I can't, even though you want to rip my face off," I add as we both choke up a little.

"Suzanne... You have to stop waiting for people to always hurt you all the time, because honestly, you're missing out on being happy. Yeah, I want to kill you for being horrible to me and Mack, and especially to Z. But that's life and family and friends. I'm going to scream bloody murder at you because I love you. Because if I didn't love you, I would do nothing. I don't have any friends I keep around who I don't care for, so screaming at you makes *me* feel better and then we move on together."

"Okay," I exhale understanding her suddenly.

"As for this little one? I would do anything to help her and love her and keep her safe, even *if* I want to punch her mother in the face."

"I know..." I cry a little smiling. "I know that. I knew that, I just-"

"Not right now, Suzanne. But we'll have this out and then we'll move forward as friends and really as sisters- like the *only* sister I even like," she adds with a laugh as I huff my quick sadness. "But we have to go now. I'm so sorry. We've been here for a few hours and Z really has to get going." A few hours I stared at my baby?

"I understand. Thank you again for this. And please thank Z for me."

"Nope. You call and thank him yourself. He misses you, Suzanne. He's happy with Mackenzie but sad and lonely without you. He's a mess, just like you are. So *call* him."

"Okay."

Watching Kayla redress Mackenzie in Matthew's huge looking snowsuit, I don't speak. There's nothing to say but sad things, so it's best to stay quiet before they leave. Afterward however, I know I'm going to totally lose my shit and cry until I simply pass out.

"Here, hold her for a sec," Kayla passes me my strangely bulky newborn and I almost laugh again at this funny little game they're playing.

Kissing her cheek, I inhale deeply Mackenzie's baby smell and hold it in my lungs. I want to remember it always, especially if I'm not going to see her for a while.

Handing her back to Kayla, I watch Mack swing Matthew's diaper bag over his shoulder and I want to cry that he's still not speaking to me. I want to beg for his forgiveness again and plead that he still love me. I want to be in such a drama, I know to keep my mouth shut. But damn it's hard, I almost giggle.

"Okay. We're going and you have to call Z," Kayla glares until I nod. "We'll bring her back as soon as we can. It's a little over the top, but we don't know who's watching us and now that the press knows all about everything there are reporters everywhere." Nodding, I knew that too, I just wouldn't read or watch any news regarding me.

"Thank you for bringing her to me," I say robotically as I hold the emotion is check. Reminding myself over and over again this isn't forever, this is just for right now like a chant, I'm able to watch them open the door to leave with my baby.

"You can always call me to talk, Suzanne. I tried calling you as I'm sure you recall, then I stopped trying. But I've been waiting for you to come around. I miss you too, Suzanne. And I think you need to understand you're not the only one missing people. We're suddenly all without you as well. But I'm still your speed-dial, okay?" He touches my arm as I exhale.

"I know. It's just been so hard."

"For *everyone*, not just for you. Though I do recognize your pain is much deeper and stronger than ours. But we feel it too, Suzanne," he says so sadly I step right into his hug.

"I do miss you very much."

"Ugh. We have to go, and you two are going to make me cry," Kayla leans in to quickly kiss my forehead as I kiss my own daughter's forehead goodbye again.

"Go. I'll be okay," I smile lamely and they do.

"Call Z," Kayla adds walking to the elevators with Mack's hand on her back and my daughter nestled between them.

Closing and locking the door, I smile cry my way back to my room to lie down beside my daughter's memory.

ϘϘϘϘϘ

"Have they left yet?" Z asks so anxiously I smile. He sounds exactly the same as he always did with me.

"Yes, 5 minutes ago." When Z exhales he sounds so worried about Mackenzie, I know I made the right choice, not only for picking him as the father of my child, but when I stepped out of the equation for him. "Thank you, Z. That was very kind of you."

"It wasn't kind of me, Suzanne. It was *right* of me."

"Well, thank you. That was an amazing surprise- almost like a special Christmas gift I'll never forget."

"I don't want you to ever forget Mackenzie... or me," Z whispers painfully as I tear up to the sound of his voice.

Desprately trying to lighten the mood I ask, "How could I forget you? You're super sexy Z Zinfandel."

Now what? I don't know what else to say, and Z isn't replying or teasing me back. For once the silence is very thick between us, and we both seem almost stuck in the nothing and everything between us.

"Well, I should-"

"You know what this reminds me of?" Z asks cutting off my goodbye.

"Um, *hell*?" I ask seriously until we both laugh sadly.

"Yes, that. But more importantly, I keep thinking of that bible verse about the king who threatened to cut a baby in half when 2 women were claiming the baby as their own. I don't know how it goes exactly, but I get the jist of it, and I keep thinking of it over and over again."

When there is another painful pause I finally ask, "Why?"

"What you did when you walked away last Friday. Ah, I really didn't know what to do right away. I mean I knew we'd win eventually, but that day, after the judge had changed the emergency custody hearing to Monday, I didn't know what to do. Monday seemed forever away, but weeks or even a month without Mackenzie seemed like an eternity. And as of that moment with you, I really didn't know how to get her back quickly. And even if I did know what to do, I never could've asked it of you. That was something I could never ask you to do, but you didn't make me ask. You offered, then pushed, then just made the decision without me so I could get her back quickly. *You* made the selfless choice I could've never done myself or ever asked you to do for her. But you did it. And I'm so grateful, Suzanne," he finally exhales choking up again while I desperately hold all my own sadness inside for him. "You were the mother who would rather walk away without her baby alone in agony, then see her child cut in half."

"I didn't do that. I, ah, just wanted her safe with you."

"Which is exactly the same thing, love. And I can never thank you enough."

"She's your daughter, Z."

"And she's *your* daughter, Suzanne."

"I know, but it's not the same thing."

"Actually, it's *exactly* the same thing. Except you were willing to make the ultimate sacrifice for me and her. And I will never forget what you did. I'll never let Mackenzie forget what you did for her when everything around us turned into this nightmare."

Feeling exhausted suddenly, I need to end this. Talking to Z hurts every part of me that misses him like an agony I'm drowning in. Talking to him and hearing his dark chocolate voice tell me I did a good thing actually hurts because I want to cry 'I made a mistake, and I want her back, and I didn't think it would take this long.' But it *has* taken long and it probably will take much longer. And I don't know how much longer I can stop from begging Z to give her back to me. I don't know how to stop myself from walking into my old home and stealing her right out from under him.

"I have to go," I whisper before the pain is heard in my shaking voice.

"I understand. Please just wait a little longer, Suzanne, and I promise I'll

We are US...

fix this. Soon, okay?"

"Sure..." I whisper back like I actually believe in soon.

CHAPTER 38

Sitting on the couch knitting I honestly feel the insanity coming. Like last time, I know it's near and I know it's going to get me, but I don't know what's going to set it off completely or what I'm going to do with it when it comes. I know it's almost here, and though I'm fighting it with everything I have left, it's getting really hard to keep fighting.

2 days ago I bought a new beautiful little journal I found in a cheesy New York gift shop down the street. The store itself was cheesy, but surprisingly the journal wasn't. I remember knowing I needed it and wanting it for her so badly, I was shaking at checkout.

And when I returned home with the soft pink leather journal I began writing to Mackenzie.

Crazily, and often without rhyme or reason I wrote everything I felt when I first saw her. I told her of the fear and happiness and the complete love I felt when I held her finally. And I even wrote about everything I've thought and felt for her since.

I told her about me and Z together before her and I told her about me and Z apart. In a continuous stream of what the fuck, I cried sometimes, giggled, and even blushed when I explained how her dad could make me blush with just an eyebrow wiggle. Obviously, I didn't write to her the dirty things I do with Z, but I did explain that together Z and I had an intensely passionate, crazy, exhausting relationship filled with love. And then I told her that's how she was made.

I told Mackenzie everything, without all my nasty past details in specifics but everything nonetheless. From my ugly past, to my current uncertainty in their lives I told her where I'm at and what I would love, which is to know her.

I told her my good, bad, ugly and beautiful honestly. I told her I loved her, no matter what happens or what the future holds for all of us.

Afterward, I simply cried my eyes out holding Mackenzie's journal.

We are US...

Later when Z called to update me on nothing, he could tell I was breaking down and when he asked, I told him what I did. I told him about the journal and though I heard his voice change to sad, he kept it together long enough to promise me I'd be able to give her the journal myself soon.
Soon.
God, everything in my life is completely dependent on soon. And soon is killing me. The court date for Z is soon, Christmas is soon, Kayla will come around soon (according to Chicago Kayla) and I won't always be this sad and lonely... *soon.*
But I'm losing it, I know it.
When I went to the store yesterday for a baguette and some Nutella which I was craving like I was still pregnant with Mackenzie, I felt off. I became paranoid and stressed in the store and I had that creepy feeling of being watched. I felt it all over me and inside me again until I had to take a pill to stop the paranoia from making me mental in the store.
It was so bad I called Z to ask if I was still being followed. And thankfully he said yes. In his ever calm voice dealing with me these days, he promised I was safe and I was relieved. Knowing my creeped out feeling was just a feeling that couldn't turn to a bad situation relieved me enough to stop the shaking in the store.
Thanking Z once again for looking out for me, I paid for my baguette and Nutella, enjoyed his laugh when I told him what I was craving and I left the store quickly without incident for the hotel. But Z stayed on the phone with me the whole time anyway. Talking about everything Mackenzie and what his lawyers were working on Z stayed with me until I quickly closed and locked the hotel door behind me.
And then we both exhaled.
Loudly and obviously, we exhaled together my fear, and his uncertainty about my mental health. I knew he was worried I'd lose it and I didn't even blame him. Because realistically I know an 'episode' is coming, just as I know any public *anything* concerning crazy Suzanne Zinfandel is going to hurt all of us, but most of all Mackenzie.
So here I am the very next day, sitting on this couch alone, knitting quietly, crying and screaming inside while the insanity slowly grows threatening to break me if I don't get out of my head soon.
It's December 22nd, my daughter is 18 days old, and I've only seen her twice in 18 days.

Jumping at the sudden knock, I wait for her voice. Kayla Lefferts is the only person who visits me and she always announce herself so I don't go for a knife to protect myself.

"Suzanne?" Kayla yells knocking again.

"Coming. Just a sec."

Dropping my knitting, I run for the bathroom quickly to check my face. Wow, thank god I checked. Crying and foundation are NOT friends and sadly I can't have both.

Quickly reapplying the thick foundation on my scars, I'm so fast I'm worried it looks too gloopy, but I also don't have time to make it perfect. Kayla has never been known for her patience, and I can't handle the constant door knocking or yelling her impatience always turns to.

"I'm coming!" I yell rounding the couch as I reach for the door.

Opening to both Kaylas I'm a little surprised, but not really. They often tag-team like the Rinaldi sisters do, and I think I always knew this was coming. *Shit*.

Walking right past me with Kayla MacDonald following, Kayla asks, "Can you go get dressed properly so we can get out of here?"

"Out of here?" I ask like a moron staring at a quiet New York Kayla.

"Yup. We," she says pointing between themselves, "have last minute oh shit gifts to buy for Christmas and we want you to come with us."

Gasping, I can't tear my eyes away from New York Kayla. "But..." Ugh. I have NO idea what to say here. "I thought you hated me."

"I never hated you. I'm fucking pissed at you, and if I could actually slap your face to feel better, I would. But I don't hate you Suzanne. I hate who you become when you lose your shit, and I hate how dark you turn on us when you can't deal. But I don't hate *you*."

"I'm so sorry, Kayla. I *never* meant what I said. I was just so stunned and heartbroken and angry and I know I was horrible to you, but I never believed for even one second you had anything to do with everything that happened. Never."

"I know-"

"Wait. To tell you the truth, I'm glad Mackenzie has you. Like so thankful she has a mother like you in her life." Keeping in the tears, I force myself to continue even when she steps a foot closer to me. "I love you and I think you're just so amazing, and with the way you are with Matthew I want you to be her mother," I burst into tears. Holy SHIT, this is *killing* me. "You're way better than I am and she needs a good mother

We are US...

and I'm so grateful-"

"*You* are her mother, Suzanne. I'm just a stand in," Kayla says reaching to squeeze my hand.

"But you shouldn't be her stand in. You should be her mom because then she won't be screwed up." Am I actually saying this? "Um, maybe Z should just stop trying to figure all this shit out and leave it the way it is. He has custody and he's happy, and Mackenzie will be happy, and if you keep standing in she'll have a good life." Exhaling, I see everything so clearly again, I wish I could stop this bout of clarity, but I can't. For Mackenzie I can't. "You should tell Z to leave things the way they are..." I moan.

Gasping a quick breath, both Kaylas stare at me and no one moves. I don't know what else I can say, and I don't know how to make this happen.

"Talk to Z for me," I whisper touching her coat sleeve. "Convince him I'm right. Tell him he needs to keep doing what he's doing with Mackenzie- parenting her, loving her, and caring for her. Tell him to keep me out of her life so she can *have* a good life. Z has never done anything wrong, except love me. And he shouldn't be punished for that anymore. And neither should Mackenzie."

"He's not being punished for loving you. He's being fucked over by your crazy bitch of a mother for loving you."

"But it's basically the same thing. It is," I push until she understands. "Whether I'm screwing him up or she is screwing him over, it always comes back to me, and I think it always will. She may have been quiet for a couple years but I should've always known she wasn't finished with me. She'll never finish until I'm either dead or locked away forever. Until I'm broken completely she'll find more to use against me or she'll use more people to hurt me with. And that shouldn't be Z's life, or especially Mackenzie's."

Waiting for something to be said, Kayla is looking at me like she actually wants to slap my face, or maybe hug me. I really can't tell anymore what she's thinking by her facial expressions, and I don't have much more patience to give this. 18 days is less than 3 weeks, I know. But it may as well be an eternity in hell as far as my heart is concerned.

"Are you really willing to walk away from your daughter, Suzanne?"

"I-"

"Think long and hard about what you say right now. Be really fucking sure about the answer you give me right now, because I'm telling you what you say right now is the absolute end of everything between not only me and Mack, but Z and Mackenzie as well. So make damn sure you know what you're saying right now."

"I am-"

"THINK!" She yells at me as I flinch. "Think before you speak, or so help me Kayla won't even be able to pull me off you. I will beat the fucking shit out of you before you even finish speaking. So be sure, Suzanne," she snaps at me again as I stare at her stunned.

"What? Um, why are you so mad at me?" Honestly, I don't get it. I'm telling her she's the better mother and I'm telling her to help Z let go. "What am I doing wrong here?"

"Giving up? Being a pushover? Being a total pussy because things are hard?"

"Things aren't *hard* Kayla, they're all-consuming, and exhausting, and painful, and almost deadly for me," I moan.

"For your child and husband?"

"No. Not for them. To let them go," I finally cry.

"Be really fucking sure, Suzanne. Because this will be forever. Z will never forgive you or love you again. And I guarantee when Mackenzie is old enough to understand, she'll know only a mother who walked away when things were tough for her. That's what she'll know, and that's what neither Z or Mackenzie will ever forgive."

"It not about me, Kayla. It's for them!" I scream until she shuts up and listens to me. "What are you talking about? Why the hell wouldn't they forgive me for walking away and leaving them in peace? Why wouldn't they see my sacrifice?" I yell shaking at her aggression. What the hell is going on here?

"What sacrifice?" She yells back.

"Saying goodbye to them so they're safe from me, and everything that comes with me."

"Safe from what? Your bitch mother?"

"Among other things."

"Like?"

"You *know*, Kayla."

"No, I don't. Tell me."

"Kayla?" Chicago Kayla suddenly intervenes, but neither Kayla or I acknowledge her.

"Tell me. What will they be safe from if you pussy out and step aside like a fucking martyr?" A *martyr?* "Tell me! You chose to have this baby. You carried her and birthed her, and she's alive. She a beautiful little girl and *now* you made a mistake? So tell me, Suzanne. What the fuck are you keeping them safe from?" She screams so loudly her voice actually cracks.

"Me." Shit. There it is again. As usual. "From *me* okay. From the crazyass mother with the even crazier past. From the screwed up wife who exhausts her husband, and from the mother Mackenzie will be embarrassed by. From the woman who wears death and insanity around her neck like the goddamn necklace she loves. *Me,* Kayla. Because let's face it, even if Z figures this out, or fixes it, or works his Zinfandel magic all he and Mackenzie will gain is me. And that's not safe for them, or sane for anyone."

"Because you're scared?"

"Of course I'm scared. Jesus *Christ!* I'm living in a hotel with hope the only thing keeping me from popping pills or *accidentally* falling on my metal knitting needle through my chest. Hope is all there is keeping my insanity away, and hope is for me very lonely. Z doesn't need hope because he has everything he wants."

"Except you," she pushes.

"Without me, look at where he's at. His life is exactly the same but better. He has a daughter he loves without the emotional bullshit being with me requires. And Mackenzie will be raised with love and safety and support. She has all of you without all my crazy mental crap following her around."

"And you?"

"I get to stop hoping," I exhale slowly. "I get to stop being mad and sad, and lonely and unhappy all the time. I get to say goodbye so I can move away from this life I wanted but wasn't meant to have. I get to say goodbye to my husband and daughter so they can have good lives away from the unhappy crazy that is me. They get to be away from the demons and past that always comes back to slap me whenever I think I'm finally happy. That's what they get. And I'm not being a martyr, Kayla, I'm trying to do the right thing for once. I'm trying to exit their lives so they are free to live them."

"Without you?"

"Yes. See, it's not about being a pussy, or weak, or whatever else you

think of me. It's about finally being strong enough to leave. I know I'm not good for them, I *know* that. So I'm making the choice to stop the back and forth, we're together, we're not together merry-go-round that has been my relationship with Z."
"That you always created between the 2 of you."
"Fine. That was always *my* fault."
"That isn't what I meant."
"It doesn't matter what you meant, it's the truth. Every single bad thing or episode or moment taken in my relationship has been by me. Z has never changed or wavered. He says he loves me and he stays put, no matter what happens or what I do. Even with all this- look at him. Z has the baby and the life, and he could cut his loses- he *should* cut his loses, but he never does. He just always comes back to me."
"Because he loves you."
"So?"
Glaring, she actually repeats, "So?"
"So nothing. And so everything. So I'm stepping aside now. Period. That's the point of all of this. All these words and all these tears, and everything I've known and felt for the last 18 days without them is what made this decision. This is the end, and it's my decision to make because once again for whatever reason no one can understand, he won't make the decision that is best for not only Mackenzie but for himself as well."
"So that's it?"
"Yes."
"After everything you've been through, all the challenges faced and the victories won? After loving and living beyond your past enough to make a child with this man you love, that's all? What was the point then?"
What *was* the point? Staring at Kayla no longer angry or disgusted, but looking more resigned to me and my shit, I need to tell her the point so she'll finally walk away and let me go.
"The point was Mackenzie, I think."
"How?" Kayla whispers with tears in her eyes.
"I finally gave back to Z the best, most beautiful gift I could for everything he's done for me. For all the times he loved the shit out of me when I was broken, and for all the times he held me when I cried. Um, for loving me enough to actually give him the child he deserves, without having to deal with all the crazy too. That was the point, Kayla. I get to be the mother of the child he loves without hurting him anymore.

And inevitably, without hurting her when she realizes what I'm really like, and will always *be* like."

Shaking her head, Kayla asks only two sentences that say absolutely everything. "So that's it? You've decided to throw them away?"

"You don't know how I feel and you've never lived the life I have. You will *never* live the life I have, so you shouldn't judge me for this."

"But you're still throwing them away?"

"I don't see it that way and I never will."

"Because you're fucked in the head," she huffs walking to the door without another word. Opening it quickly, it closes slowly because of the annoying spring in the door though it's effective nonetheless. The quiet little snap when it finally closes signals the end of our friendship like a slap across my face never could.

"Suzanne, I-"

"There's nothing to say, Kayla. We said it all, and I think you know deep down I'm right."

"Actually, I don't think you're right deep down or even on the surface. I think you are singlehandedly ruining your entire life again without your mother's help. And it's disgusting to watch."

"So don't," I actually laugh suddenly. Like she could possibly hurt me more than I'm already hurting? Whatever. She has no idea how much pain I can handle. Christ, I didn't even know until I handled it time and time again.

"Go shopping, Kayla, or Martying, or working, or whatever the hell else you do. Because there's nothing left here for you anymore."

"Okay. Bye Suzanne," she says so simply it did actually hurt quite a bit. Dammit, I thought I was immune at this point, but once again I'm wrong.

Laughing, I leave Kayla standing by the door for my makeshift bedroom to collapse on the bed with Mackenzie's journal in my hand and a lifetime of explanations and apologies to write to her so one day she might actually understand enough to forgive me.

Crying, I start my goodbye.
"Dearest Mackenzie…"

CHAPTER 39

Walking around at 7:30 in the morning, I'm a zombie. It's been 2 days since the Kayla showdown and the inevitable Kayla goodbyes. I've slept next to nothing, but I've filled the pink leather journal with my almost everything to my daughter.

I've literally told her everything. The good, the bad, the ugly and the beautiful that is me. I was graphic sometimes, and skated over some graphic events at other times. But I gave her my story, from my sad beginning to this end. And honestly, a nursery rhyme it is *not*.

Anyway, when she's way older, like maybe in her 20's, I hope Z will give it to her so she understands who I was, what I became, and who I tried to be for her. Because I really want Mackenzie to understand I was a deeply troubled, scarred woman who did her very best for her and her dad.

Actually, I need her to understand I didn't walk away because I was selfish or uncaring, or a martyr, or even worse because I didn't love her like Kayla said. I need Mackenzie to understand it was *because* I loved her that I walked away. And I think I succeeded in explaining myself as best as I could.

Mackenzie will know about *It,* and the abuse, and the hatred that was my life before her. And then she'll know about the love and friendships I couldn't keep if she was to be safe. She'll get the very best picture of the mother who loved her, and then I hope she forgives me.

I've even decided to use some of my old money, money I've always felt tainted by but for a good reason. I found a little apartment yesterday far enough away from them so we can *all* move on. I found it, made the call, and in 3 days I'm going to go look at it. It's not available until February 1st, but that gives me a month to pack and move, and to fight Z, which I know I'll have to do when I tell him I'm leaving.

No matter what he feels for me right now, which honestly I am totally confused by, I know he'll fight this, but I'll win inevitably. I'll make myself win. And really what can he do anymore? It's not like he can keep me prisoner in New York or in this hotel indefinitely. He may want to, or not, or I really don't know what he wants anymore, but I'm leaving regardless because I'm done.

Whether Z loves me, likes me, or deep down resents me for all the Suzanne shit all the time, won't matter anymore. I'll be far enough away that he won't have to see me or entertain my newest incarnation of *her*. I'll be far enough away that he can live the life he's meant to live with his daughter and friends.

Because I'll be gone.

Waiting for nothing, I'm numb from my loses and resigned to my future. Loneliness is nothing new for me, and I'm right back where it all started.

I even bought a little iPod yesterday and downloaded my only song. Mr. Cohen no longer sings to me of his Suzanne, but I listen to *her* voice cry for me everything that I am and everything that went wrong.

Oh, Sia... I hear you and I see you so clearly. I wish I could hug you and cry with you. Your voice tears me apart inside as I feel my own heart slowly die. I am alone, too. And nobody can help me.

"Suzanne... " his voice calls.

Putting down my knitting for the hundredth time to revel in his dark voice, I moan. Hearing it call to me again, I truly wish it would stop now. Hearing him whisper in the shower or whisper in my bed is making me crazier. Listening in my dark silence, he's always here speaking my name in my agony of loneliness.

"Please, love. Open the door," he calls softly. But I know this game and I know these tricks. My heart plays with me so often now enticing me to love while forcing me to breathe- but I know the truth now. And no one can help me.

"Suzanne! Please, baby. Please open the door," he yells once more as I laugh.

Do I roll over in bed to nothing again? Do I push open the shower curtain to emptiness? Do I open the door to no one anymore?

Rising, I giggle my way to the door. I know this is another mind game, and I know I can handle as many as it takes until his voice fades away like it did an hour ago. I know I can, because I've been here before and I always survive everything because I'm strong.

Unlocking the door I smile as I throw it open. Okay, more lifelike than usual, I giggle when he doesn't move.

"Stop calling my name please," I beg.

"Suzanne? It's Z," he whispers in my head again.

"Oh, I know. It's always Z in my head. Z whispering his love, and Z telling me to fuck off. It's Z who says he loves me, and Z who says he doesn't like me anymore. It's always Z," I turn to close the door once more.

"Suzanne... Look at me. It really is Z," he steps forward when I laugh.

"I know that, too. It's only ever Z who visits me in my head now because everyone else is gone. But Z always stays in my head to tease and taunt with his smile-voice and his beautiful eyes always watching."

Walking back to my knitting, I sit on the couch and resume my pink lines. When do they change to white again? I think I've lost count like I always do when Z comes to visit.

Kneeling on the floor, Z leans in like he never has before. "What are you making?"

"Your daughter a new baby blanket. But if I actually remember the lines this one will be perfect this time. Because perfection is best and good, and no one ever messes up a perfect-"

"Suzanne. *Look* at me, love. Put down the blanket and really look at me now. I'm here to see you."

"I know," I exhale my sadness across his face. God, these days are the longest I've ever known. "I miss you..."

"I. Am. Here. Suzanne. I'm right in front of you. And I need you to see me now."

"I always see you. But do you ever see me? Sia keeps asking if anybody can see me, and I know how she feels. Nobody ever sees me, and I'm all alone again."

Watching one little tear slide down his cheek Z whispers, "All I ever see is you, love. Everywhere. Always. In Mackenzie and in my heart. All I see is you, Suzanne." Oh.

Crying a quick sob, I cover my mouth and look away. I can't keep doing this all the time. I can't keep imagining these words and wishing Z was here to say them to me. I can't keep doing this to myself anymore.

"When did you last sleep, Suzanne? Like what day?" Z asks leaning to the side to shut my Sia off.

Turning back to Z I honestly don't remember. "I can't sleep anymore because you're never real when I try so I can't feel you breathing under me. I don't sleep because I can't lie on you beside the beautiful *her* on your chest anymore."

"Do you know today is Christmas Eve? Did you remember today was the 24th?"

Shaking my head I know I didn't. "I thought it was Thanksgiving I think. Oh!" Grabbing my flat stomach I know it isn't then anymore because I'm empty. "She's not here so it's not then, but- um, I think I'm confused, Z."

"I know. But it's okay to be."

"It is?"

"Yes. When did you eat last?"

"I don't know. I'm not really hungry anymore." Lifting my shaking hand to touch his soft cheek I have to be sure. "Are you really real this time? I miss you..."

"Yes, I am. And I'm here to visit you on Christmas Eve. I didn't want you to be alone tonight. Can I stay for a visit, love?"

Suddenly crying, I stay quiet. Words are always messy with me, and my head is even messier. But nodding is safe. And I can't ruin everything when I nod.

"I brought you your ring back, Suzanne. It'll fit now and I know you hated taking it off when you were pregnant."

"My ring?" I gasp. Oh *god*... "I need my ring back. I *need* it," I cry.

Reaching in his pocket, Z quickly takes out my ring and slips it back on my shaking hand. "Here, love. Its back," he smiles sweetly.

"This is us. My black and your red and the light. Um, I don't feel the light around us anymore, Z. I never feel it anymore..."

"Its there. It's still all around us, love. I can feel it."

"Oh... Okay."

"Would you like to rest with me? I need to hold you on my chest so badly, I'm hurting inside, Suzanne. And I don't want to hurt anymore."

Gasping a quick breath everything breaks free of me at once. Sobbing, Z turns to the couch and lifts me right in his arms. Holding me hard against his chest, he doesn't let me rise and I wouldn't even if I could.

Z still smells and feel exactly the same. He is so much, and I'm not enough. But right now I don't care about that, I just need to feel him against me holding me warm again.

After forever, Z lifts me right into his arms as he stands. If my weight is too much he doesn't sound like it, and if my tears are too much, he

doesn't shush me. Walking with me, Z leads me to my ugly room in hell.
  "No! Wait. I'm all dirty."
  "You're not dirty, Suzanne. You've never been dirty with me."
  "Yes, I am. And I can't lay with you if I'm the dirty her. I need to be clean with you. I always tried to be clean with you. Please don't make me dirty with you this time," I cry and thrash in his arms to get her away from him.
  "Stop! I'm going to clean you," he says calmly and the panic leaves me at once. Like a snap, he stops all the panic and makes me see.
  Placing me right on the little sink, his hand stays on my chest as he reaches to turn on the shower. Waiting, he adjusts it looking back and forth between the clean water and the dirty me.
  Joining me at the counter Z looks so calm I actually smile for the first time in forever.
  "You're gorgeous, Z. And so deep and dark and delicious, I miss you all the time you know? Even when I make my decisions to let you go, I miss you like the worst pain I've ever known. Oh, and I rhyme now, too," I giggle as he smiles that cutie crooked smile that's new for him.
  "I'm going to take your clothes off now. Very slowly, but it's just us here, okay?" He reminds me before kissing my forehead like he used to.
  When Z raises my shirt overhead, he pauses to gently touch my collarbone and neck. "You're getting so thin, Suzanne. Will you start eating for me?" He asks so seriously, I nod. I'll eat if he wants me to eat. "Thank you," he rubs his hands down my arms to grasp my hands in his.
  "Are you still bleeding?" Shaking my head, I'm too embarrassed to answer. Blushing I look away until he turns my face back to him. "Don't ever be embarrassed with me. Ever, Suzanne. There's nothing between us but us. Remember?"
  "I think I forgot."
  "Please don't forget. We're everything between us, remember? You taught me that."
  "I did?"
  "Yes, you did. Can you stand up? Will you let me get you clean?"
  "Yes, please."
  Slowly moving off the sink, Z holds my shaking hand and leans against me when I list a little forward. Keeping me between his chest and the sink, Z bends slightly to remove my yoga pants as I step out of them. Waiting in my ugly bra and huge underwear, Z keeps his hand on my

chest as he pulls his own sweater over his head one-handed.
  "I always loved that sweater," I say to myself but Z smiles anyway.
  "It's because its black," he grins.
  "I don't think so. Well, that helps. But it's because you always look so big in it. And like strong and manly, and like the man I want to love and-"
  Stopping all my thoughts, Z leans his forehead against my own and just breathes against me as I thaw a little inside. Warming to him, I feel the lonely chill fading away and the warmth of hope threatening to break me again. I know it's coming and I don't want to hope, but I know I can't stay this cold forever.
  "I'm so cold all the time now..."
  "Me too, Suzanne." Oh!
  "You are? I thought I was the one who needed your warm body wrapped around me to keep me warm."
  "No. It's both of us. And I've been so cold without you," he whispers kissing my head. "Come here. Let me help you," he offers pulling away to wrap his arm around my back as we step into the shower together.
  Oh! It's so warm here now.
  "Let me warm you," he whispers as I turn into him.
  Feeling the water slide from my hair down my whole body I shiver strangely from the warmth. Holding onto Z's body, I don't dare speak, and I hold in all the sad. I need to feel this right now. I need to feel Z keeping me warm.
  "Can you lean against the wall?" Nodding, I pull away slowly and watch him smile at my attempt to stand. "I'm going to remove your clothes, but it's still just us here."
  "I know," I smile a little finally.
  Waiting, Z unlatches and slips my bra from my arms as my breasts fall heavy and full on my chest. Covering them up, Z doesn't acknowledge them or me before he slides his hands around my waist to lower my black granny panties to the shower floor.
  Rising, he looks at my face so intensely, I can't even blink as his long lashes fill with water diamonds. "Is it still just us here?"
  "Yes."
  "I'm going to clean you now and I want you to watch my eyes. Stay right here with me. Promise?"
  "Yes..." When Z raises his arm with soap he's slow but soft. Cleaning me he doesn't touch me where he shouldn't and he doesn't linger where he

could.

"I'll turn my back while you clean yourself down there, okay?"

Placing the soap in my head, Z kisses my lips quickly but softly as I exhale the last of the dream. He IS here, and I know the difference now. This is Z because even my dream Z knows to never touch me without my real Z here.

"I'm fully awake now Z. And I know you're real now," I whisper to his back as he nods.

Touching myself, I finish cleaning the filthy from my body as the past slides away with the suds down the drain. I'm clean again, and I can now be clean with Z.

"I'm very tired, Z."

Turning to me, he says a very heartfelt, "I know," before covering my little body in his large one. "Let me get you a towel," he reaches but I point to the back of the door until he sees my black robe. "You still need to be dried first."

"No... The towels are too small and I'm never covered up. Please just give me my robe, Z. Please?" I beg as the naked shakes start.

"Here, love. It's just us, right?" Nodding, I wait to be covered and finally exhale when I am. "It's just you and me here, and I need to lie down with you."

Stepping out of the shower to pull the curtain away, Z holds the tiny towel in one hand and my arm in his other. Walking us to the bedroom, he makes weird sloshy sounds until I understand.

"Oh! Your clothes. You're clothed. I didn't see," I moan as reality surfaces completely. Sitting on the side of my bed, the complete exhaustion I feel is replaced only with the man in front of me. "I'm okay now, I think. Um, I won't look, so you can take off your clothes. I'm okay now. I *am* now." Shit! Babble babble. Crazy Suzanne. And here we go for another round.

"Get into bed, love, and don't look at me," Z says softly so I do as I'm told. Crawling under the covers, my body is freezing in my wet robe but I don't care. I'm already sleeping in my mind.

When I'm suddenly lifted, everything falls into place. He's here. And I'm alive. Snuggling into his chest and side, I touch the beautiful *her* on his chest and I wish for everything between us always as I fade away.

ҨҨҨҨҨ

We are US...

Jolting awake, I feel him and look to see his dark eyes watching me still. Looking around the hotel room, I forgot for a second where I was until everything suddenly comes crashing down around me.

"Where's Mackenzie?"

"She's having her first sleep over with Aunt Kayla." *What?!* "The *good* Aunt Kayla," he quickly amends with a grin. "And I've already called, and she's sleeping like the perfect little bugger she isn't with me."

"What does the mean?"

"Well, Kayla says because she has me totally wrapped, I can't let her even whimper without holding her, and now if I'm around she won't sleep or feed or do anything *unless* I'm holding her," Z says so proudly I smile up at him.

"Good. She *should* have you wrapped. God knows I wanted to."

"Ah, news flash, Suzanne. You've had me wrapped since the first moment I met you at that dive hotel outside of Chicago."

"I doubt it," I groan. "I was a freak, and I'm still a freak," I laugh as he turns me a little closer to him.

"Yes, you are," he smirks as I swat his chest lightly. "But I kind of like that about you," he smiles so sadly suddenly, the air changes around us making the need to flee almost unbearable.

Sitting up suddenly, I flinch as my stomach pulls until he stops my retreat. "Oh, Suzanne... Does this still hurt?" He asks touching softly my flat upper stomach above the flubby lower belly goosh I'll never get rid of now.

"Not on the outside. But I hurt always inside now," I whisper as he watches. Nodding like he understands, we both touch my stomach together. "The pain never stops. But it's okay. I like pain now because I never forget anything if I still feel all the pain all the time. That makes sense, right?" Well, it did in my head anyway.

"Yes, it makes sense. I miss you, Suzanne. And I'm struggling right now without you. You make me very happy. So without you I feel like I'm missing something good and beautiful, and it makes me hurt all the time, too."

"But-"

"There is no but, Suzanne. You are my love. So without you I feel sad."

"Wow," I exhale his beautiful confession. "Well, this sucks," I huff as he laughs.

"It does suck. But it won't suck forever. I promise."

Hearing him promise, I'm already turning away again. "I hate this and I can't keep doing this, Z. I'm so tired all the time, but not just physically. Emotionally, I'm a mess. And I've realized these past 3 weeks I'm tired of always struggling to be with you."

"I feel the same, Suzanne. I'm tired of the constant ups and downs we go through. And I'd really like a little calm now for a while."

Looking back at Z, I say the truth of everything between us. "But there will never be calm with me. Don't you understand that by now? When has there ever been, or when will there ever be calm? If it's not actually me losing my shit, it's someone else hurting us because of me. So there is no calm. There are just times when it's less stressful, but they never last and we always end up worse off and sometimes even further apart. We just can't catch a break, and I can't seem to keep it together long enough to give us a break from all the Suzanne shit all the time."

"I know. But this time wasn't you, and that's what I realized after the initial anger faded. Yes, I was pissed at you after you freaked out on me in the hospital. And I was even more pissed when I thought you were totally ignoring me with all this shit because *you* couldn't deal. But then when you stepped away so I could get Mackenzie quickly, I wasn't angry anymore. I realized how hard all this was for you and it made your freak out if not acceptable, then at least understandable to me. And after speaking to Mack, I realized just *how* hard this has all been for you."

Looking back at Z, I wish I could explain what I'm feeling, or what I plan to do. I'll tell him eventually but right now seems just too sad between us, and I don't want to add to the hurt right now.

"I understand how this situation could have made you snap. I see it, Suzanne. I understand from your perspective what made you freak out. I know you never wanted a child because of your past, then you had a child who died. Then you finally decided to make a child with me, and she lived... Only to be taken away from you again. I see everything now, and I understand why you'd feel broken inside from all the loss and disappointment," he says as I feel my silent tears drip down my face. "And I'm sorry this all happened to you and to us. But it isn't forever. I promised you, and I've almost got it worked out."

"How?" I ask quietly as hope threatens to break me again.

"On January 6th I have the custody hearing."

"You do?"

"Yes, me. And no one is going to fight giving me Mackenzie back."

"That's good," I whisper because it IS good.

"And then we're working out the you details. Child Protective Services, along with me and Mack are going to ask the judge to approve 3 supervised visits between you and Mackenzie a week for 4 weeks, until we have another custody hearing on February 2nd for you. And at that time we're going to ask the judge to allow you back into our home so you can be with me and Mackenzie."

"But-"

Shaking his head, he actually smiles before speaking. "There is no but, Suzanne. No one wants to see you away from Mackenzie, least of all me. And everyone seems to understand and accept the anonymous tip made was bullshit though it did set up a series of events that couldn't be completely circumvented once in motion. We have been able to work around them, sidestep and shorten them however. And as long as everything stays good around us no one sees any problem with you, me, and Mackenzie moving forward. But everything has to stay *good*, love."

"How? I am being good."

"You know exactly what I'm talking about. You have to keep your shit together until January 6th, and then for 12 supervised visits you have to keep it together- not that you wouldn't," he adds quickly. "But this is it, and the only way, and I need you to do this for us. I need you to be Suzanne again, the strong Suzanne you've been for the last 16 months, the Suzanne who stands up for herself and stands up to me. That's the strong Suzanne I need in my life. You have to do this for us because there's nothing else I can do if you don't."

"I am being good, Z. I'm living alone, not bothering anyone, being good and quiet and-"

"I never said you weren't good. Please don't get defensive right now. I just need you to understand that we've lasted 3 weeks apart and we have only a little while longer until we can be together and have everything we said we wanted together. But you have to stay strong, Suzanne. You have to eat and sleep and answer our calls when we check in on you so we know you're okay."

"I do."

"No, you don't. You answer maybe half my calls, you've stopped talking to the Kaylas and Mack says you rarely talk to him anymore."

"I do. But he always wants to talk talk and I can't right now. I do answer him when he calls though."

Squeezing my hand, Z looks at me desperately. "I'm not criticizing you, Suzanne. I'm just trying to explain that the bad end is near, and our good life can begin soon. But you have to sleep, and eat, and stay focused. You have to answer my calls and talk to me. Because I can't do this alone, and I don't want to. Seeing you so out of it tonight scared me. You didn't even believe I was here or real or me..." he moans so heavily I know I have to end this upset for him.

"I didn't know it was you for real this time because I always hear you whisper to me. When I try to sleep, when I shower, when I'm just sitting in the dark. Um, I always hear your voice and I couldn't be sure it was really you because you're always here whispering to me. That's all."

Exhaling deeply again, Z whispers, 'that's all', and I don't know what else to do or say. Everything is right here for me if I just hold on a little longer. If I stay strong I can have them back. If I keep the Suzanne shit out of everything I can have the future I never thought I would or even imagined was possible for me. If I just wait a little longer, and hope...

"I've got this," I suddenly announce as Z's head turns back to me. Looking down at my special Z/Suzanne ring, I know I do. "I do. Um, I will. Now that there's something, *anything* to hope for I can keep doing this alone."

"Alone for now," he pushes again as I nod.

"For now. But are you totally sure you want this? Fighting to get me back in your lives is the Z honorable thing to do, but is it what *you* actually want? And I'm not being dramatic, for once," I add with a huff as he grins. "I'm seriously asking you. I need to know if it's what you really want now. Because so far from what you've told me, I can still see Mackenzie, supervised at first, then maybe a little more, but it doesn't mean you and I have to get back together, or live together, or *be* together. We can keep things separate if you want while I see her." And that's the truth, I finally see. "We don't have to be together for me to see Mackenzie, Z. So you can make a different choice here, and I wouldn't blame you at this point. Honestly."

"I've thought about it, Suzanne." Oh, that hurt to hear, but I nod instead of scream so he keeps talking. "I have. And I know my life would be easier if you and I co-parented but didn't live together or love together anymore. But then I realized I wouldn't have you anymore, and the thought of not loving you is not worth the calm I would gain without you. Because quite frankly, I know I wouldn't be happy without you in my life."

Shaking my head, I swear he has it all wrong. His life will be exactly that- happy. "Maybe you should really think about it before the February court date. Give yourself some time to figure out if you still want me as a wife. Because we can still be friends, and I promise I'll be okay without you. Like, I won't do anything stupid ever again. I haven't even really thought about letting go, even now when I've been my saddest and loneliest." When Z raises his infamous eyebrow, I know he doesn't believe me. "I haven't, Z. Because I can't do anything like that ever again *because* of you and Mackenzie."

"What do you mean?" He asks sitting up on the bed with his arms crossed over his chest.

"I can't kill myself, because then I've told both of you I didn't love you enough to live," I whisper as the air and desperation slowly leaves my lungs. Tearing up I tell Z the truth. "If I kill myself, it meant I didn't love everything I've had with you and everything you've done for me. And it means I didn't love Mackenzie enough to live as her mother, no matter how hard it gets or how lonely I feel. And that's why I've held on these last 3 weeks, Z. I've cried nonstop, but I didn't even think about doing anything like that again because I can't do that to you or her. I *won't* do that to either of you."

"Come here," Z moans and I move instantly. Wrapped in his arms, we both exhale and hold on. This is it right here. Everything between us, always hard and heavy but just there. "We are US, Suzanne. Good, bad, ugly and beautiful. Exhausting and painful, torturous and demanding, hideous and terrible, dramatic and-"

Bursting out laughing, I gasp, "I get it, *okay*?" as he laughs against me.

"Okay..."

After a comfortable silence I realize how badly I need to feel Z with me. "I'm okay right now," I whisper hoping he understands. But when he doesn't move I force myself to continue. "Like, I'm *okay* right now. I know it's you, and I know that it's just us here. And I would like to be with you, *if* you want?" I squeak embarrassed at the end.

"Suzanne?" Turning me to face him Z looks as uncomfortable as I suddenly feel. "Listen to me closely. I want to be with you, but not right now and not like this. There are so many things going on with you and us I don't think it's a good idea if we make things more complicated by having sex. Wait!" He yells when I gasp by a mistake. "Wait. Just listen. This isn't about NOT wanting you, believe me. It's about not wanting you like this. Not when you're sad and depressed and lonely. I need you when you're happy and when you want to be with me."

"But I do want to be with you," I practically beg.

"I don't think you do. I think you're lonely and you want to be with me so you have a memory. Kayla told me you want to walk away from me and Mackenzie." Oh. "And I know you well enough to know you're stubborn enough to do it. I know you, Suzanne, so I know when you're about to make a move or a decision. I know when the sadness consumes you, and I know when you're desperate. And right now, I know you're desperate to feel something- to take something with you. I know your kiss goodbye and I know your eyes when you believe in nothing."

"I'm not-"

"I *know* you, Suzanne. And I'm not going to make love with you so you have a memory to take with you. I'm not giving you something that allows you to walk away again. I know that's what you did after the wedding, and I'm never doing it again."

"I didn't," I shake my head furiously. "I just want you, that's all."

"You can have me, love. But not now when I don't know if you'll stay. But when this is all over, when everything is the way it's meant to be I'll be with you. I'll *beg* to be with you again. But I'm not giving you a memory to leave us with," Z finally exhales and I want to cry again.

"That wasn't what I was doing. But I understand," I agree not understanding at all.

"That's all it is, Suzanne. I don't trust you to stay with me until I can fix this, so I'm not giving you a memory that allows you to leave me again."

Looking up quickly, I see Z looks exhausted, and I feel exhausted. I don't want any more sadness tonight, and I can't handle anymore loneliness, so I decide to stop all the darkness between us tonight.

"I understand. Ah, Merry Christmas, Z."

"Merry Christmas, love," he whispers holding me tighter to his chest.

We are US...

CHAPTER 40

I did it. I've done it. I made it through Christmas and New Years alone. I talked to Mack finally, and I had a very low key New Years in my hotel with Z on the phone. Holding Mackenzie the whole time or sleeping beside him, Z and I watched the ball drop together on tv. We laughed at crude Kathy and we groaned for awkward Anderson. I spent New Year's Eve with Z together though apart, and I've kept my shit together since our Christmas Eve together. I've done everything I was supposed to do and it's finally here.
January 6th.
Z's court date, which his lawyers advised I should be at to set the precedent that I may be around in the future. I'm not supposed to sit with him though, but I'm supposed to be there showing my support for him.
It's January 6th, and I need at least this battle to be over. I need to hear Z gain full custody of Mackenzie forever so I can exhale all my fear. Yes I want them back too, but I really think I'll be if not okay, at least content with them together whether I'm legally allowed to be with her or not.
I *will* be okay, because Z and Mackenzie together is right and it makes our struggle worth everything. Well, it makes my struggle worth the two of them together. Z however still insists we'll be together, and he has told me he made his decision, which wasn't really a decision at all he said sweetly. Our relationship just is- and he wants us to be Z and Suzanne with our daughter together.
Waiting for the driver to take me to the courthouse in my new clothes that I'm horribly uncomfortable in, I'm willing to play my part in fixing this for if not all three of us, certainly for Z and Mackenzie.
Looking one last time at my face and hair to make sure I look okay, I'm as proper looking as I can be, the scars and fear notwithstanding. Breathing, I smooth down my black pencil skirt for the hundredth time because my WHITE blouse under the black cardigan is making me get hives I think.
I look totally together and I'm ready for half this battle to be over.

We are US...

Walking up the steps with my security guard Heather who looks like she's a 22 year old college student, I spend more time staring at her then I do the people around us. She's distracted me enough to get through the security check point within the first doors, then through the second doors into the damn building. Ignoring the people I'm desperate to ignore, I'm dying to see the people I need to see.

Standing just inside the doors, Mack steps forward and takes my arm immediately with a slight smile that doesn't reach his eyes. Pulling me inside he doesn't hug me but he does keep himself slightly over my body like he's guarding me himself but keeping all his emotions in check.

"Don't lean in to me," he whispers and as I gasp at the rejection he quickly speaks. "The cameras. We don't want weakness." Nodding, I straighten my spine and walk down the hall beside him. "Almost there," he says softly as we keep walking probably a normal pace for him, but nearly a jog for me. Handing me a badge for my chest, I put it on while Mack continues kind of ignoring me but also supporting me with his hand on my arm lightly.

Pushing open a huge door a security officer steps forward, reads my name-tag, checks off some sheet, and then I'm suddenly in court again. It's not my first time after my father's trial but it's just as intimidating as always, and my stomach is in knots trying to stay in the present.

"Come this way," Mack says softly again as we round the back benches and sit in the fourth to last row. Far enough away that all the taller people hide me, but close enough to see Z waiting in the first row in a gorgeous dark blue suit I don't remember. I guess I wasn't the only one who went shopping for this, I giggle.

"Suzanne?" Mack whispers with a death glare forcing me to shake my head immediately to clear it.

"I'm good. Sorry."

"I have to go," he smiles before squeezing my shoulder.

Watching Mack walk away I feel so alone suddenly. Kind of scared, but mostly nervous. Everything is banking on this hearing, and if Z loses there is nothing left to do for me for a long, long while. Z can keep Mackenzie of course, but I can't be a part of their lives as a constant. Everyone thinks this should go well though, and as a last hope scenario I'll probably still be granted supervised visitation for quite a while until I'm deemed mentally well enough to be around them. So there is hope for me. Lots and lots of hope.

Sarah Ann Walker

    Turning my head slightly, I see the Kaylas a row behind Z and Mack and his lawyers and I wish so much we were still close. I miss them horribly, but I know right now isn't the time to- Oh! It's like she knew.
    Staring at me, New York Kayla suddenly smiles and gives me a very subtle thumbs up. Wow, I didn't realize how much that would mean to me until I saw it. Choking up, I just hold in a cry as my eyes fill with tears before she shakes her head no quickly turning back to the front when Z, Mack and his lawyers walk inside the gate and the hearing suddenly begins.
    Gasping a quick breath, I hold it in while I listen though I know what's coming, and I know what started this all for me. After a series of events lead to the questioning of Elizabeth, the current D.A. alongside Glenn Rose found out how and *why* this all started.
    I know the original judge was a longtime acquaintance of my mother's from back in the day. I know my mother knew the judge because there was a photo found of the 2 of them together in my childhood home nearly 20 years before when I was only 12. And then another picture was discovered. The picture of Judge Davis with my mother and Surprise! Dr. *fucking* Simmons. And that's when everything clicked for everyone. Whether my mother set it up between Simmons and Davis we don't know, but we do know Simmons made the anonymous call from his own prison, and he was the 'Physician' whose authority forced the removal of my daughter.
    Sadly, what I don't know is if Judge Davis ever touched me. We don't know for sure, and it really doesn't matter anymore I guess. He did or didn't touch me. He was either one of the bad men, or he only knew of them. Either way as Z pointed out doesn't matter though. Judge Davis is a pig who screwed me over because Simmons asked him to, either for just himself or for my mother as recorded on the prison telephone which the asshole didn't know. Ha!
    Apparently, the older Judge was an idiot, totally unaware that their conversations were admissible if a prisoner is being investigated for a criminal offense which takes place in or from prison. And honestly, no one could believe the judge didn't know or think, or maybe care that he could get caught. Z thinks it was because he was an arrogant old bastard, but Mack seems to think the asshole Judge either wanted to get caught, or finally wanted to be caught for something he may have been involved with back then.

We are US...

Anyway, the judge stepped down and he's facing conspiracy charges to commit fraud, Elizabeth is financially broke *coincidentally*, and Simmons is going to have more time added to his current sentence for the false accusations he made to CPS as 'practicing physician' which he isn't. Inevitably, it looks like my mother tried to ruin my life again but failed. Kind of.

Oh! What the hell? Z looks all stressed suddenly moving in his chair weirdly. What the FUCK did I miss?

"... I understand and accept the allegations of child abuse against Mrs. Zinfandel are untrue, unwarranted, and therefore they themselves will not be admissible in court. However, there is still the evidence supporting her mental incompetence and history of emotional disturbance which can't be overlooked when I decide what's best for the long term care of the child, Mackenzie Kayla Zinfandel. There is a precedent here which suggests placing the child in the home of a person with a history of documented mental instability causes if not an immediate, certainly the *potential* for harm to the child, therefore..."

"No! *Wait!*" Screaming, I feel the whole courtroom turn as I scream and stand. "Wait! Please." Oh *fuck*... this is bad. Z's already standing yelling my name to stop and Mack is leaving his seat to walk toward me. I'm a total freak show with all eyes on me, but I don't care. "Your honor, may I approach the bench?" I think they say that on tv.

"Mrs. Zinfandel?" The judge asks actually leaning over his huge desk to hear me I think.

"Yes. Um, may I just say a few things before you decide? Please?" Watching a bailiff walk toward me I'm scared shitless but desperate. "I won't fight if you say no but I really need to say something. Please?" I beg again as my eyes fill but my tears stay put. "*Please* your honor?"

I swear to god my breath is the only sound in the entire courtroom. There is just nothing around me or in front of me but him. Begging with my eyes, I watch for a tiny little glimmer of hope before he decides if I can speak. Please, please, please... I want to beg but stay silently standing until after forever he finally nods his head.

"You may stand within the floor, Mrs. Zinfandel," he says stretching his hand out before him. What the hell is the floor?

Stumbling over the side of my bench, dropping and leaving my purse on the floor, I walk as calmly as I can toward the front ignoring everyone, especially Z as I approach the little wooden gate. When the Bailiff actually opens it, I walk through and stop when his hand moves forward to stop me. I'm on the floor I guess, only 10 feet from Judge Mandle with everyone else behind me waiting in a deathlike silence.

"Mrs. Zinfandel?" He asks almost kindly for a change, and I nearly cry.

"Please give Z Mackenzie. If you think I'm unfit I understand, but he isn't. He's amazing and he'll care for her always. He's a really good man, and such a special person, Mackenzie deserves to have him in her life. Please don't punish him because of me."

"I'm not punishing anyone, Mrs. Zinfandel," he says in a kind tone like he's being honest with me.

"But you kind of are. I get the whole I have a crazy past thing, but Z doesn't at all. So please let him have and keep our daughter. Neither of them have ever done anything wrong and I'm begging you not to punish them because of me. *Please,* your honor?" I beg again as one tear slides down my face before I can blink it back.

"Mrs. Zinfandel I have a question I would like you to answer."

"Anything," I moan rocking on my heels.

"Do you think you would make a good parent to Mackenzie?"

"Yes." Period. Without thinking or wondering what I should say I just answer. "Yes. I think I would be a good mom."

"Why?" He asks softly and that does me in. Opening crying, I can't hold back my sadness, or misery, or my fear anymore.

"Because I love her. Um, I had a baby once who died, and now I have one who is alive, and I love her."

"I understand, and I'm very sorry for your loss. But just because you love her doesn't guarantee you won't have any other mental health issues with *this* child."

"I know it doesn't guarantee that, but I do. Um, I'm not messed up about Mackenzie, sir. She's my daughter and I love her. And she is not a reason for me to freak out. Ah, do you know about my past?"

Nodding, he says a very quiet 'yes' which though humiliating is where I needed him to be. "Well then you know I was raped repeatedly and tortured as a child," I gag out that disgusting sentence as he nods. "I was hurt badly by my parents, so I'm messed up for sure. But it's about bad men, and my past, and my mother who by the way is a total cun- uh, horrible person." Ugh. "Anyway, I'm not messed up about my daughter or my husband or about my present life."

We are US...

"But you could become unstable again."

"I could," I agree. "But it wouldn't be about them. And I'm tired of still being hurt all the time by my past. It's really not fair, your honor. My parents and their sick friends did unspeakable things to me and even now I'm still being punished for it like I did something wrong when I was little."

"Again, no one is trying to punish you."

"I know," I nod. "But it still is a punishment. I don't handle stress well, like stress about men and perverts and stuff like that. But I handle all the day to day things well. I try every day to move past all those childhood nightmares, and I did do it with Z for the most part. Yes, I may have 'episodes' and I'd be lying if I said I wouldn't ever again. But it's just not the same thing as being with Mackenzie and Z. They are good for me. They are light and happiness and finally some peace that I never had when I was young. Z loves me your honor, and I want to be better now because I didn't choose what happened to me when I was a little girl but I can choose this life now. Bad people hurt me badly and sometimes I don't handle the memories or the feelings of that time well. But they are so separate from Z and Mackenzie that I honestly think I'll be okay with them. But if I start to feel not okay again, I promise I'll get help."

"Who will you promise?" He asks quietly.

"You. Um, I promise you I'll get help if the bad stuff ever gets to me again, even though I don't really feel like it will. I don't feel crazy anymore, sir. I just feel sad without my husband and daughter. Um, I'm very tired of still being hurt all the time, especially when there's something finally here for me to love that actually loves me back."

"I under-"

"But I absolutely will walk away from Z and Mackenzie so they can be together if that's what you decide. Their happiness is still more important than my own now because I'm kind of used to being unhappy in this life against my will..."

Gasping a quick sob, I manage to stand still even though the silence is killing me and the sadness is threatening to break me apart after the last 2 weeks of hope.

"Thank you, Mrs. Zinfandel. I appreciate everything you said and I'll take it under advisement," he says suddenly sounding like a judge again. Waiting, I don't know what to do until he smiles and says, "You may take your seat now."

"Oh, sorry," I laugh turning to every single person staring at me. Almost gasping again, I feel like such an idiot staring at everyone staring at me until I see Z's sad eyes. Mouthing 'thank you' Z actually smiles at me beautifully until he nods his head to the Bailiff still holding the little wooden gate open for me to finally leave by.
And then it's done.
Walking back quickly to my seat, my purse has been lifted by someone on my seat, and my hair is covering the side of my face they can see. Sitting down I keep my hands in my lap and my face lowered.

"I'd like to speak with Mr. Zinfandel's counsellor's and the CPS representatives at the bench," I hear Judge Mandle say but I can't look up. I'm scared shitless and I'm hoping with everything in me that he'll make the decision I want. I hope I convinced him and he'll give me Z and Mackenzie back. God, I hope I proved I wasn't crazy by standing up, screaming in court, begging the judge to hear me out while crying my eyes out in front of everyone. Yup. That'll do it for sure. *Shit*.

"Suzanne?" Jumping, one of Z's lawyers I don't know squats beside my bench seat. "Judge Mandel requests that you sit with Z for this," he asks solemnly. "Would you join us, please?"
Standing, I grab my purse this time and walk up front to Z and the others without looking away from the Judge. I'm keeping the shakes in check and my crazy from surfacing.
Sitting, Judge Mandel actually smiles at me briefly and I stop breathing entirely. I'm almost bouncing in my chair beside Z until I feel his hand squeeze my knee to calm me like he always does.
"Regarding parental custody of Mackenzie Zinfandel, I've decided the best interest of the child lies with her father Mr. Zinfandel. In his home, permanently and unsupervised Mr. Zinfandel may gain full custody of his daughter."
Oh. My. God. This is it.
Leaning over the table Z keeps squeezing my leg but I don't care. I need to hear this.
"Regarding Mrs. Zinfandel and custody of her daughter Mackenzie Kayla Zinfandel I'm not ready to make my final ruling-" Gasping out loud I cover my mouth as he quickly continues. "*But* in 4 week's time I will make my final decision. I have agreed to the terms set up by the New York Child

We are US...

Protective Services of 3 supervised visits per week between Mrs. Zinfandel and her child in the home of Mr. Zinfandel, and after that time I will give my final ruling on February 2nd. I also request Mrs. Zinfandel see a court appointed Psychiatrist once a week for a minimum of a year-"

"Done! I always see Psychiatrists anyway," I yell before stopping myself. Oh *SHIT!*

Smiling briefly *thank god*, Judge Mandel continues. "Therefore my ruling is this; Mr. Zinfandel is to retain full, permanent custody of Mackenzie Zinfandel, and after a month of supervised visits, should no events occur questioning Mrs. Zinfandel's mental health regarding her daughter or *herself*," he says with clear inflection, "I will most likely award custody to Mrs. Zinfandel as well. Do you have somewhere you can stay in the meantime?" He looks at me with sympathy clearly on his face.

"Yes, your honor."

"Okay. Then my ruling is final." I can't believe it! I just can't believe- "As a side note, I would like to extend the sympathy of this court for what you went through as a child, and continue to go through as an adult for the atrocities you had to face Mrs. Zinfandel." Oh. Bursting into tears, Z takes my hand under the table as I stare at Mandel. "I would also like you to know I have made sure I was personally involved in the investigation and prosecution of those that have recently conspired against you."

"Thank you..." I moan as he nods once before rising from his bench. Feeling everything change around us, I know everyone else stood but me and Z and I wish I could, but I just can't. I'm exhausted and sad from the memories, but just so relieved I feel light-headed and nauseous actually.

"Suzanne?" Z whispers leaning into my side. "Baby, are you okay?"

Nodding, I still have no words. My heart is pounding and my whole body is shaking with the need to either throw up or scream-cry. I don't know what to do or say or how I even leave.

"Let me take you back to the hotel, okay?" Z asks quietly. "Just one month, Suzanne. You've already lasted a month, and you only have one more to go until you can come home with me. But you'll see both of us 3 times a week while you wait. Can you do that? Can you wait just a little longer?" Almost begging me, Z looks so exhausted I finally just hug him.

Squeezing him to death, he hugs me just as tightly until we both cry. Like a total psycho and a pansy, Z and I cry our relief and hope.

"I can wait another month. A month is nothing to get everything I've ever wanted with you. A month is nothing, Z."

Standing, Z takes my hand and covers me a little from whoever is left around us. "Your makeup isn't covering your face, love," Z whispers.

"I don't care anymore. This is me, Z. Good, bad, ugly and beautiful."

"*Beautiful*," he kisses my lips softly.

THE END

We are US...

Epilogue

Walking into Dr. Belanger's office, I smile and sit. Before she even has to ask though, I spill. "I'm still doing very good. I haven't had any nightmares or freak outs, and I'm still happy."
Grinning, she says what she always does. "That's very good, Suzanne."
Nodding, we each wait for the other until we smirk a little stupidly at each other as usual.
"How's that beautiful baby of yours?"
"Beautiful," I smile again.
"And Z?"
"Beautiful," I blush.
"So we have nothing to talk about today? Nothing at all?"
Leaning forward, I make sure to keep eye contact while I tell her the truth. "Absolutely nothing at all. Mackenzie is healthy and happy, Z is Z, I'm happy and for right now everything seems to be in a very good place for me. I feel next to no panic, and even when those quick little panics come they're usually over something stupid which I just as quickly recognize. And before you ask, the newest example was when Marty walked into Mackenzie's nursery with Z while I was changing her 2 days ago. Marty walked up to kiss her hello and I panicked for a split second, grabbing her in my arms to cover her little naked body but as soon as I made eye contact with Marty's surprise I quickly realized he is a safe person, I was overreacting, and Marty would never touch her inappropriately or in a bad way. I did understand quickly and I placed Mackenzie back on her change table without losing my shit."
"What did Marty do?"
Exhaling, I shake my head. "Nothing. He acted like I wasn't mental then leaned forward and kissed her forehead anyway."
"And Z?"
"He squeezed my shoulder I think both for support and maybe because I recovered so well."
"And what did you do?"
Remembering the intense moment in Mackenzie's room I admit, "I continued changing her and tried to breathe normally."

"And how did you feel?"

"Like an asshole," I grin as she laughs. "Ah, but then I was proud of myself for stopping the fear from getting me too intensely or in a way I couldn't rationalize."

"And did you stop the fear?"

"Not entirely, but I think I never really will though."

"How so?"

"Um, I'm very protective of Mackenzie," I say all duh until she nods. "Um, I love her. So I don't think I'll ever be completely normal or relaxed where her security is concerned, but I also don't really feel bad about that."

"No?"

"No. I don't. And I never will. I didn't have parents who protected me. Actually, I had evil *anti*-parents. So if Mackenzie's only complaint when she's older is her mother was too cautious with her I'm okay with that. Plus, Z balances it out a little. He's very careful with her don't get me wrong, but I think he'll always be able to talk me into realizing the difference between the good, like natural fear a parent has for their child, and the crazyass, irrational Suzanne fear I'll probably always have inside me. And again, I'm okay with that. I'd rather love her and protect her too much than ever allow her to be hurt."

"Will you let Mackenzie go to the Prom?" Dr. Belanger asks suddenly and though I'm confused by the change in topic I smile anyway.

"Of course I would. God, I want her to do all the things I didn't." Oh. Looking at a smiling Dr. Belanger I see exactly what she's done. "Yes. I want Mackenzie to have a wonderful, *normal* life- a life totally different than the one I had."

"Good, because-"

"But that doesn't mean I won't chaperone," I giggle as she laughs at me again.

Sitting back in my chair I can't help thinking of Mackenzie at her prom suddenly. With her light brown hair and dark brown eyes and with eye lashes most women would kill for, I know any color gown will look stunning on her. I can't wait to hold Z's hand while he chokes up like a pansy when she goes to her prom.

"I'm doing very well. And I would tell you if I wasn't. I still see my other shrink once I week and I see you once a week, so there's lots of help if I need it."

"You see me because you have to," she smiles.

"Yes, but I probably would anyway," I grin. "I like you Dr. Belanger, and you've been a great help adding in the female dynamic I don't have with my other doctor. But I'm still good for now, and I really would come immediately if I wasn't good. I really want to be good and *happy* for Mackenzie and Z," I finally exhale.

"I know you would, Suzanne. So it looks like we're done today. See you next Tuesday?"

"Absolutely."

Standing, Dr. Belanger, my court appointed psychiatrist, shakes my hand as usual before I turn for home for another week.

℧℧℧℧℧

Opening the front door, I already hear the crying and *wow* see the mess all over our entire living room, proof that Z tried every single toy Mackenzie owns to calm her.

"Z?" I call *calmly* walking towards the bedrooms to my screaming baby. "Mackennnnnnnzie...?" I call out in my dorky mom voice. "Where are you baby?" And suddenly the crying stops. On a dime. In a fraction of a second. Almost like a baby-mom switch, all crying stops as Z and Mackenzie round the corner to me. Oh my... they both look like hot friggin' messes.

"What the-?" I giggle looking at Z rolling his eyes at my totally silent, snotty, teary eyed crazy little baby. "Come here," I whisper as her chubby little arms reach out to me immediately. "What's wrong, sweetpea?" I soothe as she rests her head on my chest silently.

Walking the rest of the way to my bedroom, Z follows silently, and Mackenzie stays silent. Crawling on my bed, she stays in my arms and snuggles in deep. Lying sideways Z crawls in behind her and flips my favorite poo-stained for life throw blanket over us and still Mackenzie is silent. Looking at her face, I gently touch her eyebrow and with only 2 passes of my thumb her eyes flutter open and closed. Oh, yeah... she's done I almost giggle.

"How long did she cry?" I whisper watching her eyes finally flutter closed for good.

We are US...

"How long we're you gone?" Z counters with a little huff smile.

I'm not gonna lie, that feels pretty great. Well, not that she cried for so long, but totally because she cried for so long because I wasn't with her.

"I love you," Z whispers leaning over our 7 month old to kiss my scarred cheek.

"Why?" I ask like an idiot when he smirks. "I mean why did you say that right now?"

"Cuz I wanted to," he grins as I smile back.

"Did she sleep at all?"

"No."

"So she's out out?"

"Yes..."

Looking intensely at our special sex couch, I don't even need to speak before Z's eyes lower and his breathing changes. Oh, he is so on board with me.

"You go first," I whisper with a stupid grin I'm sure as he slowly tries to ease out from behind Mackenzie. Lifting a pillow over her head gently, Z stuffs it between the 2 of them as he pushes out from behind her. Watching, I almost giggle at what parents we've become. I mean seriously, dealing with a sleeping baby is like handling the detonator of a goddamn atomic bomb for Christ's sake, and yet the second the bed squeaks we both gasp and pause for the explosion.

In almost a semi-prone position Z holds his very impressive ab muscles tight while I bury my face in the bed before I burst out laughing.

"Your turn, smartass," he whispers and I'm dying. Between wanting Z and scared I'll make a noise, I can't hold in the laughter for much longer. There's no way. For 2 people who want to have sex we're like the most ridiculous looking morons ever.

"Losers?" He grins walking to my side when he's finally free of the Mackenzie bomb.

"Totally," I giggle holding in my real laugh.

Feeling his hands around my waist Z breathes *shhhhh* and just slides me sideways right off our bed backwards until my foot hits the floor.
Righting me, my laughter is right there. Almost out. Barely contained as I stare at him for one millisecond before he kisses me.

And that's it.

Z kisses the holy shit out of me and I forget everything. Well, except for my daughter, but whatever. She's sound asleep in the middle of our bed facing away from our couch, and *oh!*

  Z lifts me right off the floor by my waist as my legs wrap around his own until moving we hit our special sex couch with a quiet humph between us.

  Still kissing, I manage to yank his shirt overhead as he lifts my skirt up to my waist.

  "Making love, sex, or fucking?" Z breathes nearly silently against my lips making my arousal skyrocket. "Never mind, you can't be quiet no matter what, so I'll start slow to get to the good stuff before you scream and wake her up."

  Nodding, I wait for his slow and giggle when he looks between my body and Mackenzie's sleeping silence in fear.

  "Give me everything, Z," I moan when I feel him touch my body.

  "I plan on it, love," he growls with his intense eyes staring at my own before he lowers on the floor before me.

  "Oh *god*..." I moan covering my mouth with a couch cushion when I feel his mouth take me hard.

We are US...

We are US...

Sarah Ann Walker

ABOUT THE AUTHOR

Sarah Walker is a Scottish Canadian living in Canada with her American husband and their son.

In her real life, Sarah is a devoted mother, (semi)devoted wife ☺, and an absolute junkie for coffee, dark chocolate with sea salt, and high heels.

www.authorsarahannwalker.com

Sarah can be found on Facebook
www.facebook.com/SarahAnnWalkerIAmHer

Amazon
http://www.amazon.com/author/walkersarahann
http://amzn.com/e/B00AW22K56

Goodreads
https://www.goodreads.com/Sarah-Walker

and
Twitter
@sarahannwalker0

Made in the USA
Charleston, SC
06 November 2015